LOST HORSE
PARK

Troy B. Kechely

Though historical events, locations and businesses are detailed in this book, the main characters and the story itself are the creation of the author and completely fictitious. Any resemblance to any real persons, living or dead, is purely coincidental.

ISBN-13: 9780692793336
ISBN-10: 069279333X

DEDICATIONS

To the brave men who served in the First Special Service Force during World War II and all those who have served in the United States Armed Forces. May their deeds never be forgotten.

To a horse named Comanche, for whom no mountain was too high nor any trail too long.

ACKNOWLEDGEMENTS

First and foremost, I thank God for the gift of storytelling and the opportunity to share it. A special thank you to Anika Hanisch and Jennie Graham for their diligent guidance and editing.

To Col. Jim Kraus, retired, U.S. Army Special Forces, and Dale Moore, master saddle maker, thank you. Without your wisdom, stories, and feedback, this effort would have been impossible.

To all those who assisted in test reading, putting up with numerous interviews, and research related efforts, thank you: Kyle Blackmore; Virginia Borzellere; John Christenson; Joanne Goldstein; Zack Graham; Sandy Graveley; Pam Griswold; Phil and Mary Mooney; K. Newton; Tom Scalese; and Matthew Widdekind

I also could not have finished this book without the support and encouragement from: Tony Barton; Nathan and Haleigh Clevidence; Vicki Clevidence; Anna Constance; Amanda Crandall; Frank Crandall; Chris Forrest; Zack Graham; Brett Gunnink; Stacey Hellekson; Jim and Cindy Hoschouer; Charles Kankelborg; Darlene Kechely; Don and Marlene Kechely; Eric Kechely; Ron Murray; Ingrid Nemzek; Fred Schweitzer; Bryan Sondeno; Dana Tillet; and Bev Townsend

CHAPTER 1
AUGUST 12, 1969

Dear Mom,

Jim Redmond stared at the two words he had penned five minutes earlier. He twirled the thick barreled pen between his fingers. His mind resisted continuing, battling the urge to share his world without compromising security, without revealing too much of the truth. The struggle was heavy, suffocating, like the hot, humid jungle air. With each breath, the stench of mold, sweat, and decay permeated Jim's soul and thoughts.

The tapestry of foul air was inexplicably woven through with the fragrance of blooming flowers, and kissed by a whiff of expended Cordite from the mortar pit just outside the narrow, sandbag framed door. Such was the pungent jungle essence of Vietnam, something that Jim both loved and loathed. Home in Montana felt so far away. His journey to this point seemed an eternity, though in reality it had only been four years.

The incessant rain of monsoon season had ceased for the first time in ten days, allowing the jungle to exhale its odiferous breath in the reprieve. Jim didn't mind the rain. To him it was just a nice long cool, shower, a welcome retreat from the heat.

It also restricted movement of the enemy but that was now no longer the case. The pause in the rain allowed supplies to get to the Special Forces A-Camp once more and mail to go out. It also provided Mr. Charles time to set more booby traps and prepare for attacks. Jim and his Special Forces teammates had too much respect for their enemies to call them Charlie like the infantry and Marines did. His unit preferred the more honorable moniker of Mr. Charles when referring to the Viet Cong, whom they battled on a regular basis. Yet another detail he couldn't share with Mom.

Jim sat on the edge of his cot. The incomplete letter rested atop a rarely opened Bible perched on his knee. The pen still wove between his troubled fingers. The note from his mother lay next to him on the cot, its elegant cursive script sharing news from home, general encouragement, and not so subtle motherly reminders about hygiene and such. Jim might be a combat seasoned Green Beret, but his mother, Abby Redmond, would always see him as one of her three children, perpetually in need of motherly love and guidance.

The weather and combat patrols had kept Jim from writing his normal weekly letters, and he knew his mom would be worried. He also knew she would never let anyone back home know of her concern, even though the last correspondence from her had made it clear she was afraid for him. Well, at least one of the reasons for the rarity of his correspondence was benign enough to share: the weather. Stopping his pen in mid twirl, Jim continued to write:

Sorry that this letter is late. The mail only goes out if choppers make it in. Lots of rain here. With the heat it's just terrible, worse than when we drove down to Tennessee to visit your friend Patty and her family that one August. I know you're worried about me with all the news on TV, but don't be. I'm okay, I promise.

Okay. It wasn't exactly a lie, but it was far from the truth. True, he was alive and had no injuries at the moment, but he was far from okay. Too many memories haunted his dreams during the rare hours that he could sleep. Combat tours did that to people, forcing them into a world that most can't imagine, nor one they would want to experience.

Jim's world was a Special Forces A-Camp not far from the Cambodian border. His Special Forces team had only been there a few weeks, and they were becoming accustomed to the mountainous countryside and its thick, endless jungles that hid an ever-present enemy. The camp was Jim's home for his second tour in the Republic of South Vietnam. His first tour had been further south, where he had received his baptism by fire. Before that, more than a year of training had begun with basic, then advanced individual training, then jump school, and finally, acceptance into the Special Forces training program. Even given that experience, he still was taken aback by the suddenness and ferocity of his first contact with the enemy. Jim couldn't say it was easier now, just more familiar, less startling. Perhaps because of that reality he was, in fact, okay. The pen touched paper once more.

The men on my team are good guys, we watch each other's backs. The villagers around our camp are nice, but we learned early on not to trust anyone much. There's one villager, Tran, that you would like. He cuts wood for the camp and has a knack for attracting stray animals, just like you do. No fooling, one of the strays he has is a bear cub. Its mom was killed by a booby trap. We of course named the bear Yogi. It follows Tran everywhere, along with a scrawny mutt that we named Booboo.

The other day I was on watch with a few other guys, manning a bunker at the edge of camp. Tran was at the camp gate with some wood, and Booboo was outside the wire snooping for an easy meal, I suspect. There's a big pack of stray dogs that roam around the area, and after seeing Booboo they gave chase. Several of the guys wanted to help Booboo as he ran for his life, even getting their rifles ready. But we didn't need to do anything. Booboo came around a tree just as Yogi showed up to protect his friend. You should've seen the dogs scatter at the sight of that bear. We all had a good laugh over it.

Jim smiled as he recalled the story—one bright spot in an otherwise gloomy world. Contemplating what to write next, he gazed down at his legs. The fatigue pants were newly issued, the black and green tiger-stripe camouflage pattern not yet faded by heat and humidity or by the salt that all clothing withstood—from the gallons of sweat everyone perspired on each patrol. Blinking his eyes, Jim tried to clear his head. He could have sworn he saw caked blood appear on his lower pant legs; the blood that had coursed through his friend's veins just two days before. Rubbing his eyes, the cloth returned to normal. Then the imagined blood stains returned once again.

Jake's blood. Fellow Green Beret. A friend. Jake Gordon. The firefight that wounded him had happened on the last day of a five-day patrol. Jim had carried Jake's mangled body to the chopper and climbed in with him as the bird took off amidst a hail of tracer fire.

"Stay with me you son-of-a-bitch!" Jim had to shout over the rushing wind, machine gun fire, and the thump, thump, thump of the Huey's blades as it clawed skyward. "You hear me, Jake? Stay with me!" As Jim and a medic pressed battle dressings into numerous holes, the blood formed a crimson pool on the floor of the medivac helicopter. The chopper's vibration caused the blood to shimmer as it flowed across the metal floor. The pool reached Jim's boots and the hem of his right pant leg. It siphoned upward, saturating the fabric.

"Jake, look at me! Come on man, stay with me!"

Jim gripped his friend's wrist, felt the pulse weaken, then disappear. The fire of life that had been in Jake's eyes faded to an empty stare. Jim sat back, still holding his friend's hand.

It was not the first time he'd seen another living thing die. That didn't matter. When getting on the chopper, the man had been alive. When they landed, he was dead. That was the way of things in Southeast Asia. Jim knew and acknowledged that fact. And yet, he could never accept it. One moment you're alive, then the next moment you're gone. Four years ago, he hadn't cared about the war and all those guys dying in the far-off land known as Vietnam. Four years ago, he cared little about anything other than himself. He cared now. It was impossible not to.

Unsuccessfully trying to purge his mind of the memory, Jim looked back at his letter to Mom. The stain reappeared with each glance at his pant legs. God, how he wanted to tell his mom everything, but deep down he knew it would only terrify her. She wouldn't understand. Outside of his unit, there was only one person back home who could understand. Tom would, if he would even speak to Jim. Their last meeting had not ended well. He hoped that time would heal those wounds, but at last word from home, it hadn't. The loss of that friendship cost so many things: no more games of chess over a beer, no more World War II stories, and no more horseback rides deep into the mountains. The thought of horses brought Jim back to the note.

Thanks for the package. The Louie L'Amour books are great. All the guys are fans of The Duke so the westerns are good reading to take our mind off things. If we aren't sleeping or on patrol most everybody has their nose in some book, so send more when you get a chance. As bad as it seems on TV I'm glad I'm here. I belong here and love these guys like family. It's hard to explain the bond...not sure I can even try. Don't worry, I miss you and everyone else and I especially miss the mountains. There's no place like home.

The cookies survived the trip but were broke up a bit. The guys and I loved them just the same. Next time just send oatmeal raisin; the chocolate chips melt in the God-awful heat here.

Tell Dad, Vi, and Zack hi for me. Give Timber a pat for me as well.

Love,

Jim

Signing the letter, Jim glanced at his legs and saw the stains reappear. This wasn't the first time the images of blood stains had haunted him. That first time was almost four years ago in the mountains north of Helena, Montana as a teenager. Those earlier imagined stains rarely returned, overshadowed by the stains of more recent events. Yet occasionally, on quiet nights, when the chopper blades sounded like stampeding horses, those old memories crept back into his mind and the dark crimson stains reappeared.

Jim began to fold the letter then stopped and penned one more line.

PS. I know Tom hasn't spoken to you lately, but if you or dad see him, please pass a message along for me. Tell him he was right about the stains. He'll know what I'm talking about.

CHAPTER 2
JUNE 5, 1965

Amber light from the streetlamps on North Montana Avenue beamed through the windows of Helena Senior High School. It illuminated a stream of urine trickling onto a chair cushion and then into a coffee cup on the floor. The repulsive odor overpowered the stale air of the classroom. Jim Redmond sneered as he completed the defilement, feeling he had avenged countless students who had experienced the wrath of Ms. Woolsey. He zipped his pants, then carefully picked up the mug and returned it to the desk drawer. After one more look around the classroom, Jim was content with his efforts. He headed back into the dark hallway, locking the door and leaving the surprise to ripen over the entire summer break. If all went as planned, Woolsey the Witch wouldn't know about his prank until she returned in August.

Embraced by the shadows of the hallway, Jim felt more comfortable than in the classrooms where escape was limited. There was still time to explore more before meeting his cohorts and returning home in time for his midnight curfew. His parents believed he was at the Sunset Drive-In catching a double feature with friends. It was a flawless plan.

Lance Kramer and Marcus Trout, Jim's two accomplices, had gone separate ways after gaining access through an expertly unlocked window near the cafeteria on the north side of the school. The skills of unlawful entry were one of a few of Jim's special talents. Once inside, the boys had agreed to meet back up at the library in half an hour. Lance mentioned something about the girls' locker room, and Marcus made a beeline for the school office, intent on the petty cash box. His beer fund had been depleted earlier that day. Jim ended up in the west wing of classrooms.

While his friends ran, shouting and laughing, Jim ambled casually, calculating what illicit act he might perform. The Witch had been the first obvious choice—if not to obtain justice for himself, then for every male student who had the misfortune of suffering through her English class. No one knew what happened in Ms. Woolsey's past, what man spurned her, but her vitriolic wrath towards men was apparent, and few escaped her verbal abuse in class. It was bad enough that Jim had testicles, but the dark skin he was born with drew even more vile attention from the teacher. Three times he had visited the principal's office for daring to challenge her. Restraint of temper was not one of Jim's dominant traits.

Leaving Ms. Woolsey's classroom, Jim strolled down the hall, deciding on which classroom to trespass into next. It wasn't the first time he had walked with the shadows in the high school after hours. But it was the first time that friends had joined in the fun.

Stopping at his next target, Jim tried the door. Locked. A few seconds with his pocket knife granted access. A practiced thief, he quietly sorted through Mr. Goodman's desk in search of the prize. The small cardboard box was tucked in the back of the top drawer, as Jim expected it to be, having seen Mr. Goodman remove it many times. Inside the red felt-lined box rested a seemingly ordinary pen but Jim knew better. The Parker Arrow Clip ball-point pen was a cherished item. Everyone who had Mr. Goodman for sophomore math heard about how Mr. Goodman had been given the pen. It was a gift from President Kennedy, presented at an education conference in Washington, D.C.

It held no value for Jim. It was just a pen. Then again, none of the items obtained through five-finger discounts had value to him. They were only trinkets, trophies to commemorate all the times he had thieved and never been caught. He certainly wasn't taking it to spite Mr. Goodman. He actually liked this teacher. But the appeal of this particular trophy was just too much to pass up.

Jim looked at the dark barrel of the pen in the dim light and made out the engraved, inlaid white signature of the president, the words underneath: THE WHITE HOUSE. He twirled the pen between his fingers a couple times then pocketed it and returned the box to where he had found it, careful to leave the desk's other contents undisturbed. Before exiting the room, he paused at the chalkboard and wrote, "Kilroy was here" as a parting joke. The click of the closing door echoed like a dropped pebble on the floor of a medieval tomb.

With a quick swipe of annoyance, Jim pushed his long black bangs clear of his eyes as they adjusted to the dark hallway. Though irritating at times, the bangs were a small price to pay to emulate Mick Jagger. Jim's long, gangly build and thick mop of hair lent themselves well to that effort, though his darker skin hampered his Rolling Stones imitation.

Walking confidently but quietly in his loosely tied Converse tennis shoes, Jim started back towards the library. He didn't want to push their trespass time much longer. He reached the intersection of the main hall that connected to the east wing and the gym. He saw the two forms of his friends approaching and heard Lance sniggering. Then laughter. A loud snort. The guy was clearly delighted about whatever depraved act he had performed in the girl's locker room.

"How'd you guys make out?" Jim asked.

"Bagged only three bucks from the cash box," Marcus complained.

"Don't matter. This will be legend," Lance declared, a bit louder than Jim preferred. "Just like when Bolton rode his Harley through the halls last year." The motorcycle incident was already teen lore throughout the town. The senior had managed to motor through the halls between classes and make his escape without being caught.

"No one's a fink, right?" Jim said. "Not a word until we graduate."

Lance and Marcus nodded, neither wanted to cross their friend and be the recipient of a pounding. "Let's split before the fuzz show up," Jim said, feeling their stay had lasted longer than it should have. The hairs on the back of his neck rose as they made their way to the window by which they had entered.

In a literal flash, the protection of the darkness vanished as harsh light filled the hallway. A man's yell reverberated off the painted steel and hard tile. The three teens didn't look back as they sprinted away. Lance managed to get to the window first but struggled to squeeze his hefty torso through the gap. His taste for burgers at the RB Drive-In proved to be his undoing at the moment. Jim wasn't going to wait.

"Out of the way sweet hog!" he bellowed as he ripped Lance from the window and leapt through it. Jim fell with a thud on the landscape rocks below. The impact slammed the air from his lungs. He gasped as he struggled to his feet.

"Help me through!" Lance squealed, but Jim was already in a dead sprint, heading north along the west wall of the school. As he ran, he felt exposed in the glare of the streetlights along Montana Avenue. His goal was to get around the corner and into the protection of the shadows in the north parking area. If his friends were caught, that was their problem not his. The break-in had been their idea anyway.

Almost home free, Jim turned the corner, then slammed into the chest of a man. Jim was almost six feet tall himself, an imposing person, able to take on anyone. Giving up simply wasn't an option. Not this close to success. Both man and boy pushed the other away, but the man grasped Jim's shirt at his right shoulder with a bear paw sized hand. Without thinking, Jim threw a left hook at his captor's face, striking with enough force to drop any boy his age. But this the man wasn't seventeen years old. His captor towered over him and barely flinched. The glint of a badge on the man's chest was a new cause for panic. As the cop grabbed his left wrist, Jim's right fist whipped up to the cop's jaw. The impact had the same meaningless effect as that of his first hit. Jim felt himself hefted upward and then dumped to the ground, the full weight of the cop landing on his back. In seconds, he was shackled.

⊷⊹⊶

The handcuffs were tight on Jim's wrists as he sat in the back of the police car. A cut lip and scrapes along his arms and legs added to the discomfort. The physical pain was tolerable. What worried him was his parents. Most of his other illicit activities had managed to pass by his parents unnoticed, outside of a few calls from the school about fighting. Fear of the law was never motivating. Fear of being caught by his parents was. Being caught meant punishment, typically being confined to home except to attend school.

"Hell of a way to start the summer," Jim cursed himself. "You're in it deep now. Should've never let those flakes tag along." Out in the parking lot, Jim saw Marcus and Lance as they were hauled past him to other police cars. He ignored Marcus's glare. With the window down a few inches, Jim heard the pigs talking. The tall officer who had bagged him, Officer Johnson according to his name tag, had his back turned to the car. The discussion seemed focused on what had been stolen or damaged and on confirming the identity of the perpetrators. Jim had given his name freely; he had nothing to hide. In fact, it would be good to know that his dad's reputation in town might be soiled a bit. This incident would prove that the mildly famous stone artist couldn't control his own kid. It was doubtful any of the officers knew his father, Frank Redmond, but word traveled fast in Helena, especially when one's father happened to be friends with other business owners.

One of the other officers glanced over at Jim. "Should have known a wagon burner would be in the group," the officer said with disdain in his voice. "Probably from down at Moccasin Flats." A couple other officers nodded their heads. So, they definitely didn't know his dad.

The neighborhood known as Moccasin Flats, northeast of Helena, had a high concentration of Native Americans. Though Jim knew he was adopted from a local orphanage, he had no idea if his birth parents were from Moccasin Flats or from one of the many reservations scattered around the state. He had no idea where he really came from, who his birth parents were. For now, he was a seventeen-year-old kid in the back seat of a police car, wearing handcuffs.

The whole fiasco had started only an hour earlier. The three boys had been cruising around in Lance's 59 Plymouth Fury. It was a typical Saturday night in June, the first weekend of summer break following their junior year. Bored after looking for skirts along the drag, banter turned to their various exploits. When Jim bragged that he had broken into the school before, his friends called him on it, daring him to do it again.

"There ain't no way you're gonna do it Mad Dog!" Marcus exclaimed. He drained his current bottle of beer and replaced it with a fresh one from the paper bag sitting between them on the front seat. "I've got five bucks that says there's no way in." Good old Marcus. The guy knew Jim well, knew that the bet was the clincher to get "Mad Dog" Redmond to do anything. Jim smiled. After he'd finessed open the school window, he took Marcus's five bucks.

"That's the last of my beer money you know," Marcus whispered as he'd passed the Lincoln along to Jim.

"Maybe you can find some more inside," Jim said as he slipped into the school.

"Hope you're right, Mad Dog."

The nickname was well earned. Jim feared little regarding his classmates. The dozen fights this past school had earned him the moniker. If Jim's opponent got a punch through, Jim would just growl before going berserk on his foe. Jim hadn't started any of the fights, he hadn't needed to. His tawny skin color, thick, coal-black hair, and dark eyes made him stand out as a fine target of ridicule among the high school filled with pale, white Montana kids. It hadn't mattered how big the opponent was, Jim always won. His ferocity and fearlessness was now legend among his classmates. Though up till now, law enforcement had never been involved.

Now he sat detained in a patrol car because of a stupid bet. Jim wondered how bad it would be. Not completely sure what Marcus and Lance had done, he figured he would get off easy—assuming they didn't find the piss on Woolsey's chair and in her coffee mug. All they had found on him was a pen, and his guilt hinged on the officers figuring out that it was indeed stolen. If they did, then it might be a problem, given the pen's presidential origin.

Jim, Lance, and Marcus spent the next thirty minutes waiting in the back of their respective police cars, watching the cops take down information from the janitor. Other officers arrived and entered the school, no doubt checking the point of entry and looking for evidence of any other theft. Jim watched as the pigs stood outside talking to one another and to the janitor. How much did they know?

Officer Johnson walked to the car and opened the back passenger side door. "Seems the cash box in the office is missing the same amount we found in your friend's pocket," the officer said. Jim glanced at the man's face and saw the dried blood where his fist had connected with the cop's mouth. At least he hadn't broken the guy's nose. That was probably a good thing.

Officer Johnson stared at him. "Anything else I need to know about before we head downtown?"

"No," Jim said, easily and natural. He was used to lying. The cop's stare gave him an unsettled feeling. Jim looked at the floor of the car. His mother's words played in his mind: *A liar can't be trusted, and I won't live in any house with someone I can't trust.* Jim, his older brother Zack, and his younger sister Vivian had heard those words throughout their childhood. Each child knew that Mother didn't bluff. When caught lying, each had felt a lightning-fast swat of her hand on their hind ends as a result. Yet, Jim had lied to her hundreds of times as he'd moved into his teen years, usually when she asked where a particular item in his room had come from. He'd long grown practiced in lying, so adept that even Abby Redmond believed him. He hadn't feared his mother regarding that matter in years. But now a chill ran through him at the thought of Mom finding out he'd lied to a cop.

"The pen," Jim nearly whispered.

The cop pulled the item in question out of a small paper bag. "This one? What about it?"

"It belongs to Mr. Goodman, room 118. It was a gift from President Kennedy."

The cop raised his eyebrows. A closer look at the pen confirmed the truth. "And why did you take it?"

"I don't know. Just did."

Marcus's parents arrived first. His mom did her best to blot the tracks of tears on her cheeks. His dad's eyes were rage-filled, and a single vein bulged along his left temple. Marcus was equal to Jim in height and build and carried himself in a cocky, almost proud manner as he was led to his parents. The arrogant manner wilted when his father charged at him and cut him short with a quick backhanded slap. Officer Johnson bolted over and took hold of the irate man, neatly persuading him to restrain himself or enjoy an assault charge himself. As Marcus righted himself, holding his hand on his red check, Jim saw the glint of fear in his friend's eyes. The cops could intervene here, but nothing would temper his father's wrath once they were home.

Lance's mom arrived next. She looked mortified to be at the police station, eyes wide with fear and hesitation. Her presence there was certainly a first, she being a fine, upstanding member of the Methodist church. Jim smirked at how out of place she looked. Lance's dad was over in Vietnam, so this little incident surely made life even more traumatic for her.

With each family, the officers explained what had happened, handed out citations, then released the delinquent to go home. Jim couldn't hear the details but figured it would go similarly for him. Hopefully minus the beating.

It had been fifteen minutes since Lance and his mom left, and there was still no sign of Jim's parents. This was a troubling fact, given that their house was only ten blocks away. Why so long? Were they arguing about whether to leave him in jail for the night? If that was the case, Jim was sure his dad would vote jail. He hoped that if they came, they did so together, figuring they would be more restrained as a couple in front of the officers. If not, he wasn't sure which parent he hoped would come to pick him up, if they came at all.

His parents. He could barely call them that. In the past few years, Jim refused to call his parents Mother or Father, preferring

17

slang terms such as Pops or Old Lady—though often he would not even use those. Both Jim and his little sister had been told about being adopted at a young age. Of course, Jim hadn't needed to be told. His older brother, the first and only natural born child to Frank and Abby Redmond, had begun to tease Jim with the obvious as soon as the boy was old enough to talk. Zack would torment his sibling about how he couldn't possibly be a Redmond due to the entire lack of family resemblance. For the first time, Jim whole-heartedly agreed with Zack: his brother was right, he wasn't a Redmond. Perhaps tonight would prove it.

Fear fluttered in Jim's gut as he thought of the person he had once called Father. Frank was tall, his body lean but strong as steel from carving stone for a living. His temper, though often restrained, was not to be trifled with. Jim's dad wasn't abusive. In fact, only eight times had he raised a hand against Jim, and all but one were swats on the butt for not doing chores or for talking back. The remaining incident was more recent. Jim had tried to leave the house when grounded, and Frank had grabbed him. Jim foolishly shoved his dad away, triggering a well-placed fist to his chest. The blow sent him to the floor.

Since then, Jim and Frank held an uneasy armistice at the insistence of the woman of the house. Abby Redmond, the peacemaker. A flower in stature compared to her husband, she usually preferred to dote on both her kids and her dogs. Usually. At first look, Abby appeared to be a fragile woman, yet everyone in the household knew better. Abby was more than willing to remind everyone she was not a force to be dismissed lightly, using only her eyes and voice to prove it. No one, not even Frank, challenged her. Despite that, Abby was generally more understanding. And she had always believed Jim's lies. His father hadn't. Still wondering which parent might walk through the station door to retrieve him, Jim decided he hoped it would be Mom.

Officer Johnson labored over the Remington typewriter, finalizing the arrest report and occasionally rubbing his jaw. He glanced regularly at Jim—making sure he hadn't what? Hadn't left his chair? Hadn't left the room? He couldn't; the officer sat right outside the holding room door. Jim leaned back in his chair. Stared at the ceiling. He waited.

A male voice thundered from down the hall, "Where is he?!"

Jim's heart raced at the sound and leaned toward the open door so he could see down the length of the office. Frank Redmond appeared with a police officer alongside, trying to calm him. Father and son locked eyes, their stares imbued with mutual disdain. The old man had apparently dressed and left the house without much care to how he looked, likely distracted by the situation and what must have been a lengthy argument with Abby. He looked ragged, his long sleeve shirt only partly tucked into a pair of faded work jeans. His gray bangs hung loosely from under his dirty Stetson. Jim's father always wore that damned cowboy hat and boots.

Frank broke the mutual glare first as Officer Johnson introduced himself and explained the incident. Jim pulled his head back into the holding room and looked at the floor, wondering if his father would insist that they throw him into jail or whether he'd pay the bail and take him home. Frank's booming voice settled into his more familiar low, dominant tones. Jim didn't know what was being discussed. He didn't look and tried to shut out all noise, staring at the coffee-stained cement floor. Minutes passed and Jim raised his head at the sound of footsteps crossing the threshold of the holding room door.

"Alright Jim, we're releasing you to the custody of your father," Officer Johnson declared. "You need to be at the juvenile office Monday morning at ten. You're charged with burglary and resisting arrest. Sign here."

The cop handed over a clipboard with three layers of carbon duplicates. As Jim signed his name on the designated line, he could feel Frank's glare. The officer removed the bottom copy of the citation from the layers of duplicates. "If you don't show up, a bench warrant will be issued for your arrest so—"

"He'll be there," Frank snapped. "I promise you that."

The officer nodded and handed Jim the paper. "You're free to go kid," Officer Johnson said as he stepped to the side. "I hope the next time we meet it's under better circumstances."

Frank about-face turned and marched out of the station. Jim followed. What choice did he have? Stepping out of the police station, he contemplated running. It was a fleeting desire, trumped by his innate hatred of cowards. No, he would face the wrath of his parents. He would take it like a man. He followed Frank to the green sixty-three Impala parked next to a patrol car. Jim climbed in and closed the hefty door with a foreboding thud.

Jim tapped the door handle anxiously as Frank started the car. The Impala thundered into the quiet city streets. They turned onto North Benton and then west onto Hauser. Jim wanted to get home and hide in his room as he often did. Could Frank drive any slower? The darkened figure behind the wheel remained silent, intent. His knuckles whitened from his grip on the steering wheel, visible in the soft light of the dashboard. At least that was something, a hint at how angry Frank was. Jim realized he wanted a fight, and the car ride home didn't provide it.

Frank turned onto Grant Street and then into the alley that led to the detached garage behind their house. The kitchen lights were on. Abby was in there waiting. Jim wondered if his sister, Vivian, was up. He hoped not. Jim didn't want her to see any of this. Being almost seven years older, he always felt like he should protect her, even from his own troubles. From the first time one of her classmates made the mistake of pulling her ponytails at recess and Jim shoved him to the ground, to the time Jim knocked a kid's tooth out for calling his sis a booger face, he was Vi's guardian, whether she wanted it or not. It was the kindred connection of adoption that made him so protective. He certainly didn't care the same way for anyone else. Vivian's relative innocence was also an oasis to Jim, an escape from a world obsessed with war and from his own mind so often filled with anger.

The car idled a moment, then Frank killed the engine and got out. A lone incandescent bulb hung from the ceiling of the garage, painting a harsh white light over the car and the work benches lining the walls. Jim climbed out. He could make a dash for the kitchen door and postpone the battle. No, he decided to hold his ground. He waited as Frank shut the wooden carriage doors of the garage. Frank avoided eye contact as he walked over to a work bench. Still silent, he picked up some tools that were scattered about, hung them up on designated spots on the wall. Hammer. Screwdriver. Pliers. As if there was nothing wrong at all. The ticking sound of the Impala's cooling engine metered the silence.

Frank stopped his tidying, still facing the pegboard, his back to Jim. "So what do you have to say for yourself?" he asked.

Jim looked down, replying with silence. Two could play at this game. Maybe Frank would raise his voice. Jim didn't want to look like the ass in the fight; always better to allow the adult that honor.

Frank did not comply, though he turned to face him with a hard gaze. Sixty years old, Frank Redmond looked even older; his interrupted sleep and the light of the garage seemed to add ten years. Jim's parents were older than the parents of other kids in his school. Jim had chosen to ignore that reality. But he thought of it now as he looked at his father. Frank's brown eyes stabbed at Jim from the creases of age that surrounded them, white eyebrows contrasted against the enlarged pupils.

"Well, cat got your tongue?" Frank asked, calm but serious.

"What do you want me to say?"

"How about 'I'm sorry dad,' or, 'I made a bad decision and I won't do it again.' Let's start with those." Frank's voice had a sharper edge to it.

Good, keep it up old man. Just a little bit more. Jim smirked. Six months ago, when Jim had earned that backhand from Frank, he wasn't prepared for it. He felt ready for it now. He actually looked forward to it. This time, he could defeat Frank, he was confident of it. Jim was about to spit out a barb he hoped would trigger the fight when the door to the yard opened and in stepped Abby Redmond. She was wrapped in a long blue house coat and wearing her favorite slippers. By her side, as always, was the big mongrel, Timber.

Abby's lips were clenched tight as she and Timber entered the garage. The spring-mounted door slammed shut behind them. She stood near the door, brushed a long strand of gray laced brown hair away from her face, then crossed her arms across her chest. Feeling his mom's stare, Jim's anger grew. Damn! He didn't want to fight in front of her, no more than he would in front of his twelve-year-old sister.

Frank looked over at Abby, then back at Jim. "I'm not sure what your problem is," he said. "I really don't. Your mother and I have provided you with everything you could want. This is your thanks, we get calls from the principle at school about your fighting and, tonight, a call telling us you've been arrested!" Frank shook his head. "Do you have any idea how your actions impact this family?"

"How? Nothing I do affects you."

"Every time you get into trouble it hurts this family. It hurts your brother and sister, your mother, and me."

"You mean it embarrasses you!" Jim spat.

Frank winced, then narrowed his eyes. "What's that supposed to mean?" he snapped.

Yeah, Jim had hit home with that one. He looked at the floor. He knew Frank was well connected in town through his business. For all Jim's life, everyone had viewed him as Frank's boy, or one of the Redmond kids, but never as Jim. It was to the point that he would omit his last name when meeting new people, so he wouldn't be tied to the man.

"You know you're going to jail over this little stunt don't you? Yes, Jim, everything you do reflects on the Redmond name. But no, it doesn't embarrass me. It hurts me—hurts us all—that you plain don't care."

Jim glared, his clenched fists drained of blood. "Can I go now?" he asked, trying hard to look like he was bored with the conversation. Frank and Abby stared at each other.

"You're grounded for the rest of the month," Abby said. "Of course, that depends on if you're even living with us."

"Whatever," Jim muttered as he walked between his parents and out the door. He had hoped Frank would grab him, but neither adult hindered his departure. He ran across the yard, yanked open the back-porch door, then stomped into the house and up the stairs to his room. As he reached the top landing, he saw Vi peeking out from her room.

"What's wrong?" she asked sleepily.

"Nothing squirt, go back to bed," he said, then slammed his bedroom door closed. Jim stood clenching and unclenching his fingers. He let out a yell as his fist hammered into the wall near his door, leaving a dent in the sheetrock. It wasn't the only such mark in his room. He collapsed onto his bed, not bothering to undress.

Through his open window, he heard his parents' raised voices in the garage, followed by silence for several minutes. The back-porch door opened and closed, then soft footsteps climbed the stairs. Abby. Jim's room was closest to the stairs, and his ears had learned to identify everyone by their footsteps. A brief shadow at the bottom of his door betrayed his mother's pause outside his room.

For a moment, Jim wanted his mom to come in, to sit on the side of his bed, and to rub his back as she had done when he was little, telling him everything would be all right. She didn't. Her footsteps continued down the hall, followed by the faint click of her bedroom door closing. Downstairs, the porch door opened and closed again, but no footsteps came upstairs. Instead, Jim smelled the aroma of smoldering pipe tobacco. It was no surprise. Frank always smoked his pipe when troubled. As the sweet smell of pipe tobacco teased in through his window, Jim stared at the ceiling, wondering what to do.

CHAPTER 3

"Good morning Tom, the usual today?" The waitress was thick-boned, a sturdy gal, but surprisingly bubbly for half-past six in the morning. She chirped away as Tom removed his Stetson and made his way to a stool at the end of the counter.

"Mornin' Barbara," Tom politely replied but without the chipper demeanor. "The usual it is." His birthday had been just the day before, but he didn't bother telling her or anyone else for that matter. He had no interest in changing his usual habits in exchange for some self-indulgent celebration. His solitary glass of whiskey last night before bed had been celebration enough.

Sitting where he always did, the sole patron in the 4-B's restaurant for the moment, Tom was content to keep conversation to a minimum. Every Sunday morning he ventured into town for something other than his own cooking. He deliberately chose that day and time due to the inherent scarcity of people in the restaurant and on the roads. He would have the place mostly to himself until the churches let out, and then the brick and window faced eatery would be full of folks in their Sunday best.

"You got this week's funnies?" he asked and sipped his freshly poured coffee.

"Yep, I have 'em in back. Got the rest of the papers too if you want those?"

"Nope, just the funnies."

"How are you going to know what's going on in the world if you don't read the paper?"

"Spent enough time in the world to know that nothing changes. But toss 'em in the stack anyway. They're always good as fire starter." The fib wasn't a big one. Tom would take the time at home to look through the news but it seemed a sore spot with Barb so he figured he'd toss a little salt onto that wound. The banter between them was a weekly occurrence that Tom tolerated in exchange for the meal and free papers.

Barbara mumbled something about cantankerous old men and left to fetch the papers. Tom grinned. Even though he was an avid reader, the news held minimal interest for him. It never seemed to change. Same anger, same corruption, same violence, the same complaining with nothing changing. It hadn't seemed to change since the first time Tom had read the paper as a kid down in Durango, Colorado. And, it certainly hadn't changed in the time since he'd gotten home from World War II. People don't change so the news don't either; no point in wasting too much time confirming that. The funnies were a different story. Even if they commented on current events, they did so in an entertaining fashion.

Barbara returned with a stack of newspaper sections from throughout the prior week. Tom needed to catch up on the strips' storylines before he bought the Sunday edition of the *Independent Record* from the dispenser out front. Though Tom enjoyed the quick humor of *Beetle Baily*, he was most engrossed with the latest drama in his favorite strip: *Rick O'Shay*. Tom scanned the other strips and then caught up on the deputy sheriff's fist fight with the scoundrel, Gentry. They were duking it out for the hand of the fair maiden, Gaye Abandon. Tom grumbled under his breath as the story unfolded; Gentry easily defeated the out-matched Rick O'Shay.

"Why the hell aren't you helping him, Hipshot?" Tom hissed, hoping that Barbara didn't hear him from where she stood by the coffee machine. With each panel, Tom wondered if Rick's friend, Hipshot Percussion, would step in. By Thursday's strip Tom's disappointment was realized—Rick had been beaten, and Hipshot had done nothing. Tossing the paper to the counter, Tom rolled a cigarette to calm himself. He chuckled as he took a puff. Getting all worked up over a comic strip. What was he coming to? Tom liked the character Hipshot, a hardened gunfighter who often let his fists and guns do his talking, not unlike Tom himself. His favorite character hadn't even lifted a finger to help his friend. He pushed the papers away in anger.

Barbara brought Tom his usual fare of bacon, eggs, and toast. "Pepsi doesn't take her eyes off you, does she?" the waitress asked. Tom looked over his shoulder to see the nearly black cow dog staring at him from inside the cab of his Ford truck.

"Nope, she's just wondering if I'll bring her something."

"Oh, that reminds me, we've got more soup bones than we'll use this week. You want one for Pepsi?"

Tom nodded yes as he shoveled food into his mouth. The arrival of a few people signaled to him that he needed to hurry. They were probably just fishermen heading out for a day on the local waterways but they were enough to violate Tom's solitude.

Barbara left to tend to the other customers and get the bones. She returned several minutes later, just as Tom was enjoying his last few bites. She set the butcher paper-wrapped gift next to the stack of papers.

"That dog never makes a peep, does she?" Barbara asked. "Such a well behaved pup."

The woman had a soft spot for animals, as Tom had learned over the years, but she had never once asked if she could pet Pepsi.

Tom figured she was waiting for an invitation, which he would never extend. Pepsi was his dog. Aside from the horses, Pepsi was Tom's companion, confidant, friend. Things that Tom never had in great supply and wasn't keen to sharing with others.

"No, she only barks when herding the horses and mules or at the cars down at Ehler's when I'm getting groceries." Tom wiped his mouth and stood to dig in his pocket for the cash required to cover the tab.

"Hard to beat the friendship of a dog."

"Yep, much preferred over humans."

"You know Tom, if you stayed around a little longer you might actually meet some people you get along with. Heck, you might even make a friend or two if you put a little effort into it."

"I tried that once. The work wasn't worth the wage. Besides, I got enough friends." Tom grumbled as he collected the bones and newspapers. "Thanks for the breakfast Barb, see you next week."

"You stubborn old coot. See you next week."

Stepping outside, Tom returned the Stetson to its proper place and fished out the correct coinage for the Sunday paper. A copy of the latest *Record* in hand, he climbed into the truck, awkwardly since Pepsi was nearly crawling on him to lick his face and investigate the package that hid her bone.

"Back up girl, you'll get it when we get home."

The dog retreated to the passenger side window. She stuck her head out as Tom pulled onto the street and began the journey home. Pepsi maintained her stance the entire drive.

Once home, Tom brewed another pot of coffee to enjoy while reading the Sunday funnies. His coffee was a touch stronger than the Nash Coffee served at 4-B's, probably because he didn't bother throwing out yesterday's grounds. He just added a few scoops on top before brewing another pot. No point in wasting good coffee. Besides, it gave the brew a mule's kick, as Tom liked to say to those who were foolish enough to accept a cup.

Tom settled in and skipped the rest of the Sunday comics to read *Rick O'Shay* first. Gentry managed to beat up Rick O'Shay and then audaciously proposed to Gaye Abandon.

"That slimy sonofabitch!" Tom cursed, slamming the paper down. The impact on the table rattled the coffee mug and splashed a little onto the tabletop. Pepsi let out a yelp and withdrew to the darkness of the utility room just off the kitchen.

"I'm sorry girl. I ain't angry at you." Tom coaxed the frightened pup from the shadows. She timidly approached, and Tom petted her bluish black fur. The smudges of white and gray gave her coat a mottled appearance, like the soda after which she was named.

The phone rang and poor Pepsi jumped again. Tom decided to let her outside before answering. He held the front door, and Pepsi grabbed her soup bone then darted out onto the porch. The phone rang a fourth time before Tom picked it up with a gruff hello.

"Tom, Frank Redmond here, sorry to bother you this early."

"No bother at all Frank, you know you can call anytime." Tom's tone immediately softened. As he had said to Barbara, he had just enough friends, and Frank was one of them. "How are you, Abby, and the kids doing these days?"

"Abby and I are fine, thanks," Frank said and paused. "The kids, well, that's what I'm calling about."

Tom listened to Frank tell of his son, Jim's arrest and impending likelihood of jail time. Halfway through the tale, Tom regretted not having taken his coffee mug with him when he'd gotten up to answer the phone.

"You don't say. Well, sounds to me like he's just feeling his oats. I was the same when I was about his age." Tom would never tell a soul that he was much worse at that age, having already lived on his own for many years by the time he was eighteen. Tom stretched the phone cord as far as he could and reached out a single finger to nudge the coffee mug closer until he could retrieve it. Mug in hand, he took a pull from it, then added, "You know Frank, a little jail time might do the kid some good."

"We're not talking a few days at the county jail; he'd go to Pine Hills. Yeah, he might get scared straight there, but you and I both know that he might come back more crooked than when he went in."

Frank was right on that count. Pine Hills, over near Miles City, was known for being a harsh youth facility, and it was a coin toss as to how a kid would come out of there.

"So what can I do to help?"

"Deep in my bones I know Jim just needs to learn some responsibility—the kind that comes from a hard day's work. You and I both know what that's like. Work from sunup till sundown so that you're too tired to think about getting into any kind of trouble. That life is behind me now, and I can't offer it to him, but you've still got contacts. Maybe you could set him up with one of the local ranches or the Forest Service? Maybe I can convince the judge to consider three months of community service instead of jail time."

Tom pondered Frank's idea and rubbed his unshaved chin. "Yeah, I might know of something," he said. "Maybe a big trail repair or construction job for the Forest Service. I'm running pack strings and helping them set up and move camps all summer. Roy Zimmer is in charge, you know him. I can give him a call this morning and see if we can get Jim a spot on the crew. If that's what you want?"

"Given the short notice I'll take it. Let me know as soon as you talk to Roy. Jim goes to juvenile court tomorrow morning. I know the judge, and I think I can convince him to give Jim a choice. I don't want to force the kid into this. He won't learn anything that way." The line was quiet for a moment. Tom took another sip of coffee, and then Frank spoke again. "I really appreciate this. It means a lot to Abby and me. I won't forget it."

Frank had been a friend for almost twenty-three years. Apart from Tom's dog, his horses and mules, and members of his old army unit, Tom had only five people in his life he considered friends. Two were people he would die for and Frank Redmond was one of those. If Frank needed a favor, Tom would make it so.

"I'll see to it," Tom said. "You've got my word. I'll give you a call tonight or tomorrow morning after I get things sorted out."

"I owe you for this one."

"You don't owe me nothin'. Tell Abby hi for me, and anytime you and her want to come out and take the horses for a ride, you're always welcome." They said their goodbyes, and Tom hung up the phone. He swallowed down a big gulp of coffee, then headed out to the enclosed porch. He looked to the east. The tattered screens fogged the view of the valley and the surrounding mountains, and the numerous holes and rips did little to keep the insects out. He needed to replace those screens or tear them out one of these days.

Pepsi noticed Tom and raised her head from her bone. She was curled up on an old horse blanket in the corner. The dog's triangle ears stood erect as she listened for a command. When none was given, she returned to gnawing on the hunk of cow femur. Pepsi wasn't a big dog by any stretch, being a Blue Heeler mix. The giant soup bone dwarfed her small head, but it didn't deter her any more than the horses or mules did. The soda pop dog might be timid with people, but she was fearless when it came to herding or taking on the occasional beef bone.

Tom returned to the kitchen to refill his mug, and Pepsi followed him, the bone firmly in her jaws. She curled up in a corner and continued her pleasurable work of reducing the bone's size.

The coffee was needed this morning. Like many nights, Tom's sleep had once again been visited by past horrors. It had been so bad that Pepsi had even left her usual spot, right next to Tom's feet on the bed, retreating to a place absent of thrashing legs and arms. Waking in a cold sweat at a quarter past two in the morning,

Tom had sought solace in the only place he could always find it: outside with his animals. Pepsi had followed him out, like always, as he shuffled his way to the corral. Even with his denim jacket on, Tom shivered as he struggled to light a cigarette. His heart was still beating fast from the nightmare. His breathing calmed with each long drag of tobacco smoke and each stroke of his hand on the head of Molly, one of Tom's big mules. Molly had been first to come over to the fence. The herd was accustomed to Tom's intrusions on their sleep. They seemed to know that their care-taker needed the peace of the stars and the herd's protection, and they always made their way over to the fence at his approach. For that Tom was thankful. He hated when he was like this—anxious, nervous about what nightmares awaited him. With Pepsi yawning at his feet and horses and mules huddled near, Tom admired the trail of sparkling dust that stretched from the south horizon to the north. Damn beautiful. The anxiety subsided. After giving each member of the herd one last pat, Tom and Pepsi retreated back to the house to try and sleep the rest of the night away.

Now, after the call from his friend, Tom didn't think much of last night's dreams. This trouble with Jim was something new to mull over. In all the years he'd known Frank, he had never heard or seen the man be flustered about anything. He was flustered now.

Tom wasn't surprised by the recent events. On the day they had adopted Jim, he'd tried to warn Frank and Abby that the half-breed boy would be trouble.

"He's got Injun in his blood, you'd best take him back," he'd said. Tom's off-the-cuff comment had earned him a slap across the face from Abby.

"That is my son you're talking about," Abby rebuked him. "If you ever say anything like that again, I'll knock your head clean off! You hear me, Tom McKee?" Tom's arm muscles tensed, about to raise a hand in automatic retaliation, but he held it in check.

Any other time Tom would have struck back, unconcerned with whether it was a man or woman. Tom lived by the creed that no one laid a hand on him. Ever. Still, as Abby had stood there, the young child in her free arm and without a hint of fear, Tom knew he had been wrong. He also knew that any further words or actions would cost him a valued friendship. A quiet apology and retreat were his only option.

Since then, Tom had kept his opinions to himself. He would never admit it, but he had even grown to admire Frank and Abby's dedication to their kids, regardless of the aesthetic differences that existed. In a way, he was even jealous, not having been raised in a home where loving parenting was the norm. Given the current situation, Tom couldn't help but wonder if he had been right about the half-breed. He still thought it might be good to let the kid sit in jail for a few months. He knew that Abby had to be behind this alternative plan as much as Frank was. Well, they loved their kids. Tom had to admire Abby and Frank for that. Now the question was whether Frank had enough pull with the judge to provide the option of community service in lieu of a trip to Pine Hills. Of course, first Tom had to convince Roy to take on a juvenile delinquent for the summer. None of this would matter, though, if Jim didn't like the sound of a summer of hard work.

Tom never did understand kids or the people who had them. When he had met Frank and Abby, their first boy had been a couple years old. Their meeting hadn't been the most pleasant introduction. Tom's fault. It was back in January 1943, and Tom was in training with an army unit out at Fort William Henry Harrison, west of Helena. Like all the men in the unit, Tom was a scrapper and a drinker. On one particular weekend pass, he had lit it up good, having closed down the bar and survived three fights on the way out the door—bloodied lip, black eye, rubber legs and all. He stumbled down the road with the foolhardy intent of walking the four miles back to his barracks in the freezing cold. Tom only remembered waking up on a couch with a tall man sitting nearby, glaring at Tom with a watchful eye.

"Where am I, and who the hell are you?" Tom moaned, rubbing his temples to dull the explosions inside.

"I'm Frank, that's Abby, and that's my son Zack," the tall man said and pointed to fuzzy forms standing in the threshold of the room. Sunlight glinted off a stove and sink behind the woman. "You're in my home."

Tom had rubbed his aching head as he sat up. Looking around he saw a simple but tidy home. A young boy clung to the petite woman's leg. The child stared back at him, wide-eyed. The woman gave Tom a reserved smile and turned back to her chores as her husband dealt with the wayward soldier.

"What day is it?"

"You must've been on a real bender son. It's Sunday morning."

Tom had breathed a sigh of relief knowing he was still on his weekend pass and not AWOL. "Oh Lord, I hope I didn't barge in on you..." He looked at the floor, wondering if he might have kicked in the door in a drunken rage. It wouldn't have been the first time he had done such a thing.

"No, you wouldn't be breathing if you had done that."

Frank's answer made Tom chuckle.

"But you darn near froze to death out in the street. Figured I would do my part for the war effort and keep one of Uncle Sam's soldiers alive so they could get you killed later."

Again, Tom had laughed. He'd liked the man; they thought the same. Frank's stern face allowed the slightest smile. Embarrassment set aside, Tom was treated to breakfast, a might tastier than what he would have gotten from the chow hall at the fort.

Tom was a hard man with few manners, since running away from home at the age of fifteen. But he had enough smarts to be thankful for the kindness shown him that day. During the next three months of training, Tom stopped by and chatted with Frank and Abby any time he was in town. Each visit they had welcomed Tom into their home, and not once had they brought up the circumstances of how they'd met. After Tom's unit shipped off to war, regardless of where he was in the world, he received regular letters from Frank and Abby. It was the only mail he received while deployed, and such devotion had gone a long way to strengthen their friendship. After the war, Tom was aimless, uncertain of where to go and what to do. He had no desire to return to Durango, Colorado, his birthplace. His family had disowned him long ago. So, Tom settled on the one place where he had friends, Helena. He learned that he wasn't alone in that decision. Many of the men from the Devil's Brigade, as his unit had come to be called, returned to the place of their creation and initial training. The love of the mountains and the people of the area tempered the war memories.

Tom got along with Frank Redmond because both shared common traits: loyalty, devotion to friends, love of animals, and a strong sense of honor. Both men believed that keeping their word was more important than anything else. If true friends were a measure of wealth, then Tom felt rich with the few he had.

Tom glanced at his watch and decided it was too early to make calls. Most people were church-goers and all. Draining the last of his coffee, he stood and headed for the door. Pepsi sprang up and darted across the linoleum, her nails clicking and clacking as she went. Once at Tom's side, she looked up eagerly as he donned his mangled, dirty Stetson hat and his denim Storm Rider jacket. This would ward off the chill from the cold snap that had moved through the region the day before. As he opened the door to head outside, Pepsi darted past him and pushed through the torn screen at the bottom of the porch door, sprinting around the dirt driveway in jubilation. She knew it was time to work. Tom let the screen door slam closed behind him. He pulled a pouch of Bull Durham tobacco and a slip of cigarette paper from the left chest pocket of his Pendleton shirt. With well-practiced motions, he had a cigarette rolled, lit, and the pouch returned in less than twenty seconds. Tom walked at his normal, confident pace towards the corral, a thin ribbon of smoke trailing behind him. After her initial burst of energy, Pepsi fell in line next to Tom's leg, her gaze always turned up to him. The six horses and twelve mules that milled around the corral perked up at their approach. Sil, a tall, silver roan mare, trotted up and hung her head over the fence for the neck scratches she took for granted. Tom's favorite, Comanche, stood off a bit. As always, the pale Morgan and Appaloosa cross looked at him with a defiant eye. Tom needed to check all the horses' hooves today to make sure they were ready to start hauling camp supplies for the big Forest Service job. All his stock was shod, so Tom would be checking for slack or missing shoes, tacking on replacements, or resetting loose shoes as needed. As always, he had a full day of hard work ahead of him, and Tom wouldn't want it any other way.

CHAPTER 4

The rancid smell of cigarette smoke seared Comanche's nostrils. Though he had smelled it hundreds of times before, he still hated it. The odor tainted the cool morning air and overpowered the sweet smell of fresh hay. Comanche snorted to purge his senses of the awful intrusion. He watched the man walk away from the corral to the building holding the saddles and other tack. They were going out again. Comanche tossed his head in excitement and hopped to the side. The rest of the herd spooked and trotted around nervously. Time in the corral was torture for the big Appaloosa but the knowledge that they would be going out on a trip again thrilled him.

Though he hated having a rider on his back, Comanche made an exception for this man, the one he called Boss. Even with the stinging smoke the man breathed at times, Boss was tolerable because he had earned his trust—unlike Comanche's first owner. His previous owner had been a cruel man whose method of control had been a harsh hand and a violent manner. Comanche was not one to tolerate such treatment. When it came time for him to be broke, Comanche nearly killed the man. It had been a war of wills, and Comanche had won. Shipped off for sale, it was then that Boss came into his life, and their journey as rider and horse began. That first time they'd met at the auction pen, Comanche could see that Boss' eyes had a fire in them, but it wasn't the fire of anger. Instead, it was a fire of calm determination. It was a look that Comanche respected.

The sound of Boss' voice echoed from inside the shed. Though the man was out of sight, all ears were turned toward the open door. The talk wasn't for the horses or the black dog that had taken post outside the shed. The talk was just Boss being who he was. The animals were used to it, but listened intently anyway. Boss always talked more when animals were the only ones there to listen. They liked that: the man's voice, steady and strong, was as soothing to them as the warm morning sun. It was the voice that helped most with Comanche's training. There was never any fear or anger in it. Just confidence.

Training had dominated the first few months with Boss. It had started with halter breaking and eventually led to skilled riding. All the effort and time together earned Comanche's trust, to the point where the horse knew what the man wanted with just a press of the knee or touch of the leather rein on his neck. By the time they made their first journey into the mountains, the bond between man and horse was permanent.

Never before had Comanche had the chance to push himself as hard as he wanted, and this rider not only allowed it but encouraged it. Up one mountain they would go, only to look for another to climb. While the other horses would rest and eat whatever grass was nearby, Comanche was impatient. He wanted to continue the journey; there would be plenty of time to eat back at the corral. The two complemented each other. The horse comforted and carried the rider, the rider tempered and paced the horse. The relationship went beyond that of typical saddle horse and master.

Boss came back from the shed wearing a thick leather apron with tools sticking out of its pockets. At his feet, the ever-present dark dog trotted around, as excited as the horses. Boss carried a metal stand, which meant he would examine their hooves. Comanche didn't like this, but he knew it was necessary before a trip into the mountains. At the sound of a gentle whistle, the whole herd to trotted over to the man. He entered through the gate, latching it behind him. Comanche led the herd with Sil behind, followed by the others. The whistle meant food.

Not disappointed, the horses were each given a nugget of compressed alfalfa. Their soft lips lifted the nugget daintily from the man's open palm. Though careful with the man, all the horses and mules jockeyed for position, hoping for more than one treat. But Boss scolded and pushed away each selfish offender, ensuring that each animal received the allotted treat.

The man had no hesitation mingling with the herd, even being so small among the four-legged beasts. His movements and posture conveyed his confidence. That is exactly what Comanche respected. The man was confident in who he was, and he made it clear he was alpha in the herd, absent of fear. Comanche despised cruelty, but he also hated fear in riders. The smell of it was as repulsive as the smoke Boss exhaled. The horse had learned to sense fear long ago, and he played off of it with any human, besides Boss, who dared ride him. The man who stood among them now had no such fear. Boss was welcome in the herd, and he was worthy to be followed and trusted.

The man looped a thick rope around Comanche's neck to keep him close then strapped a halter around the pale horse's big head. Comanche pulled back a little and then swung his head to push Boss away, forcing him out of his space. Every day, every new interaction, Comanche tested the man. Was he still leader or not? As much as he liked Boss, Comanche wasn't going to submit completely; it just wasn't in his nature. The man gave him a firm push in return and talked quietly as he fastened the halter. Yes, he was still in charge. Boss led Comanche to the fence where he tied the rope to one of the railroad tie fence posts.

Something was wrong. Boss was more tense than usual, though Comanche couldn't ascertain why. It wasn't fear, it was something different. His voice, his movements, and his mind were elsewhere. When the man grabbed the tuft of hair at the back of his right rear hoof, Comanche gave a quick kick. It didn't connect with the man and certainly wasn't meant to. It was only meant to get Boss' attention. The man stood up and looked at his horse. Comanche turned his head and locked eyes with Boss. The man nodded, spoke a couple words, and patted Comanche's rump. With the man's mind back where it needed to be, he took hold of Comanche's hoof again and lifted it so he could clean and inspect the shoe. Comanche allowed it this time, now that his rider was focused. He couldn't let the man go soft on him now.

CHAPTER 5

J im wrestled with his dreams throughout the night. His nightmares were fueled by emotions that tumbled like an autumn leaf
in free fall. Thick blinds shielded him from the Sunday morning
sunshine. Semiconscious, he entertained the hope that he could
remain hidden in his darkened room, that his problems would just
go away. Abby Redmond had other plans. In the hall, just outside
his bedroom door, commanding words rallied the family to head
to church. The clock on his dresser revealed that Abby had let him
sleep past eight. A rarity for a Sunday morning, or any morning
for that matter.

Driven more by the rumbling of his stomach than Abby's demands, Jim pulled himself out of bed. Still wearing the clothes
from the day before, he trudged downstairs and into the kitchen.
Vivian was already seated at the table in her Sunday best, her blond
hair pulled back into a pony tail. She smiled at Jim but didn't stop
her conversation with Abby. Something about what she wanted
to do that summer. Abby faced the counter, her back to Vi as she
flipped misshaped banana pancakes on the electric skillet. She
caught sight of Jim as she turned with a plate stacked high with
pancakes.

"Glad you are awake," she said and set the plate on the table. "Sit down and get some breakfast in you. We need to hurry so we aren't late for Sunday School." There was surprisingly no strain in her voice. She sounded as though it was any other Sunday morning.

Big-eyed and hungry, Vi stabbed three pancakes with her fork. Jim sat down at his spot, across the table from Vi. The only out of the ordinary element was that their father was nowhere to be seen.

"Where's pops?" Jim asked. He grabbed four pancakes with his fingers, dropping them onto his plate.

"Use your fork Jim, you're not an animal!" Abby scolded. There was the edge. Jim felt oddly satisfied at her losing her cool. "Your father has some business to take care of. He won't be joining us at church."

Everything was falling apart at home, and the old man was working extra, that figured. Though it was welcome news for Jim. Now bleary-eyed and sleep deprived, he wasn't feeling as eager for a fight anymore. He drenched his pancakes in maple syrup. The first bite was blissful, a reprieve from everything. Jim's hunger pushed aside his anxiety. He ignored the female conversation and voraciously ate his first stack of pancakes. Then a second.

Jim didn't speak a word as he ate. Forks clanked and scraped on the plates, Vi smacked her lips, mother and daughter chatted about what friends were doing over the summer break. No mention was made of last night's events, though Jim suspected that Vi had inquired about the disruption to the family's normally sedate evenings. His sister seemed chipper enough, but something about her smile and casual conversation seemed a little forced. Yeah, she knew. That reality weighed on Jim; he didn't like that Vi was impacted by his actions. It left him feeling as though he had failed in protecting her. Nothing he could do about all that. Right now he just needed to eat the pancakes. He doused his last few bites in extra syrup and caught a fleeting glare from Abby.

After breakfast, Abby insisted Jim go back upstairs to put on a clean shirt and at least attempt at taming his hair, which showed clear evidence of his night of wrestling with his pillow. Once Jim was groomed well enough to glean a single approving nod from Abby, the three loaded into the car. The drive to the First Baptist Church of Montana took them past the police station at the Civic Center. The copper-domed spire appeared less imposing to Jim than it had the night before. He wasn't wearing handcuffs this time, though he was packed into a car, going somewhere against his will.

No one spoke during the drive, and the only sound was the noise of the engine. Abby did not approve of having the radio on while driving. Normally Jim would have liked the distraction of music. Today he was grateful for the silence. On Warren Street Abby maneuvered the big Impala along the narrow historic road. She pulled to the curb a block away from church, killed the engine, adjusted her hair, and gathered her small purse and well-worn King James Bible. Then she ushered Jim and Vi out of the car.

Jim held back, standing near the car while Abby and Vi stepped into the street. "Do I have to go to Sunday school?" he asked. Abby and Vi paused. The blaze behind Abby's eyes made it clear that Jim's attendance was non-negotiable.

Reluctantly, Jim followed Abby and his sister. Jim had sat through countless Sundays, Frank and Abby's presence preventing his escape. Sunday School and church were like school to him: something he was required to do until he moved out. Just one more year and he could decide for himself what he did with his time. That is, if he survived whatever the judge threw his way tomorrow.

Jim followed Abby and his sister into the sanctuary, where he would endure the theological diatribes of the weekly Sunday School lesson. Vi hurried off to the children's class in the church's new educational building. The smell of fresh paint was almost overpowering. A major expansion and remodeling effort had been underway most of the year. A new coat of light aqua paint covered the walls, giving the appearance that the stained-glass windows and cross behind the pulpit were floating in a big sky. Jim sank onto a hard wooden pew.

The forty-minute-long discussion on the book of Ecclesiastes left Jim nearly numb. Staying awake through adult Sunday school and the following service was officially the least of his worries now. Probation or perhaps jail? He wondered what the juvenile officer and judge would say. Would he go to jail? Of course he would; he had broken into a school and had punched a cop. Life, as he knew it, was officially over. Even if it was juvenile jail, he would miss his senior year. Occasionally, his ears caught scraps of the teacher's Ecclesiastical musings: Life is meaningless. Pleasure and pain, work and play, riches and poverty. All meaningless. Well, sure as hell there was some truth to that.

Between Sunday School and the main service, Jim grabbed a cookie and a cup of juice from the newly renovated kitchen while Abby went to find Vi. The crowd milled around Jim, everyone smiling and chatting, none saying hello to him. He felt invisible. He stared at the side door and thought of making a mad dash. Start running and never stop. Then he caught sight of Abby returning with Vi. He swallowed his pride and ate another gingersnap instead.

Abby shepherded him and Vi into the sanctuary. They had just sat down when the organ started playing, causing the entire congregation to rise. In mind-numbing repetition, Jim recited a prayer that preceded a herd of hymns. He mouthed the words as usual, not bothering to put any effort into singing. Despite the troubles he'd brought to his family, both his mother and sister belted out the hymns as usual, seeming to delight in how well they could hold a note in perfect harmony. Finally, the congregation was told to sit, and Jim stared off at the stained-glass windows. His mind wandered as an elder read a Scripture passage and Reverend King presented his sermon. As always, Jim heard none of it. However, unlike any other Sundays, his mind didn't wander to school, girls, or other trivial things. His thoughts were on his immediate future, and on whether he would even have one.

After the service, Jim exited the church quickly, leaving Abby and his sister to socialize. Walking south towards the car, Jim looked across the street. In the distance, beyond the ornate stonework of Central Public School and all the other downtown buildings, loomed Mount Helena. A green cloak of trees draped its slopes and ended in bare gray cliffs near the top. Jim had hiked to the top a dozen times with his siblings and friends, and he wished he could be hiking it now. What he'd give to be away from everything—if only for a minute—to be free of his troubles.

Jim waited a good ten minutes before Abby and Vi showed up. Their chatting seemed subdued as they approached. Perhaps they'd talked to church friends about him. Whatever the case, the drive home was as quiet as the drive to church. Arriving home, Vi walked quickly into the house and headed to her room to change out of her Sunday clothes. Timber trotted alongside her, barking in excitement at the return of his humans and trying to coax Vi to play. The slamming door denied the dog such pleasure. Jim ignored Timber's nudge at his hand as he entered the back door, and Abby headed in right behind him. Not a good day for the dog.

There was no sign of Frank in the house, but the court papers from last night now lay on the kitchen table where he always sat. Jim stared at the papers. Absently, he rubbed his palms on his jeans. Suddenly he switched from fearful to irritated. He exhaled loudly, stomped over to the fridge, and grabbed a bottle of Coke. Stealing past Abby before she could say anything, he retreated upstairs to his room. He sipped the sweet soda as he thumbed through his collection of vinyl records, trying to find some suitable escape. Several Beatles and Beach Boys albums held no appeal. Their way-too-cheerful tempo and lyrics made him cringe. Definitely not a day for love ballads; his last attempt at asking a girl out had ended with her laughing at him then callously, saying that her parents would never approve. He was depressed enough without revisiting that moment.

Jim settled on the Rolling Stones. He could tolerate Mick Jager bellowing *Everybody Needs Somebody to Love* and *Down Home Girl*, knowing the rest of the album would work for him. He ignored the lyrics as he picked up a stack of comic books and lost himself in an issue of *Sergeant Fury and his Howling Commandos*. His retreat into the colorful pages was interrupted by both the end of the first side of the album and the growling of his stomach. He shut off the turntable and listened to determine who was in the house.

Hearing no one, Jim slipped downstairs long enough to make a sandwich. Lunches on Sunday were a help yourself matter, with the Sunday family dinner occurring at six in the evening without fail. For now, the house was strangely quiet. Abby and Vi must have gone for a walk. Frank was still gone, ever devoted to his work. To heck with him. Jim was grateful for the solitude. Back in his room, he munched on the ham and cheese pressed between two slices of Sweetheart white bread. He switched to a *Captain America* comic and found himself increasingly distracted by his worries. The fitful sleep of the previous night had taxed him. Unable to focus on reading, Jim collapsed on his bed. He noticed the time on his bedside clock: 2:43. A short nap would be good. Exhaustion overtook him and he slipped into a deep sleep. Three hours later, he woke to Abby shouting that it was suppertime.

He heard Vi's quick steps descending the stairs, opened his bedroom door, and caught a glimpse of her bright red shirt as she spun around the banister on her sprint to the kitchen. As he followed, the aroma of the usual Sunday dinner wafted up to him: ham and fresh baked bread. Entering the kitchen, Jim saw that Frank had returned from wherever he had been all day. He sat at the table reading the *Independent Record* and glanced over the top edge of the paper at Jim. Frank gave the paper a shake and returned his gaze to the pages. Not a hint of emotion. Jim's throat tightened. This reserved silence was way worse than an all-out fight. He walked the few steps to the table and sat down opposite Vi.

"Frank, the blessing please," Abby requested as she sat down.

Her husband gave the paper one more shake, folded it twice, and set it on the counter behind him. Bowing his head, Frank reached out his hands to each side as did Vi and Abby. Jim bowed his head, ignoring the open hands on either side of him.

Frank exhaled, then recited their standard nightly prayer, the one they said at every evening meal in the Redmond household.

"God, we thank you for this food. For rest and home and all things good. For wind and rain and sun above. But most of all for those we love." Another weary exhale, then, "Amen."

What, was Jim supposed to feel sorry for him? Didn't anyone realize he was the one going to court tomorrow? Didn't they realize he was the one who had never felt loved a day in his life? Jim felt no love, for or from anyone in the world, except for his sister. Even with her, what he felt was more like a protective solidarity. He wasn't sure it was actually love.

Jim didn't feel like eating. That morning, worry had driven him to eat more. Now, for some reason, the unspoken tension at the table drove his appetite away. He picked at his food and ignored the conversation between his parents and Vivian. Supper was notably less exuberant than normal. Some of that was because his older brother Zack and his wife were absent. Typically, they joined them for Sunday dinner, but with a new baby at home, they had opted out for a few weeks. Ever since Zack had become a partner at their father's stone shop, Jim felt even smaller in his brother's shadow. His absence at tonight's dinner was a small relief.

He wondered if Zack knew about the pending court date. He hoped not. His brother was a source of constant torment and insults. All in brotherly love, Zack would claim. Though they were brothers by name, Jim had never felt a bond with Zack, not like he did with Vi. The bond between Jim and Vi was one of kindred spirits, kids who shared the commonality of having been adopted. Zack liked to rub in the fact that he was the true Redmond, always reminding Jim that he was bought at an orphanage like some toy at a store. These torments were never directed at Vi. She was spared such teasing, likely because she was white and because she was a girl. Regardless, it was a good thing that Zack was not here this evening.

Each bite was an effort. The ham seemed bland and the bread dry. Conversation between his parents and sister transpired as if he was not even present at the table. With half his plate still piled with food, Jim set his silverware down.

"Can I go? I'm not hungry," he said and pushed back from the table.

Abby looked from him to Frank.

"Go ahead," Frank begrudged.

Jim could feel all three of them watch as he carried his plate to the sink and walked upstairs. In his room, he sat on the floor, leaning back against his bed. Through the floor, he soon heard the TV, the familiar tune of the *Bonanza* theme song. It was a re-run, as the season had ended, but Jim knew his parents didn't care. Though neither watched much TV, they devotedly made time for westerns.

The solitude began to tighten around Jim as if the hand of some dark being had encircled him, closing its grasp tighter and tighter. His thoughts fixed on Monday: the crime, the punishment, and how his life would be over at ten a.m. What was the point? Life was hell and was only about to get worse. He pondered what future awaited him when he got out of jail. What would it be like to go back to school a year older than every other senior? And after school, if no one would hire him, he'd have to join the military. That idea didn't entirely bother Jim, but the likelihood of being sent to Vietnam was unsettling. Jim held his head in his hands, his fingers weaved through his thick black hair.

What, indeed, did he have to live for? Nothing. He sat with that reality for a while, that question. He let it pound into him. For several minutes, he shook, fighting the sobbing knot in his chest. Slowly, the desperation subsided; he felt numb. Rubbing his face dry of tears, Jim got up and walked to his door. Downstairs, he heard the harsh whistle of a tea kettle and then a soft melody, his mother humming as she prepared her nightly cup of Earl Grey. No one knew how he felt. No one cared. Incredible.

The light of the hallway flooded into Jim's room as he cracked open his door and peered out. Both Vi's and his parents' rooms were dark. The sound of Little Joe and Hoss Cartwright bantering on the TV echoed up the stairwell. With the television as loud as it was, Jim didn't worry about the floor creaking as he walked into his parents' room and opened their closet door. Tucked in the back corner were three bolt action hunting rifles and an old double-barrel shotgun that had supposedly belonged to his grandpa Redmond, who had died long before Jim or his siblings were born. Jim grabbed the Savage 30-06 that he normally carried while elk hunting with his dad and brother. He quietly slid it out of the closet, snatched a box of shells from the top shelf, and then snuck back into his room and closed the door.

Sitting down on the bed, Jim admired the well-used rifle. Its deep blue barrel was mottled with rust spots from when they had gotten stuck in a heavy, wet snowstorm and hadn't been able to get the rifles dried and cleaned quickly. The stock had several small dents and scratches from walking through dense timber in the effort to get a jump on a big bull. Good memories, but they faded quickly, lost in the darkness of the moment. Jim pulled a cartridge out of the box and opened the bolt. He heard nothing but the cold metallic click of steel as the bolt slid back and revealed the chamber. His hands shook as he placed the cartridge in the gun and closed the bolt. He turned the gun around and looked into the emptiness of the hole at the end of the barrel. Jim paused for a moment and wondered where he should put the barrel, under his chin or in his mouth? Concerned that the gun might shift at the last moment and fail at the task, he chose his mouth. Crazy thoughts. Crazy life. Yeah, he was crazy, but he was just sane enough to know what he had to do.

Raising the barrel to his lips, Jim smelled the distinct odor of Hoppe's No. 9 gun solvent. The odor triggered strong memories of cleaning guns on the kitchen table with his brother and dad, and of the laughter they had shared as they'd told Vi of their hunting adventures. She always listened intently to each tale. Then, last fall, she'd insisted she would join them next autumn, now that she was almost old enough to hunt. Zack and Jim chided her, insisting that girls didn't hunt and couldn't shoot anyway.

"I can too!" she bellowed. Near tears, Vi ran to her mother who had assured her that she could go hunting if she wanted, as long as her father approved. To Zack and Jim's surprise, Frank immediately shattered their exclusive club of male adventure.

"If Vi wants to hunt, then she gets to hunt," he said. "If she's anything like your mother, she'll outshoot the both of you."

Vi hugged their father, thanked him, and shot an I-told-you-so smirk at her brothers. The shock was twofold: the fact that their sister would be hunting with them and the realization that their mom had not only shot a gun before but was skilled at it.

Jim needed no skill now, not with the barrel inside his mouth. The cold steel felt strange on his tongue, the taste a combination of solvent, rust, and metal. Not entirely unpleasant, just unfamiliar. Steadying the gun with his left hand, Jim reached down with his right and rested his thumb on the trigger. He took a breath.

The safety had never been set, so only a few pounds of pressure were needed now. Jim sat there, thumb on the trigger, barrel in his mouth, and a new batch of crazy thoughts: Would Captain America do this? Would any brave man? Doesn't a real man own his mistakes instead of running from them? From the back of his mind, fighting through the despair, came a shrill, clear accusation: *Coward.* Only a coward would do this. He hated cowards!

Carefully, Jim lifted his thumb from the trigger, pulled the gun from his mouth, and set it on the bed. He stared at the rifle. Once again, he rubbed his face dry—when had he started crying again? Jim opened the bolt to remove the cartridge, the ejector sending the round to the carpeted floor with a dull thud.

There was a gentle knock at his door and Jim jumped. Light from the hallway filtered in as the door opened. Vivian. She never asked if she could come in. Jim never required her to. He quickly pushed the rifle away from him on the bed and snatched the cartridge from the floor. His little sister took a step into his room, blinking at the dark.

"You missed *Bonanza*," she said softly. Her right hand nervously twisted her sun blond hair.

"Yeah, it was just a summer rerun," Jim grumbled, trying to sound casual.

"It was good though. Hoss got in a fight with some horse wrangler," she said and sat down on the bed, between him and the gun. "Hey, Mom said they know of a guy who has horses and said that he'll let me come out and learn how to ride. You want to come too? It would be fun, don't you think?"

"Yeah, sounds like fun." Jim couldn't look at his sister. She must have been sneaking up the stairs while he held the gun in his mouth. She would have been the one who had found his body. Shit. What had he been thinking?

"Are you okay?" she asked. "Mom said you got into some trouble, and you have to go to court tomorrow."

"Yeah squirt, it's nothing big. I'll be fine."

"Why do you have the gun out?"

Jim glanced at the rifle. "Oh, I was thinking of going hunting next weekend. I was just cleaning it." Jim looked at his sister hoping she'd buy his lie. She didn't.

"Hunting season isn't till fall, stupid."

"What do you know, squirt?" Jim gave her a playful shove with his shoulder and tried to shore up his lie. "You can hunt gophers any time of year, silly."

She pushed back with a giggle and then got up to leave. "It'll be okay," Vi said as she paused at the door. Her voice quavered a little. "Tomorrow I mean."

She knew the court date was serious. He wasn't surprised. She might seem innocent, but she was also observant. Thoughtful.

"Thanks squirt. I'm sure you're right."

Vivian closed the door, leaving Jim in the darkness. He got up, turned on the light, and quickly returned the cartridge to its box. Peeking out the door, he saw that Vi was in the bathroom. His parents were still downstairs with the TV on. He grabbed the rifle and box of shells and swiftly returned them to his parents' closet. In his mind's eye, he saw his lifeless body, brains all over the wall and ceiling, and Vivian standing at the door, screaming. He shivered. Never again. Jim returned to his room and turned on his radio. The sound of the exuberant DJ announcing the next song drowned out his thoughts—what had almost happened and what might happen tomorrow. Only when he heard his parents go to bed did he feel confident that Vi hadn't tattled on him about the gun.

The rapid knocking on his bedroom door yanked Jim back to a state of consciousness on Monday morning. Abby entered his room and pulled open the blinds, flooding his room with sunlight. He dragged the covers over his head.

"Jim, it's after eight, so get out of bed and get cleaned up," she said, all business. "I want you to wear a nice shirt and clean pants. You're not going before Judge Cannich looking like a vagabond."

Jim felt her yank the bedspread away from his head. He groaned.

"I said get up!" She didn't leave the room till he had pulled himself upright, sitting on the edge of his bed. When she left, he considered lying back down, but the last time he'd tried that Abby had returned with a glass of cold water, which she unceremoniously poured over his head. And that had been on a good day.

Jim showered, and in keeping with his Abby's orders, he dressed in clean clothes, making sure he looked at least a notch above his usual appearance. He combed his long dark bangs off to the side, looked at himself in the mirror, then took a deep breath and headed downstairs.

"Here's your breakfast," Abby said and set a plate of eggs and bacon on the table. "Eat up. We need to drop Vi off at the Watson's before we head to the courthouse."

"Where's dad?" Jim asked. He sat down and starting shoveling in a forkful of scrambled eggs. Apparently, he was hungry once again.

"He's at work," Abby answered as she washed a frying pan in the sink. Jim must have really been asleep if he hadn't heard his dad's shop truck start up and drive away. The hole in the muffler was as good an alarm clock as Abby was most of the time. Jim wanted to ask if Frank would be at court, but Abby's stern brow made him think it might be better to remain quiet.

As Jim finished off his breakfast, he heard Vivian practicing her piano scales in the living room. The notes immediately stopped when Abby called to her. It was time to go. Jim, Vi, and Timber headed out the back door, Abby shepherding them all along. Vi was already in the back seat when Jim slid into the front passenger seat. Abby gave Timber a goodbye pat and then ushered the dog back into the yard. She got into the driver's seat, slid behind the steering wheel, and scowled at Jim.

"What?" Jim asked.

"Do you expect me to drive through the doors?"

"Usually you—"

"Do not talk back to me today. Open those doors, or we're going to be late."

This day was awful enough as it was. Jim was astounded that Abby was so set on making it even worse. She wasn't the one going to court. He got out of the car, stomped to the back of the garage, and hefted open the carriage doors. He stood impatiently at the doors while his mother adjusted the two pillows she used to shift herself higher and closer to the pedals. Finally, Abby backed the car into the alley. He closed the garage doors and climbed back into the passenger seat.

"If you have that kind of attitude before Judge Cannich you'll end up locked up for good," she said. "Don't question anyone today."

Jim stared out the side window, leaving Abby to burn a hole through his head with her eyes. He didn't care. None of it mattered now.

The drive to the Watson's house was quick since they lived just a few blocks away. The Watsons were family friends from as far back as Jim could remember, and the two mothers watched each other's children whenever needed. Vi dashed off to play with the Watson's daughter, Jenny, who was just a year younger than her. Vi didn't even look back at him. Good. Maybe she had believed him after all when he'd said the court date was no big deal.

As the car drove on, Jim continued to look out the window, wondering what the next hour might hold. Annoyingly, Abby seemed to read his mind.

"We have to meet with the juvenile officer first," she said, breaking the silence. "He will explain things. I think he might be able to give you probation and maybe keep you from going before the judge at all."

Jim wondered how realistic that option was. Would they just give him probation, a slap on the wrist?

"If that doesn't happen, then you'll have to go before the judge. I think you have to plead guilty or not guilty then. I don't know which is best in that case. Maybe the juvenile officer can answer that?"

Guilty or not guilty. He had a choice? Jim had never considered that he could plead not guilty. His mind processed what would happen if he chose that option, taking the charges to court and hoping the judge or a jury would have mercy on him. What about Lance and Marcus; would they be there too? How would they plead?

Pulling into the parking lot of the city courthouse, Abby shut off the car and reached over and grabbed her son's hand, giving it a squeeze. He was too shocked at the sudden contact to pull his hand away.

"It'll be okay," she said. "Just be respectful."

Jim extracted his hand from hers, got out, and walked toward the stone-framed double doors. He heard Abby fumble with her keys and purse, asking him to wait. He didn't, but she caught up to him easily when he paused just inside the building, unsure of where to go. Abby looked at the papers in her hands and then at the directory on a wall by the entrance.

"It's room eight," she said. "It should be down that way." She pointed to the left.

Jim led the way but paused at the frosted glass pane with the number eight in the middle of it. Abby reached past him and knocked on the door.

"Come in," a man's voice called from inside.

Abby opened the door and ushered Jim in first. A bull of a man, in a white dress shirt and poorly knotted black tie, sat behind a desk with several foot-high piles of papers and files stacked on both ends. Abby introduced herself. The man stood and extended a hand to her.

"Larry Burkland, I've been assigned your son's case." Larry shook Abby's hand then reached over to Jim, who hesitated a moment, stared at the pudgy hand, then shook it. "Sit, please."

They sat on a pair of steel chairs with cracked vinyl seat covers. The stuffy air reeked of stale coffee, cigarette smoke, and body odor. Wretched. This was the man who was supposed to help him? Larry muttered something to himself as he rummaged through his files.

"Here it is," he said after finding Jim's file. Opening it, he reviewed its contents, his eyes scanning quickly back and forth. "Hmm, I see."

"What's that?" Abby asked.

"Well, a couple things," Larry set down the file and looked over the rim of his plastic framed glasses, first at Abby and then at Jim. "Normally, with a first offense like this, I have the option of placing you on probation till you are eighteen like I did with your two friends. They were here earlier, and since these were their inaugural delinquencies, they have probation for a year and will pay restitution for damages."

Closing the file, Larry sat back in his chair and let out a sigh. As he continued, he took his glasses off and cleaned them with a handkerchief wrestled out of his back pants pocket. "For you, a few things complicate the situation. First, it seems you have a nice record of trouble at school. And that pen you stole? Well, the owner has demanded that its value be set rather high since it has ties to JFK. Those two issues, the vandalism, and the fact that you hit a cop—twice—raise your little escapade to a higher offense.

Given all of that, I don't see much choice but to refer you to Judge Cannich in youth court." Larry returned the hanky to his pocket and looked at his wristwatch, then jotted a quick note on the paperwork in the folder. "Youth court starts at eleven."

"What happens then?" Jim finally spoke.

"Well, you can try and fight this and plead not guilty, but I wouldn't recommend that since they caught you in the act. Not much of a defense there. If you plead guilty the judge will impose a sentence."

"What is the worst sentence I can get?"

"Pine Hills, over by Miles City, till you're eighteen." Larry fumbled through his file to find Jim's age. "So, next May. You don't want that, son, they only send the hardest cases there, and it isn't a pleasant place to spend any amount of time."

Jim glanced at Abby. Her face was calm and strangely void of emotion at the options posed. No hint that she might come to his defense or ask any questions herself.

"The judge might also impose nontraditional punishments. Sometimes the defendant is required to join the military or do some type of community service. You'll just have to see." Larry stood, wrangled himself into a suit jacket, and straightened his rumpled tie. "I'll walk over with you since I need to give your file to the clerk."

Jim and Abby stood as Larry opened the door for them. Abby piped up then, asking Larry several more questions, but Jim didn't hear them. His mind, like his body, was lagging many steps behind. Pine Hills. The state boy's school was a source of countless nightmare stories told by those who had been sent there and had come back to Helena Senior High: Stabbings, boys beaten with socks stuffed with bars of soap, stories of older boys raping some of the younger boys. Jim had not considered those tales worth giving any credence, but now he desperately tried to remember the details. Following Larry and his mom, Jim turned down the hallway and saw the dark, stained wood doors, the lettering on the frosted glass identifying the courtroom.

"Jim, I'll be there when your name is called, since I have several cases on today's docket," Larry said. "If you have any questions, don't hesitate to ask me. I'll warn you now, Judge Cannich won't tolerate disrespect. Always call him 'Your Honor.' Who knows, he might be in a good mood today."

The strong odors of nicotine and caffeine hitchhiked on Larry's laughter. The man gave Jim a slap on the shoulder, jokingly, like they were pals on the same football team or something. Jim saw no humor in the moment, and the man's laugh sent a wave of anger coursing through him. They paused at a small window just outside the door, where Larry handed files to the clerk for the day's cases.

Abby thanked Larry, then turned to her son and took a deep breath. "Well, here we go."

Once inside the courtroom, Jim felt a twinge of fear burrow into his stomach. A bailiff asked his name and his purpose. The gruff old man told Jim to take a seat up front and told Abby she could sit in the back. Jim fought off the fear and found a seat among the small crowd of young people who were there for similar reasons. The bailiff would call out a name from the docket and that teen would approach the bench, stopping about fifteen feet away, near one of two tables that faced the judge. Then the judge would read off the charges, the defendant would plead either "Guilty" or "Not guilty, Your Honor." After that, the judge either set a trial date or imposed punishment. It was evident that the names were being called in alphabetical order, so Jim had time to repeatedly observe the protocol for addressing the imposing old man behind the towering, cherry-stained desk. Jim looked behind him. Abby had found an empty bench at the back of the room. Name after name was called, each one drawing closer to the Rs.

"Redmond, James Clayton," the bailiff finally boomed. Jim stood up and walked to the defendant's table where the others before him had stood. Larry was there and stood up next to Jim. The judge had yet to look up from his review of the case file. Finally, he glanced over the top of his glasses at Jim.

"You Frank Redmond's boy?" the judge inquired.

Jim felt a flash of anger. He couldn't go anywhere in this town where his father wasn't known. "Yes, your Honor," he said.

The judge only nodded. What did that mean? An uneasy feeling swept over him. Yes, Frank was well known, but not everyone liked him. In fact, there were some in town who outright hated his dad because of his success. Many attributed the success to Frank's friendships with people high up on the political ladder, connections made through numerous jobs making memorials and other stone monuments for the state. If the judge was one of the latter, Jim was certain that his goose was cooked. The judge read off the charges and explained each one. Though some of the terms were beyond Jim's understanding, he did catch that both fines and jail time were possible options for sentencing.

"In response to these charges, how do you plead?"

Jim looked at Larry briefly, but he knew what he had to do.

"Guilty, Your Honor."

"Very well. Given the value placed on one of the items stolen and the assault on a police officer, I believe a sentence at Pine Hills might be the ticket." The judge stared at Jim. If he was expecting a plea for mercy, Jim was unable to respond, frozen in uncertainty. Then a voice came from behind him.

"Your Honor, my apologies for interrupting. With your permission, may I approach the bench?"

Jim turned at the sound of Frank's voice. There he was, at the back of the courtroom. In one hand, Frank held his faded Stetson and in the other hand was a plain white envelope. Jim looked back at the judge, who smiled and motioned for the bailiff to allow the man forward. Larry approached the bench alongside Frank. Jim could only stand back and watch as the three men debated his future. A minute into the conference, Frank handed over the envelope. The judge opened it and read the letter inside. When finished, he nodded at Frank and Larry. With that, the two men retreated from the bench. As Frank passed his son, he gave him a squeeze on his shoulder.

Larry returned to his position next to Jim. "Looks like you might have a choice to make, young man."

Jim looked up at the judge as the man in the long black robe wrote several notes in the file. Then he cleared his throat. "James Clayton Redmond."

"Yes, Your Honor?"

"Given this is your first legal offence, I'm giving you a choice. Three months in Pine Hills, followed by six months of probation, or three months of community service during which you will be assigned to a trail repair crew for the US Forest Service in the Gates of the Mountains wilderness area near Nelson. Before you answer, know this: if you take the community service option, there will be strict guidelines that you must follow. Any deviation from them will result in an immediate transfer to Pine Hills. Those restrictions are…"

Jim was numb as the constraints were detailed: no alcohol, no fighting, no entering the city limits except every three weeks when the trail crews were scheduled to come into town for a weekend— at which point Jim would only be allowed to go home and nowhere else. "After the community service term, you will remain on juvenile probation until the age of eighteen. In short son, if you so much as even fart wrong, I'll send your ass to Pine Hills so fast your head will take a week to catch up. Do you understand your choices now?" Judge Cannich glowered over his thick wire-rimmed glasses.

"Yes, Your Honor."

"And your choice is?"

Jim looked back at his parents. He knew enough about the horrors of Pine Hills to not want to go there. How bad could it be working on a trail crew? Frank and Abby made no motion to their son one way or the other. The choice was his and his alone.

"I choose community service, Your Honor."

CHAPTER 6
JUNE 14, 1965

The shop truck shuddered violently on the transition from paved York Road to the washboard gravel of Nelson Road. Frank slowed down abruptly to maintain control. Jim had left home with his father forty minutes earlier on their way to the trail crew drop-off point. The truck's tired suspension and the rough road resulted in a deafening clatter, leaving little chance for conversation. Not that there had been any since they'd started the journey. The less than ideal road conditions sent Frank's coffee-filled, green thermos rolling across the bench seat. Frank reflexively reached for it and pulled it back to his side of the truck. The intrusion into Jim's space caused him to press closer to the passenger door. He glanced at his dad, then returned to looking out the rolled down passenger window.

With each mile, he realized that soon he would be out in the wilderness for longer than just a day. This was no hunting trip. Although he enjoyed his short outings in the woods during hunting season, he always preferred to be in town with his friends, cruising the drag, getting drunk, and cat-calling girls. The next three months would be devoid of such pleasures. Reality was truly sinking in.

A week before, the judge had given him the sentence. Since that day, Jim's time had been filled with preparations under the watchful eye of his parents. His Converse tennis shoes had been replaced by a pair of work boots. His bright colored tee shirts were supplanted by jeans and a few old button up, long sleeve shirts that Jim's mom had pulled from a box stored in a closet. They smelled of mothballs and age with a hint of hay dust and leather. She told him they'd belonged to his grandfather, Clay Redmond. They were a little big but Abby insisted they would work just fine. From the same box came an old straw cowboy hat that looked as if someone had stomped on it for hours and then used it to wipe grease and dirt off an engine. Abby straightened it out then set it on Jim's head. It fit, only because Abby had insisted the day before that Jim get a haircut, shearing most of his thick, black locks. Jim had protested as Abby had removed inches of his mane, but she told him that he would thank her for it while up in the mountains, working all day in the summer heat.

"Besides, short hair makes it easier to find the ticks before they latch onto you," Abby said and winked.

Ticks? Jim didn't like the idea of some bug sucking his blood, but he kept his distress to himself. As he adjusted the hat, his mom had stood back and smiled. Jim saw her eyes glisten, but she didn't say anything further. Leather work gloves completed his ensemble. The entire pile of tragic clothing was stuffed into a Korean War army surplus backpack Frank had bought from a friend for two dollars.

That pack now bounced in the back of the truck along the rough road. As the truck quaked and fought up a long hill, Jim glanced over his left shoulder to make sure the pack hadn't fallen out of the back of the truck. Jim saw his father glance at him, only to quickly return his eyes to the road. The noise of the struggling truck engine increased with the steep grade. On each side of the road, the mountain slopes rose sharply. The road dragged Jim in like a hungry beast, its fur the thick pine forest climbing up to the early morning sky.

The last set of switchbacks presented a final grueling effort for the truck as it crested the pass and began a shallow descent into one of countless mountain valleys. More curves on rough roads were filled with continued silence between father and son. The road narrowed as they turned to the northeast at the mouth of a canyon.

Besides an occasional ranch house nestled in the troughs of the terrain, there was little to resemble civilization. Even when they passed through the spot on a map named Nelson, it felt as though they were far from anything familiar. The town, if one even could call it such, was comprised of a cluster of a few houses, and it did boast its own post office. Other than that, Nelson offered little proof that the modern world existed. Further up the road they passed the Checker Board Ranger Station, which was the last structure they would see on their route. The road hugged the north wall of the canyon as it gently climbed up from the creek bottom. Stone cliff fangs jutted out from dark green slopes, grinning at Jim in ravenous expectation as he was carried further into the mountain's gullet. Jim anxiously rubbed his fingers on his Levi's as the road climbed yet higher. On the left was a near vertical cliff of rock, which rose to the sky from a narrow ditch along the shelf road. To the right, just a few feet from the truck, the slope dove down almost one hundred feet to the creek bottom. Jim's nerves didn't calm until the road meandered back down to the canyon bottom.

After crossing two roughhewn timber bridges, they rounded a curve and Jim saw several vehicles parked in a widened stretch of the road. Dozens of young men stood around with packs at their feet. At a distance from this sea of youth, huddled a group of older men, all with cowboy hats and weathered faces. Two stock trucks were backed up to an embankment. Jim watched as a cowboy unloaded a large mule from the back of one of the trucks and walked it around to the side of the truck where he tied it up. A mid-sized, dark colored dog escorted the pair. The mule stood compliantly as the man headed back to unload another.

Frank pulled his truck to a stop near the group of older men who seemed, by age and demeanor, to oversee things. Jim stayed put for a moment as his dad exited the truck and strode over to shake hands with the men. Frank blended right in; his worn jeans, cowboy boots, faded Stetson, and Pendleton shirt all could have been pulled from any of the other men's wardrobes. From a distance, Frank, the stone carver, looked like any other cowboy.

Rubbing his hands on his pants one last time before exiting, Jim climbed out of the truck and grabbed his backpack from the bed. He struck the bulbous army surplus pack several times to rid it of the layer of road dust. Slinging the pack over his right shoulder, Jim walked to where his dad stood but was careful to stay back a few paces as the men talked. Looking around, Jim noticed that many in the group of young men were sizing him up. They all looked to be in their early twenties. Jim ignored their stares and tried to listen in on his dad's conversation. From what he could glean, Frank was giving the men the rundown on his son and the reason he was there. Jim edged closer but then suddenly felt uneasy. He looked to his right and saw that one of the old cowboys—the one who had been unloading horses and mules—was now staring at him. The grizzled horseman wielded the look of a person with a personality as malleable as the granite cliffs surrounding them. The man's air made Jim uneasy, but something else inspired actual fear in him: the large white Appaloosa horse standing near the man. The animal eyed Jim with a contempt that drove deep to his core.

"Son, come here," Frank's voice broke Jim's stare. "I want you to meet the trail boss."

Turning away from the old cowboy and his pale horse, Jim saw his father standing next to a domineering man near a green Forest Service truck. "Roy, this is my boy Jim. He's here to work for you this summer. He won't be no trouble, will you son?"

"No, no trouble." Jim approached them and shook Roy's hand. He was glad to get his hand back in one piece from the man's vice-grip.

Apparently not one for pleasantries, Roy immediately addressed him regarding the rules of the camp: "No alcohol allowed, no smoking due to fire danger, no fighting..." the man looked up from his clipboard to emphasize that rule. He continued to explain additional rules and described how the days would go. He recited the list from a stack of papers held to a clipboard that looked as if it had been dragged behind one of the pickups on the way up the mountain.

The man's words became a dull drone as Jim glanced around, his attention pulled back to the pale horse. The animal continued to watch him, not with the soft eye of an old trail horse, but with a predatory glare. What was with that creature?

"Are you listening boy?" Roy demanded.

"Yes sir," Jim answered. But as soon as Roy started up again, Jim glanced over his shoulder. The creepy old cowboy was still staring at him too.

"Listen breed, up here you need to keep your head on straight. Lots of things can get you killed if you aren't paying attention."

Breed. That got his attention all right. Jim hadn't been called that in years. The first time he'd seen the word was when he'd found his adoption papers in Abby's file cabinet. He and Zack had been snooping for Christmas presents and had found the papers instead. Under race was penned "Breed". Zack had explained, in his typically harsh big brother manner, that it stood for half-breed because he wasn't white and he wasn't Indian.

Jim saw Frank tense a little and his lips tightened at Roy's insult. But he didn't say a thing to Roy.

"Pay attention son," Frank whispered, his back to Roy, his face awfully close to Jim's.

His fists balled up at his sides, but Jim gave Roy the full attention he demanded.

Once the briefing was complete, Jim hoped Frank would leave. He didn't.

"Come with me, I want to introduce you to someone else before I go."

Frank strode over to the cowboy with the frightful, pale horse. Jim fell in five steps behind, in no hurry to be close to Frank or that unpleasant cowboy with the powerful horse.

Though Jim had seen Frank wear cowboy boots every day of his life, he had never seen him near a horse. He assumed Frank knew just about as much about horses and riding as he did—very little, if anything. Jim remembered vague stories about his parents once living on the west side of MacDonald Pass. Those stories had not been detailed, just general references recounting how hard things had been. Those stories were usually told whenever the kids complained about household chores or having to walk to school. The older Jim became, the less the stories had been told until, finally, they'd stopped altogether. He didn't recall his parents ever mentioning working with horses, so Jim was surprised as his dad walked right up to the big, evil-eyed Appaloosa and began petting him as if he had been around horses his whole life. The horse snorted and jerked its head at the first touch but calmed quickly as Frank confidently rubbed its powerful neck.

"Good to see you again," the old cowboy said. He shook Frank's hand firmly, with barely any motion.

"Tom, thanks again for helping out. Abby extends her thanks as well. I see Comanche is still hauling you all over creation. Pepsi still tagging along too." A dark, speckled dog had been resting in the shade under the truck, but ventured out to sniff Frank. She quickly withdrew to the security of Tom's side, taking a seat next to the man's legs, her body leaning into him.

"Yep, same old team. Is this Jim? Damn sight taller than the last time I saw him."

Jim had no memory of meeting the old man before. Who was he? Frank motioned for Jim to come over for a formal introduction.

"This is Tom McKee. He's a friend of mine, and he'll be stopping by camp on occasion."

Jim reached his hand out, and the cowboy spit to the ground before providing a handshake on par with that of the trail boss. The hand felt like leather that had been in a soaking rain and then left to dry in the sun. "You know the rules, right?" the old man stated more than asked.

Jim nodded.

Frank chimed in, "If Tom tells you to do anything, you do it. He can teach you a lot."

Jim looked at the old cowboy. Like the other packers there to help haul in supplies, Tom wore a cowboy hat, a threadbare button-up, long sleeve shirt, Levi jeans, and a pair of light tan chinks. The fringe-edged leather covered his legs from the waist to just past the knees. He was the same height as Jim but broader in the shoulders. His skin was nearly as dark as Jim's, though the ghost-white that flashed from his open collar revealed that the hue was due to constant sun exposure, not bloodline. Tom's posture and air gave the impression that he was near the same age as Jim's dad, perhaps younger by a few years. But the weathering on the man's face and hands made him appear as though he had been around much longer. Tom's eyes were what bothered Jim most. The twin blues stabbed at Jim with a derision not unlike the Appaloosa's. The weather-beaten, U.S. Army leather pistol holster hanging off the man's right hip only reinforced the man's intensity and imposing stance.

"I'll watch him for you, Frank. You got my word." Tom's raspy words sneaked past a hand-rolled cigarette. Jim, again, rubbed his palms on his jeans.

"Okay son, they're heading up," Frank said and ushered Jim toward the young men who were beginning to don their packs. The two stopped short of the group, and Jim pulled on his shoulder straps, adjusting the pack. He looked at Frank, who wore his ever-present, stoic expression.

"Do good. I'll pick you up in three weeks," Frank said and rested a hand on Jim's shoulder.

Then he was off, heading back to his truck. Jim watched Frank drive away. As the truck disappeared down the narrow canyon, Jim took a deep breath and made one more readjustment of his pack, then turned to join the trail crew. The group hiked toward a dark wedge in the cliff, through which snaked a trail and a narrow stream of fast, clear water.

Jim stood at the back of the group waiting to cross the stream. A young man wearing dark aviator shades introduced himself. He reached toward Jim for a handshake. His name was Matt Person, and the mirrored lenses made it impossible to see his eyes. Jim, however, didn't feel the least bit threatened, given the fellow's overt friendliness.

"First time on a trail crew?"

"Yeah. That obvious?"

"Well, now that you bring it up…" Matt smiled and shrugged. "You do stand out like tits on a bull, but no more than some of the other guys." Matt surreptitiously pointed and nodded toward one long-haired crewman wearing frayed jeans, leather vest, and a bead necklace. The guy had slipped off a rock and drenched his boots and pants in the cold creek.

Jim's baggy western shirt and straw hat actually helped him fit in with this assembly. As he continued to struggle with the pack, he realized his awkwardness revealed he was a total novice.

"It's my third year," Matt said. "I keep signing up because the pay is good, which helps with school. That and it keeps me outdoors instead of behind a desk." Matt expertly bounded across the stones that provided a haphazard path over the ice cold, snow melt water. "Why are you here?" he asked.

Jim tried to think up a decent lie, but decided against it. His mess was what it was, no point in denying it. He followed Matt's path across the boulders, then said plainly, "It was here or Pine Hills. Hoping I made the right choice." Jim explained only the most vital details of his crime: the dare, the break-in, the fact that they were caught.

The group threaded their way through a narrow stone passageway. As they entered the shadows between the two high cliffs, the walls grew so close that only a ten-foot-wide gap existed. Water splashed as the men walked through the stream, forced there by the stone barriers.

"Damn, it got cold fast." Jim shivered.

"That's why they call it Refrigerator Canyon. Don't worry, it'll get warm soon enough for you," Matt said. His words ricocheted off the rock walls and mingled with the sound of water over cobble. "It's lucky that you got to choose. I hear Pine Hills is the pits."

"Yeah, I've heard that too. Actually, the only reason I got the choice was because my dad knew the judge."

"That's cool, lucky you."

"Yeah, I suppose." Jim didn't like the idea of Frank helping him at this point, but the reality was impossible to ignore. It didn't matter anyway, not now.

"So all this because you snuck into school at night, huh?"

"Well, it wasn't just that." Jim then shared about the vandalism and stealing the pen. He paused his tale whenever he needed to concentrate on his footing. When he got to the part about slugging the cop, Matt let out a laugh.

"A cop? Damn Jim, sounds like you live an exciting life. Was it worth it?"

Jim shrugged. Not because he didn't have an answer, but more because his breathing had become labored as the weight of the pack and the chaotic footing took its toll. Fifteen minutes of hiking brought the group free of the soaring cliffs and into a narrow mountain valley stretching to the north. The rising peaks and dense timber were as intimidating as they were beautiful.

Some of the men talked, but most everyone remained quietly focused on their steps and breathing as the trail grew increasingly steep. Matt spoke for several minutes about his dream of getting a Pontiac GTO once he was done with college and about his current focus on rebuilding a Fairlane. Then even Matt turned silent and settled into the rhythm of breathing and trudging upward.

Jim paused a moment to catch his breath. He glanced back and saw the cowboy on his pale horse, several hundred yards down the trail. They had exited the canyon, along with a string of laden mules. The distance gave Jim some comfort as he hoped that the greeting half an hour ago would be his only encounter with this strange man.

CHAPTER 7

Once free of the narrow rock walls and the slow-paced creek crossing, Comanche tried to pick up the pace as the trail opened up. To his annoyance, he felt a tug on the bit. Boss never reined hard. Instead, it was all soft pulls and pressure from the knees. With a snort of disapproval, Comanche slowed his powerful steps. He could see the group of humans ahead on the trail and desired nothing other than to race past them. Boss wouldn't allow it. Humans! So small, so slow. The slightest tug on the leather reins communicated clearly through the steel bit and smothered Comanche's desire to show the group of struggling humans how powerful a horse could be. He chose to obey the bit, to obey Boss.

As the trail meandered further into the mountains, Comanche often knew when he was going too fast, even before Boss corrected him. The tension on the lead rope, which connected his saddle to the first pack mule, made it clear that he had accelerated beyond the herd's pace. This was not a natural skill, but one he had learned over ten years of working with Boss. Before that, Comanche had been wild and hateful toward the two-legged creatures that dared to try and ride him.

Like all horses in the herd, Comanche had been forced through the typical breaking process. The men involved had demanded that he submit to the feel of a saddle and bridle. Unlike the other horses of the herd, however, Comanche never submitted. It wasn't until he met Boss that he learned to tolerate the hands of a man, the feel of the tack, and the weight of the rider.

As a colt, he had observed the process of breaking. He'd watched in fright as a wrangler wearing a black hat lassoed the front hoof of a young mare and then looped the rope over her back, pulling her leg up. Though she tried to buck and jump, she wasn't successful with one leg restrained. For ten minutes, man and horse fought until, at the point of exhaustion, the mare surrendered. The man strapped a hackamore on her head, cinched the saddle, and then climbed on her back as another man held the rope tied to her neck. The restrained leg was freed and, though the mare fought the man, she was too drained to have any impact. Soon, with the mare barely able to trot, let alone buck, the man gained full control.

Comanche's dread of his own meeting with the man in the black hat had morphed into anger and disgust. This anger fueled him. When the impending occasion arrived, he hoped no wrangler would be able to tire him out. Each day, he ran, sprinted, and goaded the other colts to race him, and he always came out victorious. While other horses galloped excitedly to the humans whenever they offered food, Comanche held back, recognizing the deception. This garnered laughter from the humans who tried to woo the glaring, pale horse into coming closer. He refused. He had grass to eat. Oats, though pleasant, weren't worth the compromise.

When the time came to be broke, Comanche was ready for it. Not able to coax the Appaloosa, the men mounted their tamed horses to herd him into the pen. Even that was no easy task. Three times he broke free of their encirclement, racing back into the open pasture where he had grown up. It took five riders and several hours to force him into the high-fenced pen. Two of the men had to cast short lariats around his neck to help with the effort. In the pen, he broke free from the ropes, and pranced around in defiance, stomping at the soft dirt, and challenging the humans who clung to the top rail of the corral in expectation of the spectacle to come.

With slow, smooth, looping motions, Black Hat circled his own rope over his head and walked toward Comanche. He could not stand there and be caught, he had to run. It was a horse's only defense. Running was life. With a snort and a jump Comanche took off like a shot. The circular corral forced his path to follow the fence. Post, rail, cowboy hats—all flashed by as he ran from the ribbon of rope spinning above Black Hat. The man stepped further out from the center of the pen with each of Comanche's circling laps until, with a quick flick of his wrist, he sent the rope through the air. Comanche saw it coming but could not move his head fast enough.

Panic crushed him as he felt the loop tighten around his neck. He'd expected to feel the man apply pressure, to try and force him to stop using his own muscle and mass. But Black Hat allowed Comanche to run as another man jumped into the pen and grabbed hold of the long trailing rope. With another lariat, Black Hat took aim at Comanche's front hoof. Five times the loop missed due to Comanche's well-timed leaps. Black Hat was more patient than Comanche expected. He persisted until the loop finally caught his front right hoof. Comanche struggled but not as hard as he could have. He was saving his strength. He knew the fight had just begun.

A few weak leaps and snorts preceded Comanche's apparent kneel of submission. With a glaring, calculating eye, Comanche watched Black Hat approach and drape a blanket and saddle on his back, then strap a hackamore on his head. As the cinch was tightened, Comanche pinned back his ears, but Black Hat didn't notice. Perhaps he was tired from breaking the other horses, as well as from the long battle to capture the pale horse. Regardless, as Black Hat climbed into the saddle, another man removed the loop from around Comanche's hoof, and the real battle commenced.

Comanche did not intend for the first lunge to unseat Black Hat; he would deal with him later. No, his first charge was aimed toward the man in the center of the pen, the one restraining him with the loop around his neck. No doubt expecting Comanche to flee rather than fight—like a typical penned horse—the man's mouth gaped and his eyes went wide as the pale horse charged straight at him. In panic, the man dropped the rope and ran, only to absorb the brunt of Comanche's massive head as he swung it violently against Black Hat's vigorous attempts to rein him in. Rope Man flew at the impact and hit the fence with a groan. The men who stood outside the corral reached over and helped the stunned wrangler to safety, leaving Black Hat and Comanche in the pen.

Comanche bucked hard but Black Hat was good, remaining centered through the storm of jumps and snorts. Fighting hard, Comanche felt his head pulled toward his chest by thick ropes connected to the hackamore. This severely limited his jumps. But, the horse had the advantage of strength and speed. Comanche felt the weight on his back shift, the smallest of mistakes on Black Hat's part. Taking his chance, the pale horse spun with a hard kick of his hind hooves and stretched his neck out straight. The hulking weight on his back suddenly disappeared as Black Hat soared skyward for an instant, landing with a thud in a cloud of dust. Then Comanche spun around and attacked. Hooves slashed down, striking flesh and dirt. It took the whole mob of men to spook Comanche away so they could retrieve their cowering friend.

Alone in the pen, Comanche snorted and pranced in victory. Those outside stood glaze-eyed with shock and scowling in anger. Black Hat was carried to the house, and one of the men returned carrying a gun. Others stopped him. The men shouted heated words at each other and cast glares and sharp gestures toward the pen. Comanche didn't care. He was the victor.

After several minutes, a gate was opened, and Comanche trotted out—not into the pasture, but straight into a fenced chute, that narrowed down to the point he barely fit. A small gate hindered his advance and a log was thrust through the rails behind him, preventing his retreat. From the safety of the other side of the fence, men reached through the rails and loosened the cinch and removed the saddle. They removed the hackamore and the lasso still around his neck. Free of the oppressive articles, Comanche was released into a larger pen.

The next morning, a truck backed up to a loading ramp and Comanche was herded up into its back, accompanied by plenty of yells and whip cracking. Men who had once tried to befriend the pale horse with food, now stared in anger as the truck pulled away. It was nearly sunset when the truck stopped at a large compound of corrals that housed hundreds of horses. Comanche also heard cattle mooing in distress. Relieved to be free from the confines of the truck, he galloped down the ramp. Men shouted and waved their arms, forcing him to head through an open gate to a holding pen. There he found fresh water and a manger filled with old hay. Anxious about these new and sparse surroundings, Comanche sniffed and greeted the horses who were in the pens next to his. Their heads reached over to investigate the newcomer. Though other horses were near, and he had plenty of food and water, Comanche hated this new home. He wasn't able to run.

Finally, on his third day there, he was herded down a chute to another pen. The voice of a fast-talking human echoed out of a sheet metal barn. One by one, the horses were prodded into the barn. Finally, it was Comanche's turn. Waving arms and snapping whips spurred him into the building. He found himself in a small, fenced area surrounded by bleachers, filled with cowboy hats and inquisitive eyes. The fast voice was loud and hurt Comanche's ears. That, the bright lights, and the foul smell of men and cigarettes overwhelmed him. He snorted and stomped the sawdust on the ground. The voice gained speed, and excitement flowed through the crowd as men flashed brightly colored cards. The card-flashing slowed and the voice that rattled from the speakers took on a slower, more serious tone. The voice picked up again with only three in the crowd raising their cards, then only two, and finally one.

Comanche didn't pay attention to the man who held up the last card. His focus was on the men who opened the gate and who now released him from the pen. Relieved to be ushered out of the loud building, Comanche kicked as he galloped back to his pen. Once there he pranced around, happy enough to be in the open air and again near other horses. The next morning, the stockyard workers opened several more gates and harassed Comanche toward the loading ramp on which he had first arrived. His steps were not as quick as they'd been the day before. A sleepless night, filled with strange sounds and smells, had robbed him of his usual defiance. A snort of protest was all Comanche could muster as the large stock truck backed up to the loading ramp next to the corral. The opened gate didn't motivate him to venture up the ramp, but the crack of a whip did, and with a slam of the gate, he was headed to a new home.

Countryside rolled by, and Comanche grew curious about the new landscape and its scents. From the flat open plains, they entered forested hills, which eventually grew to mountains. The truck struggled over several mountain passes, slowing at times to a point at which Comanche thought he could get out and outrun it.

The truck made three stops during the long day of driving. At each one, as the truck was fueled, a man climbed up the side panel to hang a bucket of water in the corner of the truck. Comanche wouldn't go near it if the man was there, but he took hard pulls of the water as soon as the man had jumped down to tend to the truck.

The sun was just setting in the west when they slowed and turned down a narrow dirt road. Other horses whinnied at Comanche while the truck backed up to a loading ramp. He returned the greeting and stomped the floor impatiently as the man opened the gate. Hesitating until the man moved far enough from the gate so as not be a threat, Comanche trotted out of the truck and down a fenced chute to a larger circular pen, adjacent to the corral holding the other horses. The pen was big—almost sixty feet across—big enough to let him run and kick, which he did. The man and a dark colored dog watched Comanche run around the corral from the other side of the fence. The man checked the supply of hay and water for all the stock and then retreated to the small house near the corrals, his dog always at his side. Comanche sniffed the clean air, noting the smell of the other horses, the mules, the fresh hay. For the time being, he was content.

The following morning, the man and dog exited the house and immediately headed to the corral that held the other horses. The man petted each one, pausing just long enough to roll and light a cigarette. Comanche snorted in disgust at the odor that drifted to his corral right along with the man, and he refused to approach the fence. The man and horse stared at each other for a few minutes. Then the man and dog left to attend to the chores of feeding the animals and working on the large stock truck.

Later in the afternoon, the man stepped into a small shed and returned with a loop of rope. Fear flooded Comanche at the sight of the lariat, as the memory of Black Hat filled his mind. The man gave the dog a command; she immediately lay down in the shadow of a stock tank. Then the man climbed the fence and dropped down into the corral. Unlike Black Hat, this man didn't spin the rope, instead he made a large loop and approached slowly, never making eye contact with Comanche. Holding the loop in his right hand, the man calmly brought it up to his left shoulder. Two more steps and Comanche felt it was time to run. But his reaction wasn't quick enough. With a smooth motion, the man's right arm swung across his chest, ending high above his hat, and a single swing over his head sent the loop flying. His aim was perfect, and the rope cleared Comanche's head, tightening slightly around his neck.

Panic consumed Comanche, sending him running along the perimeter of the circular pen. The man stood in the center, almost thirty feet away, but holding the rope. Comanche expected the rope to be pulled tight, but the man didn't take up the slack. Instead he allowed Comanche to run without any pressure at all. Slowing to a steady trot, Comanche noticed that the man moved closer, keeping the tension of the rope only tight enough to remind him that they were connected. The man spoke, not the long string of sounds that Comanche was used to hearing from the two legs, but just a word or two. Calm and slow. With each pass, Comanche felt his fear ebb, his trot slowed to a walk, and then Comanche stopped. Horse and man held eye contact for a moment before the man looked at the ground in front of Comanche. The diverted gaze calmed Comanche more. Predators stared, herd members looked away, helping each other search for threats.

The man took a half-step towards Comanche who sniffed deeply, reading the man's scent before snorting. Another step, never looking the big Appaloosa in the eye. The slow approach took several minutes, and the entire time the man spoke softly, until he was within arm's reach of Comanche. Soft words preceded the touch of his hand. That slight fingertip touch sent a tremor of fear through Comanche's shoulder muscles, but he took deep breaths, trying to detect the smell of fear or aggression in the human. There was none. The tremors calmed.

Initially fear-induced, now Comanche's tense shoulder quivered with the contact more out of tolerant annoyance as it did when an insect had landed in search of a meal. Comanche shifted his weight, his head turned just enough to watch the man. The contact continued. Touch of fingers transitioned to the entire hand stroking and patting him gently. No pain. No fast motions that implied a threat. Comanche's quivering muscles stilled. He grew curious.

The man's hand moved toward his jacket. Comanche glared. The hand pulled a handful of oats out of the pocket. Comanche snorted and inhaled deeply. The oats smelled so good. Despite himself, Comanche sampled the treat. For half an hour, the man repeated this process. Touch, oats, touch. For the first time in Comanche's life, he felt calm around a human. At least until the man moved the rope up towards Comanche's head.

As the loop cleared his ears, Comanche jerked back out of reflex, the desire to run welling up inside him. The desire was quelled as the man didn't move but instead whispered calm words. Comanche held his ground, eyeing the man as he stood just a few feet away. It was the man's confidence that earned Comanche's trust. Confidence and no fear. Because of that combination, that day Comanche came to view the man as the herd boss.

Every morning for the next two weeks, Boss and the black dog would exit the house, and the man fed and watered Comanche and the other horses. Then the man would disappear into a small structure next to the corral. Comanche would stretch his head over the top rail to see and smell what the man might be doing. The odor of oats was something Comanche grew to appreciate. It meant the man would enter his corral, and the oats would be a reward for each time he didn't flinch when the man touched him.

The first few days were the most trying for Comanche. Boss spent more time each day getting Comanche accustomed to human contact. Sometimes he used his hand and sometimes a long, thin stick with a cloth tied to the end. Comanche hated the cloth bird that fluttered with every move the stick made. It took almost an hour to learn not to jump at its motion. Comanche slowly learned to accept it touching his body: under his belly, over his back, and around his neck. Understanding that the touch wasn't painful, Comanche relaxed. He trusted Boss more with each successive interaction. Sometimes, when Boss petted Comanche, the horse tried to act stoic at the contact, but he eventually found himself enjoying it, leaning into the man's scratches as they neared his ears.

On the third day, Comanche walked up to Boss instead of waiting for the man to approach. There was comfort in being around the calm, confident man, but that comfort was to be seriously tested. That afternoon, Boss slipped a leather halter over Comanche's head. The feel of leather straps around his muzzle and neck triggered hard head shakes, but the straps became tolerable as Boss scratched Comanche's ears and neck. Several times Boss took off and returned the halter to Comanche's head. Each time, Boss provided a reward of oats.

The last time the halter was strapped on, there was something different with the weight. A long lead rope was attached and dangled to the ground. Comanche stepped back as he eyed the foreign object. Boss' calm words steadied Comanche. The man took hold of the rope. A slight pull gave Comanche reason to jerk back a few feet. Boss didn't fight it but let the lead rope drag on the ground. Oats came out of the coat pocket. Snorting in the aroma, Comanche calmed and returned to the man. The horse nibbled the treat, then glared at the man as he took hold of the rope once more. More calm words and a palm of oats were enough to persuade Comanche to willingly yield to the subtle tension on the rope.

Every day, Comanche's tolerance for human contact increased, partially because the touch was enjoyable, but more because the horse had grown to trust Boss. He now understood that this man would not hurt him, even when Boss put the bridle on. The smell of steel and leather was not unfamiliar to Comanche, but the taste of steel was new. As the cold metal was pushed to Comanche's lips he recoiled. But then he smelled and tasted something different, something sweet smeared on the mouth piece. With licks and nibbles, Comanche allowed the steel into his mouth and the leather bridle was secured to his head. More brushing and pets. Another handful of oats.

Once again, Comanche's trust was tested after the first week, when Boss set a blanket on his back. The sensation was more than he could handle and resulted in a swift spin and kick with his back legs, sending the blanket airborne. Comanche calmed quickly, though, with the soft words, the man's calm retrieval of the blanket, and his steady return to Comanche's side. Five times the blanket was placed on Comanche's back and four times it flew off. Then, like every other new encounter, Comanche chose to tolerate it.

The next day, the man brought out a saddle and hung it on the fence. Approaching slowly, Comanche sniffed it. The memory of Black Hat caused Comanche to recoil at first, but his curiosity overtook him. He kept sniffing. Though the smell of the leather was like that of the saddle back at his original home, there was no smell of Black Hat. Only Boss and the horses and mules in the other corrals. Because of that, Comanche didn't buck when he felt the weight of both the blanket and the saddle across his shoulders. He barely noticed the weight; what caught his attention were the dangling stirrups. The leather straps under Comanche's belly gave him cause for concern. Still the eight preceding days with Boss had built solid trust between them. After being led around the corral with the saddle on for several minutes, Comanche was rewarded with oats and ear scratches. Then, tied at a fence rail, Comanche watched the man retrieve a strange new object: two sandbags tied together with a length of rope. Comanche sniffed at the bags as the man offered them to him. Content they weren't anything bad, Comanche calmly watched the man hang the bags over the saddle. The weight was strange, and Comanche pranced to the side a little, but Boss' hand on his neck calmed him. The man freed the lead rope and led Comanche around the corral a dozen times. He let the long lead rope out to its end and waved the fluttery evil cloth flag to encourage Comanche to a trot. The weight wasn't heavy, just different. The feel of the saddle became more pronounced and the bags shifted with each step, especially when running.

The next day, Comanche was almost bored with the routine. Halter and lead rope on, followed by a good brushing. Then blanket and saddle, followed by the bridle. But Comanche noticed that Boss didn't bring the sandbags this time. As the man tightened the cinch, Comanche sensed that he intended to ride him. Fear and anger swept through him, just like the day Black Hat had tried to ride him. Comanche licked his lips quickly, in contemplation of what he should do. But with the touch of the man's hand on the side of his neck, like all the times they'd tried something new, the fear subsided. Comanche watched Boss clasp the reins and then grasp the saddle horn. The saddle pulled to the left a little as Boss put his boot into the stirrup. Before Comanche could react, Boss had swung up onto the saddle. Despite the trust that had been built between them, Comanche didn't like having a human on his back. No horse did; it wasn't natural to tolerate another creature on one's back. All of equine history had instilled such fear—the fear of a predator dropping down from the trees.

Dipping his head quickly, Comanche leapt upward, hooves kicking, snot flying, launching a thirty-second battle that ebbed to a run, then a gallop, with an occasional kick. But the weight of Boss was still there. All the while, the calm words from the man reached Comanche's ears. The gallop slowed a little, and then Comanche felt Boss' hand on his neck. Comanche slowed to a walk. He felt a little pressure from Boss' knee on his side as well as a gentle pull of the rein. Comanche resisted, his desire to never be tamed flaring. More calm words from Boss. A stronger pull on the reins, and Comanche allowed his head to be turned. In the next hour, Comanche learned to accept the guidance from Boss, the pats to the neck reinforcing the bond and trust with each successful maneuver. It was that guidance, that trust, that Comanche had grown to respect and follow.

That day had been ten years ago. Now, having arrived at the trail crew camp, Comanche, Boss, the dark dog, and their string of pack mules caught up to the group. The young men had stopped and were dumping their packs with groans and complaints. Comanche wasn't even breathing hard. Boss dismounted and led the horse to a shady spot beyond the camp, securing him to a tree. The man then led the pack mules to the shade at the edge of camp and tied the lead mule there, near the large tent that breathed smoke. Comanche was content to stay in the shade of the tall pine; he knew they wouldn't be there long. He was not bothered when Boss' dog came and lay near the base of the tree. Both dog and horse had long grown accustomed to one another. Boss was their common tie.

Comanche watched Boss remove the heavy manties from the pack mules. He grunted as he lifted the canvas and rope-wrapped plywood boxes, untying them from the pack saddles. In steady repetition, Boss lay each manty on the ground next to the mule that had carried it, then repeated the process on the other side. In this manner, he progressed down the line. When the entire string had been freed of their loads, Boss moved the mules further from the camp, tying them near Comanche.

While Boss talked with an older man near the smoking tent, Comanche and the dog watched the young men. They were all heading to a group of five large tents. The younger man Comanche had noticed at the trailhead looked at him. Eons had conditioned

Comanche and his entire species to sense a stare from another animal, an early warning of predators. But, the look in the eyes of the young man was not a predatory stare. No, what Comanche saw there was fear. If a horse could smile, he would have.

CHAPTER 8

"Did they add another form, Chuck?" Tom grumbled as he shuffled through the small stack of papers at the Forest Service office near the Helena Airport.

"Afraid so Tom, the bean counters need their pint of blood you know."

Tom cast a glance at Chuck and shook his head. Damned paperwork! Tom kept his attitude to himself as he filled out the forms required for hired stock contractors like himself. He knew it had to be done, but dear Lord, why did there have to be so many? Only government could take a simple task and complicate it to the point of absurdity. As much as he hated paperwork he did like having a paycheck. It allowed him to do what he loved: ride horses and run pack strings, all while getting paid. The extra money was a boon, given the small veteran's stipend he received each month. That stipend was a pittance for the peppering of shrapnel across his back, his souvenir from his visit to Italy during the war. The pain kept him from walking very far, but he was able to lift a saddle and pannier, and he could still plant his foot in the stirrup. He was thankful for that. He had it better than the poor bastard on the other side of the counter who was sorting paperwork for a paycheck.

Tom had started working as a packer almost twenty years before, but the steady summer work hadn't started till 1955, when the U.S. Forest Service had gone into high gear to make wilderness areas accessible by trails. The rangers and trail crews were taxed by the short work season and needed all the help they could get. Their stress was only increased by visits from every mucky muck congressman or government department head who thought they were someone important. These 'Show Me' trips were where Tom had gotten his start, leading politicians in on horseback to show them the progress of the work. Each trip had served to grow Tom's disdain for people who thought highly of themselves just because they had a fancy title. They were bags of hot air in his opinion, most of them falling below a leech in Tom's ranking of God's creation. After five trips of hauling these windbags up on the sightseeing tours, he let a few too many honest words fly toward one thin-skinned state representative. Thus, Tom was restricted to hauling supplies instead of people.

If he wasn't running strings for the trail crews, then he was hauling supplies for firefighter crews who battled forest fires around the state. The work was steady but it was seasonal, only offering Tom employment from June through October. The rest of the year he worked odd jobs as needed, but he preferred making money by training horses around the valley. All this only to bide time till trail construction resumed in the spring.

After three years, the main trail construction push had ended in 1958, but Tom stayed on as a packer, hauling supplies into remote ranger stations or fire towers around the state. This year was different because trail crews were now returning to the Gates of the Mountains to repair existing trails which had washed out during spring rains. The crews had also been tasked with building a few new trails that had been deemed desirable. For Tom, this meant steady work closer to home. He hauled weekly supplies in to the trail crew working up by Nelson and hauled out any garbage not burned. During each trip Tom chatted with Roy, usually over a cup of strong camp coffee. Tom shared news from town, and Roy detailed how the trail work was going. Now, since Frank's boy was installed in the crew, Tom also asked about the kid. He never got the chance to see Jim, himself, since the kid was always up working on the trails when Tom came into camp. As of the last week in June, the kid had managed to keep his head down and mouth shut, which Tom passed along to Frank via a phone call after returning home. Tom hoped that this week's chat with Roy would yield similar news.

The current haul was like all the others: food and supplies. Tom checked the same boxes on the paperwork, wrote the same dull phrases. Well, the paperwork ensured he'd be paid. It was a necessary evil. With the last signature, he thanked Chuck and turned to leave.

"Tom, before you go, do you want more work?"

"What ya got in mind?" Tom looked back, pulling his half-finished cigarette from his mouth and flicking the ash into a bucket by the door. The ranger pulled out a file and opened it on the counter.

"Seems that the engineers from Washington didn't do a very good job of marking the proposed trail routes. The boss wants someone to map out a new trail, from over on the Heller Ranch, to the current base camp south of Moors Mountain." Chuck pulled a folded USGS Quad map from behind the counter and unfolded it so he could show Tom the area in question. "They also want someone to flag the locations where water bars should be installed to stop the trails from washing out. Chuck scanned the map then pointed out a few key landmarks. "Let's see, right now the crew is repairing the trails heading to Bear Prairie. The new trail is meant to connect the Refrigerator Canyon trail to the Moors Mountain trail, which cuts over Windy Ridge. Think you can do that for us? Probably take a couple days' riding to do it all."

He didn't need any time to think about that one. It was his kind of work—riding in the mountains, camping overnight, in total solitude. "Yeah, I think we could do that." Tom never spoke of just himself when his dog and horse were part of the group. It was always 'we'.

"Good, let me know how long you think it'll take, and we'll settle on compensation for you and your stock. It'll need to happen in the next few weeks. I'm sure it'll be an easy job for you compared to repairing the washout and rerouting that spring two years ago."

Tom certainly hadn't forgotten that one. An artesian spring had wreaked havoc on the trail work two summers ago, its endless flow of water saturating a slope the trail traversed. Tom was asked to haul in equipment for the job, including explosives. The government engineers came out and wasted a lot of time and money coming up with a complex design in which a deep trench had to be dug or blasted along the upslope side of the trail and then backfilled with rock. The drain would collect the spring water, keeping the trail dry. Once their directions had been made clear, the engineers left, assuming Roy, the trail boss, would follow their orders. Tom had been up there that day and watched with a smile as Roy assured the government guys that the job would be done as directed. Tom knew the man too well. As soon as the engineers were gone, Roy called Tom over.

"Those damned engineers got a big problem; they know so much they don't realize how stupid they are," Roy said and grinned. "Come on, I need your help."

Tom assisted Roy in gathering up several bags of explosive ditching powder. Using one of Tom's mules to help haul the load, the two men ran a 400-foot line of the explosive from the head of the spring down to a depression in the slope that would divert the water to a culvert they were planning on putting in anyway.

Making sure both humans and animals were clear, Roy set the explosives off.

Great fun. Except, in an instant, Tom was inundated with memories of his time in the Army. The good times: training with the First Special Service Force, later dubbed the Black Devils by the retreating Nazis. While in Helena, the Force held "training drills," blasting every abandoned mine and old bridge within fifty miles of town, including, inadvertently, a few bridges which were still in use, much to the surprise of the locals. Then there were the not-so-good times: the memory of the explosion on the steep slopes of Monte La Difensa particularly, the one that had given him the scars across his back. As the wave of air from Roy's detonation rushed over Tom, all those memories forced their way into his consciousness in a single clamoring rush.

Monte La Difensa. That night had been over twenty years ago. Tom and hundreds of other Force members used the cover of night to scale the unguarded cliffs of a heavily fortified German position on the steep Italian mountain. The Nazi position had blocked the entire Allied advance to Rome. The initial battle lasted only four hours, but there was no time to celebrate their success. The ensuing battle to secure the adjoining mountain tops took several more days. It was on the second day that Tom was injured. He was sprinting from a shell crater to a small rock outcrop when the mortar round exploded behind him. The heat and blast wave tossed him through the air. When he landed, he could barely move, and he felt the blood from a dozen shrapnel wounds soak into his uniform. Tom was just another statistic at that point. In that fight, over half the men of the Force were either killed or wounded.

Though the events had occurred twenty years earlier, Tom found himself experiencing them as if yesterday; the sight, sound, and smell of the ditch blast brought them all back. Roy's shouts and backslapping yanked him back to the moment. He forced a well-practiced smile, an approving nod. As the dust settled, it was clear their efforts had worked, and a fire-charred ditch now ran from the spring, diverting the water away from the trail bed.

Tom was silently thankful no explosives were needed for this new work that Chuck was proposing. He thanked Chuck with a handshake and stepped out into the sunlight, grateful for the prospect of more work, another decent paycheck. Outside, Comanche and the three mules—Cecile, Molly, and Bart—strained their heads over the top rail of the stock truck to catch a glimpse of him. Pepsi was in the cab as always, content to be out of the sun.

Countless cars raced by on Interstate 15, just two hundred yards away. Obnoxious throughway. It had taken years to construct, during which it had been close to impossible to get to the ranger station. When the interstate was dedicated in 1963, Tom hoped life would get back to normal; instead it just seemed to speed things up. Taking a drag from his cigarette, he watched several cars whiz by on the overpass. Just a whole lot of people in an awful big hurry to get somewhere. Though he needed to get somewhere, he was in no hurry—not that the 1957 LCO Chevy livestock truck could be hurried anyway, especially with thousands of pounds of equine muscle in the back.

As always, during the one-hour drive to the drop off point, Pepsi barked at creatures unseen by Tom, and the horses and mules shifted footing every now and then. Tom checked them regularly in the rear-view mirrors. Having an animal go down in such close confines is bad, but having it happen on a steep mountain road was worse. Every chance he had he did a head count to make sure all passengers were upright. When they reached the trailhead, the Forest Service truck was already there, its bed full of canvas panniers stuffed with the food needed to keep the trail crews fat and sassy for the week. With the help of the Forest Service ranger, Tom unloaded his horses and mules, tightened cinches, and strapped the panniers onto the thick, steel D-rings affixed to the top of the pack saddles. After a final check of the string, Tom swung up onto Comanche's back, bid farewell to the ranger, and headed up through the narrow gap in the cliff walls.

Comanche was his normal, impatient self, but a quick tug on the reins brought him in line, allowing the three mules to keep pace despite their heavy loads. Tom didn't bother to keep tabs on Pepsi as he knew she was never more than a few leaps beyond the trail. Still, he kept an eye out for cougars, who would find his forty-pound dog a nice meal. Tom patted the leather flap covering his 1911 pistol. Always good to know he had that on hand. Any predator that chose his dog or one of his pack animals for a meal would be in for a fatal surprise.

This day, the trip up the narrow dirt trail was uneventful. They encountered no forest critters larger than the occasional noisy chipmunk. Pepsi darted after any chipmunk that dared perch at ground level, barking as it retreated to high branches. Once the dog realized the futility of her effort, she would race to catch up to the string. Aside from these auditory intrusions, the ride was peaceful, hypnotic even: the gentle clip, clop of horse and mule hooves methodically working up the trail. This was one of the few times Tom didn't mind not having a smoke, the strong smell of pine and horse caressing his senses. That was drug enough. Tom wasn't sure there was such a thing as heaven, but with blue skies, mountains, trees, a good dog, and a great horse beneath him, he figured he was as close to it as possible.

As they climbed further up the narrow valley, the constricted drainage widened into a timber-filled bowl. The trail meandered up the middle of the bowl, through the towering pines. Comanche's ears perked, turning to identify noises filtering through the timber. The horse's nostrils flared, taking in the odors of the forest, and the base camp. After less than an hour, they were almost there. They could smell it a few minutes before they saw it—wood chips from newly cut logs and smoke from the camp stove.

The dozen canvas tents were the color of sun bleached driftwood. Their exterior A-frames, made up of lodge pole timbers, supported the canvas shelters. The roofs sloped down from the top and terminated in a short vertical wall, which was anchored to the ground with logs. Loose door flaps stirred in the breeze, but no occupants were around other than the cook and his assistant. The crews would be half a mile away, up the side of the mountain working the trail.

Tom guided his string to the cook tent where he stopped and dismounted, tying up Comanche. He loosened the half hitch knot that held Bart's lead rope to the braided loop on the back of Molly's pack saddle and led Bart to a tree near the tent. There, Tom effortlessly tied Bart's halter rope to the tree, then did the same with Molly and then Cecile. With the animals secured, Tom unhooked the panniers and left them on the ground next to the mules. With all the mules freed of their burdens, he moved the string back near Comanche and tied them there, then headed back to the panniers to help haul them to the cook tent. As he set down the last of the panniers, he heard a fellow call to him.

He turned and saw Roy, the trail boss. The mountain of a man smiled at him and said he was hoping to run into him that day.

"Looks like you did." Tom said, smiling as he shook his friend's hand. "How far away are the crews?"

"Still up on the south face, but we're almost to the saddle, so we can start dropping down into Bear Prairie soon. We'll probably move camp when the crews go out this coming weekend."

"It's only been three weeks. Giving them a break already?" Tom scoffed. "That's the problem nowadays, we keep coddling these kids. Back when I was in the Army there was no rest. You just kept fighting until someone remembered to tell you to stop."

Roy shrugged. "Can't argue with you, but it's a decent crew, and they've made good headway. A break will do them good, and it'll only be for a couple days. Besides, they need to get out and wash their clothes. Most of 'em are as ripe as a roadkill skunk."

"I'm sure that's the truth," Tom said and chuckled. "So how's the Redmond kid doing?"

"Okay. He works hard, but I suspect there might be trouble brewing. One of his bunkmates and him have been less than cordial to each other." Roy narrowed his eyes. "So far, Jim hasn't done anything stupid, but I'm not putting it past him."

"Work him harder then."

"Well, there is only so much sun in the day. I just hope he keeps it together until they get the weekend off and maybe cool down a bit."

Tom rubbed his lips and chin. He suddenly wanted a cigarette, but didn't dare smoke when out in the woods. He had helped pack supplies in to forest fire fighters on many a summer's day and remembered well the Mann Gulch Fire of 1949. Thirteen firefighters died in that blaze. He didn't want something like that on his conscience, not with all the war memories already hitching a ride there.

"Might be good to remind him of why he's here and what happens if he breaks the rules."

"Yeah, I have. Not sure it got through."

Both men walked over to the scatter of chairs outside the cook tent. They sat, and Pepsi took that as an invitation to take her post at Tom's side—the one farthest from Roy. Not the greatest guard dog. She always used her human to protect herself from strangers. As Tom patted the dog, he mulled things over. Jim had been doing well, but one mistake would end it for him. Tom didn't want that to happen. His concern wasn't for Jim so much; he was just a selfish kid. Tom's real concern was for Frank and Abby. He knew they didn't want their son in Pine Hills. When Tom had given his word to Frank about looking out for Jim, he'd meant it more than most people would have. Looking out for someone meant stepping in, fighting for them, and even fighting with them if necessary to prevent a bad choice from causing harm.

This was something he had learned with his unit. They had all been brawlers, the worst of the worst, but that was why they'd been chosen for the Force. Their fearlessness was needed, and their tendencies toward disobedience could be tempered and redirected, even if never fully removed. So, they looked out for each other, forcefully when needed.

How prideful, arrogant, and foolhardy Tom had been at that age. Leaving an abusive home as a teen, Tom had learned to survive any way possible. That included lying and stealing. The Army had changed those habits. The camaraderie with his fellow soldiers who shared pain and spilled blood, both their own and that of the enemy, had taught Tom the importance of keeping one's word. You had to be able to trust one another every hour and every minute of every battle. Keeping your word was both a matter of honor and a matter of life or death.

"Roy, I got a favor to ask."

"Anything Tom, what is it?"

"If the Redmond boy does anything stupid, I want you to keep it up here and let me know the next time I come in, okay?"

"Tom, that's asking a lot. There is a court order, you know."

"I know, just let me handle it. Please." That word was not one that slipped past Tom's lips often.

Roy nodded. "You got it, Tom. Not sure why you'd put your ass on the line for a half-breed, but as long as he doesn't kill anyone I'll let you handle it."

"The 'why' is my business. And 'nobody dying' is always a good thing," Tom said with a thumbs up and a grin. Few people understood Tom's trademark thumbs-up, his constant response to trying situations. He never shared that he'd started doing that when his unit was pinned down in Italy by a Nazi machine gun nest. The withering fire had wounded two men seriously and making the rest hug the ground so tightly only their uniforms kept them from getting any more intimate with the fertile Italian soil. A brief lull in the incoming fire had allowed Tom to look at his men. He could see the concern in his men's faces so he called out each name, asking each one if they were alive. One by one, all shouted back, confirming they were alive. Tom responded with a grin and risked raising a thumbs-up. "Good, let's keep it that way," he shouted. "No one dies today!"

His voice was loud enough to be heard over the MG-42 that continued to send short bursts of fire their way, kicking up dirt at the edge of the crater they found themselves in. No one died that day, at least not in his squad. From that day on, a thumbs-up had been Tom's answer to whatever problem he faced. No one had died on the trail today so it was, indeed, a good day.

Tom stood to ready his string to leave. He'd be back in just three days to help Roy and the crew move camp. Hopefully, for Frank and Abby's sake, the news about Jim would be good.

CHAPTER 9

The two knife-edged ridgelines were connected by a low saddle. Turbulent wind currents funneled through the rough landscape and, high above, a hawk ascended on the thermals. With effortless ease, the bird of prey soared over the drainage where the trail crew's basecamp sat. Jim looked down the valley at the small whiff of smoke that marked the location of the cook tent. In the distance, he could see the cliffs where his journey into the mountains had begun almost three weeks earlier. How he envied the bird and its freedom. From his section of trail, on the broad open face of a steep mountainside, Jim looked over an expanse of timber-lined slopes occasionally interrupted by sharp outcroppings of light gray granite. It was an expansive landscape, but the mountain ridgelines were effective prison walls nonetheless. Jim watched with resentment as the hawk disappeared into the distance. From somewhere to the west, Jim heard the ominous rumble of a summer thunderstorm.

"Hey red man, the trail won't build itself," Josh shouted up to him. The insults from Jim's bunkmate were a regular occurrence, only ceasing when the long-haired, spindly braggart was snoring. Jim tried to ignore the bastard, remembering the promise he'd made to Frank and Abby as well as the jail time that awaited him if he didn't uphold that promise. His grip was tighter than normal as he resumed swinging his mattock in a long arc till its pick sunk into the hard soil. Jim continued his work, leveling out a twenty-foot stretch of trail that had washed out during the spring rains. The first section had begun back at the head of Refrigerator Canyon and had progressed up to the camp. The work within the timber had afforded some protection from the sun. The tasks were simple enough: widen and reinforce the existing trail they had walked up almost three weeks earlier. Now the crew was repairing washouts and removing blown down timber that blocked the trail on its steep traverse along the ridge. This new work exposed the crew to broiling summer heat for much of the day. Most of the men worked in rhythmic weary silence. But Josh never shut up. He spewed endless stories of his travels around the country, telling of how he had been in the demonstrations against the war, including the burning of his draft card like they did at Berkeley in May. He also shared plenty about how he was working to save money to go to San Francisco to join in the revolution, as he called it. According to Josh, there was no drug he hadn't tried, no place he hadn't traveled to, and no woman he couldn't ball.

Matt often tried to calm Jim down. In hushed tones, he spoke to him even now. "Don't let that candy ass get to you. He's so full of sheep dip it's a good thing we're working up slope from him." Matt was working just a few paces away from Jim. He paused in his own work and stretched his back. "I can tell you this, he ain't no hippy no matter what he says. There's about as much peace and love in that guy as there is cheese on the moon."

"Yeah, I'd still like to pound him."

"Only if you want to see the inside of Pine Hills. If that happens you won't get to see my Fairlane when I finish it."

Jim steamed, but he knew Matt was right. He was grateful for the guy's occasional reminders to keep his cool. That was hard to do with nothing but physical labor to give vent to his rage. There were no walls to punch when you lived in a tent, and there were several fist-sized holes in the walls of his room back home. He was proud of them. The first hole he'd lied away by saying he had stumbled over his school bag. The others were neatly concealed behind two Rolling Stones posters. Thus far, while working with the trail crew, Jim's temper had come to a boil a couple times over Josh's bullshit, but Matt was there each time to calm Jim down. After three weeks of working together, Jim considered Matt a friend, the only one he had on the crew, maybe the only one in the world. Their friendship existed mostly because Matt didn't seem bothered by Jim's past or ethnicity. In fact, the only time Jim's new criminal record came up was when Matt was talking him down. Otherwise, Matt preferred to talk about rebuilding a small block 289 engine for his hotrod Ford Fairlane or about his plans to earn an engineering degree.

Ultimately, Jim's desire to break Josh's jaw was strong, but there wasn't time or energy to do so. It had been that way since day one. After settling into camp, the hard work and long hot days left little time for conflict. The routine was highly regimented. Wake up at six, eat a big breakfast, then hike up to where they'd finished construction the day before, and start working once more. Rest was limited to water breaks. Every worker carried a jug with him. Bathrooms didn't exist, so the nearest bush or tree sufficed, except when the crew was back at camp, where they'd built a latrine. At noon, the entire crew would find whatever shade they could and eat a box lunch prepared by the camp cook. With only an hour to eat and rest, many of the crew inhaled their food and then dozed off, cherishing the few minutes of rest out of the harsh sun. After lunch, they were back up on the trail working and wouldn't come down until the sun was setting. Then, in the twilight, they ate and retired to their tents, only to pass out and begin the process again the next morning.

It was a steady routine interrupted only by the regular insults from Josh. The only thing more irritating than Josh were the flies. Small deer flies darted from one patch of exposed skin to another, triggering an immediate swipe of Jim's hand. As frustrating as the deer flies were, they paled in comparison to the horse flies that seemed to view the trail crew as a bountiful buffet. The thumbnail-sized demons would land and take a painful bite of flesh before retreating. Occasionally, Jim was lucky enough to swat one while it took a taste. The first swat usually only stunned the pest. It would tumble to the ground and rally for an encore if Jim didn't stomp on it to finish it off. If only Jim could stomp Josh out of existence so easily.

Most of the time, he could ignore the ass. Though the work was physically taxing, Jim was starting to enjoy it. That is, he'd begun enjoying it once his blisters had healed up from never having done any manual labor. He felt himself growing stronger, and he liked that. He also appreciated that each day, as they headed down the mountain, he could look back and see that he had accomplished something. Each worker was assigned a section of trail to clear and dig out. On every hike up and back, Jim saw that his sections were better worked than some of the others. Laboring close to Matt helped. The guy was three years older than Jim, but he didn't lord it over him. The college student's attention to detail was motivating enough; it drove Jim to complete his sections as well as Matt's.

While working on the trail and back at camp, Matt asked Jim about his life in Helena, and Jim liked hearing about the engineering classes Matt was taking and about how he hoped to become involved in the space program. Because most of Jim's teen years had been spent living in the moment, with no thought of the future, he was fascinated by Matt's dream to be an engineer at NASA.

During lunch break, as he and Matt sat in the shade of a big pine tree, Jim asked about Matt's NASA goal. "That's some goal, isn't it? Not everybody can get into the space program." Jim said.

Matt didn't answer right away. They were watching a pair of camp robber jay birds tag team in an effort to steal food from a few other guys. The gray birds worked beautifully together as if by design. One would swoop in and make an attempt at the crumbs, only to be shooed away with a stick or rock thrown at it. It would fly a short distance away and perch on a tree branch, keeping the attention of the workers. Meanwhile, the other bird made his move for a larger prize. Jim chuckled at his crewmates' frustration with the small, yet cunning, feathered pests.

"Dreams gotta be big my friend," Matt said. He flashed a cheesy smile. "Nothing's worse than settling for average. I don't know about you, but I want to be the best in whatever I do. In engineering, that's the space program."

"I guess that makes sense," Jim said and shrugged. Sometimes he wasn't sure how to take Matt's enthusiasm.

"Come on man, I'm gonna help put a man on the moon! That is so cool! What about you, what do you want to do? Who do you want to be?"

Nobody had asked Jim that question till now—not his teachers, not his parents, not even himself. He had been so busy just living day-by-day he hadn't thought about what he wanted to do down the road.

"Hell, I don't know. For now, I'm just someone working up here to stay out of jail."

"Well, then be the best at it." Matt grinned as he hung his water jug back up on a tree branch. They'd burned the whole lunch hour yacking. No time for a snooze this time. Matt waved to Jim, coaxing him to get up. "Come on, let's show these guys how it's done."

><+ +>~

Shadows sped across the mountains as the sun dipped low to the west, ending another day on the trail. The thunderstorm Jim heard earlier had passed a mile or two south of the crew. Not a drop of relief for them. On their way back to camp, Jim and the others watched the far off lightning in silent awe. The quick stabs of light flickered between ground and cloud. After several seconds, the angry rumble of thunder reached them. The distant thunderstorm seemed to add to the crew's energy. They knew that tomorrow they would move camp, and the next day they would hike out for a two-day break.

Jim didn't share the crew's anticipation. The thought of returning home was not a pleasant one. Though he missed certain things—his mom's cooking and his sister Vivian's laughter—he dreaded being in the same house as his father. He knew that, once home, he would immediately retreat to his room. There, he was master, if only the master of his own prison. Here, among the towering peaks and dense trees, he was master of nothing.

Since the first trek up from Refrigerator Canyon till now, trudging down the trail in the fading daylight and distant storm, Jim had moments when he felt trivial, meaningless. It happened anytime he was outside and not working. Looking up through the lattice of branches, Jim saw the first glints of stars in the darkening sky. As more stars appeared, he felt smaller and more insignificant. What did he want to be? The question vexed him. He knew who he was, or at least he knew what people thought he was and what they already assumed he would become. He saw Josh up the trail and clenched his fists. The three weeks of intermittent taunting unearthed memories of the torment he'd received from Zack. His brother was the original master of propagating Jim's feelings of not belonging.

When Jim was only six, he and Zack were in the back seat of the car when Abby had stopped at the orphanage for some reason. Zack took the opportunity to bring Jim to tears once again. Their legs strained while standing on the rear bench seat, the two boys crossed arms resting on top of the front seatback, as they watched their mom enter the orphanage. Zack flashed a sly grin.

"You know why we're here don't ya?" Zack poked Jim. Though their mother had left strict orders to not fight or leave the car, that warning had no impact on Zack.

"No, why?" Jim wondered.

"She's going in to see if they will take you back."

"No she's not!"

"Yeah, they thought they were going to get a clean kid, but you're a dirty kid so they are going to give you back."

"I'm not dirty, I took a bath last night!"

"See my arm, see yours? You're dirty. Mom and dad don't want a dirty kid so she's asking the nuns to take you back."

"No she isn't," Jim sobbed.

"Yep, see, here she comes to take you in."

Jim's eyes grew big and his lip quivered under tears and sniffling nose as Abby got into the car. At the sound of Jim's sobbing, she looked into the rearview mirror.

"What is going on here?" she demanded. "Jim, why are you crying?"

"Zack says I'm dirty and you're giving me back to the nuns," Jim wailed through deep sobs. Abby spun around and leaned over the back of the seat so that she could grab her oldest son by the arm.

"Zachary Logan Redmond, how dare you say such a thing to your brother?" Abby's grip and angry stare left him fumbling over denials. Abby got out of the car and came around to the door on Zack's side. Without a word, she opened the door, hefted a stunned Zack out of the car, and gave him a firm swat on his hind end. She returned him to the car and climbed back into the driver's seat. The elder Redmond boy pouted in his corner of the back seat.

Abby took a couple deep breaths, then turned back to face Jim. "I am not returning you to the orphanage, ever. And you are not dirty, you hear me? God just gave you darker skin so I can tell you two boys apart." Jim could see his mother's eyes in the rearview mirror when she turned back to drive. They still had a flash of anger in them.

She started the car but didn't shift it into drive. She sat quiet for a moment and then turned around. Her face was calmer than it had been moments before. "I was going to save this news for later, but now is as good a time as any, I suppose. I stopped at the orphanage because your father and I are trying to adopt a baby sister for you," Abby turned back then shifted the car into drive. She glanced at Zack in the mirror. "Zack, you and your father will have a talk tonight about how you treat your brother."

The boys sat in their respective corners of the rear seat. Zack looked at the floor. Both boys knew that a talk with dad usually ended in a spanking much more severe than the one their mother had just delivered. The news of a possible little sister joining the family could have distracted Jim. It didn't. All he could think about was how pale Zack's arm was compared to his own.

As Jim grew older, that difference became more evident. It wasn't just his brother, but also other kids in school who chided Jim for being different. Slowly, steadily, Jim felt as though he didn't belong anywhere and never would. Even here on the trail crew, with Matt as a friend, Jim found himself feeling like an outcast.

Drawing closer to camp, the crew was greeted by the smell of canned stew bubbling in the large enamel pot on the camp stove. Normally, this was as pleasurable to Jim as it was to the rest of the crew. Yet now, even knowing that they would be leaving camp for a break in just two days, Jim found himself fixed like a wolf in a leg trap, by the reality of who he was, or more importantly of who he seemed destined to be. He was hungry, but he didn't give a damn about the stew. His mind simmered on the fights with his dad, the arrest, and on a future devoid of any prospects other than jail.

Jim ate his meal alone, avoiding Matt. The young man's boisterous demeanor and pep talks would be too much at the moment. Truth be told, he didn't want anyone to dampen his foul, yet comfortable mood. Yes, comfortable. That's what the anger was. Comfortable like an old pair of shoes, fitting well.

After dinner, Roy gave a brief lecture explaining the logistics of moving camp. It was going to be another full day, but all the workers agreed it would be easier than digging trail for twelve hours straight. When Roy was done, the crew retired to their tents. After getting ready for bed, Jim wormed into his sleeping bag and stared at the canvas roof above his head, its pale color now nearly black since the lanterns had been extinguished. In the dark, Josh was still yammering. Somehow he still managed to elicit laughter from the other five men in the tent.

"Yeah, I was talking with Roy about moving camp tomorrow," Josh continued in an overly expert tone. "He's not a bad guy once you get to know him." Yes, Josh now claimed to be buddy-buddy with the trail boss. Jim knew he was full of shit as did most of the trail crew. That truth was common knowledge in the camp, but it was Josh's way—to turn things around to make himself look better and smarter than all the rest. Jim's anger grew as Josh carried on. "He said we're moving three miles deeper into the wilderness, to a place called Bear Prairie. Maybe the red man will feel more at home there, him being a prairie nigger and all." Josh laughed at his own oh-so-clever insult. In the darkness, Jim heard a few others laugh as well, but he couldn't tell who. For the hundredth time that day, Jim clenched his fists

"Or perhaps we can start calling you a timber nigger. How about that red man, would that be a good title for you?"

More laughter.

"Shut up, Josh." Matt's voice silenced the laughter.

"What college boy, are you the injun's bodyguard now? Come on red man, can't you speak English, or do you only speak injun?"

Jim rose from his bunk, his eyes adjusting well to the lack of light. He had grown fond of the darkness, even the darkness of a tent in the wilderness, in thick timber with no stars. Like the anger, it was comfortable. While others feared it, Jim had grown to accept the dark and to use it to his advantage.

"My name is Jim Redmond. If you call me red man again I'm going to knock your goddamned head off."

The gentle flapping of the tent walls in the breeze was the only sound for several seconds.

"I don't think you will," Josh hissed as he sat up. "I bet I can say anything I want, and you won't do a thing, because you're a pussy who's scared to go to jail. Ain't that right, red man?"

Jim strode down the narrow isle of cots, towards Josh's corner bunk. A challenge had been issued, and Jim loved a challenge. The floor of the tent was just the ground, but Jim's bare feet didn't bother him as he closed the distance. He felt only a sense of pure purpose. Josh stood up just in time to catch a fist to the nose, and then the fight was on. Shouts and flashlight beams soon filled the tent, spilling out until the entire camp was in an uproar.

CHAPTER 10

As always, Tom relaxed with the melodic beat of horse hooves on the trail. Once again, he and Comanche led their line of mules into the wilderness. Their group was behind three other pack strings making their way up the trail to the camp just two hours past sunrise. As usual, Pepsi darted from one clump of grass and tree trunk to another in excited pursuit of those mocking and elusive chipmunks. Both Comanche and the mules ignored the soda pop dog as she crisscrossed the trail between them. They were long since accustomed to their canine outrider. Tom kept an eye on the black and blue dog, but mostly he just enjoyed the ride.

It would be a busy day of hauling tents, cots, and other gear deeper into the wilderness. Tom looked forward to it since most the day would be spent riding, and there was nothing better than that. He couldn't imagine sitting in an office chair instead of experiencing the gentle sway of a horse beneath him. Reaching down, Tom patted Comanche's thick neck muscles. The horse whipped his head up and down and then shook it in frustration at being at the end of the procession. Tom knew that Comanche wanted to be out front which was exactly why he'd elected to take up the rear. They had a long day ahead of them, and Tom didn't want all the animals tired out with Comanche setting the pace.

Voices and the sound of hammering sifted through the pine needles as the pack train approached the camp. Tom was encouraged to see that most of the tents had been dropped from their lodge pole frames, nails and twine already removed. The only evidence that would remain of the camp would be the logs themselves and the trampled grass. It wasn't that Tom was averse to helping tear down the camp, but he was there to pack and ride, so if he could keep it to that then he was happy. The packers split up, each leading their string of mules and horses to a different section of the camp site.

Tom led his string to the cook tent, which was still standing but looked as though it had regurgitated its contents out the front door. Given all the canned goods, pots, pans, stoves, and provision boxes, it was going to be a heavy haul. He was glad he brought mules only to bear the load. Their strength and long legs made them ideal for such work. Heading the string was his best pack mule, Cecile. Having him there meant he had a strong, calm lead mule. It also meant that the big guy wouldn't cause any trouble back home. Cecil had the habit of escaping from the corral and wreaking havoc with the neighbor's gardens—something Tom didn't want to have to deal with if he didn't have to.

Stopping near the cook tent, Tom dismounted and looked around as he tied up his string. From across the camp he could see Roy storming around, pausing every now and then to bark orders at the trail crew. The ire on the trail boss' face told Tom that things were not going as well as they appeared. Roy saw Tom and immediately stomped his way.

"You wanted to know if there was trouble with Frank's boy," Roy huffed, wiping a layer of sweat and dirt from his forehead.

"Well, there was. Last night. He just couldn't hold it together for one more goddamn night."

"He ain't dead is he?" Tom asked, only half joking.

"No, but damned near close, as I wanted to kill him. Got into a fight with a bunkmate."

"How bad was it?"

"For Jim? Not a scratch. The other guy? He won't be winning beauty contests anytime soon."

"How do you want to handle it?"

"If I had my way the little half-breed would be off to jail. But you asked to take care of any complications, and I said I'd let you. He just can't stay in this camp. Not if he's gonna beat the hell out of every worker who doesn't know when to keep his mouth shut. I know he's Frank's boy, but why on God's green earth did they want to adopt a redskin boy?"

Tom kept his thoughts on the matter to himself. He snorted deeply and spit, then rubbed his chin, wishing like hell for a cigarette. Regardless of how he or Roy viewed Jim, Tom had given his word to Frank and that was that.

"I'll take him out with me," Tom said. "The Forest Service wants me to re-mark some trails for your crew. Between hauling in supplies and trail-marking and work around my place, I can keep him busy for the rest of the season. He can come out with me today. I'll call his folks, and hopefully Frank can get things squared away with the judge."

"Do you think he is going to stay put at your place? Up here he's got nowhere to go. In the valley his friends are only a phone call away."

Tom nodded as he broke a thin branch off the lodgepole pine nearby. "Yep, but that'll be his choice."

"If you're sure about this Tom. I didn't figure you for a babysitter."

"Yeah, me neither," Tom growled. But now he was just that. Damned little shit couldn't keep his temper in check. Tom snapped the twig in two and then tossed the pieces to the ground. "Suppose we should let the kid know."

Jim was not far off. Surprisingly sedate, he was helping a crew-mate fold one of the giant canvas tents.

"Jim, get over here!" Roy shouted and the kid came running. "Change of plans for you boy. Because of your little stunt last night you can either go out with the crew tomorrow and have the sheriff waiting to take you to Pine Hills, or you can go out today with Tom here and finish out the summer working with him. As long as the judge approves it."

"Work with him? Doing what?" Jim asked.

Tom saw the defiance in the kid's eyes, but also the flicker of apprehension. That was good; a little fear would serve the kid well.

"He's running pack strings all summer. You help out, and do whatever he wants you to do," Roy declared. "What'll it be? Pine Hills or finish out your summer working for Tom McKee."

"Doesn't look like I got a choice," Jim mumbled and he looked away.

"There's always a choice. Now what'll it be?" Roy demanded.

"I'll head out with Tom today."

"You might have some brains after all, boy," Tom said and grinned.

Roy instructed Jim to return to breaking down camp. The boy shuffled away. Tom was certain he heard him cursing under his breath as he left.

"Bye-bye, red man," a long-haired crew member chided Jim from nearby. Tom figured, from the bruising and dried blood on the kid's lip, that he had been the one on the receiving end of Jim's rage the night before. The battered trail worker had been off to the side, helping tear down a tent frame and eavesdropping on the conversation with Roy. Apparently, the brat wasn't a fast learner.

Jim spun, with fists clenched, looking fully intent on finishing the job he had started the night before. He was only stopped by Roy's thundering voice.

"Josh, shut your damn pie hole or, so help me, I'll kick your ass off this crew right here and now!" The trail boss stormed over to Josh. "You've been flapping your jaws since day one and I'm sick of it. If you so much as make a peep the rest of the summer your ass will be out of here, you got me?!"

Tom snickered as the blowhard withered before the trail boss. He looked back over to Jim, who was retreating from the situation, but smiling. Roy's face was flushed as he stormed back toward Tom.

"Goddamned kids! Josh is an utter imbecile, and that Redmond boy has got a temper. You sure you know what you're doing?" Roy asked as he wiped his brow with his once-white handkerchief.

"Nope, but I got a few ideas."

With a nod and firm handshake, the men set off in different directions to help with the packing. Tom, with the help of the cook and his assistant, began carrying the canvased bundles to the pack string, where he hefted the manties onto the saddles. The two lightest manties, holding duffle bags full of the cook and assistant cook's clothes, he strapped onto Cecil. On top of those, he set the larger cook tent across the Decker pack saddle, letting the manties act as a shelf for the folded and tied jumble of canvas. Molly would carry the smaller cook tent, and the remaining mules would carry the rest of the panniers of food and cook gear.

An hour later, the pack strings were burdened with their loads and stood stoically as they waited to depart. Even laden as they were, the horses and mules would outpace the trail crew, whose own packs were filled with their personal belongings. Tom and the other packers would arrive at the next campsite first and unload everything in time for the trail crew to show up and start assembling the camp. With a gentle tap of his boot heels, Tom let

Comanche set out, leading their line of five mules out of the old camp. For almost forty minutes the ease of the newly repaired trail sped their travels, but as they merged onto old trails they were limited to a slower pace. Well-traveled game trails intersected the main trail. But the packers knew the way, each one having lived most of his life navigating the wilderness as easily as a townie might stroll along a big city street. All the men had been part of the original crews that built the first trails in the area, in the 1950s.

Roy rode near the head of the procession on a spare horse brought in just for his use. He, like the packers, was a man who had spent much of his life in the woods, on horseback. Tom knew that Roy was enjoying the ride after three weeks spent babysitting the trail crew. It took a special man to handle such a command. When in the Army, Tom had led men, but that was different. The soldiers had been disciplined, focused, and dedicated. Nowadays, the pictures on the nightly news, when Tom got to see it, showed a generation of people that he couldn't relate to or even understand. The war protests infuriated Tom. What did these slovenly kids know? It seemed they only cared about drugs and rock-n-roll. They had no concept of discipline. At least up here, in the woods, Roy had some influence over them. Tom wondered if he would have the same sense of command over Jim once they were out of the mountains.

There was no time to think about it now; Tom brought his mind back to the ride and looked at the string ahead of him, checking to make sure the D-rings were centered. The Decker pack saddle, on the third mule from the rear, looked a little catawampus, probably from an uneven load and a loose cinch. Tom called up to Milt, the packer leading that string, telling him of the issue. The cowboy turned and confirmed the problem.

"I see it. I'll take care of it at the park," Milt said and pointed to the expansive clearing up ahead. The park. It was an old wilderness use of the word. Any large meadow qualified. The path they were traversing was pocked with exposed rock and an inordinate amount of dead fall. This forced multiple delays as each string picked its way over or around the obstacles. On each side of the trail were steep slopes covered in a labyrinth of trees, most no farther apart than a man's outstretched arms, not the best place to try and fix a pack. Tom watched the teetering load closely, wondering if it was going to make it to the clearing or if it was going to prematurely slip too far, causing total panic for the mule. With each step, the panniers swayed. Again, it shifted a little more. Tom had seen his share of pack strings explode and broadcast their loads all over a mountainside. It was an occupational hazard, and every packer feared having a problem in an area in which they couldn't get to the animal in time to prevent injury. The list of troubling landscapes included: river crossings, rocky terrain, shelf trails, and thick deadfall forests such as the one they found themselves in now. If one animal panicked, then more would follow suit; that's what herd animals did. They only had two speeds, really, graze and panic. Tom stared intently at the pack, as if his will alone could keep it steady.

As the first two strings made it out of the shaded trail and into the sunlit park, Tom figured they were in the clear. His hope was quickly shattered as he watched the mule with the loose pack slip a hoof on the soft soil at the trail's edge. The panniers worked up the momentum they needed to cause the saddle tree of the Decker to slip over the mule's wither. The pack on the left side of the now-lopsided-saddle caught the trunk of a mature lodgepole, pulling the mule off the trail.

"Aw hell, here we go," Tom cursed, as his right hand gripped the reins tightly and his left freed the loop of his pack string's lead rope. His body tensed in anticipation of what was about to happen. The troubled mule grunted and then brayed wildly as it felt itself dragged down to the side. Panicked now, the animal hunched over deep before erupting in a tornado of canvas and leather, fur and hooves. As it kicked and bucked, the twine that connected the mules in front and behind snapped as intended, but that didn't stop them from joining the chaos. Tom could do little but rein Comanche back and try and keep his string from adding to the violent dance. Snorts and grunts of bucking mules rose to meet the shouts of packers as everyone tried their best to keep their own animals under control.

Like so many times before, Tom watched as saddle straps ripped, and the panniers and manties flew upward. The freed mules bolted into the timber. The trail mule nearest Comanche managed to keep his packs attached but spun around on the trail with full intent on running back to the trailhead and the safety of the stock trucks. With Comanche blocking his path, the mule dove down into the trees, only to become wedged in the timber where it protested with loud braying.

In only fifteen seconds, the main brunt of the blowup had passed. Here and there mules stood trapped by dead fall or with lead ropes snagged on trees. Believing the situation safe enough, Tom dismounted and tightly secured Comanche to a tree using a slipknot. He made sure to put the loose end through the loop to guarantee that Comanche didn't pull it loose and thereby free himself—an annoying trick Tom's horse had learned and used regularly if Tom wasn't paying attention. A quick look at his own string convinced him that his mules were calm enough and not thinking of holding their own little display of equine acrobatics. Pepsi had found a safe place under a rock outcrop near Comanche.

With his charges safe and secure, Tom set about helping clean up the ungodly mess. Keeping calm and talking softly, he approached the closest mule, who was now entrapped in a jag of crisscrossing logs. Letting his hand run along the side of the animal, Tom calmly stroked her until he could grab the lead rope and guide her out of the log jam and back onto the trail. He tied her to a tree and was in the process of catching another wayward mule when Roy rode up to help.

"Anyone hurt?" he asked. His concern was as much for keeping on schedule as for the riders and animals.

"Nobody died," Tom winked with a thumbs-up, "I think we're good."

CHAPTER 11

Exhausted was too weak a word to describe how Jim felt as he trudged down the trail in the failing light, almost twelve hours after the crew had started breaking down camp that morning. More than a football field's length ahead of him, he could see the dark shapes of Tom's mules. With each tired step, the straps of his pack bit deep into his shoulders. He did regret, if only briefly, his refusal to allow one of Tom's mules to transport the load. The old man had even offered Jim the option of hitching a ride on one of the pack saddles, but he had opted for the safety of walking the trail rather than climbing atop some beast of questionable temperament. As for carrying his own pack? That was a matter of pride, pure and simple—that and he didn't mind the excuse to lag behind a little. He preferred some distance between himself and Tom. He'd soon be spending more than an hour in a truck with the man. And then the rest of the summer. He kept walking, but slowed his pace even more, allowing the gap between him and Tom to increase even further.

Jim's exhaustion stemmed from a near-sleepless night. After several of the crew had pulled him off Josh, the trail boss had charged in, threatening to kill both boys. He made Jim swap cots with someone in another tent. The morning was filled with disdain among the crew because of the disturbance and resultant sleep deprivation. Some supported Josh, and some supported Jim, but all were tired and facing a long day.

After breaking down the camp, they hiked over three miles to the new campsite. Jim helped set up for a while before he began his forced march, following his new boss out of the mountains. In all, he figured he'd hiked nearly nine miles with his pack. With six hours of work added to that, Jim felt beyond drained, as though his soul had abandoned him for less painful realms. He wanted to rest but didn't dare. He didn't want to give the bastard riding ahead of him the satisfaction of seeing him quit. No, he would make it to the truck. He just needed to keep walking.

Entering the narrow canyon, Jim knew he was almost at the trailhead. He'd lost sight of Tom and the pack string ten minutes earlier, but that didn't matter. The finish line was near. Splashing through the creek, Jim's legs almost quit him, but he caught himself on the cliff wall. Just a few more steps. Free of the water-carved cleft, he walked out onto the road and saw Tom loading the last of the mules into the truck. Even before Jim got to the truck, he was taking off his pack, liberating his frame of the burden.

"Where do you want me to put this?" Jim panted out the words.

"Up there," Tom pointed to a rusted tube steel rack on top of the cab. It took all of Jim's remaining strength to heave the pack up into the rack. It landed with one end sticking out, but he didn't care. Even if it fell out on the way home, he just didn't care. Opening the passenger door to the cab of the truck, Jim was startled by a dark shape that yelped and leapt over to the driver's seat.

"What the hell did you do?!" Tom roared from behind the truck as he fastened the rear panel.

"Nothing, I just opened the door," Jim said, now hesitant to enter. He closed the cab door and stood outside, waiting till Tom came around and climbed in on the driver's side.

"Come on, get in," Tom said, now more gruff than intimidating. "She won't bite. Pepsi is just scared of people is all."

"She seems okay with you," Jim observed as he climbed into the cab and yanked the heavy door shut. He leaned away from the fearful dog now huddling on the seat next to Tom.

"Yeah, well that's a long story."

The truck's engine rumbled to life, and Jim allowed himself to succumb to the fatigue. As the truck traveled down the road in the last light of day, and with nothing to look at in the darkness outside, Jim slipped into slumber. For how long he wasn't sure. Other than rousing briefly when they transitioned onto the paved road heading towards the York Bridge, Jim only remembered waking and seeing the lights of Helena to the south. It was the first time in three weeks he had seen electric street lights, and they were like a beacon of comfort to him.

Just as they neared Helena, Tom turned north onto Green Meadow Drive and then west onto Lincoln Highway, leaving Helena to slip behind the hills. The landscape was dark again, other than a few solitary lights that marked a possible ranch house or barn. The truck slowed. Tom downshifted, turning the big steering wheel to pull the truck off the highway and onto a narrow dirt road. A few hundred yards after that turn, the headlights revealed a small, single story ranch house with peeling paint and a few outbuildings and corrals.

Turning the truck in a giant arc, Tom lined the back up to a loading ramp made of railroad ties and dirt. Calm and obviously well-familiar with the task, Tom backed the truck up to the ramp and stopped at the first bump of contact. With a turn of the key, the rumbling engine went silent, and the headlights and dash lights flicked off, leaving nothing but quiet darkness. Tom got out first and Jim thought he saw Pepsi leap out after him, though he couldn't be sure. Opening his own door, Jim hefted himself to the ground and felt his legs nearly give out from exhaustion as they tried to bear his weight. He shuffled toward the house, hoping for nothing more than some food and a bed.

"Where the hell do you think you're going?" Tom demanded. "We've got mules to unload."

Jim reflexively clenched his fists, but far too tired to argue, he staggered back to the loading ramp. From the darkness, Jim heard the click of a switch and suddenly the back of the truck was awash with light from a pole next to the ramp. The illumination called forth an immediate frantic dance of insects zipping around the bulb. As Jim walked up the loading ramp, the smell of horse and manure became more pungent than his own sweat and dirt.

"Come on, give me a hand," Tom ordered vaguely as he un-latched the truck's stock gate. Swinging it open, he walked into the back of the truck and untied the mule that was standing calm-ly just inside the gate. "Here," he said holding the rope out toward Jim. "Lead her over to that hitching rail and tie her up. We'll get 'em unloaded and take the tack off, then wipe them down and turn 'em loose."

Jim stood dumbfounded as he looked at the rope in his hands, and at the twelve-hundred-pound animal connected to it.

"Well go on, she won't hurt you. Just tie her up over there."

White knuckling the rope, Jim walked away, glancing over his shoulder, still unsure whether the hooved beast would decide to turn his smelly, exhausted body into a doormat. He reached the thick, log hitching rail unharmed and tied the mule up using a square knot then returned to grab the next animal. He repeated the process with all five mules. It actually wasn't so bad. Tom led Comanche out. Which was good. That horse scared Jim, there was no doubt about it. The look in the beast's eyes was unsettling enough in the daylight but now, in the shadows of the dull lamp high above, it was fear-inducing. Jim was not accustomed to fear, and the vulnerable feeling made his current circumstance all the more frustrating.

Jim stood by the loading ramp, unsure of what to do next, yet not daring to go into the house until given permission. He watched as Tom tied Comanche to the rail with effortless ease.

"Where the hell did you learn how to tie a knot, boy?" Tom bellowed as he inspected the mules' knots. He didn't wait for an answer as he went down the line and retied the animals' ropes to his own satisfaction. "Come here, I'll show you how to take this saddle off and then you can do it on your own."

Tom's hands moved quickly, unclasping buckles and loosening leather straps as he gave names and directions for each part. Jim's mind was a fog but he tried to pay attention—especially when Tom told him how to avoid getting kicked or bitten. Tom unsaddled the first mule and placed the saddle on the ground with the blanket resting on top.

Jim thought he understood the process by the time Tom unsaddled the second mule; he even remembered a few of the saddle parts. Unsnap the breast collar, pull the slipknot on the latigo to free the cinch, walk around the rear to the off side while slipping the britchen over the tail. Lay that between the D-rings, lay the cinch between the D-rings, and then run the breast collar through the front D-ring. Then, run the collar through the cinch ring and through the back D-ring. Now, grab, lift, and pull.

Just as Jim began to feel almost confident, Tom barked more orders at him. "Here. Take this and the other pack saddle and blanket to that tack shed. The light's on the left when you go in the door. Hang the blanket on the fence rail outside to let it dry."

"Okay," Jim said, beyond weary.

"Mind the ears when you come back."

"Ears?"

"Yeah, make sure the mules' and horses' ears are following you so you don't startle them. That'll get you kicked. And if both ears flatten back then it's best to keep clear, cause that means the critter don't take kindly to anyone for the moment."

"Got it. Watch the ears."

The pack saddle was light enough that Jim could hold it with one arm as he placed the saddle blanket on the top rail of the corral and then groped for the light switch inside the shed. Once found, the shed lit up, revealing wood plank walls with two rows of thick two-foot long logs protruding from two of the four walls. One row was at belt level, the other at about Jim's shoulders. Many of the log pegs already held saddles. Jim found an empty slot and set the pack saddle on it.

Returning to the hitching rail, Jim noticed the row of animal ears pivoting quickly, tracking each sound in the dark. As he moved closer, he saw all six pairs of ears training neatly on his steps. He slowed as he saw Comanche's ears flatten and then relax. Damn that horse. The mules were content, aware of his approach, even glancing back as Jim moved between two of them. He picked up the second saddle and put it away then returned to unsaddle one of the mules by himself for the first time.

Pausing for a moment, Jim looked at the buckles and straps. First the breast collar—but wait, disconnect the strap to the cinch first, then the breeching, then the front and trail cinch. Jim maneuvered around the mule, trying hard to mimic Tom—not out of desire to be like the bastard, but out of fear that if he didn't he would invoke the wrath of a mule. After nearly triple the time it had taken Tom, Jim removed the saddle and hauled it to the tack shed. Returning yet again, Jim found that the other mules were unsaddled, and Tom had just finished taking the riding saddle off Comanche. Jim didn't need to be told to haul the pack saddles to the tack shed. That done, he returned to the hitching rail, hoping he'd finally be released to shower and sleep.

"Grab a towel, there, and start wiping them down," Tom commanded with a nod of his head. Then he walked away, hauling Comanche's saddle to the shed. Jim looked around and saw some towels hanging on nails pounded high up on the light pole.

He pulled one down and approached the nearest mule. He began wiping the mule's neck, figuring that was as good a place to start as any.

"No dammit!" Tom's voice made Jim jump. "You clean up where the saddle was, where the sweat is." Tom grabbed the towel from him and quickly wiped the mule's back, switching sides by walking around the rear of the animal, always keeping a hand on the animal's body. "Go with the direction of the hair, see," he said, sounding maybe an ounce less perturbed.

Jim nodded.

"Good, now get to it." Tom tossed him the towel and headed back to the tack shed, returning with a brush. Jim followed Tom's directions, and Tom worked along behind him, brushing down each animal after Jim sopped up the sweat. On the last mule, he felt he was getting the hang of it, even becoming comfortable around the towering beasts. That was until he turned to Comanche. Jim paused. He could feel Tom watching him, waiting to see what he would do. Under the horse's steely glare, Jim approached, reached out with the towel, and touched the horse. Only Jim's disdain for his own fear kept him moving. He began to wipe down the pale horse. Surprisingly, with each swipe of the cloth, Jim thought he felt the horse's tense muscles relax. If he didn't know any better, he would've sworn the horse was enjoying it. Still, once finished, Jim was relieved to back several paces away and let Tom come in to brush his horse. Finished, Tom set the brush on a fence post and told Jim to hang the towel back up.

"Pull the loose end of the rope and the knot will come undone. I'll grab three and you grab three," Tom said as he untied the knots for Comanche, Molly and Cecil, talking to each of them by name as he led them.

Jim did roughly as Tom had and followed with his three mules—one he thought was named Bart but he couldn't be sure. Once in the corral, Tom unbuckled each animal's halter, turning them loose among the half dozen horses that were already there. Several newly freed mules trotted around the corral in excitement, only to stop and drop to the ground, rolling on their backs in the dirt. Jim watched in amazement as the powerful beasts frolicked like kids in a sandbox, their dark shapes melting into the shadows as they moved further away from the loading ramp light.

All the mules that had been on the day's trip now mingled with the herd that had been left behind. The animals pranced and nuzzled, all apparently excited at being together again. All except Comanche. His haunting form stood stock still just at the edge of the light, watching Jim. Then, with a sudden snort and a fling of his head, Comanche trotted off to join the rest of the herd. Tom waved Jim out through the gate, closing it behind them.

"You gotta make sure the gate is latched and the latch tied down. If you don't do both, that damned Cecil will open it and head over to Mrs. Jacobson's garden. Last time he scared the dickens out of her when he ate all her sunflowers, then stuck his head in her kitchen window. I've faced down more hospitable Nazis than that woman and won't dare do it again if I can avoid it."

Jim almost smiled. He didn't dare laugh. Tom led him to a stack of squat, rectangular hay bales. With a quick slash of his pocket knife, Tom cut the twine on two bales and told Jim to toss the wedges into the corral with the horses. As hay dropped to the ground, horses and mules trotted over for their meal. Finally, with all the animals cared for, Tom went about shutting off the lights in the tack room and at the loading ramp. Jim stood by the truck waiting for further direction.

"Grab your pack. I'll throw some soup on the stove while you get cleaned up. No way you're staying in my place smelling like you do," Tom said and walked toward the house. Pepsi darted out of the shadows and fell in step with her master. Jim was far from offended by the jab about his smell. It was true. He did want a shower, and any kind of food sounded good. Struggling to maneuver his pack off the high cab, Jim finally freed it with one final, exhausted yank, slung it over his shoulder and wearily followed Tom.

The porch door opened right into the kitchen. It was nothing like Abby's well-kept kitchen. Rather, the galley looked more like something out of an old *Gunsmoke* episode, with the addition of an antiquated, white metal Frigidaire and a dingy electric stove. The bare wood cabinets sucked the light away from the three working bulbs that hung from a cobweb-covered, five-light fixture. Jim's nose wrinkled at the smell of old coffee and cigarettes.

"Set your pack in the washroom," Tom said, pointing to an open door on a side wall of the kitchen. "Go ahead and put your clothes in the washer there. It can run tonight and you can hang them to dry in the morning."

Jim headed into the washroom with its Philco top-load washing machine. That thing looked like it had more miles on it than Frank's shop truck. In all his years, Jim had never washed his own clothes. It was just something Abby always took care of. Looking back into the kitchen, he thought about asking for help, but pride overruled that idea. Emptying out his pack, he stuffed what clothes he could into the small tub but saw quickly it would take two loads. Jim had at least watched Abby do laundry, so he knew soap was part of the process. On a shelf above he saw a box of Ajax laundry soap and poured what he thought was a proper amount into the tub. Closing the lid, Jim stared at the knobs for half a minute before figuring out what to push, turn, and pull to start the machine. Back in the kitchen, he saw Pepsi curled in the corner on a pile of blankets and Tom stirring a pot. The old man looked up at him and pointed to dark hallway opposite the front door.

"Bathroom is first door on the right, go get showered up," Tom said. He turned his attention to the soup, but continued his verbal directions. "The wash should be filled by the time you start. You only got a minute or so of hot water so make it quick."

"I don't have any clean clothes."

Tom twisted his lips in thought while he stirred. Leaving the spoon in the pot, he strode down the hallway and came back with a neatly folded pair of jeans and a threadbare Pendleton shirt. "This will keep you till morning," Tom said as he thrust the clothes at Jim. "Now go get cleaned up. Soup will be ready in a minute."

Walking down the hallway, Jim found the bathroom. Flicking on the light revealed a room barely large enough to stand in. A small hard water-stained sink was cluttered with a shaving cup, brush, and razor. The toilet looked as though it had never been cleaned. Just inches beyond that was the curtain for the shower, the stall about the size of a phone booth. Balancing the clothes on the sink edge, Jim did his best to undress and use the toilet— a small, weird enjoyment after three weeks of a log latrine in the woods. Tom was right about the hot water. Jim had barely soaped up when the water turned frigid, bringing an abrupt end to that momentary civilized pleasure. He gritted his teeth as he quickly rinsed off. Still, it felt good to scrub away the layers of dirt and sweat. The pants and shirt were a bit loose and smelled of cigarettes, moth balls, and, well, Tom. All repulsive. Only better than being naked he supposed.

Carrying his filthy clothes to the washroom, Jim returned to the kitchen, where Tom had set the pan of soup on the table with a couple bowls and a plastic bag of hard rolls. Tom had already dished up his own supper and motioned for Jim to do the same. No words were required. Campbell's chicken noodle soup had never tasted as good in Jim's life as it did that night. Four rolls and a bowl of soup finally silenced the rumbling in his stomach. When Tom finished, he set the pot and his bowl in a sink filled with dirty dishes. Jim followed suit, and realized how tidy Abby kept their home compared to this pit.

"You got dish duty tomorrow," Tom said, seemingly reading Jim's mind and using the contents against him. "Come on, I'll show you where you'll bunk." Down the hall, the old man opened a door to a small room, cluttered with boxes and dressers. An old metal army cot sat wedged in a corner. On the end of the cot was a thin mattress, rolled up and tied with twine. Some sheets, a couple wool blankets, and a pillow rested on top of the mattress. "I don't get much company other than an old Army buddy every now and then. It ain't much, but it's better than the ground. You know where the crapper is. I'll wake you in the morning."

Tom left Jim standing in the room. Unrolling the mattress, Jim did his best to drape the sheets over the mattress. It didn't take much to qualify it as sleep-worthy in his mind. Jim would have curled up in the corner if that was his only choice. Shutting off the light, he collapsed onto the cot, not even bothering to remove the borrowed clothes. The last thing Jim heard was the clicking of Pepsi's claws as she made her way down the hallway toward Tom's room.

CHAPTER 12

The next morning, Tom hardly knew how he was going to tell Frank that his boy had gotten into a fight and been kicked off the trail crew. As he drove his old Ford pickup into town, each version he played over in his head ended badly. By the time he was knocking on Frank's door, his gut felt as if he had taken a swig of turpentine chased by a lit match.

"Tom—awful surprised to see you! I was just getting ready to head up to get Jim." Frank shook Tom's hand and invited him inside. Abby came out of the kitchen, wiping her hands on her apron. She smiled and greeted Tom cheerfully.

"Yeah, about Jim," Tom removed his hat and held it in both hands.

"What about Jim?" Abby asked immediately turning pale. "He's okay, isn't he?"

"Yes ma'am, he's fine. It's just... he got himself into a bit of trouble the other day and was kicked off the crew. I was up there delivering supplies, so I talked Roy into letting him come down to work for me and—"

"Dammit, that little..." Frank was fast coming unglued. "Is he here with you now?" He looked past Tom to see if Jim was in the truck.

"No, he's at the ranch house. I wanted to talk with you about things first."

"What's to talk about?! He's bought himself a ticket to Pine Hills. After all I did to give him a chance, the kid just throws it away." Frank threw his fists up and then rested them on his head. He paced to the middle of the living room, and stared out the big picture window to the street. They were all silent for a good minute.

Abby spoke, measuring each word slowly, "Tom, would you like some coffee?"

"That'd be nice ma'am. Thank you."

"Frank, maybe you and Tom need to talk?"

Tom didn't move until Frank agreed with his wife and headed to the kitchen himself. Once at the table, Abby poured the men tall mugs of strong black coffee. She set a plate of freshly baked blueberry muffins on the table then removed her apron and sat at the table with them. Tom had hoped she would find some chores to do elsewhere. All women made him nervous, even Abby. Maybe especially Abby. She settled in with them. No, she wasn't going to miss a word of this discussion.

"So what did he do?" Frank asked, a touch calmer.

"A fight. Some guy kept egging Jim on, and I guess it got to the kid."

"What did Roy say? Was it his idea to send him out with you?"

"No," Tom said and took a sip of coffee. "That was my idea. Roy was damned near fit-to-be-tied. Couldn't decide if he should kill 'em both or just send a packer to call the sheriff about Jim."

"Well it might just do the trick for Jim," Frank said. "Some hard time is what he needs."

"Frank!" Abby snapped.

"I know," he sighed, not bothering to look at his wife. "Tom, do you want me to come get him? I'll take him to the judge first thing Monday and let the chips fall where they may."

"Well, I was thinking." Tom paused and looked Abby and Frank in the eye in turn. "I was thinking about having him help me the rest of the summer. I got some contracts with the Forest Service, and I could use him on those. It would be the same as if he was on the crew. He would only have to deal with me is all, and I'm sure I can keep him in line. I'll work him as hard as the trail crews, and if things get bad then we can call the sheriff."

Frank rubbed his chin, his mouth contorting as he mulled things over. He looked at Abby. "What do you think?"

She nodded in agreement, though Tom noticed her furrowed brow. She held reservations about the idea. She spoke up. "If he got kicked off the trail crew for fighting, then who's to say he won't take a swing at you?"

The question surprised Tom, not that he hadn't thought about the same possibility. But he was surprised that Abby would be so blunt. "If that happens, then I think Jim and I will come to an understanding right quick ma'am." Tom smiled. Abby did not.

"I'm up to it if you are," Frank surrendered. "I'll call Judge Cannich Monday morning and square things away. You sure this ain't no trouble?"

"No trouble," Tom said and took a drink of coffee.

The remainder of their conversation revolved around packing some fresh clothes for Jim and asking Frank to chip in on the food during his stay. Abby was as quiet as a church mouse the rest of the time, and Tom could feel her concern even after he pulled away from their house. There wasn't much he could do about it though. On the way home, he stopped at the grocery store to get supplies and to allow Pepsi some time to bark her heart out at people in the parking lot. Done with his errands, Tom breathed a sigh of relief as the truck wheeled towards less populated areas. With all the people and traffic, the weekly drive to get food and gas tried Tom's nerves. Ventures into civilization were on par with a date with the dentist—they only occurred when necessary.

There was one pressing concern as he headed home. Would Jim still be there? The question vexed Tom as he drove north out of Helena. In a way, Tom hoped the kid had skipped out. He'd left it an easy choice for the kid. A test. Tom hadn't hidden his departure. He'd left his phone connected and his keys to the stock truck in the ignition. In his mind, it would be a good thing if Jim did leave—clearly running from the law, and leaving Tom, Pepsi, the horses, and the mules out of the circus for good.

"It's all your fault, you know," Tom declared to Pepsi, who lay curled up on the bench seat next to him. "You were supposed to talk some sense into me."

Pepsi tilted her head curiously, making Tom laugh. He gave the dog a pat as he slowed down for the stop sign at the intersection of Green Meadow and Lincoln. "Yeah, I know, it was my idea. What the hell was I thinking?" Pepsi stood up and scooted closer to Tom, arching herself away from the gear shift as he accelerated onto Lincoln Road. Almost home.

Pulling onto the dirt drive that led to his house, he could see that the stock truck was still there. That didn't mean that Jim was. A phone call to a friend was a quick escape. Time to check the house. As hopeful as Tom was for such an easy out, muffled snores from the spare room informed him that his guest hadn't even been conscious to contemplate an escape. Tom put away the groceries, then took the bag of clothes that Abby had sent with him and entered Jim's room without knocking.

"Rise and shine sleepin' beauty! I was nice and let you sleep in, but that'll likely be the last time." Tom tossed the bag of clothes onto Jim's head, eliciting a groan. At least there was some evidence of life. "There's some clean clothes so you can get out of mine. Get moving, we got work to do."

Tom left the door open as he went back to the kitchen to start another pot of coffee. Several minutes later, he saw a shadow lurch from the bedroom to the bathroom and then finally, like some B movie monster, the boy shuffled into the kitchen.

"Coffee's on the table. There's cereal in the cupboard by the sink. Your mom said it's a kind you liked."

"They were here?" Jim perked up.

"No, I went to town this morning. Where do you think those clothes you're wearing came from?"

Jim looked at his shirt and pants and realized they were, indeed, clothes from his room back home. "Oh," he said and rubbed his eyes.

"We're trying to get things ironed out for you to finish out your time here."

"What if I don't want to?"

"Then it's Pine Hills for you. You know that."

"I don't believe you," he said, now quite awake. "They can get Roy to give me another chance. They wouldn't leave me out here, not with you."

"There's the phone, call 'em yourself."

Tom enjoyed his coffee as Jim stomped across the kitchen and dialed his parent's number. This was interesting. The kid had been almost helpful the night before. He'd been ignorant of all the tasks, but he'd tried. And he hadn't acted like the raging idiot that stood before him now. Clearly, it was not good to allow this boy to get too well rested. The rotary dial wound up and then spun back to the start with each number. Jim spoke softly at first.

"Hi, it's me, Jim. Yeah, I'm fine. Are you coming to get me?"

Tom watched the boy clench a fist.

"No, I don't want to talk to him. I want you to c—Hi Pops…" Pops? Tom felt his temper rise at the disrespectful title Jim used for Frank. Silence. Muted shouting on the other end, then Jim snapped back. "But it wasn't my fault."

The anger in the teen's voice didn't sit well with Tom. He slowly set his coffee mug on the table.

"Dammit, why won't you come get me?" This fruitless volley continued for another half minute until Jim huffed and hung up the phone violently.

"I can't believe this shit!" his skin turned darker with fury. Then, quick as a rattlesnake, he roared as his right fist slammed into the wall.

Spooked by Jim's rage, Pepsi leapt up and raced across the floor towards Tom. From the corner of his eye, Tom saw Jim turn toward the dog. Tom didn't know if the boy was going to storm outside or kick Pepsi, but the scared cattle dog looked to be a very possible target as Jim took a step in her direction. It didn't matter what Jim intended, no one was going to harm one of Tom's animals. He leapt up between Jim and the dog, grabbed the boy by the throat, and slammed him into the wall. The look in Jim's eyes told Tom that the teen was absolutely stunned, but aware enough to understand his words.

"Listen here you little bastard, you're stuck here or else you can spend the rest of your pathetic year with the other vermin in Pine Hills. You stay, then here's how things are gonna be: you even look at me wrong, or don't do what I say when I say it, then I'll kick your ass so damn hard you'll look like a ringed-necked pheasant for a week!" Tom released his grip and stepped back a pace. The boy gasped, but didn't move an inch. Good. Tom stuck his trigger finger in Jim's face. "And if you ever hurt one of my animals, I'll kill you."

Jim's eyes told Tom all he needed to know. The kid believed him. "There's the door kid. You want Pine Hills? Then get walking. I'll call the sheriff so you won't have to walk far. What'll it be?"

Jim rubbed his neck. Amazing. The rage still flashed in the kid's eyes. The boy was rallying and clearly wanted to take a swing at him. No, kids did not learn easily these days.

"Stay or go, your call," Tom reiterated. Jim looked at the door and then back at Tom. Something cooled in the boy's demeanor. He was far from resigned though.

"I'll stay."

"We understand each other then?"

"Yes sir."

"Fine. And don't call me sir. I wasn't no damned officer." Tom paused at the door on his way out to roll a cigarette. "Get some grub. When you're done, tend to those dishes, and take care of your laundry. We can start work after that."

"I wasn't going to hurt her," the kid muttered. "Your dog, I mean. I was just angry and was heading outside."

True or not, it was the right thing to say. Tom gave a curt nod, then held the door for Pepsi. Once outside, he rolled a smoke to calm his nerves, his hand still trembling slightly as the adrenaline subsided. He lit up and walked out to the corral. The horses came to him, curious. While petting Moonlight's muzzle, Tom looked back at the house and then down to Pepsi, who sat nearby. The soda pop dog had recovered from the incident much faster than Tom had. She casually scratched at her neck with her hind leg.

It had been years since Tom had felt such rage, or the desire to snuff the life out of someone. It was not a comfortable feeling, though it was unfortunately familiar. He was thankful that Jim hadn't tried anything. Restraint only lasted so long with Tom, and once a certain line was crossed it meant someone was going to either the hospital or the grave. How would he explain that to Frank and Abby? With Jim committed to being there for the summer, Tom hoped this would be their only conflict. Maybe the teen would now realize that his odds were better if he didn't test his keeper.

After ten minutes, Tom finished his smoke and tossed the stub to the ground, snuffing it with the toe of his boot. Comanche approached him then. Tom rubbed the horse's neck as he glanced around the forty-acre spread. The perusal brought to mind a whole list of chores Tom could have Jim complete during his stay.

The screen door screeched open and out tumbled the kid, hauling his wet laundry to the clothesline. Tom watched in silent laugher as the teen fumbled through the simple process of hanging his clothes. Abby had indeed mothered him too much. Yes, it would do the kid good to earn his keep.

Watching Jim continue to struggle with the simple task of his laundry, Tom felt no sympathy but, rather, disdain. He had no such ignorance of chores in his youth. No, Tom's childhood had been entirely different. For that he was almost jealous of the teen. Frank and Abby loved their kids. Though strict, they provided for all their worldly needs while asking little in return. Tom knew they had struggled to have kids, so when they finally did have them, they treated them as though they were some literal blessing from God. The shadow side of that adoration was this: Jim was a spoiled brat.

Tom's parents, Patrick and Martha McKee, had not been of that mindset. A proud Scotsman, Tom's father was also a drunkard with a quick and violent soul, a man hell-bent on enforcing rules that he never followed himself. Martha, Tom's mother, was far from submissive to her husband's demands. On the contrary, she seemed to feed off of the man's anger. Several times a day they would fight, each one dead set on being right and on getting the last word in. Tom knew that all couples fought, even Frank and Abby, though he suspected they did so in a more civilized manner. He didn't see Jim as having any fear of his parents, not after hearing him demand that they come pick him up. For Tom, it hadn't been that way.

Much of Tom's youth had been spent trying to find a way to avoid a melee of shouts, slaps, and hits. They had lived in Durango, Colorado, where Patrick and Martha ran a saloon that catered to the tourists visiting Mesa Verde National Park. That kept them busy in the afternoons and late into the night. When they were home during the day, Tom retreated from their house, withdrawing to the outskirts of town where a hunting guide kept his horses. Once away from the screams and yells, Tom found peace, if only for a few hours. That was why he retreated to the corral even now, after his bout of rage at Jim. Peace always came from the calm of a horse herd.

From the edge of the corral, Tom watched as Jim continued to curse and fumble with his heavy, wet clothes. Tom understood Jim's anger and the desire to rebel and be on his own, but he also knew that the kid had no idea how good he had things with Frank and Abby. Tom hadn't had another option by the time he'd left home.

As Tom grew older, his father's anger began to manifest itself against his sons, Tom and his older brother, Michael. Patrick McKee would remind his boys of the McKee motto with each drunken punch: *Manu forti. With a strong hand.* When Michael reached sixteen, he struck back at his father, knocking him to the ground. Patrick McKee just smiled and told Michael to get out and never show his face in town again. Tom watched in terror as his brother, the only one he trusted, left. What shocked Tom most wasn't that his dad exiled Michael, but that their own mother said nothing. Tom even thought he saw her smirk as Michael walked out the door.

It was another full year of beatings before Tom had enough. At fifteen, Tom, himself, struck back. Not just once, though. He'd pummeled his drunk father till the monster lay unconscious on the floor, his mother screaming at Tom to stop. He didn't wait to be formally banished. Tom had his few belongings already packed and immediately set out on his own.

He spent the first year looking for his brother but gave up somewhere in California. From there, working as a cow hand and laborer, he made his way up to Alaska, where he learned how to run trap lines while surviving in the harsh climate. After that, Tom returned to the lower forty-eight just in time for the Great Depression. He was one of the lucky ones and got on with a ranch in central Idaho, where the dust bowl didn't hit quite so hard. There he learned the craft of horsemanship and running pack strings.

Working the horses and cows and packing into the mountains each hunting season helped temper Tom, teaching him that fists and cursing didn't work as well on horses as they appeared to with men. Even in those early days learning horsemanship, Tom's violent past haunted him and showed itself during weekend benders at the bars. Though not as big as some men, he liked fighting and found himself skilled at it. He even managed to make some money in back room brawls for cash bets, his size tipping the odds against him but giving a bigger payoff when he won. Despite the fact that Tom was finding a beneficial outlet for his violent nature, the local law enforcement didn't feel the same. It was while he was facing jail time for breaking a man's jaw in three places, that Tom was given the option of joining the army.

Everyone knew war was coming, so Tom didn't think twice about it. Why not get paid to fight? It was a good fit, other than the fact that Tom had to learn to obey orders, something he had never quite got the hang of. A list of reprimands went side-by-side with his achievements. Both were plentiful. Tom's savage nature kept him from advancing and resulted in him being swapped from one unit to the next. It wasn't until the summer of 1942, while Tom was stationed at Fort Lewis in Washington, that he received a recruitment letter for special duty.

While the war raged in Europe and the Pacific, Tom had been frustrated with getting stuck on guard duty back in the States. The recruitment letter asked for single men between the ages of 21 and 35, with the preferred occupations of woodsmen, loggers, hunters, and others with outdoor experience. It fit Tom to a T. He hadn't asked the unit's purpose and he hadn't cared; he just knew it was something special and he wanted to be a part of it. That and, if he accepted, the position would pay an additional fifty dollars a month. Upon acceptance, he rode the train to Helena, Montana, where he started his training with the First Special Service Force, a mix of Canadian and American soldiers and officers intended to be dropped into Norway to harass the Nazis. That however, didn't happen. Instead, following their training, they briefly deployed to the Aleutian Islands in Alaska then changed climates entirely, heading to southern Europe to help the Allies push up through Italy.

As difficult as the training had been, Tom enjoyed it, even relished it during the brutal fifty mile marches. He loved the hand-to-hand fighting, testing his skills against others. All this while being paid. As part of the unit, his tendency toward rage was strengthened, honed, and restrained by training, like the effect of a bridle on a spirited horse. Tempering had been the very thing Tom needed, and he credited his time in the Army as the one thing that kept him from ending up in prison or dead. However, death had come near enough while in Italy with his unit.

Tom tried not to think of those times. He preferred to remember the training and his friends from the unit. Those were good memories. The good memories helped keep the demons locked away for the time being, though Tom's confrontation with Jim had tugged at the latch a bit. That was why he had retreated to the horses. He breathed in time with them, and felt in control again.

Tom's peace was broken by the slamming screen door, as Jim completed his twenty-minute battle with his laundry. Tom stayed outside for another half hour or so, walking around the ranch and making a mental list of things for Jim to do. When Tom knew that his nerves were calmed enough that he could at least talk with Jim and not envision seeing the young man's eyes roll up in his head as he died, he headed back to the house.

As he and the dog entered the kitchen, Pepsi steered clear of Jim as she scurried over to her bed. The dishes were indeed washed and stacked in the drying rack. Jim sat at the table with a mug of coffee in his hands. The washing machine ground away at another load of Jim's clothes.

"What else do you want me to do?" Jim asked in a careful monotone.

"You got some food in your gut?"

Jim nodded.

"Okay, we'll work on some fence repairs, and then I think we'll start you with some riding lessons. You can't do me any good if you can't ride." Tom hung his hat on a hook by the door then poured himself half a cup of coffee. "You ever been on a horse?"

"No. My sister always wanted one though."

"Let's get you riding then. And after this court mess is done, you can bring Vivian out and take her for a ride. Casey or Moonlight are calm horses, either one would be great with her."

"Not sure my folks would be up for that."

"Why not? They're horse people."

"They are?"

"You really don't know a thing about them, do you? Before you kids came along, your mom and dad had a ranch on the west side of the divide. I can't believe they never told you about it."

"They told us a few stories, but I guess I just can't see them as ranchers and knowing horses."

"Boy, they've probably forgotten more about horses and ranching than most people will ever know. Mark my words, if they could still be ranching they would be. But they had some hard times and had to sell their spread and move over here before World War II started up. Might be worth your while to get to know them better. They are your parents after all." Tom stood up after finishing his coffee. "You come from a strong family name, even if you don't want it."

"I'm not a Redmond," the kid said. Same careful monotone, but this was definitely a topic that got to him.

"What nonsense are you speaking, boy?"

"They're no more my parents than they are yours."

"That so? You gonna play the adopted card or the poor Indian card or both? Want to tell me which half of you is Injun? Is it the pig-headed, stubborn half, or the foolhardy, ignorant half?"

Jim remained silent, sitting back in his chair with his fists on the table, his eyes avoiding Tom's.

"Your skin just keeps all your guts inside. Don't make you who you are any more than wearing a particular shirt. Trust me, you poke a hole in someone you'll see we all bleed the same." Tom shook his head, frustrated at the boy. He took another drink of coffee and set his mug on the table. "I'll give you a bit of advice. What you do makes you who you are and will make your name a good one or a bad one. You don't want the Redmond name, then go make your own, but don't soil your mother and father's name in the process. They adopted you, which makes you their son by choice; they wanted you. Don't you ever cheapen that." Tom didn't wait for a reaction to his tirade. Pushing his chair away from the table, he quickly added: "Now let's get to work."

Grabbing his hat, Tom headed for the door. The boy stood and followed. On their way out, Tom pointed to a small end table in the living room. On it was a dust-covered chess set. "You know how to play chess, kid?"

"No."

"Well, you'll learn. I can't play with Pepsi anymore; the little bitch cheats too much." Tom headed out the door as Pepsi darted past his legs, giving Jim a wide berth.

CHAPTER 13

The breath rushed from Jim's lungs as he hit the ground. The big silver roan mare stood a few steps away, looking back at him with large, soft brown eyes. Gasping for air, he wished he was still fixing fences or, better yet, back in bed. His day had been frenzied from the start, beginning with that not-so-pleasant call home, and his not-so-friendly run-in with Tom. God, that old codger was insane. They'd at least kept busy with house chores and mending fences until a lunch break around one o'clock. As long as they were working or eating, the old man was almost civil. After lunch, they'd worked for two more hours, replacing ten-foot long wood rails on the main corral. Then Tom halted that work and told Jim it was time for his first riding lesson. So far that was going just fantastic.

"So, you want me to tell you what you're doing wrong or just let you keep makin' a fool out of yourself?" Tom ribbed from the edge of the corral. "If you can't get on a gentle nag like Sil, then I don't know how you'll manage a bronc."

Jim slapped the dust off his jeans as he leaned over, trying to refill his lungs. Tom was right, of course. Sil hadn't bucked or jumped, she'd just started walking right as he'd stepped into the

stirrup. Like some gangly scarecrow, Jim flailed and, grabbing for
the reins, only succeeded in going over the other side—kissing the
ground for the second time.

"Okay," he said, "show me." Jim swallowed his pride.

Tom hopped off the corral rail and strode to the horse's left
side. Jim joined him there. "You grab the reins with your left hand
and the horn with your right. Then put your foot in the stirrup.
Don't grab the cantle if you don't have to," he said, pointing to the
back of the saddle, "that way, when she walks, you aren't fighting
your arm to swing your leg over. That's the best way to mount a
horse. Anything else will make you look like a fool, or if the horse
goes rodeo, you'll get yourself hurt. If you've got a horse that's a
walker, like Sil, then run that inside rein ride outside your elbow,
like this."

Tom demonstrated, going from standing next to the horse
to sitting in the saddle in one smooth motion, even though Sil
started walking the moment he put weight in the stirrup. The
pressure on the rein pulled her into Tom, allowing an effortless
mount. Tom got off in just as fluid a movement and handed the
reins to Jim.

Trying to mimic the flawless demonstration, Jim clutched Sil's
reins with his left hand, then grabbed the saddle horn with his
right. As he put the toe of his left boot into the stirrup, he remembered to route the inside rein around his elbow. As before, Sil began to walk, but Jim let the motion pick him up. With surprisingly
little effort, he swung his right leg over the saddle. His knuckles
were white, gripping the horn, as he struggled to get his right foot
into the other stirrup. But, once his feet were secure, Jim found
himself sitting high off the ground, heart pounding, as Sil calmly
walked around the corral.

"Now tighten up the reins, but not too much. Remember, she'll
mind your knees and heels as much as the bit, so don't get rough
with either of them."

Jim let go of the saddle horn and fumbled with the reins, though he could tell Sil needed no guidance from her rider. With leather in hand, Jim smiled. He realized he was, in fact, riding the half-ton animal.

"Now what?" Jim asked.

"Rein her. Do some figure eights. Remember, gentle with the reins, and always pull the reins back to your belly, never your head. Keep those heels down. Sit on your back pockets. There you go."

Jim did as he was told, and Sil responded perfectly to his direction. Never in his life could he have imagined being around, let alone in control of, such a large animal. "Kind of like driving, right?" he asked. "Just steer it where you want it to go?"

"I guess so, but a car don't have a mind of its own. A horse is a strong, fast, and loyal creature, but they're used to being food."

"What?" Jim brought Sil to a stop.

"They are prey animals, used to being hunted. Their only defense is to run, and if they feel threatened, they'll do just that. Run. That's why if you're out in the pasture catching one, you can't act like a predator. You gotta be calm, which means keeping your emotions in check even if you're having a bad day." Tom backed away to the edge of the corral. "Now get her walking again, and then give her a little kick with your heels to bring her up to a trot."

"A trot?"

"Yes, a trot, you pansy. You'll be fine. Just lean forward and keep your weight on your toes. Don't fight the motion. Find a rhythm and ride it."

Jim's heels nudged Sil's flank, causing her to resume walking. Another nudge sent her into a gentle trot. At first, the motion was jarring; Jim's body bounced up and down, his butt slamming into the saddle with each step. He was about to rein her to a stop when his legs found the rhythm that Tom spoke of. A push with his legs at the right moment allowed his body to move up and down with each stride. Each step allowed him to feel more at ease, rising and falling in unison with the horse. Confidence growing, he shifted the reins to the left and Sil altered her course almost before he'd tugged on the reins. At a trot, Jim rode five big, lazy figure eights before bringing Sil to a stop in front of Tom.

"Not bad. Later in the week we'll take you two out to the field. You might find her less predictable then." Tom spoke through the haze of a newly lit cigarette.

"I don't know, she seems nice enough," Jim proclaimed, patting the mare's neck.

"Don't get complacent. Even a horse as nice as Sil will dump you if you become lazy. If you get too cocky, I'll have to put you on a real bronc."

"Like Comanche?"

"No, I wouldn't put you on him. I promised your parents I'd keep you alive. Keep riding. Do some loops around those barrels and remember, light on the reins."

Jim nodded. Something about the moment put him at ease, despite the conversation topic, despite sitting on a horse for the first time in his life. A casual question popped out of his mouth before he could think it through, "Is Comanche the leader of the other horses?"

"No. The brood mare leads the herd, and Sil has that title. If you mean is Comanche the stud, no. He's gelded, though he's proud cut."

"Proud cut?"

"Yeah, he had his balls cut off, but no one told him so," Tom said matter-of-factly. "He still thinks he's the herd stud, which is why he can be a stubborn cuss sometimes. Hey, don't start slouching. Sit back on your pockets and keep your weight centered."

Once again, Jim straightened himself and nudged Sil into a walk. They transitioned from walking to trotting and back to walking again for the next thirty minutes, both learning to understand the directions they were giving each another. Tom watched and smoked silently, just outside the corral. Sometimes Jim forgot he was there. Slight pressure with his knees, a touch of the rein on the side of the neck, a brush of boot heel on Sil's flank, all translated into movement and redirection. Jim smiled, thinking of how fearful he had been at the start, but now he felt in total control of the animal he was riding. Again bringing Sil to a stop in front of Tom, Jim slid off the side of the saddle with a grin, though his legs quickly morphed into an awkward stance. His muscles rebelled from the time in the saddle. Jim stood tall though, proud of his accomplishment.

"It's like she knew what I wanted her to do before I did," he said. "Are all horses like this?"

"No, Sil is a good horse. She's had a few riders on her, so she knows the game. Other horses will require you to pay a bit more attention to them."

"What happens if a horse bucks?"

"Goes rodeo? Well, you got a few choices there. Grab the horn like a city dude or step off like a coward—"

"I'm no coward," Jim interrupted.

"Well then, you go the cowboy way: rein and spur, and see how the ride ends. Either you win or the horse wins. The horse only wins if he dumps you, and you're too afraid to get back on."

"You ever been afraid to get back on a horse?"

"Ha. Still see me ridin', dontcha?"

A rumble of thunder from the western horizon drew both Jim and Tom's attention. "Storm's a brewin' on the divide," Tom said. "Go and get that saddle off so you can get her wiped down and let out."

Jim walked Sil out of the corral and led her to the hitching rail. He tied the lead rope to the log with a loose square knot.

"Finish up. Then I still need to teach you how to tie up a horse properly."

Tom's tone led Jim to believe he had done something wrong, leaving him with an uneasy feeling about the next lesson. He tried not to think too much about it; instead he focused on taking the saddle off Sil and wiping her down. Once that was done, he untied the lead rope, led Sil to the corral, and released her to be with the other horses and mules. He secured the gate on his way out and walked over to Tom, next to the corral. The cowboy had a thick rope in his hand. Behind them, roiling over the Continental Divide, the thunderstorm flashed and boomed.

"Now watch, I'm only going to show you once, and I don't want you to come back into the house until you can do this with your eyes closed," Tom said. "You don't get this right, it could mean the death of one of my horses. Or you." He took the rope and flipped it up under a rail, allowing the loose end to drop on the left side of the taunt end—which would presumably be tied to a horse. "Reach across and grab the tail end, twist it to form a loop over the top. Leave enough of the tail dangling down. Reach through the loop and grab the tail. Pull it through the first loop but just enough to make another loop and tighten the first one around it. This'll let you untie it quick with just a pull of the tail. To keep the horses from untying it, slip the tail through the loop, that way if they pull it, it'll just tighten. Got it?"

"Uh, yeah, got it," Jim said. The truth was, he'd only caught glimpses of the technique. His attention was mostly focused on the lightning strikes in the mountains near the old mining town of Marysville, just seven miles to the west.

"Well then, do it. Don't come in till you can do it with your eyes closed, you understand? You never know when you'll have to tie a horse up in the woods during the pitch black of night." Tom untied the knot in single quick pull and handed the rope over. Then he left Jim standing there.

Jim watched as Tom and Pepsi retreated to the protection of the covered porch. The old man sat down on the bench swing and rolled a cigarette. Jim gripped the rope and tried to mentally replay the steps required to tie the knot to the fence. The first attempt elicited a smoke-filled chuckle from the porch. A glance over his shoulder confirmed that Tom did not approve. Even Pepsi had taken to watching the test from her place next to Tom. Attempt number two also failed, but Jim knew he had the first part right. He just couldn't remember how Tom had grabbed the rope to make the loop.

Heavy, imposing raindrops fell, slowly at first, an impact every couple of seconds, like an artillery unit bracketing the target to find the correct range. Jim felt several drops hit his shoulder, and then the barrage started in earnest. He didn't bother to look toward the house. He knew Tom was still there; he could feel the bastard's stare. As the torrent continued, Jim considered calling it quits till it dried out, but pride kept him attempting the knot. He wanted to prove he could do it, and he certainly didn't want Tom to think he was a quitter. On the ninth attempt, he was soaking wet and his fingers almost numb, but the knot looked right. He tested it, pulling the loose end. The knot came cleanly undone.

Smiling, but still not looking back at the house, Jim tied it again. Once more, the knot looked right and came undone when the loose end was pulled. Again he did it, five times, six times. Then, yes, twice with his eyes closed just to make sure. Content with his work, Jim took the rope and slogged through the muddy puddles back to the house, where Tom and Pepsi sat unimpressed on the bench. Jim tossed the rope to the floor.

"Good enough?" he asked.

Tom gave him a single nod, which Jim took as permission to go inside and change into some dry clothes. After changing, he came out of his room to find Tom frying two hamburgers in a well-seasoned cast iron skillet. A bag of Sweetheart white bread sat on the table alongside a tub of butter, a home-canned jar of sweet pickles, thick slices of onion, and two Kessler beers. Interesting.

Was this the old bastard's idea of a test or something? Surely one of the beers couldn't be for him, being only seventeen and all. Tom told him to get the bread ready as the burgers were nearly done. Jim sat down to butter the bread and added a double layer of sweet pickles and onions just in time to accept the two thick burger patties dripping with grease.

"This beer for me?" he asked.

"It is if you want it. If you don't, it won't go to waste," Tom said, sitting down to his meal. "I figure you earned it. Just don't tell your folks."

Jim let a hint of a smile cross his face. "Don't worry, I won't."

The beer and burger were plain, average at best. Yet, after three weeks in the mountains and a day of work and riding, they tasted better than the finest fare of any eatery that Jim had been to. As the summer thunderstorm passed overhead, a drum roll of rain and thunder filled the house.

⚊⊰⊱⚊

The next morning, Jim thought he heard Tom's truck leave long before the first glints of sun made it past the tattered drapes. Exhaustion pulled him deeper under the covers; he willed himself to ignore the noise. But soon enough, sunlight invaded the room. He buried his face under the wool blanket. The rays of sunshine filled his room completely by the time he heard the Ford truck returning. Though his body felt immobilized, Jim's mind was alert. He heard everything. The truck door closed with a deep metallic thud, and the screen door creaked as Tom and Pepsi walked in. He heard the clicking of the soda pop dog's nails on the filthy linoleum in the kitchen, then the clanking of iron pan on stovetop, and the rustle of a newspaper. After another ten minutes, he heard boots coming down the hallway. Hmm. His time of restful slumber was officially over. Tom pounded on Jim's door three times then opened it, letting in the smell of fresh-brewed coffee and cooking bacon.

"Let's get moving, it's half past eight. I let you sleep in a bit," Tom grumbled then headed straight back to the kitchen.

Rising from the cot, Jim's butt and thigh muscles screamed, constricting painfully in further protest as he struggled to get dressed. The riding lesson had exacted its revenge on his body. With every step, Jim wanted to groan in agony, but he didn't dare. He entered the kitchen, standing as straight and walking as normally as he could.

"Legs sore?" Tom glanced up from a section of the newspaper comics.

"No, good as new," he said and walked to the table, where his coffee mug sat waiting to be filled. His fib was exposed as he sat down too fast, a moan of pain escaping his lips.

"A day of bucking bales will cure that."

Jim didn't answer. Sore muscles, a growling stomach, and the prospect of hefting heavy bales of hay all day killed his inclination to speak.

Following breakfast, and after ensuring all the animals had food and water, Tom directed Jim to shovel the horse manure out of the stock truck. Oh joy. When that was done to Tom's satisfaction, Jim and his keeper and the dog all climbed into the stock truck and drove east, towards the Helena Valley, to pick up a load of hay from the first year's cutting. Jim asked why they were getting more hay when the stack next to the corral looked plenty big to him.

"Gotta stock up for winter," Tom said. "I'll get another three loads before the snow falls. Once the cold settles in, food is the only way the animals can stay warm."

Unlike the night that Jim had come out of the mountains, the town was clearly visible to the south, its sprawl climbing the base of Mount Helena. The mountain sat majestically, its gray cliffs adorning its top. Jim couldn't see his home but he recognized where it'd be in relation to the rest of the town. It was Sunday. Frank, Abby, and Vivian would be sitting down to Sunday breakfast before heading to church.

It all seemed a lifetime ago. Strange as it was, Jim couldn't help but think that things were better now than when he had been with the trail crew, and they were certainly better than Pine Hills. He had a bed, a shower, and a toilet—even if they were filthy—and he even had some solitude at night. It was the solitude that he hadn't realized he'd missed. At home he could retreat to his room, but up with the trail crew there was always someone nearby. Solitude allowed him to mull things over quietly. This, combined with the work so far, made Jim figure he just might make it through the summer.

But what would the judge say tomorrow? Jim realized, with no small flash of fear, that it was all too possible a sheriff deputy might pull up the next day, slap handcuffs on him, and haul him to Pine Hills. That reality smothered him as he continued to look out the window at his distant hometown. Eventually, the sound of the truck gearing down to turn off the highway pushed the worry aside. A sign on the side of the road advertised hay for sale, confirming that they had reached their destination. Tom maneuvered the truck so the back end lightly bumped the foot of a gargantuan stack of hay bales. In front of a barn, near the west end of the stack, two men worked on a tractor. One waved and walked over to them.

"You stay in the cab, Pepsi," Tom ordered. "Rosco don't take kindly to other dogs."

Jim assumed Rosco was the scraggly mutt that had just launched himself from the porch of the house a hundred yards away. The beast barked wildly as he fell in step with his owner. Tom climbed out and greeted the man who wiped his hands on a rag dangling from the front pocket of his denim overalls. They shook hands and chatted. Jim grabbed his leather gloves from the dashboard and got out to join them.

"Go ahead and start loading," Tom said to him. "Put 'em in tight so they don't shift. I'll help in a bit."

"How do I get them into the truck?" Jim asked, looking up at the stack, towering at least twice as high as the truck.

"My hand'll help ya," the hay farmer interrupted. "Charlie, come on over and give the kid a hand, will ya?" The man back at the tractor nodded and gave a quick wave, then set his tools down and cleaned the grease off his hands with a rag. Tom and the hay farmer walked off toward the house, leaving Jim and the ranch hand to the task.

"Charlie Goodhorse," the ranch hand said. The man's grip was one that would have caused a blacksmith to shed a tear. A good three inches taller than Jim, he was imposing in his flat-brimmed Stetson. Two large feathers were tied on the left side of the hatband. Jim couldn't help but notice that they shared the same color skin.

"Jim Redmond."

"Nice to meet you." Charlie smiled, a warm smile that seemed out of place on such an imposing man. "Come on, we can get to the top of the stack from over here." Jim followed Charlie to the end, where the stack had been taken down a bit by other buyers, the rectangular bales forming a makeshift stairway to the top. "You working for Tom?"

"Yeah, for the summer."

They walked along the top of the long stack and stopped at the edge, looking down to the stock truck. A wave of vertigo washed over Jim, but he steeled himself and took a step back.

"Bucked bales before?"

Jim shook his head, wondering how many bones he would break if he made a wrong step this high up. Charlie showed him how to free a bale from the stack by grabbing both strands of twine, standing up with the bale in his hands, and then using his legs to launch it down to the truck. Jim looked down into the truck bed. While cleaning the inside of the stock truck earlier, he'd felt small surrounded by the open topped, six-foot-high steel and wood walls. Yet, now the eight by eighteen-foot deck looked small from so high up.

Charlie tossed another bale and Jim joined in. After two dozen bales, the two climbed back down to the truck to straighten the jumble into a neat bottom layer. Then Charlie scrambled back up top and tossed bales down to Jim so he could continue with the layering.

"So, what tribe?" Charlie called down to him as he sent a forty-five-pound bale flying. It dropped into the truck with a heavy thud and a cloud of hay dust.

"Tribe?" Jim looked up, confused as he grabbed the strings to reposition the bale.

"You're Native, aren't you? You know, Injun. What tribe you from?"

"Don't know, I'm adopted. And my mom said I'm only half Indian."

"An apple, huh?" Charlie grinned as he launched another bale.

"An apple?"

"You know, red on the outside and white on the inside."

Odd, it didn't feel like an insult coming from this man. "I guess so," Jim said and laughed. "How about you, what tribe?"

"Apsáalooke."

"What?" Jim asked, confused by the strange name.

"Crow. Down by Hardin."

"Oh. Why are you up here?"

"White man don't make us stay on the reservation anymore, Apple." Charlie grinned, launching another bale down.

"That's not what I meant."

"No jobs. If you stay on the reservation, the only thing to do is drink and complain. No one in Billings would hire someone from the rez, so I came up this way. Been working here three years now."

"Why can't you get a job in Billings?"

"Most people off the rez that those whites know are drunks and troublemakers. They see me and think I'm the same, so no job. That's the problem with makin' trouble; it affects other people. Like a rock tossed in the water, the closer you are, the bigger the waves. So, I came here. Smaller waves."

"At least you know who you are and where you're from."

"And you don't?" Charlie paused for a minute to let Jim catch up in the sorting of bales.

"I don't know. I'm adopted so…"

"You got a family don't you? Where'd you grow up?"

"Here in Helena. But, really, I don't know who I am."

Charlie let out a laugh. "You've been in the sun too long kid. You're you." Charlie tossed two more bales, then jumped down to help Jim finish layering the stack that was now a half bale over the top of the stock rail. "You're you," Charlie reiterated and poked a finger in Jim's chest. "So, be you."

Jim didn't know what to say to the big man. He was actually thankful when Tom returned, and his presence permanently ended the discussion. Charlie and Jim lowered themselves down the side of the truck then jumped the last four feet to the ground. Jim cast a quick thanks to Charlie.

"Good meeting you Jim Redmond," he said. With long strides, the man returned to the tractor.

Tom handed the ranch owner some cash, shook his hand, then turned back to the truck. Jim tried to shake the countless hay seeds and dust from his shirt and jeans, then started to reach for the passenger door when Tom stopped him.

"Nope, you're driving," Tom declared, pushing Jim out of the way. "You do know how to drive don't you?"

"Yeah, just not a truck this big," Jim confessed.

"No better time to learn. Let's get going, I want to stop at Ehler's and get some things."

With leather gloves tucked in his back pocket, Jim climbed into the driver's seat of the truck. Everything was bigger and harder to manipulate than in Frank's shop truck back home. Already tired and sore from riding yesterday and bucking a couple tons of hay today, Jim winced as he pushed the clutch in with his left foot and started the truck. Pepsi retreated toward Tom as Jim reached for the gear shift and battled to find first gear. Confident he'd found it, Jim started to release the clutch while pushing on the gas pedal with his right foot. All three occupants lurched forward and then back into the bench seat as the truck stalled.

"This ain't no hot rod," Tom barked at him. "You gotta go slow on the clutch and give more gas since it's loaded."

Jim shook his head in frustration. He knew how to drive; his old man had taught him a full two years before he was allowed a license. Frustration quickly grew to anger, but the memory of being slammed into the wall the day before strangled the feeling into silence.

Jim started the truck again, doing as Tom instructed and, with a shudder, the vehicle rolled forward. The truck lacked power steering, so Jim waited till it was moving before he attempted to wrestle the wheel to turn the truck down the driveway. As the engine revved, Jim shifted to second gear, the shudder less pronounced as he got a feel for the clutch. Nearing the end of the driveway, Jim slowed enough to check for traffic, then pulled onto the paved road heading toward town. Tom gave directions, guiding him onto Sierra Road where he turned west. Nearing the intersection of Sierra Road and Montana Avenue, Tom told Jim to turn into the parking lot of Ehler's Corner Market.

"You've got a big truck with a heavy load, so give yourself plenty of time and space to slow down. There are too many fatheads on the road who think they can pull out right in front of you and expect you to stop in time," Tom said.

Jim was surprised at the number of cars out and about on a Sunday morning. He saw a spot in the parking lot that looked big enough for the truck and navigated off Sierra Road, rolling to a slow stop and shutting off the engine. A sigh of relief escaped his lips. The tension of driving the big truck was almost as much as that of learning to ride a horse. Tom got out of the truck and told Pepsi to stay as he closed the door. She watched Tom walk into the market and then looked at Jim, the concern in her eyes palpable.

"Hey pup," Jim reached across to let her sniff him, but Pepsi cowered and forced herself closer into the corner, between the seat and the door. Jim didn't push the issue and returned his hand back to the steering wheel. Pepsi relaxed a bit, but maintained her position until Tom returned.

"You like apple fritters?" Tom asked as he climbed in with a small white paper bag in his hand.

Jim nodded.

"Good, I got us a couple to have with coffee after we're done unloading."

Leaving Ehler's, Jim turned north onto Montana, following the road back to Tom's place. The entire trip home, Tom sat looking out the passenger window, his left hand petting Pepsi—who stood on his lap with her head out the window, nose to the wind. The lack of constant oversight was fine with Jim as he struggled to keep the colossal truck and its hay load on the narrow road while not running into anyone. He wanted to wipe his palms on his shirt to dry the sweat but dared not take his hands off the wheel. His heart raced with each car that sped by, his stress increasing with the honking horns from vehicles trapped behind the metal behemoth and the cloud of hay dust. Jim's anxiety eased only upon pulling the truck onto Tom's drive, where the old man told him to back up to the haystack. Before backing up, Tom and Pepsi jumped out of the cab. Jim struggled to wrench the truck into reverse. He strained to see Tom through the cracked and dirt-covered side mirrors as he let the clutch out and gave the engine some gas. Finally, the truck rolled backward towards the stack. Jim followed Tom's hand signals until he saw the man's palms push toward the truck. Perfect. Stop.

When Jim joined Tom at the stack, he noticed that the activity and smell of new hay had drawn the entire herd of mules and horses to the edge of the corral. Tom handed him a pair of hay hooks, demonstrating how to use the S-shaped steel tools. A quick swing buried the sharp tip into the narrow end of the bale with one hand while the same was repeated with another hook to the other end. The stalks of hay acted like rope as they filled the curve of the hook, allowing the bale to be hefted without having to grab the strings. Their use made the task of pulling the bales up and out of the truck a fair bit easier than grabbing the thin, hand-biting twine. As Jim unloaded the truck, Tom grabbed the tossed bales and set them onto the stack near the corral. For thirty minutes they worked, until the last bale had been placed. Jim jumped out the back of the truck, and his sudden landing sent Pepsi scampering.

"Has she always been like that?" Jim asked, dusting himself off.

"Like what?"

"Scared of people. Has she always been so fearful?"

"No, her first few years she was friendly as could be. It's been eight or nine years, now, that she spooks like that."

"What happened?"

"Some bastard stole her. I made a trip to town and left her here to watch the place. When I came back she was gone." Tom knelt as Pepsi tiptoed up next to him. He patted her side. "I figured coyotes or a cougar got her, but my neighbor came over and told that me that some guy in a truck had stopped on the highway and grabbed her. She'd been sitting at the end of the drive waiting for me to come back, I suppose."

"How'd you get her back?"

"Went to every bar in the valley asking around." Tom grabbed the bag of fritters from the cab and started walking toward the house. Jim followed. "A few days later, I was at the Corner Bar, and I overheard some guy trying to sell a dog. I asked him what kind of dog he had, and he told me, so I asked to see her. He walked me out to his truck, and there she was, locked in a small wooden crate, scared to death."

"What'd you do?"

"Beat the shit out of him, of course. No one was watching, so I didn't stick around to explain things. I just grabbed Pepsi and hightailed it out of there."

"Did you get into any trouble over it?"

Tom paused as he opened the screen door. "No one ever came asking about it, which is probably a good thing. I heard the bastard died."

Jim reached out to catch the door before the rusty spring could slam it shut. Nice try old man. Jim wasn't going to let Tom scare him. There's no way the old guy killed someone over a dog. Though. The memory of the day before flashed through Jim's mind—both the pain of being slammed against the wall and the look in Tom's eyes. Jim hesitated before following Tom and Pepsi into the house.

He tried not to think about the story of Pepsi's rescue but it was hard given that he was living in the house of a man who had just confessed to killing someone over a dog. True or not, Jim decided he would toe the line for the summer and not tempt fate, if the judge even let him.

When Jim was roused from his slumber at six the next morning, he half expected to see a sheriff's car waiting at the front door. There wasn't. But it was awfully early; his date with destiny would probably arrive later in the morning. Jim helped with the morning chores and then, with Tom's oversight, began prying off and replacing the horse-chewed top rails of the corrals.

It was almost ten when they heard the harsh ring of the phone carrying out through the open windows of the house. The first ring was nearly muted by the clang of the five-pound sledgehammer hitting an eight-inch-long fencing spike. The second ring was crystal clear. Jim paused mid swing and looked at the house.

"You keep working. I'll see to that." Tom spit as he walked away, leaving Jim at the fence to wonder if the repeated rings were indeed his summons, his fate for the summer. He thought of sneaking over to the house to listen in, but feared retribution from Tom almost more than another handcuffed ride in a cop car. There was nothing he could do but work. So, that he did. Holding the short sledge handle with both hands, Jim struck at the fresh nail that already stretched through the fence rail and another inch into the vertical railroad tie post. Each sharp ping of steel on steel carried under it a deep thud as the energy of the hit transferred from steel to wood. His swings were deliberate, steady. Raise the hammer, eye the nail, strike. Repeat. He heard Tom's muffled voice rise at one point, a raucous noise that could have been laugher. Jim kept swinging the hammer. Two more nails. Three.

Tom returned and stared at him, stone-faced. "Looks like you're mine for the summer," he said. With that, the old man carried on with his directions for the fence repair, as if nothing noteworthy had happened at all. Jim was relieved. And scared to death too. He was suddenly no longer sure he'd been dealt a better hand.

CHAPTER 14

Five days after the boy joined them on the ranch, Boss gave the teen his third riding lesson. Comanche and the others in the herd watched as Sil politely tolerated the boy's rough fumbling, though Comanche could see that his skills were improving. The boy handled Sil as they transitioned from walking to running and taking hard turns, each time with more control. It was then that Boss entered the corral and brought Comanche in for a ride. After being saddled, the pair of horses and their riders trotted off into the field. Comanche pranced in excitement as Boss talked to the boy. The pasture was one of the few places Comanche was allowed to run. Its vast expanse was free of rocks and gopher holes—those obstacles being the only things Comanche feared as leg breakers. This field was safe, its soil soft and level from being turned by the neighbor every year.

Once in the field, Comanche leapt forward even before his rider's heals touched his belly. The horse knew it was time, as he had felt Boss lean forward in the saddle. Now the boy would see what a horse could do! Now Comanche could run free. Sil, with the boy, did well to keep up. Though as sure-footed as Comanche, Sil nearly lost the boy on that first all-out gallop, he so obviously unaccustomed to the motion of a running steed. On the second sprint, the boy improved. His grip was no longer on the horn of the saddle, and his weight was centered such that Sil could hit full stride. The third lap across the field, the boy apparently thought he could catch Comanche. Foolish boy. Comanche could hear Sil drawing close, the boy encouraging her with yells and hoots of joy. A stronger touch of his rider's heels pushed Comanche to his top speed, leaving Sil and the boy well behind. The cannonade of hooves impacting the sod matched the cadence of Comanche's deep, powerful breaths, as he drew a full two lengths ahead of Sil and her young rider. Boss neither whipped nor spurred him, as such motivation was rarely needed. The edges of hooves cut into the sod for an instant before propelling the horses and their riders in smooth levitation across the stubble grass.

As the horses neared the fence at the far end of the pasture, Comanche braced himself to jump the obstacle, only to feel pressure on his bit, pulling his head in closer to his neck, hindering his stride. He jerked his head in protest, extending his stride all the more, intent on the jump and intent on the win. Once more the bit pulled, forcing Comanche to slow just a little. The touch of rein on the right side of his neck deflected Comanche's approach into a gentle curve, causing him to decelerate even more. Sil and her rider caught up, the mare's heavy breathing mixed with her rider's laughter.

The rapid pummeling of sod dissipated into a gentle trot and then finally a walk. This only irritated the winner of the race. Comanche thrashed his head in protest, yet Boss would have none of his attitude. He gave a quick pop of the reins while telling him to settle in a stern voice. Obeying both bit and words, Comanche calmed to the point that Boss slacked the reins. The horse held his head high and drank in the cool morning air.

Sil and the boy drew up alongside, and the riders began to talk as they guided their mounts around the pasture. Comanche did not understand most of the words his rider spoke. Some he did, especially the ones that he knew preceded a journey into the mountains: pack, truck, mules, morning. He understood tone too, his keen ears perceiving the highs and lows and the pace of words, all hinting at Boss' mood. Today his tone was calm, even pleasant, which enticed Comanche to pick up his pace a little, testing to see if Boss was up for another run. A slight pull on the reins told him otherwise, and Comanche returned to his steady, proud gait. Boss continued to talk to the boy, words as steady as hoofbeats.

Once back at the corral, Comanche watched the boy, still un-sure whether he belonged here. The tension between the man and boy was easily felt by the herd and had begun the very day the boy arrived. Since then, the humans lived with an uneasy truce that sometimes failed. Sometimes Boss lashed out at the boy, yelling at him for some task done in a manner not to his lik-ing. Comanche knew the boy would learn; he would have to if he wanted to be part of the herd. Boss would teach him that laziness would not be tolerated. The herd already knew this fact. For the most part, all the horses and mules worked hard when tasked, but a slap of leather strap on flank motivated those who didn't. The whip was not out of anger—Comanche knew that well. His rider expected his animals to work as hard as they could, as hard as he himself did. In exchange, Boss ensured that the herd was fed, wa-tered, and protected from weather and predators. This was a fair exchange in Comanche's mind. If the boy didn't learn this, then he would never be part of the herd.

The boy's next test came the following day when they made an-other supply trip into the mountains. Three mules accompanied Comanche and Boss and Sil and the boy. After unloading at the trailhead, the man showed the boy how to tighten the cinches on the saddles, demonstrating on Comanche's saddle and then leav-ing the boy to the task with the remaining saddles. Comanche could see that the boy was not pulling on the cinches hard enough. Perhaps he was afraid of causing the mules pain, or maybe he hadn't understood Boss' directions. Either way, the straps were not as tight as needed. When the heavy canvas-wrapped bundles were slung and tied to the steel rings, the saddles strained and then shifted.

Heading up the trail, Comanche and Boss led the string as always, followed by the three pack mules. Sil and the boy brought up the rear of the line. It was after fifteen minutes on the trail that the fallout of the boy's error came to pass. On a steep hillside, festooned with thick grasses, the first mule, Cecil, brayed as his pack saddle shifted even further. Fifteen years' experience of hauling loads with Boss prevented Cecil from panicking. Instead, the big mule simply stopped, resulting in the untimely halt of the entire string. The boy cried out in warning, but Boss had already seen the possibility of impending disaster. Comanche watched as Boss dismounted and walked back to fix the pack saddle. The boy came to help, only to be loudly chastised. Sharp words punched their point home as the boy struggled to assist in the work.

Each animal's saddle had to be checked, requiring the removal of their loads and the retightening of cinches. The entire time, Boss' rage grew, so much so that Comanche thought he might just whip the boy as if he was a horse instead of a rider. Mercifully, no whip was used. Surprisingly, the boy neither challenged nor defied Boss. Instead, he did as commanded without a word, until they were riding again.

Entering the camp, Comanche could sense the boy's unease. As packs were removed and unloaded, the boy stayed away from the other people in the camp, especially the big man who Comanche knew was a friend of his rider. The boy helped unpack the loads, all the while never looking up. Comanche was confused by the boy's behavior. He had not been whipped, so why was he so submissive? It was only when Comanche's rider and the other man laughed that Comanche saw the boy flash a glare at the men, an ember of defiance in his eyes. So, he wasn't defeated. Though Comanche still did not care for the boy, he now respected him, if only a little. To Comanche, obedience was not surrender, not if your spirit was still defiant. His respect for the boy grew as he saw the boy's spirit drive him to work harder.

It was only after the packs were loaded with the camp trash, and they were riding out of the mountains, that Comanche felt the tension lift. During a gentle part of the trail, Comanche allowed himself a glance back at the boy and confirmed the change. The boy looked off into the distance, his shoulders relaxed as his body swayed with Sil's steady steps. The entire ride down was silent, except for the sound of hooves on dirt. Comanche felt his rider's weight in the saddle but not an ounce of pressure from his knees or reins. All in the pack string seemed content to rest into the rhythm of the slow journey back to the truck.

Comanche didn't know if his rider and the boy talked during the drive home. The wind that rushed by muffled all but the rumble of the road and the hum of the engine. Once back at the ranch, only a few words were spoken as the animals were unloaded and unsaddled then turned loose into the corral. As the man and boy worked, Comanche watched them closely and sensed no anger between the two. Still, there was something about the boy—it seemed there was a much deeper anger in him, only waiting for the right moment to manifest itself.

The next day there was no riding, much to Comanche's dismay. At first light the boy came out, alone, to feed everyone and check the water trough, ensuring it was clean. This had become the boy's task in recent days, initially completed only under the watchful eye of Boss. After the morning chores, the man and boy commenced to working on bigger tasks: fences were torn down and rebuilt, and the pair worked to mend the weathered roof of the small barn. Several times during the day, Boss lost his temper at the boy, yelling and even throwing tools in frustration. The boy had not responded in kind. Instead, he kept his eyes trained away from Boss and did his best to make right whatever Boss had been angry about.

That evening, long after the house had darkened and the herd stood sleeping, Comanche heard the screen door of the house open. Boss must not be sleeping well again. It seemed that such episodes were growing more frequent. As the figure approached the corral in the light of the waning gibbous moon, Sil and a few other horses and mules wandered over to console him. Comanche stopped short. It wasn't Boss. It was the boy. The smell of rage stung Comanche's nostrils, a powerful odor as pungent as the foul smoke that Boss bellowed at times. The other horses and mules smelled it too and paused a few steps from the fence. In the dark, Comanche could see the boy clenching and unclenching his fists while looking to the east, toward the big town where all the people lived.

Sil was the first to approach him and lean her head over the fence. She was, after all, the most familiar with the boy and the wisest of the herd. The boy looked at her dark silver head and reached up to touch her. She sniffed his hand and allowed him to pet her. Comanche inhaled deeply, sensing that the anger in the boy was subsiding. A few of the other mules and horses reached over the top rail of the fence as well. Most were looking to see if the boy offered any food, and when they learned there were no treats to be had, they departed. Others stayed, allowing the boy to pet them. With each passing moment, Comanche could sense that the initial rage emanating from the boy had cooled, dissipated into the calm of the night, the calm of the herd.

From the safety of the center of the corral, Comanche walked over to the fence and pushed his way between Sil and Molly. The horse sniffed deeply as he reached his head over the top rail, to the boy. Hesitating, the boy lifted his hand up toward Comanche.

The horse jerked away from the touch, but Comanche did not flee back into the center of the corral. Instead, he lifted his head back over the top rail. More slowly this time, the boy raised his hand, his fingers touching Comanche's head. There, in the cool night air, Comanche and the other animals allowed the boy to take solace in their company. From the shadows of the porch, unbeknownst to the boy, Comanche saw Boss silently watching.

CHAPTER 15

The nightmares of Monte la Difensa woke Tom shortly after three on Sunday morning. He blamed the resurfaced memories on the stress of having to deal with Jim all week. Unable to sleep, he shuffled down the hallway with Pepsi in tow, through the kitchen, and then out onto the screened porch. As usual, he was on his way to the corral and the welcoming peace of the herd. Standing on the porch, he began to roll a cigarette but stopped mid effort. There, standing by the corral, was Jim.

"What the hell is he doing?" Tom whispered, looking down at Pepsi. From the shadows, he watched as Comanche approached the boy. A flash of anger flickered in Tom's mind at the thought of Comanche, his horse, taking to the boy. It was part jealousy and part spite, following such a frustrating day of trying to teach Jim how to repair a roof. How damned hard was it to learn to use a hammer correctly? Though, he had to hand it to the kid, Jim had never once snapped back at him. He was at least learning to keep his mouth shut.

Tom was now fully awake, and the oddity of seeing the boy out there somehow squelched his cigarette craving. He stood gaping like a fool, wondering what he ought to do. The kid wasn't doing anything wrong *per se*, just petting the horses. Tom shook his head. He had no hankering for a middle of the night confrontation, so he slipped back into the house with Pepsi and returned to his room. He sat stock still in the dark. Ten minutes later he heard Jim return to his own room. Tom lay awake the rest of the night, wondering why the boy had been unable to sleep after such a long day of work. Perhaps he was thinking of running. If that was the case, then good riddance. But that couldn't be it. He was still here. He had his chance to bolt any night, and hadn't. Still, he'd worked Jim dawn to dusk every day, and no one could be worked non-stop. Maybe they both needed a day off from the heavy work. The chores of caring for the stock would still need to be done, but a rest day might do both of them a bit of good.

Finally throwing off the covers just after the sun peeked over the hills, Tom dressed quietly. He didn't bother to turn on any lights, except for the one in the bathroom so he could shit and shave. Jim was still snoring away in the spare room. With Pepsi at his side, Tom headed out to the corral to have his moment with the horses and to enjoy cigarette. Then, he and Pepsi made their usual Sunday pilgrimage to 4-B's for breakfast and the weekly comics.

When they returned, the sun had been up for over two hours. Tom didn't bother to tiptoe now, letting doors slam shut and clattering about in the kitchen as he made a fresh pot of coffee. After minutes of not-so-subtle noise making, Tom saw his efforts pay off. A bedraggled Jim shuffled from his room to the bathroom and then back to his room again. Several more minutes passed before Jim walked into the kitchen, his eyes still sleepy but at least open. Tom continued to read his comics as the kid poured himself a mug of coffee and a large bowl of Fruit Loops. He tried to ignore the teen's obnoxious chomping and lip-smacking, but his restraint only lasted so long.

"Didn't your mother teach you to chew with your mouth closed?" Tom grumbled without taking his eyes from the comic strip.

The sound of Jim's masticating decreased to a tolerable level, now replaced by the sound of Pepsi gnawing on her new soup bone—her prize from their venture into town. When the boy finished, he silently took his bowl to the sink, washed it, and set it in the drying rack. He took another sip of his coffee, then donned his boots and headed out the door. Tom kept his head in the comics, though he could hear the prancing of the horses through the open window. They jostled to get at the fresh hay Jim tossed to them. Tom had finished all the comics by the time Jim returned and sat down at the table to pour another cup of coffee.

"So what are we working on today?" the boy asked. He glanced at one of the comics laying on the table.

"You need to get some burger out of the freezer for supper, first off. I think we've got the makings for chili. Don't suppose you can screw that up like you did those taters the other night?" Tom wasn't about to let Jim live that one down. The kid had filled the house with smoke because he'd forgotten to check on a pan full of cut potatoes. Helping with meal-making was one of many chores that Tom had assigned to Jim to keep him busy. The kid was about as talented at cooking as he was at swinging a hammer.

"I said I was sorry," Jim said. He wasn't defensive, rather his response seemed light, more like the episode had turned into a running joke between the two of them.

"After that, we're gonna work on some saddles. But before all that, you need to give your folks a call."

"What for?"

"To invite them and your sister out for a ride this afternoon."

"Really?"

Tom nodded.

Jim rose and dialed his parents' number as fast as the rotary dial allowed. The call was downright hospitable compared to the last one Jim had made. Tom didn't stick around to hear the entire conversation. The pull of a cigarette craving drew him outside, and he took his time enjoying his smoke. He flicked the small remnant to the ground just as Jim came outside.

"They couldn't talk long because they were heading to church," Jim said. "But they said they could come out around one."

Tom stomped the cigarette stub into the dirt. "Well, I suppose we should get some tack ready."

"Do we have a saddle that will fit Vi?" Jim asked as they walked to the tack shed.

"The saddle fits the horse, not the person," Tom said. "She can ride Casey this first go 'round; we'll adjust the stirrups when she gets here. Let's pull out all the riding saddles and set 'em on the hitching rail. It's nice weather out, so it's a good time to oil them all up."

Jim did as directed and, for the next two and a half hours, Tom and Jim rubbed every piece of leather with saddle oil. Three saddles had broken straps, and Tom showed the boy how to fix them using leather tools and large scraps of tanned leather he kept in an old army footlocker. Once the riding saddles were repaired, Tom and Jim swapped them out for the ten pack saddles. The work on those took half the time, since the Deckers didn't contain much leather other than the cinch, tail strap, and breast collars.

"A little past noon, Tom decided it was time to clean up, get out of the sun, and grab some lunch. They had just finished their simple meal of cheese and sausage, Tom's smothered in black pepper as always, when Pepsi let out a warning bark. Moments later they heard the crunch of gravel as a car turned into the drive.

"Sounds like your folks are here," Tom said as he set down his paper. "Best go out and greet them."

The kid hesitated for several seconds, then headed outside. Tom followed, with Pepsi darting past to bark at the visitors. Jim tolerated the exuberant hugs from his mom and sister, then exchanged polite nods with Frank.

"Frank, Abby, good to see both of you again." Tom shook Frank and Abby's hands in turn. Abby reminded Vivian to be polite and greet Mr. McKee.

"Are all those horses yours?" She asked as she shook Tom's hand.

"Yep, all the horses and mules are a part of my herd. Jim, why don't you take your sister over to greet Casey before we saddle 'em up?"

With glee, Vi grabbed her brother's hand and dragged him to the corral. Tom invited Frank and Abby into the shade of the porch and offered them a beer, which they declined.

"How's he doing?" Frank asked, as they watched Jim show Vi how to offer a treat to the horses and mules.

"He's still alive ain't he?" Tom chuckled.

Frank laughed. Abby didn't. She fidgeted with the blue stone hanging on her thin silver necklace. She seemed lost in a distant memory as she stood off to the side, watching her two youngest children interact with the horses.

"It's only been a week," Tom continued in a more serious tone. "I've got to run some horses up north for the Forest Service tomorrow, so it'll be a day in the truck with me. If he can behave himself for the duration of that trip, then I'd say he's got a fair chance of surviving the summer with me."

Abby shot a withering glance at him. Tom liked Abby and considered her a friend; he ignored the glare. Years of solitude made him immune to the influences of women, good or bad.

Frank spoke up. "You know I appreciate you doing this. It took a lot to convince the judge. Damn near had to beg, and even then it was a stretch. It helped that he knows your reputation Tom. But just so you know, the only reason he signed off on this was because I gave him my word that Jim wouldn't get into any other trouble this summer. He can't come into town or anything. It's my ass on the line now," he said. "Are you sure you can do this?"

Tom nodded. "Shouldn't be a problem. Gonna start marking trails later this week. Between that and hauling supplies in I think I'll keep Jim busy for the rest of the summer. How he acts is up to him, but so far we seem to have a healthy understanding of each other."

Thankfully, Frank and Abby didn't inquire about the details of that understanding. Tom had no desire to lie to them, but he knew he couldn't tell them the entire truth about Jim's first day on the ranch.

"He appears to be taking to the horses," Frank noted, his words carrying a touch of pride.

Tom smiled, then stood and called to the kids, "Go ahead and saddle up Sil and Casey. You and Vi can ride in the big corral today." Jim jogged to the tack shed to retrieve two halters and lead ropes. While Vi sat on the top rail of the fence, Jim caught the two mares and led them out of the corral to the hitching rail. Everyone watched as Jim expertly saddled the two horses, cinching them well. All the while, Jim taught Vi the names of each part.

"Might make a horseman out of him yet," Tom said, "that is, if he don't get too cocky. Still, the herd likes him, which says a lot."

"You always said that you trusted your dogs' and horses' judges of character more than anything else," Abby said.

Tom chuckled. "Sounds like something I'd say. Might just be true. Even Comanche has warmed up to him."

"Comanche, huh? Few people earn that trust," Frank said and stood a bit taller. Jim took the horses to the corral and helped Vi up onto Casey, a chestnut mare with a black mane. He adjusted the saddle stirrups for his sister's legs. Tom saw Abby inhale and hold her breath.

"She'll be fine," Tom said. "Casey is as good as they come. I wouldn't put either of them on a horse that was flighty."

Abby looked at Tom and nodded once.

"You two know that you can come out anytime to ride. I'm sure you miss it."

Abby looked away and bobbed her head thoughtfully.

Frank's jaw tightened. "That's the past," he said then sighed. "It was hard giving up the ranch and the horses, and I do miss the saddle. You do too, don't you Abby?" He touched his wife's shoulder.

She smiled and shrugged, "Yes, but with the kids and the house, there's just no time it seems."

"No excuse now," Tom insisted. "Your kids want to ride. You can just join them. I've got plenty of horses for everyone."

He hooked them with that. Frank chuckled and agreed that they'd all come in their riding jeans the following weekend. Then the three walked out to the corral to watch the kids ride. By the end of the hour, Vi was getting the hang of things, keeping turn for turn with Jim. Occasionally Vi grinned at her parents and waved. Before dismounting, Vi leaned over the saddle horn to hug Casey.

"When can we come back?" she asked before she even got out of the corral. Abby told her about their plans to ride as a family. Jim led the horses out of the corral, to the hitching rail, where he tied them up with decent quick-release knots. Not bad at all. The kid was coming along. Saying goodbye to his parents, Jim once again tolerated a hug from his mom and a bit more willingly bent down to hug his sister. As the family left, he waved goodbye and seemed in fine spirits.

Tom told him to brush and put away the horses and then come back inside to start the chili. The kid gave him a quick nod and got to work. As Tom headed into the house, he could hear the boy whistling some tune as he unfastened the saddles. In the house, Tom set out the makings for chili then headed into the TV room to finish reading the news of the week. Jim returned to the house half an hour later, and Tom soon heard burger frying on the stove and the sound of chopping on the butcher block. It wasn't so bad having help around the place, now that he didn't feel the need to throttle the kid ten times a day.

"When you finish, come on in here," Tom called. Several minutes later, Jim stood at the threshold to the TV room, wiping his just-washed hands on his shirt.

"Pull up a chair," Tom said as he seated himself at the chess board.

Jim grabbed the cracked, leather-cushioned chair from the corner and joined him. The busy week had prevented Tom from giving Jim a lesson on his favorite game. There was no better time than now as they waited for the chili to finish cooking.

"This ain't checkers. You gotta use your brain for this one," Tom said, explaining each of the pieces and their movements. Jim leaned in, his interest in the game evident. They started playing, and Jim glanced around the room as Tom contemplated his next move.

"Hey, does the TV work?" he asked.

"Yep, I only get one channel on a good day though, so it's not really worth it. Got plenty of books if you ever want to read."

"What's that?" Jim asked, pointing to a wood carving on the wall. Its ornate shapes were painted bright yellow and blue. At the top was the head of a medieval knight and a hand holding a sword that pointed upward to the words *Manu forti*. Below the knight's head was a stag's head, surrounded by the heads of three wolves. At the bottom was the name McKee.

"Scottish Family Crest."

"What do the words at the top mean?"

"With a strong hand," Tom muttered. He'd moved his knight, hot on the kid's tail. Jim was still staring at the crest. "You gonna move or what?"

Jim apologized and hastily moved his rook. As they played, Pepsi entered the room and sniffed around, then came closer to them. Jim glanced at her but looked back at the board, intent on determining his next move. Tom watched in surprise as his dog edged closer to Jim and sat down. Absentmindedly, Jim's hand reached down and scratched Pepsi between the ears. Tom could see a flash of fear in her eyes, but it quickly fled when she glanced at Tom and saw no concern on his face.

"She seems to like you," Tom said.

Jim looked down and realized that he was, indeed, petting Pepsi. "Wow, I'm so used to Timber back at home. I guess I did it out of habit."

Tom nodded. Well, if Jim had earned the trust of that skittish dog, maybe he could be trusted with some bigger responsibilities. Time would tell.

That first game consumed half an hour, and Tom was just about to move his queen into check on Jim's king when Pepsi barked and bolted to the door. Then the humans heard it: galloping hoofbeats heading down the drive. Tom jumped up and ran to the door in time to see all the horses and mules stampeding toward the highway.

"Dammit boy! How many times have I told you to tie the latch on that gate?"

Jim stumbled out a denial, but Tom would have none of it.

"Don't bullshit me. Get your hat, we gotta get to them before one of 'em is hit by a car!"

Tom, Pepsi, and Jim rushed out of the house, heading towards the pickup. Tom told Jim to run to the tack shed and grab a couple lead ropes.

"Should I bring a bag of oats?" Jim asked.

"No, to a horse an alfalfa field outbids a bag of oats any day. Just grab a couple halters and lead ropes."

As Jim sprinted to the tack shed, Tom opened the truck door and let Pepsi jump into the cab, sliding himself behind the steering wheel. The truck roared to life and Jim jumped in on the passenger side, holding an armful of ropes and halters. He had barely closed the door when Tom let the clutch out to rumble down the drive.

The whole herd of horses and mules ran inside the borrow pit along the highway, clearly enjoying their new-found freedom. Cars honked as they passed, and thankfully, no animals stood in their paths. The herd galloped through an open gate and into the neighbor's alfalfa field. "Dammit," he said. Tom gunned the truck out of his driveway and onto the asphalt. "I knew they'd do that."

All but one ran into the food trough of a field, all but Cecil. The big, cunning mule trotted past the field gate in a beeline for Mrs. Jacobson's house, just off the highway. Tom slammed on the brakes as he turned toward the gate the main herd had passed through.

"Take a lead rope and halter and catch Cecil. Fast. Pepsi and I will get the rest of them," Tom ordered. The kid pulled a rope and halter out of the tangle on the truck's floor and then jumped out. "Watch out for Mrs. Jacobson. She won't take kindly to Cecil bein' there."

Tom goosed the Ford and rattled into the field, staying close to the fence so as not to drive over the bright green crop that was near time for cutting. Looking back at the highway, he saw Jim jogging down the road to retrieve Cecil.

Tom had no intention of jogging anywhere—not that his scarred body would allow him anyway. Instead, he waited until the herd had settled down and began to partake of the alfalfa. Pepsi sat rigid on the seat next to him, her eyes locked on the animals in the distance. Shutting off the truck, Tom got out and stood by the open door. Still on the truck seat, Pepsi quivered in anticipation.

"Pepsi, get the horses." Tom hadn't finished the command before the black and gray speckled dog had leapt from the truck. She might be a complete failure as a guard dog, but this situation was one where Pepsi shined. With fast, leaping bounds that propelled her toward her quarry, she made her way to the herd. They'd already heard Tom's command and stopped eating. They knew that the sneaky herder was on her way. Tom grinned as Pepsi slowed and moved closer. The dog began to circle to the left, around the herd. Her movement spooked the horses first. The mules were more confident in their size as the canine pest flanked them. Using the cover of the alfalfa, Pepsi stalked closer, darting in to nip at a mule's rear hooves and retreating before a swift kick was delivered. Three times she used this tactic. Finally the mules, out of fear and frustration, followed the horses towards the gate. At one point the herd veered off course, only to be quickly brought back in line by the diligent dog.

Tom started the truck and moved it out onto the highway to prevent the horses from heading east. Like a dozen times before, the herd passed through the gate and trotted along the fence, back to Tom's place. Pepsi faithfully nipped at their heels along the way. Yes, the animals knew this drill. Yes, Tom himself, had left the gate latched-but-not-tied at times, but the kid should know better. He was young. What could possibly cloud his mind to make him forget something so simple? Tom drove alongside the equine mass until they turned up his drive. Only then did he look down the road to check on Jim's progress.

He shook his head as he watched the boy feebly trying to catch Cecil. Mrs. Jacobson stood nearby, screaming at him as the mule trampled her rhubarb. Up the drive, Pepsi was still pushing the main herd along. Tom accelerated the truck to catch up to the dog. Most of the mules and horses trotted through the open gate into the corral. Comanche, Sil, and Moonlight remained outside, extending their time of freedom just a bit longer. Pepsi paused in confusion at her failed attempt to get the three stragglers into the corral. She looked back to Tom for guidance.

"Well get 'em girl," Tom encouraged as he walked over to help her. Seeing that she had support, Pepsi renewed her efforts and streaked in, barking at the horses. Comanche kicked as Pepsi nipped at him, but she was speedy, avoiding his sharp hooves in a blur of dark fur. Sil and Moonlight galloped into the corral as Comanche followed, bucking in disapproval at his capture. Tom closed the gate just as he saw Jim walking along the highway, Cecil in tow.

"You did good, girl." Tom knelt and petted the rapidly panting dog. When he stood back up, Pepsi walked over to the horse trough and jumped right into it—much to the dismay of the horses who were drinking from it. Standing belly deep in the trough, Pepsi lapped quickly at the water. She finished and jumped down to the ground, shaking out a veritable cascade. Tom leaned against the truck as Jim arrived with the obstinate mule. The boy's face was long and his eyes wide, like a man who had just shook hands with the Grim Reaper himself.

"How'd you get along with the old hag?"

"That woman scared the hell out of me. I really thought she was going to kill me." Jim released Cecil into the corral and closed the gate—making sure to tie the latch this time. "She came out of the house with a butcher knife! I told her over and over that I was sorry, but it didn't help. I think it actually made her angrier."

"Yeah, she and I don't get along too well," Tom chuckled. "I swear, that damned Cecil knows it too. That's why he goes there—to rile that foul woman up. Her husband, Harry, is so whipped that he can't even look another person in the eyes. Poor bastard. That's why I'll never marry. I wouldn't want to end up with a devil like her."

Jim laughed, seemed to relax, seemed to catch that Tom figured the encounter with Mrs. Jacobson was punishment enough. He must have felt comfortable to ask the question that followed. That or he was looking to change the subject in a big way.

"Were you ever married?"

"Nope, close once. She wised up before I could pop the question. Headed back to her family figuring she would be better off there than with me, I suppose. No matter, though. Saved me from ending up like Harry down the road. I got Pepsi and the horses and mules to keep me company. Nope, I'm good with bein' a bachelor."

"My old lady says that it isn't good for man to be alone."

"Old lady? She's your mom boy. Don't let me hear you call either of your parents anything that ain't respectful, you hear?"

Jim jumped at the sudden rebuke, but nodded yes.

"Your mom's a smart lady, and I don't want to encourage you to question her judgment. But it just might be that some men aren't marriage material is all." Tom turned away from Jim and headed to the house. There was no sense in talking about the past. Damned kid was poking his nose in places that were none of his business—just to divert attention from his own mistake. Well, two could play at that. "Come on," he shouted over his shoulder. "We've got a game to finish."

Back at the chess board, in only four more moves, Tom cleanly defeated the kid. Not deterred, Jim quickly reset the pieces. Laudable. Tom started with the same opening moves he had during the first game, simply to test Jim. Moving his pawn forward to E4, Jim countered as he moved his pawn to E5. Tom moved his knight out to F3, wondering if Jim would panic and try to cover his pawn with another pawn or a bishop. Instead, the boy countered with his knight to cover the threatened pawn. He was learning. Tom moved his bishop to B5 to threaten Jim's knight. The boy paused, weighing his options. Tom smiled. This opening was one of the first strategies he had been taught by his friend Marcus while in the barracks back in Helena, during the war. Jim moved his other knight out to F6 to protect his pawn and to extend his defenses. Tom moved his left pawn out to A3 to free up his rook.

He really had missed playing the game all these years. The distraction of chess had been essential to his sanity during the war, especially while on long transports across the oceans to distant battlefields. The game worked its magic now, slowly steering his mind away from the very memories Jim had just poked at. Yeah, after the woman left, Tom had accepted that he was meant to be alone till he died.

Feigning bravery, Jim moved his bishop out to D6. Tom didn't hesitate, and he moved his other knight to C3. Then the phone rang. "Shit," Tom said as he stood. "No cheating. I'll be back in a moment."

He walked to the kitchen and picked up the phone. He didn't recognize the voice on the other end of the line. But hearing the familiar name in this stranger's mouth sent a chill down his spine. This couldn't possibly be good news.

CHAPTER 16

Jim's instinct told him to attack with his knights, but he had made that same mistake during the first game. Now, he leaned toward a more defensive approach. The phone call was a blessing, and Jim welcomed the time to figure out his next move. Tom's side of the conversation drifted out to him as he pondered the board.

"Hello...Yes, I'm Tom McKee."

Jim wondered if it was worth moving his knight to the middle of the board where it would be a more powerful deterrent against Tom's attacks.

"What happened, is he alright?"

Jim looked up from the board. The tone of Tom's voice grabbed his attention. The old man's face fell as he listened to the caller.

"I see. Thank you for letting me know. When's the funeral?"

Tom's jaw tightened, and he reached across to the left chest pocket of his Pendleton shirt where he kept his bag of tobacco and cigarette paper, as if he wanted to roll a smoke.

"Will he have an honor guard? Good, good, he deserves a proper send off. Oh? What is it? No, that will be fine; I'm glad he thought of me."

Tom provided mailing instructions for something and thanked the caller, hanging up the phone. The man stood silent for a moment, his hand still on the phone, slumping forward as though he was bearing the weight of a fully loaded pack on his shoulders.

"Is everything okay, Tom?" Jim asked, knowing full well it wasn't. He didn't know what else to say. The man didn't respond, didn't even look at him. Tom just straightened up and walked out the door, Pepsi at his heels. Jim rose and went to the window, watching as Tom strode to the corral and rolled a cigarette.

Thinking that Tom wouldn't be outside long, Jim stirred the chili on the stove and then returned to the chess game, running several strategies through his mind. After thirty minutes, he rose again and looked outside. Tom was still by the corral. Jim wasn't sure but it looked like he was either talking to himself or holding an earnest conversation with one of the mules. Another half hour later, about six that evening, Jim walked out to the porch to ask Tom if he wanted some chili, but the man wasn't anywhere to be seen. The light was on in the tack shed, and the door was closed. Jim ran through his mind the facts that he knew. Someone Tom knew had died. He'd mentioned an honor guard, so it must have been someone in the military. Had they been in the war together? Which war? World War II or the Korean War? After just over a week with Tom, Jim realized how little he truly knew about the man. He knew enough, though, to conclude that Tom wasn't one who would take kindly to being disturbed. Jim retreated to the house where he ate dinner alone.

It was nearly dark when Tom came back inside. He said nothing and went straight to his room, Pepsi close behind. It was near ten o'clock when Jim decided to put the pot of chili into the refrigerator and go to bed. Tom's light was still on.

The following morning, Jim didn't ask about the phone call when he entered the kitchen and saw Tom sitting at the table, staring at a half-finished cup of coffee. His eyes looked bloodshot. Jim said good morning, and the man grunted a greeting then took a sip of coffee.

"Get some grub," he rasped and cleared his throat. "We've got a full day."

"What are we doing?"

"Gotta haul some horses up to Kalispell for the Forest Service. We're gonna be gone all day, so I want the stock well-fed before we leave. Also, make sure their water is flowing. That damned float valve sticks sometimes."

Jim confirmed he would do as asked and then poured a bowl of cereal. Tom headed outside before Jim could even sit down, leaving him alone to his meal. The thought of spending all day in the truck with Tom was unsettling but not for the same reasons as three weeks ago. Jim couldn't put his finger on it. He didn't hate Tom. The old guy was tough, but he was still human. And someone he knew had died. Jim felt he should say something, but was at a total loss as to what, and that was scarier than putting up with Tom's usual barking anger. For now, all he could do was complete his ranch tasks. At least that stuff made sense.

Breakfast downed and dishes washed, Jim grabbed his grandpa's hat and headed outside. While Tom worked under the hood of the stock truck, checking oil and belts before the drive, Jim went about his chores. After he finished feeding the herd and checking the water tank, Jim waited by the corral, petting Sil and Molly, who had wandered over in hopes of some oats, apple slices, or carrots—treats that Jim now regularly carried in his pockets. Not this morning. He'd entirely forgotten to grab a couple carrots on his way out of the kitchen.

"Let's go!" Tom hollered from the stock truck. Jim gave Sil one last pat on the neck.

"See you all tonight," he said and headed to the truck. He didn't look at Tom as he climbed into the cab. He could feel the man's glare though, no doubt upset with him for not moving faster. Or something. Jim didn't say a word. Probably best to keep quiet today. For the moment, the old man was silent too. Pepsi took her usual spot between man and boy as the truck rolled out onto the highway toward Helena.

"Might be violating the judge's orders a little by taking you into town, but I don't have much choice," Tom said as they drove up Montana Avenue on their way to Cedar Street. "You think you can behave yourself?"

"Yeah," Jim answered, just loud enough to be heard over the truck's engine. Tom's words were always gruff, though for the past week the gruffness sometimes had a teasing tone. Jim could take that. But this morning, the old man just sounded pissed off. Jim wanted to ask him about the phone call, but didn't dare. It was going to be a long enough day without both of them wanting to kill each other right from the start.

After crossing over the interstate, they made a quick stop to top off the gas tank. When Tom climbed back into the truck, his face had changed. The angry furrows had honed into a focused, work-minded stare. Jim had seen that look before. He knew to keep his mouth shut from this point on, unless he was asked a specific question.

Tom maneuvered the truck across town. At Washington Street, he strong-armed the steering wheel to turn the massive truck south and then west, to the ranger station.

"Get out and guide me back," Tom ordered. Jim jumped out, glad to be free of the foul mood and cigarette smoke filling the cab. Signaling the direction to steer and how much distance remained, Jim guided Tom's truck till it pressed against the ramp. Tom killed the engine and headed into the ranger station, while Jim waited near the horse-filled corral.

The boy looked to the west and couldn't help but wonder what his friends were doing. For a brief moment, he considered running, following the railroad tracks that stretched under the interstate. But to where? Lance and Marcus would punch him in the nose if he dared to show up at their houses, considering how he'd left them in a lurch. He couldn't run home; his dad would take him straight to the judge. And he had no desire to live the hobo's life. So, Jim waited.

Several minutes later, Tom appeared. His pace was fast as he returned to the truck, so fast the short ranger had to jog a few steps to catch up.

"Jim, it's those five," Tom yelled, pointing to one of three corrals that connected to the fenced loading ramp. "Get 'em loaded."

The ranger helped open the necessary gates as Jim jumped into the corral behind the horses. Walking slowly, waving his arms up and down, and giving a soft whistle, Jim approached the herd, making them spook toward the open gate. Their hooves pounded the dirt and then the thick wood planks that made up the truck bed. Jim arrived just in time to close the gate. As he connected the chain to the load binder, Tom stormed up and pushed him aside.

"No dammit, that's too loose!" Tom made some minute adjustment and secured the gate. With the truck's gate closed and locked tight, he rushed off to the cab, not bothering to return the departing wave of the ranger. Jim offered a wave and a quick shrug then climbed into the truck. The ranger gave him a single, understanding nod.

With a lurch, the truck pulled clear of the loading ramp and headed west, through town. The windows down and the cool morning air rushing by, Jim looked at the businesses and homes they passed; all were familiar to him yet entirely distant at the same time.

"Sonofabitch!" A Buick pulled out in front of Tom and instantly became a fresh target of profanity. "Come on, dammit! Where'd you learn how to drive?" The expletives only increased until they made it past the Kessler Brewery, where traffic became less congested. The buzz of the tires, the straining engine, and the wind passing through the open windows would make conversation challenging and unlikely. That was a relief; Jim didn't have to think about whether he ought to voice his thoughts. Last night's phone call would have to remain a mystery for now. Maybe forever.

Twenty minutes after leaving town, Tom downshifted to a slow crawl—the best the old truck could do going up MacDonald Pass with its load. The narrow, serpentine, two-lane road demanded all of his attention. Jim felt nervous as they climbed higher and higher, the drop-off to the valley below seeming to beckon to the truck on each curve. Almost to the top, they passed by the turn into Frontier Town, a favorite stop for tourists hoping to experience a taste the wild west. Jim smiled slightly, realizing he was actually living the wild west in a way, doing things the city dudes from back east could only dream of.

Cresting the top of the Continental Divide, Jim finally relaxed his grip on the armrest. He certainly saw the beauty of the wide-open meadows. Though his family had driven over the pass on trips to Missoula, he had never really paid attention like he did today. Grass, once-green, was transitioning into waves of tan in the hot summer sun. Cattle grazed behind the fences paralleling the road. Pepsi noticed the cows too. She jumped onto Jim's lap and barked out the window. Apparently, Jim was now fully dog-approved.

Tom remained silent as he piloted the truck on the downhill side of the pass. The drop-offs weren't as steep, but the curves were just as demanding as the east side. Once free of the grade, he upshifted, managing to get the truck back up to highway speed, though not quickly enough for the line of cars that had stacked up behind them during their descent. Just before the small town of Elliston, the highway straightened out as it cut through the narrow valley at the base of the pass. The open road allowed the impatient cars to rush by, some with horns blaring. A Cadillac with Kansas plates rushed by and swerved in front of the stock truck to avoid an oncoming car. The driver thrashed his fist at them before zooming off. Tom retaliated with what was surely an extensive and creative curse. Jim couldn't be sure. The road noise drowned it all out.

Ten minutes after Elliston, Tom began to downshift again. On the south side of the highway, the Little Blackfoot River flowed steadily to the west. Tom turned north and crossed the railroad tracks that had been paralleling the highway for the last ten miles. A small, white building stood next to the tracks, the word "AVON" painted on its side. The small town ran alongside the railroad tracks for about a quarter mile. The highway cut through the cluster of small houses. A couple hundred yards to the west stood a small church, with a tall green-shingled steeple. That was the extent of Avon. In just seconds, they were clear of the town.

The road curved gently along the low hills of an expanding valley that stretched for miles on both sides. Less than three miles north of Avon, Tom pointed to the northeast where a dirt road branched off of Highway 141. Just down that road sat a two-story, white farmhouse and a barn. Behind it, rolling hayfields stretched into the distance, until they met the pine-covered sides of the mountains.

The truck slowed and the road noise quieted enough that Jim could hear Tom speak. "That's where you're from," he said, the first words he had spoken to Jim since leaving Helena.

"What?"

"That's where you're from," Tom insisted, pointing again.

Jim looked, seeing only the giant stacks of hay resembling unsliced two-story high loaves of bread. Next to some of the stacks there was a tall, wooden contraption, an enormous slide whose top hung over the stack. Jim looked back at Tom. "I was born in Helena, not here."

"This is where your family comes from. Your folks' ranch was up that road."

"I came from an orphanage."

"What is the name on your driver's license?"

"What?"

"Dammit, what's your name on your driver's license?"

"James Clayton Redmond."

"That's where you come from then," Tom pointed and returned to his steely silence. The truck accelerated and the wind noise resumed, closing the door on any further conversation. Jim looked to the mountains in the distance before the road veered to the west and dropped down to a creek bottom, the hills blocking the view. He'd never seen that landscape before in his life. Tom must be really coming unhinged. Still Jim wondered about the land, about the ranch where Frank and Abby used to live. He could barely picture them as ranchers. What, indeed, had their lives been like? He pondered that till Tom stopped for gas in Seeley Lake.

At their fuel stop, Tom bought two Hershey's bars and two bottles of Coke—one of which he gave to Jim. Back on the road, his mood seemed to improve slightly. He explained where they were heading as he ate one of the chocolate bars. Their destination lay just outside of Kalispell—a small corral leased out by the Forest Service that held horses on their way to the remote ranger stations in the million-acre Bob Marshall Wilderness. After the almost pleasant description, Tom sank back into his quiet concentration on the road.

It was just after two in the afternoon when he backed the truck up to the loading ramp, under Jim's guidance. Jim unloaded the horses while Tom passed the paperwork to the ranger and signed off on the transport. Closing the corral gate, Jim paused to watch the newly-loosed horses prance and explore the corral. He, too, felt he could breath for that moment, away from Tom and the confines of the truck. The old man's shout ripped him away from his daydreaming. He obediently walked to the passenger side of the truck, but Tom stopped him and told him he was driving home.

"Gotta fill up the tank before we go," Tom said as he climbed into the cab's passenger side. "And how about we grab a couple burgers to eat along the way?"

Food! Jim's stomach had been uttering its own obscenities at him for the past two hours. He felt nervous about driving the behemoth truck again, but the hope of food tempered his anxiety some. Tom gave Jim directions to a gas station that had plenty of room for the stock truck and also happened to sit across the street from a burger joint. At the gas station, as Jim started filling the tank, Tom came around the front.

"Here, pay for the gas and get the receipt," he said and shoved a crumpled wad of bills into his palm. "Then, go get us a couple burgers for the ride home. I'll meet you back here in a few minutes."

Jim lost sight of Tom as he walked down the street and turned a corner. As her owner disappeared, Pepsi whined from the cab of the truck. "It's okay girl, I'm sure the crazy old coot will be back," Jim said.

Tank filled, Jim paid the attendant and then walked across the street to order two burgers, fries, and a couple Cokes. While he waited, he tried to ignore the sneers of the summer teens who had walked in after him. Jim realized how much his faded Pendleton shirt and straw cowboy hat contrasted with the scantily clad youth. Swim trunks and bikini tops made it clear they had been, or were on their way to, enjoying some time in Flathead Lake nearby. Jim looked more like the old cowboys who sat in the corner chatting over coffee than a high school-aged kid enjoying his summer vacation. One of the girls looked at Jim and then looked away with a haughty air. Jim didn't fit in, even more than ever. But in the mountains or with the horses or in the truck with Tom and Pepsi, even though such moments had been tense for other reasons, he had never wondered if he belonged. It wasn't even a relevant question. It had been only ten days since his arrival at Tom's place, but already he had to admit he preferred the ranch to the halls of his high school any day.

One last glance at the cackling teens made Jim glad he was heading back to the truck. The grease-stained, white paper bag he held in his hand bulged with cheeseburgers and fries, along with two more bottles of Coke. He was damned hungry and hoped Tom would let him dig in right away. But when he arrived at the truck there was no sign of the man. Under the glaring eye of the gas station attendant, Jim started the truck and moved it onto the street. He parked in the shade of a tree that dominated the yard of a small house. Hopefully the tree-lined street was one that led back to the highway. He sure didn't want to have to navigate the beast of a truck through narrow city streets to turn around. Well, first things first. Jim dug a burger and bag of fries out of the bag. Tom be damned, he needed to eat.

Pepsi whined as she looked out the window. Jim momentarily wondered if it would be worth driving off and bearing the consequences of such a choice. He could let the authorities know that Tom had simply left, and since he didn't know what to do, he'd headed back to the ranch. He quickly decided against that. Tom would walk all the way back to Helena and probably kill him in his sleep if he left him behind. Resigned to wait, Jim dug into the bag of fries.

"Here Pepsi, want one?" Jim offered the worried pup a fry. At the sound of her name, she turned and sniffed the treat, then cautiously took it. Jim continued to devour his meal, smiling at Pepsi as her pyramid ears stood alert and focused, her eyes watching every motion of his hand as it brought food to his mouth. Drops of dog drool formed a small pool on the cracked vinyl bench seat. Jim couldn't resist the begging dog and offered her a fry each time

he ate one. At the end of the burger, Pepsi leaned forward hopefully. Jim ripped the last bit in half, giving her a piece as he finished the remainder.

Almost half-an-hour later, Tom returned, carrying a large
brown paper bag. He climbed into the truck and set the bag on
the floor by his feet. "Where's my money?" he demanded between
bites of his burger. Jim dug into the pocket of his jeans and handed
Tom the remaining money. "Well, let's get going. You can have my
soda since I got my own beverages," he said and pulled a Hamm's
beer from the bag.

His strong fingers removed the pull-top tab. The foam didn't
even have a chance to make it past the rim as Tom hastily brought
the can to his mouth. That first beer was drained before Jim had
even gotten the truck into third gear. The second beer was finished by the time they were back on the highway. Only after he was
halfway through his third, did Tom slow his consumption. After
the fifth can, Tom paused in his drinking long enough to look out
the window and pet the dog curled up next to him.

"What are you afraid of?" Tom suddenly belted out over the road
noise. He wasn't looking at Jim, just staring out the windshield.

"I don't know," Jim answered, not willing to name the things
he was truly afraid of: Tom for one, and doing something wrong
while driving the truck, or messing up while working with the
horses. Jim couldn't confess that he was also, for the first time in
his life, afraid of disappointing people. He wondered what Tom
was afraid of but didn't ask.

"A good friend of mine died yesterday," Tom said to the windshield. "I survived the war with him. After all we went through,
he's gone just like that."

For several seconds, the sound of the truck's engine and the
tires on the road filled the cab. Once again, there was that great
feeling of not knowing what the hell to say.

"I'm sorry," Jim said.

"Sorry?" Tom shouted, glaring directly at him now. "What the hell are you sorry for? You got your whole life ahead of you. Marcus is done. Over! He'll be six feet under in just a couple days."

Jim didn't say a thing. Thank God the road demanded his full attention. Anything he said at this point would only spur Tom's wrath.

"What the hell is it all worth?" Tom's voice was more a whimper than a rage now. He cracked into Hamm's number six. The other empties littered the floor at his feet. "Can't even get there for his funeral. Some fine friend I am." His words were becoming slurred, but Jim got the gist. "At least his family was there, lucky bastard." The old man shook his head and took another drink. "Not for me! Nope, I'll die alone." Tom offered a toast to the windshield and then drained the can.

"Dammit all to hell anyway," Tom muttered as he progressed into the second half of his twelve pack. He drank in silence for the next hour, stopping only to demand that Jim pull over so he could relieve himself. The highway through the Seeley-Swan Valley was lined with thick forest, leaving Jim few options for pulling off the road. After another mile of Tom demanding they stop, Jim came upon an ideal pullout. It appeared to be an abandoned logging business, with plenty of room for the truck to get off the road and get back on. Tom stumbled from the truck, and a clatter of aluminum cans struck the running board as they cascaded out of the cab. Pepsi daintily jumped out of the cab to explore the woods near the truck. Jim took the moment to empty his own bladder, pissing out the two Cokes he'd enjoyed with lunch. He chuckled at the cars and logging trucks that rushed by, some honking their horns at the roadside show. Tom, a dozen feet away, stayed standing only by letting his shoulder rest against the trunk of a tall pine tree.

"Pepsi, come here," Jim called as the dog wandered awfully close to the side of the road. She darted back over some deadfall, her bright smile gleaming against her dark fur. Jim zipped up and walked with the dog back to the truck. With a pat of the seat, Pepsi jumped into the cab. Jim glanced toward the trees and saw that Tom was still standing. He settled in to wait for the guy. While waiting, he dug through the glove box, finding a road map he had seen earlier. In the late afternoon shadows, he struggled to figure out where they were on the map. He found the highway they were on and then whispered to himself, in proper order, the names of the roads he needed to take to get home. Soon enough, it would be dark, and reading the map while driving would not be an option anyway. Jim also knew, full well, that Tom's navigational capacity was nonexistent at this point.

When Tom finished pissing, he stumbled back to the rig, struggled to climb back in, and slammed the door behind him. As Jim maneuvered their ride back onto the road, Tom began to chuckle. "Home Jeeves, my mansion awaits," he sniggered.

Jim ignored him. Being around drunk people was thoroughly unenjoyable when one was not personally drunk. Another hour and two more beers later, Tom left behind his momentary foray into being the happy drunk and began to complain that he was hungry. Damn hungry.

"Turn here!" Tom demanded, pointing toward a dude ranch sign.

"What—here? Why?"

"Dammit kid, just turn. I'm hungry."

Jim muscled the steering wheel, forcing the truck off the highway and down a dirt road leading to a large wooden lodge with smaller log cabins scattered about. Pepsi barked at the horses in the corrals around the property. Jim felt very out of place as he pulled the truck in front of the main lodge. Some of the guests, who were relaxing on the front porch, recoiled as Tom stumbled out of the truck.

"I have hunger!" he roared.

Shit. Jim killed the truck and jumped out in an attempt to head off Tom before something bad happened. Pepsi remained in the truck, cowering at Tom's booming voice. "Dammit, I have hunger!" He railed at the folks on the porch. "Bring me food!"

Jim rounded the front of the truck to find Tom slumped against the front wheel, still bellowing his demands. A man in a well-starched western shirt and too-clean jeans came down the stone steps of the lodge. "I'm the ranch manager," he said, working hard to sound polite. "Can I help you?"

"We have hunger! Feed us!" Tom shouted. He climbed up the side of the truck cab so that he was standing, above everyone, on the running board.

"I'm sorry sir, our dining room is only for lodge guests."

"What? Are you denying me food, you Nazi bastard! Don't you know I fought in the war? I bled for pansies like you. Feed us!"

"Sir, if you don't leave, I will have to call the authorities."

"Call them, you sonofabitch. I'll kick their asses and come back to kick yours."

Tom stumbled forward probably intent on emphasizing his point with the manager. Instead, Jim stepped in and put Tom's arm around his own shoulder to keep him from falling to the ground.

"I'm really sorry, sir," Jim apologized, trying to usher Tom toward the truck. "Come on, Tom. I'm sorry, sir, we'll be leaving."

"I really wish you would."

"To hell with you all! Bunch of goddam Nazi bastards!" Tom yelled, spitting his final words before Jim could close the truck door. Jim apologized again as he ran around to his side of the truck, hopeful he could start the engine before Tom decided to cause more of a ruckus. Starting the truck and dropping it into gear, Jim shook his head in frustration. Tom continued to curse both the manager and the guests from his window.

Back on the highway, Jim imagined reaching over and opening Tom's door as they rounded a curve, just to let the drunk bounce along the highway for a bit. So tempting, if only to be rid of his continued railing. Then the profanity stopped. Tom had passed out, his head slumped against the doorframe. Pepsi, seeing that the storm had passed, curled up next to her now sedate master. Jim drove the remaining two hours in silence, stopping once for gas. He tried to wake Tom to get some money from him, but was unsuccessful. He resorted to digging through the pockets of the man's sheepskin vest to find the required fuel money.

It was dark by the time Jim pulled the truck in front of Tom's house. There were no horses to unload and no tack to put away. He was eternally grateful he didn't have to back the truck up to the loading ramp alone, but there was still the matter of unloading Tom. Jim got out and called Pepsi to follow him, then went to the passenger side. Bracing himself, he opened the door. The last three beer cans tumbled to the ground, and then Tom's dead weight fell into Jim's arms. The smell of beer, cigarettes, and sweat made him cringe.

"Come on Tom, we're home."

Jim slung Tom's right arm over his own shoulder and coaxed the man to walk to the house. The fall out of the truck had roused him just enough to stagger along. At least Jim wasn't carrying the man's entire weight. Close enough though. Pepsi followed them through the door, and Jim hauled Tom across the dark kitchen till he got to the hallway, where he was able to turn on a light. At that point, Tom passed out once more, and Jim half carried, half dragged the old man to his bedroom. Not having been in there before, Jim groped around for the light switch. The sparsely-furnished room suited its occupant: simple, meager, and effective. A twin-sized bed, its head centered on the far wall, filled most of the small room. A dresser sat against the near wall, pictures and trinkets on its top, all covered by a thick layer of dust. Tom's body fell to his bed as Jim released his grasp. He was content to leave Tom as he lay, having no desire to remove the man's boots or make him more comfortable. He'd done enough favors for the old bastard today.

Pepsi stood watchfully at the door. Jim asked the dog if she was hungry as he left the room. He returned to the kitchen and turned on a light. A scoop of dog food and a freshly-filled water dish seemed to be just what Pepsi had hoped for. She ate slowly, as she always did, chewing each nugget loudly before swallowing. She paused every few bites to take a quick drink—such were the odd eating habits of the soda pop dog. Jim left Pepsi to her meal and headed outside to check on the horses. A quick headcount confirmed that all were present and well. He tossed a couple bales of hay over the fence, and double-checked the water. Then he headed back into the house to warm up a bowl of leftover chili for himself. He ate in silence, Pepsi standing nearby, her small brown eyes convincing him to let her finish up the last few bites of his meal.

"Don't tell Tom, okay?" Jim whispered as the dog licked the bowl. With all the animals and himself fed, Jim walked back to Tom's room to check on him. The man had shifted further onto his bed and was snoring loudly. The click clack of Pepsi's claws on the hardwood floor echoed off the walls as she worked past Jim's legs and jumped up onto Tom's bed. She turned around several times before resting near the man's boots. Dog fur and a dingy stain on the comforter indicated that this was her usual resting place.

In the dim light from the hall, Jim looked more closely at the pictures on Tom's dresser. Some showed him in military fatigues, a few with horses, and another was a young woman. Maybe it was the woman he had almost married. Jim left Tom and Pepsi alone, closing the door partway behind him.

In his room, Jim sat on his bed, tired and confused after the long day. Despite total exhaustion, his mind was far from sleep. He looked around the room at the boxes and old furniture crammed into the space. Till today he hadn't given the clutter a second look. The boxes had only served as a place to set his clothes. With absolutely no concern about rousing the owner of the boxes, Jim began to explore.

First he tested the weight, as a child does on Christmas morning, trying to guess the contents of each box. The ones that were taped shut he left alone, not wanting to leave a trace of his activities. But most were not taped, the four panels of cardboard simply folded in overlapping fashion. The first box contained old papers, receipts for horses, and other ranch-related business. Refolding the flaps and setting that one aside, Jim tested the weight of two more, both heavy, probably more paperwork. The next one was lighter and the contents shifted as he lifted the box. This one seemed promising.

Taking the box to his cot, Jim opened it and immediately found souvenirs from Tom's world travels. He held a shapely, plastic hula girl. "Honolulu" was inscribed on the base. Tucked into an old sock were several coins and folded bills, the markings of which appeared to be Italian. One coin, with bold lettering and the head of a bald man, caught Jim's interest and he set it aside on his bed.

Finishing with that box and securing the flaps, Jim returned it to its original location and continued his search. He found a good prospect that had some heft to it, but not the dead weight of paper stacks. Jim opened it and found several old, neatly folded, olive drab army uniforms. A large spearhead-shaped patch was sown on the sleeves of the jackets, just below the shoulder. The bright red patch had the letters "USA" at the point of the spearhead and "CANADA" beneath that, in a vertical column, forming a T that filled the entire patch. Jim examined the stitching that attached the crest and then noticed a similar patch tucked along the edge of the box, this one free from the uniforms. Jim picked up the spare and looked at it, wondering if this was from the unit that Tom and his friend had been a part of. He had seen many unit patches on the news, as troops were being deployed to Vietnam, but he'd never seen this one. Maybe it didn't even exist anymore. The patch might be valuable. Even if it wasn't, it was certainly interesting.

Setting the patch on the bed, Jim rummaged through the uniforms to see if there was anything else that might catch his eye. He was not disappointed. Buried under several layers was a long, menacing dagger in a well-worn leather sheath. Jim let his fingers run along both the leather-wrapped handle and the sharp, broad spike at the end of the pommel. He unsnapped the strap and pulled the stiletto out, revealing a dark metal double-edged blade, wickedly pointed and razor sharp on both edges. The flat of the blade was indented with ridges, perfect for placing a thumb while gripping the blade. Below that were the letters CASE. On the opposite side of the blade were stamped V-42 and USA. Jim admired the weapon for several minutes, and he couldn't help but wonder if any men had been killed with it.

Looking at the door, Jim considered taking the blade, then thought better of it. The worn handle and markings on the blade told Jim that this was no souvenir. A few nicks and scuffs from hasty sharpening was the only marring on its edges. This blade had seen war. It was something special, something earned. Fighting temptation, he returned the knife to the box, but he took the patch and coin and stuffed them into the bottom of his backpack. After today, he'd earned a couple souvenirs, fair payment for bringing that drunk old fool home safely.

CHAPTER 17

The explosions arrived in perfect intervals, each one sending waves of pain from the top of Tom's head all the way to his feet. A shrill whistle pierced the air, preceding every impact. Tom saw Marcus on the other side of the foxhole where he was firing his M-1 rifle at the unseen enemy. Yelling to his friend, Tom struggled to reload his rifle to join in the fight. Further explosions rocked the earth. A swarm of tracer-laced machine gun fire zipped over their heads, the deadly crackle like that of intense static electricity.

The scream of the next incoming mortar round was unlike the others; it was louder, and it was coming down right on top of them. Tom crawled across the foxhole, trying to reach his friend. As he stretched his arm out to grab Marcus and pull him to safety, the mortar shell hit. The explosion filled Tom with pain and his vision momentarily faded to black. The unmistakable smells of smoke and burning flesh flooded his senses. His head hurt, pounding as though a herd of a thousand mustangs were running across it.

Tom reached a hand up to his face to see how badly he was wounded; he felt no helmet as his fingers brushed through his thin hair. His hands became wet as he moved them along his head. *Oh*

God, I'm hit. He pulled his hand away and looked at it in the dim light. No blood.

Slowly, with each painful blink of his eyes, Tom began to recognize his room as he regained consciousness from the nightmare. At his feet, Pepsi twitched and let out muffled, whining barks that matched the intervals of the explosions from his dream. Her legs moved in a dream-fueled chase. Sitting up on the edge of his bed, Tom's head spun worse than any bronc he'd ever ridden. He fixed his eyes on his dresser. He tried to swallow and felt as if he'd been chewing on an old horse blanket all night.

The feeling called to mind a line from one of his favorite books, *Trails Plowed Under.* In one of many short stories, a cowboy awoke from a long night's bender at the bars, and while trying to regain his senses said, "I got a taste in my mouth like I had supper with a coyote. I ain't quite dead, but I wish I was." Head still throbbing, Tom smiled weakly. Good old Charles M. Russell sure knew how to put it. Tom looked at Pepsi, now awake and yawning, and he could only hope he hadn't actually shared supper with the dog.

"Morning girl," he tried to whisper, instantly regretting the bedraggled wheeze that escaped his lips. Rising to a standing position was a monumental effort, demanding all his concentration to ensure that the floor didn't swallow him face-first. With dizzy steps, he staggered, first to the bathroom and then into the kitchen. Lord, he wasn't just hung over, he was still a bit drunk. Thankfully, there on the table, was the coffee pot. Steam rose from it. Fresh then. Good. Tom sat down and filled his mug. Images from the nightmare still haunted him. Unlike in the dream, he and Marcus had survived the war. Like in the dream though, Marcus was now gone.

Since first meeting in 1942, Tom and Marcus had survived hell together in both training and combat. Both had been wounded, both had helped one another, and both had killed to stay alive. Marcus was one of the few members of the unit that Tom kept contact with at least once a year, by letter or a phone call. Too often Tom had wished he could just sit down with Marcus and share memories of the war, something impossible with Marcus living near family in Pennsylvania. The last time Tom had seen his friend was almost four years ago at a memorial for the First Special Service Force at Fort Bragg, North Carolina. Tom and Marcus had felt so out of place on the viewing stand, not more than a stone's throw from President Kennedy. They all watched the new U.S. Army Special Forces soldiers march in parade in front of them. Marcus joked how he and Tom would never have made it into this new outfit, since most of the men had college degrees and spoke multiple languages. These new soldiers were truly elite.

"So what did that make us?" Tom elbowed his friend as the troops marched by.

"Fodder for the dogs of war."

Tom knew he was right. They were both a couple of trouble makers, foolish to volunteer and too stubborn to quit once in. Still, Tom knew that Marcus shared his sentiment; their experience in the First Special Service Force was one they wouldn't trade for anything.

He shook the memory off. It was a good one, but even the good ones only made the sting of Marcus' death more intense. Tom got up and pulled a bottle of blackberry brandy from the top shelf of the cupboard. Returning to the table, he poured a little into his coffee and grabbed a stale doughnut from a box near the coffee pot. As he gnawed on the donut and consoled himself with the spiked coffee, he tried to take comfort in knowing that Marcus had not been alone in the end. His family had been near, and his brothers from the Force would be at his funeral to fold the flag that covered his casket. When Tom's time came, he knew Force members would be there to bury him as well. However, he wouldn't have any family present. Tom looked down at Pepsi, who sat at his feet, leaning against his leg and gazing up sweetly. She probably wanted an ear scratch; she couldn't possibly be begging for the old donut.

"I've got you, I guess," Tom said and patted the dog. "And a bunch of horses and mules. More than some I suppose." He finished his coffee. Looking around the kitchen, he saw that the dishes were already cleaned and put away, and a package of frozen burger was on the counter, thawing for dinner. Tom glanced at the clock on the wall. Nearly ten. He hadn't slept that late in at least twenty years. Looking back down the hall, he noticed that Jim's bedroom door was open.

"Well, someone made the coffee. Where do you suppose the boy's at, Pepsi?"

Struggling to his feet, Tom shuffled across the kitchen and through the door to the screened porch. Both trucks were still there and nothing seemed unusual, other than the pounding in his head and the churning in his stomach. Finally, he saw the kid standing by the corral gate, most of the herd stretching their heads over the fence. Comanche was in the middle of the group, his big, white head standing out amongst the line of bays, blacks, and chestnuts.

Jim walked down the row of horses and mules and stopped at each animal. He'd pull his hand out of his pocket and flatten it out, palm up, a slice of carrot resting in his open hand. Each horse and mule would stretch soft, velvet lips and gently nibble the prize, testing it before snatching it out of his hand. Tom watched as the boy made his way to Comanche. Surprisingly, the horse took the treat just as the others had. After Jim finished doling out the carrots, he went back down the line to pet each animal. When he came to Comanche, the horse snapped his great head around Jim's hand, trying to bite at the boy's shirt fabric.

Jim responded with a soft slap to the horse's nose.

Rage flared inside Tom. He was about to shout and walk over and smash his coffee mug over the kid's skull, but what happened next gave him pause. With the slap, Comanche shook his head and then bit at Jim once more. Again Jim gently slapped the horse on the nose. After three more such exchanges, Tom realized that they were playing. He had never seen Comanche do anything like this before, but it was unmistakable. The horse that hated most humans was playing with Jim. It couldn't have been the first time either. This was clearly a game they'd played before. How had Tom never seen it? As quietly as he could, Tom opened and closed the screen door and crept towards Jim. Before Pepsi or the other horses gave away his approach, he let out a yell.

"Damn you boy, stop picking on my horse!"

Jim turned, his eyes wide. His shocked, fearful look faded as he saw Tom's crooked smile.

Jim grinned. "He started it."

"Yeah, I don't doubt that he did." Tom walked up and started petting the horses. "Seems like you got us home safe enough last night. Anything happen that I need to know about?" Tom's memory of the evening had ended somewhere in the Seeley-Swan Valley. He wasn't ashamed of himself, more just angry. He knew better than to let his grief over Marcus impact him as it did. It was a lot to ask Jim to drive the truck all the way home and take care of a cantankerous old drunk.

"You called some people at a dude ranch a bunch of Nazis," Jim answered. "You were hungry and they wouldn't feed you. They were gonna call the sheriff, but I got us out of there."

"Didn't kill anyone, did I?"

"No..."

"Nobody was hurt?

"No."

"Hmmm, if the worst of it was calling some cowboy wannabes a bunch of Nazis, then I'd say I had a slow night." Tom turned and ambled back towards the house while rolling a cigarette. He paused, looking back over his shoulder. "Thanks, by the way."

CHAPTER 18

AUGUST 13, 1965

Jim strained to heft the manty up against Cecil's side and hold it there while he pulled the loop connected to the front D-ring of the Decker pack saddle. He shimmied the loop about two thirds of the way up the canvas-wrapped food boxes and cinched it tight by pulling the tail of the rope and twisting the manty back and forth. This twisting movement took up the slack like a ratchet. When it was tight enough, he pulled the tail of the rope under the bottom of the pack, tying a packer's knot in the middle of the first loop. After placing a half-hitch over the loop, Jim moved around Cecil's rear, making sure to keep his hand on the mule so as not to surprise him. Once on the other side, he repeated the process. When done, he went over every knot and shifted the pack around to make sure it was stable and not causing the mule any discomfort—just like Tom had taught him.

This was Jim's fifth supply run up to the trail camp with Tom. Each time things became easier, or at least, less unsettling. Fear and concern about the horses, mules, and Tom lessened as familiarity and comfort set in. It wasn't as though Tom and Jim were best friends now. No, they continued to coexist as task-master and worker, teacher and student. Jim was okay with it, though. Despite the long days and despite Tom himself, the work wasn't half bad, even though it qualified as punishment by the law.

When they weren't making supply runs, Tom and Jim spent time re-marking trails for the crews. It was important to find the original red ribbons the government surveyors had placed earlier in the spring. Most of those original ribbons had now faded or disappeared, requiring replacement. These trips, though the most enjoyable for Jim, were also the most tiring. It was demanding to get on horseback just after sunup and return to the truck at twilight.

Jim was amazed by how at ease Tom was in the mountains, how he never seemed to get lost or even disoriented. Often, as they picked their way through heavy timber, it was impossible to even see the sun to orient themselves toward east or west. Several times Jim had felt a shot of panic rise in him, but he only needed to look ahead and see Tom and Comanche, their direction clear, their focus set. They had marked out over five miles of trail earlier in the week. This supply run would be the last ride till Monday, when they would head back in to continue marking trails.

"This'll be a cakewalk today," Tom said as he saddled Comanche. "But next week you'll be a bit saddle sore. They got the Moors Mountain trail done last year. Now they want us to look at a route that comes back this way from there. You'll see a lot of new country: Sheepherder's Monument, Windy Ridge, and Crow's Nest. If there's a heaven, that land is a glimpse of it." Tom flipped the left stirrup of his saddle up over the seat so he could tighten Comanche's leather cinch, then he added, "Make sure those cinches are tight. I don't want any rodeos on this trip."

"I will," Jim said, though it was a task he hated. The more he grew to like the horses, the less he liked causing them discomfort, even though he knew it had to be done. With every tug of the strap, Jim could see unease in the horse, but he did as he was told. With cinches tight, manties secured, and a beautiful August day to enjoy, Tom, Jim, and the string of mules headed back up to the trail camp. The ride was routine now, the newly-constructed trail letting them make good time. As with the previous trips, Jim rode drag, following the string of mules, led by Tom and Comanche. Jim's duty was to watch the packs and ensure they remained centered. This simple task permitted Jim to enjoy the ride, to look at the beautiful mountains and forest, and simply relax. There were times when he was nearly lulled to sleep by the melodic, rhythmic hoof beats on the trail and Sil's gentle sway. Usually a low pine branch or a whiff of mule fart snapped him back to attention.

The two-hour ride delivered them to the camp with no incidents, and like the times pervious, the trail boss gave Jim what seemed to be an obligatory glare. Roy and Tom conversed while Jim unloaded the packs at the cook tent.

"Seems you've managed to stay out of jail," a cheerful voice called to Jim. Matt Person appeared, limping around the corner of the smaller cook tent.

"Matt! What the heck happened to you?" Jim set down the last of the manties.

"Rolled my ankle yesterday. I'm having to rest it for a while, so I'm stuck here at camp. Good to see you. It's been mighty quiet since you left; no fights or anything exciting. Even Josh keeps his mouth shut. Roy cracked down on him."

"I'm glad something finally shut that jerk up. Looks like you guys have been making good progress."

"Yeah, almost too good," Matt said as he hobbled over and sat on a log to rest his ankle. "If we keep up this pace, there might not be work for me next year. I'd hate to end up getting pulled into Vietnam if I can't get work to keep on paying for school."

"You're a college brat," Jim teased, "the Army doesn't want you educated types."

"Yeah, well let's hope so. What *is* going on with the war?"

"China is threatening to send troops in against us," Jim explained as he helped the cook remove the ropes and canvas that encased the pack boxes. He summarized the war highlights he'd read in the week-old Sunday paper at Tom's house. Tom hadn't needed the paper for fire-starter of late, so Jim actually got to catch up on what was going on in the world. "I read that a Special Forces camp, someplace near Cambodia, has been under siege for two months, but they're still holding off the North Vietnamese."

"Really? Wow, two months? Must be Green Berets; I hear they're tough."

"They must be to keep fighting that long. How about you, what else has happened up here?" Jim asked as he continued unloading supplies. Matt shared stories from up on the trail—an encounter with a black bear that sent three of the trail crew scrambling up a tree, a mid-summer snow storm, an incident with a wasp nest, and a new guy's smelly encounter with a skunk.

Jim genuinely enjoyed catching up with his friend. Their time was cut short when Tom told him it was time to saddle up to head back down. After loading the trash-laden manties back onto the pack saddles, Jim tightened Sil's cinch, having loosened it to let her breathe more easily while they were stopped in camp. From high up on Sil, Jim wished Matt farewell. He could only hope that he would see him again.

Tom was already atop Comanche and holding Cecil's lead rope, with Molly and Bart tied in sequence behind him. Surprisingly, he called for Jim to come up and take the string. Jim rode over and took hold of the lead rope as Tom held it out to him. This was new.

"We've got a light load, so no need to ride drag today," Tom said. Just put one loop around your horn and tuck the loose end under your thigh, that way if the mules blow up you won't be taken down the mountain with them."

Jim took the rope and looped it once around his saddle horn as told. With a touch of his heels, he urged Sil to follow Tom and Comanche down the trail, the three mules quickly falling in behind. With the string now in his control, Jim found himself paying more attention to everything: his horse's ears, the trail up ahead, branches that might snag a pack, and any other possible hazard. With each of Sil's steps, Jim felt the lead rope tighten and loosen as the mules kept pace behind them, reminding him that he was controlling over four thousand pounds of flighty prey animals.

Jim was thankful the trail had been clear on the way up. He knew that the trip down would not involve jumping the pack string over a fallen log or any other obstacle. He had seen the string maneuver obstacles twice now, but that had been with Tom leading. When crossing logs, the pack string acted like a bull-whip, with the rider and lead horse going over slowly but the re-maining animals going over at full speed. Tom had shared with Jim that not minding such things was exactly how rookie wrecks were caused on the trail. The last thing Jim wanted was to cause such an event while he was in charge of a string.

"You and that fellow seemed rather chatty back there," Tom said, keeping his gaze forward.

"Matt's a good guy. He's going to university in Bozeman to be an engineer. We were talking about the trail crews, and I was tell-ing him about the war."

"War? That Vietnam mess? Not sure I'd call it a war, but no one asked me."

"Yeah, Matt's worried about being drafted."

Tom spit off to the side of the trail. "If your country calls, you answer. If you don't, then I say get the hell out."

"You were in World War II, right?" Jim knew that detail from Tom's drunken tirade about Nazis. This might be his only chance to weasel the topic into a real conversation.

"Yep."

"What'd you do?"

Tom was silent for several minutes, the clip, clop of the horses' steps the only noise. Jim knew that the old cowboy ahead of him had heard his question. The long pause before the answer was typical Tom.

"I was in the First Special Service Force."

"Sounds elite."

"It was."

"Did you see much action?"

"You might say that."

Jim wanted to ask more questions but waited a moment, knowing he had touched a nerve. The red, spearhead patch that Jim had seen in the box at Tom's place flashed into his mind. It had to be from that unit.

"How was it elite?" Jim finally asked. What he really wanted to know was what kind of fighting Tom had been involved in. Something about being part of an elite unit intrigued him.

"You sure are asking a lot of damned questions," Tom grumbled but then he started to talk. "What the hell, it's not like it's a secret anymore. Though it sure was at the time. The Force was a bunch of Americans and Canadians pulled together to form a unit that specialized in mountain and winter warfare. We were supposed to go into Norway and harass the Nazis, but we never got the chance. Instead, they sent our asses to the Aleutian Islands to drive out the Japanese that had landed there." Tom spit and turned to look back at Jim. "What a mess that was. Four days on a puke and piss-filled boat to get there. Then when arrived at the landing, we found that the Japs had left already. A damned waste. No, I didn't see real action until Italy."

"You fought there?"

"You can say that. It got messy as we headed north, taking out Nazi fortifications, some built up on cliffs. We gave those German bastards what-for though. They started calling us the Black Devils after a while."

"Why?"

Tom turned again and gave him a devious grin, like a small child who had just pushed his sibling into a pond for fun. "We'd put boot polish on our faces and then sneak around behind their lines at night. We'd slip in and kill one or two bastards with a knife while they slept, leaving the rest to wake up and find their buddies dead. We left cards with our unit patch and the words: "The worst is yet to come" in German. Did a number on their morale, that's for sure. Boy, did we scare the hell out of them."

Jim was amazed that Tom was even willing to share this many details with him, and the stories kept coming. His tone turned somber as he shared about climbing the cliffs of Monte la Difensa, a mountaintop fortress. They'd made the climb while wearing ninety pounds of gear, and at the top, they had dived headlong into a three-day firefight with the Germans. Tom mentioned the battle at Anzio, but stopped midsentence. For half a minute or so, only the sounds of horse and mule hooves on the trail could be heard. Finally, he began again.

"We fought ninety-nine days without a break. You can't forget some of the things you see in a battle like that, no matter how hard you try. It sure wasn't worth the fifty dollars a month extra pay, that's for damned sure." Tom wouldn't share any more about Anzio, and Jim knew better than to press him further. Still, the force that Tom had been a member of ignited Jim's curiosity.

"What did it take to get into a unit like that?"

"More balls than brains," Tom said and laughed. "At least back then. Nowadays, it takes a lot more of both. They flew a bunch of us Force members back to North Carolina years ago, before Kennedy was killed. He was inspecting the Army's new Special Forces in '61. Green Berets they call them now. We were just a bunch of dumb, fearless brawlers who were too stupid to realize we'd signed up for a suicide mission. These new soldiers, though, they're exceptional. I don't think I, or anyone else in our unit, would make the cut now. They want these new soldiers to be smart, speaking other languages and such. We just knew how to blow stuff up and kill people. They really want the pick of the litter now."

"Do you think it's hard to get into a unit like that?"

"I reckon it is. It'd take a person with a lot of will to make the cut."

Jim asked no further questions, his mind occupied with thoughts of elite soldiers undertaking dangerous missions. He wondered about Tom, trying to envision him on the battlefield. Any doubts he'd had about whether Tom had ever killed another person were annihilated by his battle stories. Jim recalled the look in the man's eyes that first day in his kitchen. He shuddered.

⟦⊹⊹⟧

The next day, the weekend unfolded in a fashion similar to all the others since Jim's arrival at Tom's: chores and special projects on Saturday, riding on Sunday. As the projects were completed on the forty acres, Tom began to invent work for Jim. He even offered Jim's labor to neighbors, who gladly took advantage of the free help. Sunday, though, was a relaxed day, one that Jim looked forward to since it meant Vivian would come out for riding lessons. She had started riding on the old chestnut mare named Casey, but had progressed to riding Moonlight, a ten-year-old black mare with white socks and a blaze across her head. As before, Jim rode Sil, guiding Vi on Moonlight as they rode across Tom's property. Sometimes Frank and Abby would ride along with Tom. Sometimes the three adults hung back at the house chatting. This Sunday, Jim and Vi rode off in one direction, while Tom, Frank, and Abby trotted down the road on their steeds. After riding for almost an hour, Jim and Vi made their way back to the ranch. They could see Tom and their parents already riding up the driveway near the house.

"When can I ride Mr. McKee's horse?" Vi asked, pointing at Comanche.

"I don't think he'd ever let you," Jim said. "He won't even let me ride him. Comanche doesn't let anyone on his back but Tom."

"That's too bad. He's pretty; I like him."

"Yeah, so do I. They're all good horses."

"Especially Moonlight!" Vi leaned over her saddle and hugged the neck of the black mare. Sitting back up, Vi looked at Jim, "Mom said that you're almost done working out here, and that you can come back home in a few weeks when school starts."

"Yeah, just a few more weeks." Jim looked west past Tom's house, toward the mountains.

"You promise that you'll bring me out riding after school starts?"

"Yeah, sure, as long as Tom allows it."

"Good. You owe me."

Jim reigned Sil to a stop and looked at Vi. "Owe you, for what?"

"For not telling Mom and Dad about that night you had the gun in your room. You're not going to try something stupid like that again, right?"

Jim was stunned. She knew. She might be ten, but she knew. The smell of gun oil and the taste of the steel barrel in his mouth flashed back from the recesses of his mind. "Of course not," he said.

"You promise?" Vi had a look in her eyes much harder, much more intense than a ten-year-old girl should have.

Jim matched her gaze. "You have my word, Vi, never again."

"Good. Now you just need to not break into school anymore."

"Yeah, that would be a good start, I suppose." He sidled up near Vi and gave her a friendly shove, relieved she'd closed the dark topic. The shove distracted her long enough for him to kick Sil into a run, giving him a head start towards the corral. Vi screamed in protest as she encouraged Moonlight to take up pursuit. The two Redmond kids pulled their horses to a stop at the corral where Tom, Frank, and Abby were already unsaddling their horses and brushing them down.

"You cheated!" Vi complained. Jim smiled as he dismounted and tied up his horse. Vi took her protest to her parents but received little support.

"If you want fair Vi, you'll have to go back to your fairytales," Frank said gruffly. With a half-hearted pout, Vi began to undo the cinch on Moonlight's saddle. Abby watched her struggle with the cinch for a little while, then came over to help.

After everyone helped put tack away, brush horses and set them loose in the pen, the family said their goodbyes. Abby and Vi hugged Jim as always. Frank gave him the nod and slight smile that left Jim wondering if his dad might actually be proud of him.

"Just a couple weeks left, so keep your nose clean, you hear?" Frank called to him from the driver's side, before they drove away. Jim didn't know what it would take to earn Frank's respect, but he decided then and there that he would not give the man another reason to doubt that he wasn't the kid he was a few months earlier. There was no time to mull such things over for too long; Jim heard Tom's boots behind him.

The next day, Tom woke Jim well before sunrise. Today, they'd take an overnight trip with just two saddle horses and one pack horse. Tom was hell-bent on finding a path from the old camp over to the Halsted ranch. Before he could do that, he needed to finish marking the last lengths of trails the crews needed to carve out before September.

With horses loaded and the house secured, Tom, Jim, and Pepsi pulled out onto Lincoln Highway and headed east, into a blood-red rising sun. The haze from a forest fire near Butte gave the horizon an ominous feel. This would be the second time Jim had gone with Tom on an overnight trail mapping run. The neighbors would come over and care for the horses and mules that remained at Tom's, allowing the duo to take their time in the mountains. Tom always said that accidents happened when people were in a hurry, so taking an extra day was justified in his mind, though Jim suspected it was just an excuse to extend their time in the mountains.

Nearing the steel trestle York Bridge, Jim yawned, trying not to nod off. He picked up the green thermos from the floor of the truck and poured himself a cup of coffee.

"Give me a hit as well," Tom said, his words muffled by the half-smoked cigarette he held between his lips.

Jim filled Tom's mug about two thirds full and handed it back.

"This should be a good trip," Tom said and crushed his smoke in the ashtray below the AM radio. "We've only got to mark another mile or so of trail up past Log Gulch. Then we can then ride up over to Willow Creek, and up Elk Horn to drop over Windy Ridge." He took a swig of coffee and set the mug between his legs. "I'll show you the Crow's Nest and where Hump Cabin is. We won't go that way, though. One of the Basque sheepherders is usually up there this time of year, and he'll talk our ears off. There's two of them sheepherders in the area. If we do run into one of 'em, don't mention the other one no matter what!"

"Why's that?"

"Those crazy bastards hate each other. They've been feuding for years over who was grazing their sheep on the other's land, or some fool thing like that. They're up there all by themselves all summer, so they become a bit irritable, so much so they even traded rifle shots across the valley a while back. I just don't want to be caught in their crossfire is all."

Jim nodded and sipped his coffee, wondering about all the places Tom had mentioned and trying to imagine what they were like. The prospect of covering so much country was exciting. Even meeting the Basque sheepherders sounded like an adventure. Jim settled into the seat. This was going to be a good trip, indeed.

CHAPTER 19

Comanche, Sil, and Moonlight were tied to trees only fifty feet from the small campfire, the darkness of the forest kept at bay by the gentle flicker of flames. The fire cast a soft orange glow over the man, boy, and dog sitting near it. It had been a long day of riding, much of it through untamed country. For the first time, Comanche was glad they had stopped, as today's climb had actually taxed him. They had made camp long before sundown, allowing the horses most of the late afternoon and evening to feed. Now, after grazing in the high country pasture near camp and quenching his thirst at the creek, Comanche was content. Sil and Moonlight were already asleep, their eyes closed as their standing bodies swayed ever so slightly. Comanche stood watch. He would wait until his rider was asleep and only then would he rest. The smell of smoke, hard rolls, and canned meat mixed with the essence of pine needles and the horses' own sweat.

Boss' voice kept Comanche awake, his strong, calm speech reassuring the horse that there was nothing to fear. Occasionally, the boy spoke as well. As the fire faded, the words grew sparse. Both humans stared at the dying fire in silence. Sparks leapt from the flames, rose toward the stars, then disappeared. With the last glow of embers, Comanche watched the man and boy crawl into their bedrolls, the man's dog curling up next to him. Only then did Comanche allowed himself to close his eyes.

The next morning sunrise came late, obstructed by the high ridgelines encircling the camp. More than an hour after the first blush of dawn, sunlight finally reached the campsite. Comanche had woken two times during the night: the first after the dog had barked and chased away a herd of elk near the creek, the second just before dawn when Boss's snoring had become especially loud. Even with the disturbances of the night, Comanche felt rested as Boss led him and the other horses out into the big open park and tethered them with long ropes, allowing them to graze. The aroma of dew-covered grass and pine needles soon intertwined with the smells of coffee and fried meat, and with the biting odor of a cigarette. His rider never smoked in the mountains during day trips, and that was always a relief to Comanche. But anytime they spent a night or more in the wilderness, Boss allowed himself one cigarette, smoked right next to the fire pit. Comanche stomped. Detestable.

The grass in the meadow was dry after a hot summer but Comanche, Sil, and Moonlight had been tethered near the creek where the grass was still lush and green. The horses ate their fill, content with their surroundings, content to not be saddled just yet. The horses were allowed two whole hours to graze in the rising sun as Boss and the boy ate their own breakfasts. Comanche enjoyed the tranquility only for so long; soon he longed to get back on the trail, to climb mountains, and he stomped at the earth to express his opinion. Boss understood. He chuckled and, in seconds, he and the boy were breaking down their camp. The fire was extinguished with a hiss as the boy poured water from the creek over it. He made five trips with the coffee pot before Boss nodded his approval. The boy then brought the horses back to camp. They were saddled, loaded, and cinched, and then Boss and the boy mounted up.

They were off once more, Comanche and his rider leading the way up the thickly timbered draw. Boss and Comanche worked together, finding the easiest route between the trees and deadfall, since there was no trail as they made their way deeper into the wilderness. At one point, Comanche could sense that Boss wasn't sure which way to go. He felt the reins go slack. His rider's hand patted his neck, and with a tap of his boot heels, Boss gave him permission to find the way. With steady, strong steps Comanche picked his way through the timber, looking ahead and finding a path through the trees.

After an hour in the shadows of the timbered ridge, Comanche and the others found the main trail traversing a steep slope along the north ridgeline of Moors Mountain. Heading east along the trail, they broke out into the sunshine ten minutes later. Before them, like a sway-backed buckskin, was a long, exposed bow of land that dipped down from the north face of Moors Mountain. From there, it curved up a bit to the northeast, like a grass-covered saddle seat. The wind howled across the golden scrub grass covering the crest. Comanche felt the reins guiding him further north, to a rock outcrop that overlooked the valley where they had camped the night before. There they stood, while Boss pointed out features. Far below, to the northwest, the dark green trees of the valley filled the arteries of the land, the pattern look-ing much like a bull elk's antler. Farther to the north was a long, knife-like, rock-covered ridge. The loose shale cased the south face, flowing down to the tree line like a frozen waterfall span-ning the entire mountain.

Boss and the boy dismounted and tied the horses to one of the few trees that had survived the harsh conditions of the exposed knob. There, Boss pointed to one feature after another, educating the boy, but Comanche didn't pay much attention. Feeling rested within minutes, he wanted to hit the trail again. Finally, Boss and the boy mounted up, and Boss turned the group back to the windswept ridge, where he led them to the trail.

The group began a slow, steep descent eastward through timber and grass-covered meadows. They dropped down into a small, tree-lined, bowl-shaped meadow. The bowl nestled at the east toe of a cliff-faced mountain. At the bottom, they stopped once more, and Boss and the boy dismounted, loosening the horses' cinches to allow them to rest and drink from an artesian spring bubbling from the base of the slope. The humans snacked on hard rolls and sliced summer sausage as the horses ate all the grass they could reach from the end of their lead ropes.

When it was time to leave again, the boy tested Moonlight's cinch but found it plenty tight. Ignoring it, he walked back to Sil, tightening the cinch on her saddle. Comanche knew that Moonlight had inhaled deeply, not liking her cinch tight. Boss, in his experience, knew that some horses played such tricks. Boss would have waited for her to exhale and then tightened the cinch a notch or two. The boy was either too impatient to wait or just ignorant of Moonlight's wily ways.

Boss, unaware of the situation, led the way into the timber on the south side of the park. Behind him and Comanche, the boy and Sil followed, with Moonlight trailing behind. Comanche glanced back at the string and could see the gap between the pack saddle's cinch and Moonlight's belly. The slack cinch was matched by the sagging breeching strap around her rump—the pack saddle was still fitted for one of the big pack mules and not adjusted for the smaller black mare; another error on the boy's part.

For twenty minutes, they picked their way through the timber, occasionally crossing narrow washes that carried only the slightest trickle of water after the long, dry summer. Entering a string of south-facing meadows high on a bench, Comanche spied a treeless ridge over a mile to the north. His keen eyes caught glimpse of a small cabin nestled just below the crest and a herd of sheep grazing near it. Boss pressed on, turning the group south through more timber. From within the trees, Comanche glimpsed a large park a hundred yards away. The high sun illuminated the meadow, a golden beacon in the dark timber. As the slope dropped toward the park, the rocky ground grew steeper. Comanche minded his pace earnestly, the rocky patches forcing him to slow his steps. He picked each step with precision so that his hoof would land on dirt and not the jagged, loose rocks. Boss adjusted his weight in the stirrups to help with their descent.

At a wind-fallen tree, Comanche paused. On each side, the path was lined with boulders and jagged granite. Boss gave a gentle touch with his heels, encouraging Comanche to make the easy leap over the log. With just enough effort, Comanche jumped, clearing the log while taking care to retain his footing and to keep his rider safe. A few strides down the path, far enough to allow Sil and Moonlight room to cross, Comanche, Boss, and the dog stopped and looked back.

Sil jumped the log easily enough, but the sudden pull on the lead rope caused Moonlight to lurch over it with more force than required. Then it happened: the loose saddle slipped over her shoulders, stopped only by the breeching strap that caught on her rump. The mare came unglued. In her furious bucking, her body slammed into Sil and the boy. Sil reared up, throwing Jim to the ground.

With a quick kick and hard reins, Comanche and Boss rushed towards the chaos. Boss was leaning over the saddle, trying to grab Moonlight's lead rope when she spun and hit Comanche in the side, shoving him and Boss deeper into the timber and rocks. Among the noise of steel horseshoes on rocks and breaking branches came the loud, terrifying snap of bone. Comanche felt his front left leg give way. He tried to stay upright, to keep his rider seated, but it was too late. Boss flew off to the side as Comanche rolled across the rocks.

Searing pain surged through Comanche's leg and shoulder as he regained his footing, only to find that his front left leg was incapable of supporting his weight. Looking down, he saw his dangling hoof, white bone protruding, a crimson ribbon flowing down his leg, and the large red drops pooling on the granite. Moonlight and Sil disappeared in a panic, heading deeper into the timber. The forest turned silent. Comanche simply stood there on three good legs, heart pounding, leg throbbing. Boss! Without changing his stance, he turned his head until he saw his rider, fifteen feet away, his unmoving body draped on the rocks. A shaking, frightened Pepsi sniffed at the man. The dark speckled dog made eye contact with Comanche and whimpered.

The horse heard one of the humans' moan. The boy. He stood, rubbing his head and looking at his hand, blood-covered after touching the cut above his eye. He looked around, lost balance, and braced himself on a tree trunk. Finally, he noticed Comanche and staggered closer. Comanche's own fear grew as the boy's face melted in horror, his eyes wide at the sight of the broken leg. The horse tried to recoil as the boy touched his shoulder, but the slightest motion caused the pain to explode anew. Comanche stumbled, almost collapsing to the ground. The boy backed off, waited a few moments, then slowly grabbed the lead rope and tied Comanche to a tree at the edge of the rocks. He then picked his way over the rocks to where Boss lay. With deep, pain-induced breaths, Comanche smelled the boy's fear and also his own.

Over several minutes, the boy pulled and carried Boss free of the rocks and down to the edge of the park just fifty feet away. The dog stayed close the entire way. The boy knelt next to the man, trying to wake him with no success. Several times the boy looked back up to Comanche with tear-filled eyes.

With every breath and every beat of his proud heart, the pain in Comanche's leg pulsated. For the first time, he didn't want to be in the mountains; he wanted to be back at the corral with the other members of the herd, with Boss. Comanche looked at his rider and then at the boy. With slow steps, the boy climbed the hill, leaving the dog to watch over the sleeping man. In the boy's hand was a pistol, the one Boss always wore at his side when they headed into the wilderness.

CHAPTER 20

The steel slide pulled back then released, closing with a harsh metallic clank. Both Jim and Comanche flinched. The cartridge was in the chamber. Jim wiped his eyes then raised the pistol. The sights wavered as he tried to line them up. His vision distorted even more as he looked into Comanche's eye. The gun shifted as Jim took a deep breath, his heart trying to punch out of his chest. He knew what he had to do, but he honestly wasn't sure that he could. He wasn't entirely sure how. The gun stilled. He saw the sights align. Saw fear in Comanche's eye.

Then the flash at the end of the pistol.

The gun jumped in Jim's hand. He momentarily lost sight of Comanche. There he was, an arc of red pouring from his head, a few inches below and behind his eye. The flow scattered as the horse reared against the lead rope. God, he was still alive! Panicked, Jim fired again, but the second shot was just as ineffective. Comanche tried to flee, but both the rope and his injuries caused him to falter and collapse. Still he struggled to get back up. In desperation, Jim lunged forward and thrust the muzzle just below Comanche's ear, releasing the final shot. He looked into

Comanche's terror-filled eye. It was the final sign of life the boy witnessed as the horse collapsed to the ground.

The gunshots echoed against the mountainsides. Then the forest was entirely silent. In a final act of defiance, Comanche's hooves continued to kick. Finally, the broken pale horse was still. Jim fell to his knees at the beast's side and sobbed. He rested a hand on the animal's great neck. Comanche's blood soaked into his jeans. The horse's eye stared blankly up at the blue sky beyond the web of pine limbs. No defiance, no life. The eye was utterly empty.

Jim had killed animals before: one elk and two deer since he first started hunting when he was twelve. During those trips, Frank had taught him how to shoot, how to aim at the front shoulder from long range, and how to take a shot only if he knew it would kill the animal. Frank always reminded him that killing was for food and never sport, that the best thing a hunter could do was to make a shot so good the animal never even knew it was hit. No suffering. He taught him that if an animal was wounded, it was best to walk up and shoot it in the head to end its misery, but Jim had never had to do that before. His first shots with his rifle had always, mercifully, ended the animal's life.

Here he was with the corpse of an animal for whom he had caused incredible suffering. No, not an animal. A friend—if it was possible to call the bond between horse and human such a thing as friendship. Jim's trembling hands touched Comanche's mane and neck, and his tears fell on the horse as he tried to understand what he'd done wrong.

He knew how to shoot a pistol because he had shot one once with his friend Lance. Hunting trips had taught him almost all the details of how to make a clean kill. But there was one crucial omission—no one had ever told him where to aim if he had to shoot an animal in the head. No one had told him that the brain of a horse only took up a small portion of the massive skull. He hadn't even known whether to aim from the side or from the front of Comanche's head.

The grief and guilt consumed him. By the time Pepsi's whining drew his attention, Comanche's body had begun to stiffen, his back leg hanging out into the air as if suspended by an unseen force. Jim looked back over his shoulder and saw Pepsi sitting next to Tom's unmoving body. Leaving the pistol on the ground where he had dropped it, Jim returned to Tom. There was no question that the old cowboy was hurt badly, his lower right leg not as straight as it should be and blood matting the white hair on the back of his head. But he was alive. Tom breathed, though only with slow, shallow breaths.

Jim looked out over the valley and the endless mountain ridges. "Help!" he shouted. "Is anyone out there?" He knew full well it was useless the moment the words were carried away by the wind. The trail crew was five miles away and at least three ridges to the north. The closest person had to be the sheepherder up at Hump Cabin, but what good would he be? Jim knew from the day's travels that he had to drop down into Porcupine Creek and back up another mountain to reach it. Without a horse, there was almost no chance he'd arrive before dark and no assurance that the occupant would even be there. Besides, to even try would mean leaving Tom. No, Hump Cabin wasn't an option. Tom's parked truck, in the opposite direction, was his best bet for help.

Jim had paid enough attention during the ride to realize they were about two and a half miles, as the crow flies, northeast of the first trail camp. Trees at the edge of the park hid what lay between them and the first trail crew campsite, but Jim could see the big peak just southeast of the old camp. He knew that peak. He'd looked at it every day for three weeks. Tom had called it Sheep Mountain and said that it was a landmark he should remember, the same way he'd called Jim's attention to Shale Rock Ridge and the grassy saddle where Hump Cabin sat. Such landmarks could be seen from most high ground and could help a rider figure out where he was and where he needed to go.

Towards Sheep Mountain was where he needed to go, but he couldn't leave Tom here. He thought about carrying him and even tried to lift the man to his shoulder, but he quickly realized the task was impossible. He needed the horses. Bad. Jim stood up and looked around for Sil and Moonlight. Distress filled him as he wondered if they, too, were injured. Would he have to shoot another horse?

He climbed back up the hill, to the log where the disaster had started. He looked around but saw nothing. He tried to whistle like Tom did when calling the horses to the gate but nothing came in response. Not a whinny, not a hoof beat. Moonlight had the food, cook gear, and bedrolls in the panniers she carried. Sil's saddle held a rain slicker and some hard candy that Jim had put there to snack on during the ride. That left only Tom's saddle. Comanche's body lay still, the saddle secured fast to his corpse.

Dreading going near the horse once more, Jim approached slowly, as if not wanting to disturb him. With as reverent a motion as possible, Jim removed the bridle and halter first, the blood that covered them now drying to a near-black crust. Then he unbuckled the cinch and breast collar of the saddle. He tried to pull it slowly at first, hoping to let the straps pass under the horse without disrespecting him, but the rocks and Comanche's sheer mass required several hard tugs on the saddle before it came free. Last, Jim picked up the pistol, unloaded it, then tucked it into his belt at the small of his back. As he hauled the tack down toward Tom and Pepsi, he saw the man's head move ever so slightly.

Jim rushed as fast as he could to Tom's side. His eyes were still shut and the shallow breaths continued. He had come to. Jim set the pistol on a nearby rock and rolled up Comanche's blanket, still wet with the horse's sweat. He placed the blanket under Tom's head to provide some comfort. The large gash on Tom's head had stopped bleeding. A mat of black, hardening blood and hair covered the wound. Jim took the bright yellow slicker from the back of Comanche's saddle and draped it over Tom's body, and Pepsi laid down next to him, snuggling her body close to her master's. Never before had Jim felt so lost. Here at his feet lay a man who could be dying, and up the hill was the body of a horse, of a friend, that he had just killed.

"God, what do I do?" Jim whispered. He hardly believed any unseen deity was listening. The pleading prayer was sheer instinct. It was what his mom would do, he knew that much. Pepsi raised her head at Jim's words and her ears perked. "What do you think I should do?" Jim asked. The dog tilted her head inquisitively. Looking back up the hill, Jim saw the white body of Comanche among the timber and boulders, a haunting reminder of what had just happened. He couldn't leave the horse like that; he deserved so much better.

Unable to discern what he should do about Tom, about the missing horses, about anything, Jim did the only thing that made sense in that moment. He climbed back up the hill to Comanche and began placing rocks around the horse's body. For the next hour, he stacked steel gray talus stones, encircling and then covering Comanche. Tearless and numb, he gathered the stones and placed them until he'd entombed the horse in a giant rock cairn. He winced once when he thought of his father's work, the stone carving shop, and of how Dad always said, "The stones aren't for the dead, they're for the living." Jim pushed the thought aside and hefted another large rock over to the horse. It wasn't until he was nearly finished that he set stones over Comanche's magnificent head, building a wall of rocks that sat a few inches higher than the lifeless face. On top of the wall he placed a large, flat stone to complete the improvised tomb. Would anyone ever come across this grave marker? So far off any main trail, he doubted any other human would see and honor the grave. But he knew that Comanche deserved something; his life demanded some sort of memorial.

With a jagged rock, Jim scratched two-inch high letters into the flat stone.

Comanche
A horse like no other
8/17/65

Standing up, Jim tried to remember the prayer that Mom had recited when they buried one of their family dogs. He was eight at the time, and the words were long lost to the past.

"I'm sorry," he said. The words slipped past Jim's trembling lips. Wiping his face, he returned to Tom and Pepsi. The old man was still unconscious, the bend in his lower right leg was frightening. Jim wondered if it would help if he made a splint and realized it was probably better to do that now, while Tom was passed out. He gathered a few long, sturdy branches and retrieved the coil of manila rope Tom kept in his saddlebag. He also found Tom's two-bladed Case pocketknife. Jim cut half a dozen arm-length pieces of the hemp rope and trimmed and smoothed the branches. He set them next to Tom's leg and then stared, struggling to remember his minimal first aid knowledge. Zack had been the Boy Scout. At least Jim had gotten to act as the patient while his brother practiced making splints for his first aid badge. That was the memory that guided him now. Trained or not, this much was vividly certain: the leg wasn't straight but needed to be, and the stiff, wood splints would help keep it as it should be.

As carefully as he could, Jim pulled and turned Tom's boot, drawing the leg over and down till the calf seemed straight once more. The harsh movement triggered a moan, but the man thankfully retreated back into unconsciousness. Jim threaded the pieces of rope under the injured leg as gently as he could, from the knee down to the ankle. Then he placed two of the smoothed branches between the ropes and the back of Tom's calf and set two more branches on the front. He tied the ropes that were closest to the knee and the top of Tom's boot first. Then he weaved the remaining sticks along the sides of the break. He tightly knotted the last strands of rope, completing the makeshift cast. As Jim stood up from his task, the last rays of sunshine waned through the timber.

He'd just splinted a broken leg, but that was now the least of his concerns. Dark was coming. He shivered, not from the cold, but from plain fear. Already it was dark in the trees that lined the meadow. Dammit, he had to keep his head together. What would Tom do? A fire, he had to build a fire. Though the days were hot, the high mountain temperature dropped quickly once the sun went down. The warmth would be critical for getting through the night, but he also wanted flames to keep the darkness at bay. And any predators. God, they were stuck near an enormous corpse in the middle of bear country. He could only hope a fire would help in that regard, but he really didn't know.

With his boot, Jim cleared a large patch of ground near Tom, kicking away all the pine needles and branches. He stacked several large stones to form a fire ring, then gathered sticks and clumps of dried grass to use as kindling and dry deadfall logs for fuel. Following Tom's example from the night before, Jim pulled a pitch stick from the saddle bag. With that and Tom's Zippo lighter, he managed to entice the flames to life.

Shadows devoured the trees surrounding them. Even with the fire, Jim found himself looking quickly in the direction of every sound he heard. He grabbed the pistol and took his post near Tom, Pepsi, and the fire. Now a fear worse than bear formed in his mind. In the orange flicker of the flames, Jim envisioned the vengeful spirit of Comanche rising from the rocks, stampeding down to exact his revenge on the one who had taken his life.

As night cloaked the mountain, Jim dared not close his eyes. Every time his head nodded in exhaustion, that last gunshot tore through his mind, and the look in Comanche's eye burned into his thoughts.

Fighting sleep for hours, Jim's grumbling stomach forced him to rummage through Tom's saddle bags. He found an old can of Spam, which he opened and shared with Pepsi. The salty, canned meat made him wish he had the canteen from his own saddle. Indeed, how long could he go without water?

In the dead of the night, Jim heard an animal in the trees. Something big. His heart raced. Then relief: horse hooves, the shake of a head, and the jingle of bit and halter. Jim stood, looking into the timber, wondering if it was just his imagination. For a moment, he found himself hoping it wasn't Comanche coming back to haunt him. He shook off the fear and whistled, but heard nothing in reply. The meadow was silent. It had to be Sil or Moonlight. If only one of them came closer to his crude camp, he could catch one, and then he might have a chance at getting Tom the help he desperately needed.

As he tossed another large branch onto the fire and pushed a big deadfall log deeper into the flame, Tom stirred. Jim slipped the pistol into the saddlebag and then sat down next to him. Tom mumbled, asking repeatedly where he was and what he was doing there. Jim answered as best he could, aware that the man's mind could not be right after the fall he'd taken. Tom tried to sit up once but quickly returned his head to the horse blanket pillow, a look of agony on his face. Jim placed a hand on his shoulder to keep him down, explaining to him that he had a nasty cut on the back of his head and that his leg was likely broken as well. Tom shook his head slowly in disbelief.

"What happened?" he groaned once again. "Where are the horses?"

The question that Jim dreaded.

"I don't know exactly what happened. I remember going over the log on Sil and then waking up and seeing you on the rocks.

"Comanche."

Jim's mouth quivered. He couldn't look Tom in the eye as he told the man about the horse's broken leg. He told Tom that he had shot Comanche, but omitted the detail of the dreadful deed requiring three shots. The crackle of the fire muffled Tom's sobs.

"Comanche, I'm so sorry I failed you," Tom wept.

Jim pulled his knees tighter to his chest and cried as well. He wished that he could undo the day's events and that men and horses were all well and back home. Eventually, Tom's sobbing subsided. He spoke.

"Where is he?"

"Up the hill. I piled a bunch of rocks on him to keep the animals away. I'm sorry, Tom. I really am." Again the sounds of the fire filled the silence.

"What about the others?"

"I don't know. They ran off when you went down. I thought I heard one of them in the dark a little bit ago, but I couldn't see."

"Are you okay?" Tom finally asked.

"Yeah, I got a bump on the head is all. I'm alright, though."

"We need a horse, son. You need to catch a horse."

"I know."

Jim stirred the fire, placing another piece of deadfall on it to keep the flames fed and the darkness away. He wished he was home. He wished that the image of Comanche's eye did not appear every time he closed his eyes. Jim wiped his face and rested his hands on his jeans. He gasped. His jeans were covered in Comanche's blood from the knees down. Panicked, he turned away from Tom, grabbed a handful of grass, and tried to rub the crusted blood away. He heard Tom breathing behind him.

"Those stains don't go away," the man said. "That kind stains down to your soul."

Jim stopped his scrubbing, turned back, and tossed the grass into the fire. It was immediately consumed. The men watched the flames flash brighter for a moment. Then both heard it—the sound of horse bridle and hoof steps teased from the dark.

"There it is again; did you hear it?" Jim asked.

"I did. One of them is back," Tom said. He took a couple labored breaths and added, "They're spooked. Don't try and catch 'em tonight. Morning. First light. Might give you a chance." The man slipped back into unconsciousness.

Jim looked as far as the firelight carried, hoping to see either the black or silver roan mare but only saw a charcoal veil of darkness. Looking upward, he let his eyes adjust skyward, out from the light of the fire. The black of the sky was cleaner than that of the trees. A flawless canvas for the fleeting sparks of the fire. With each blink the stars came into focus. First one, then hundreds more. Sparks weaving between them. One more blink opened up the jeweled sky. For a moment, Jim lost himself in the expanse of it, despite the day, despite everything. A thread of light briefly flashed. Brilliant, but then gone. As a boy, he had always made a wish when he saw a shooting star. He shook his head at the thought now.

Faint hoof steps in the trees off to his left brought his thoughts back to Sil and Moonlight. Turning toward the sound, he hoped they were unhurt and simply scared. Looking back up at the stars, he prayed again, just a few words. He prayed he could catch even one of the horses so he could get Tom out of the mountains and to a hospital.

Utterly spent, Jim tried to lie down and close his eyes, but once again he heard the gunshot, felt the terror, as real as ever. So he stayed awake, fighting sleep and the cold. At some point in the pre-dawn hours, the waning flames forced him to venture to the farthest reach of the firelight to retrieve more deadfall logs. Otherwise, he spent the night huddled close to the warmth and light of the flames. Tom slept. Even the dog nodded off. Jim kept watch.

Never before had he been so grateful to see the sky in the east lighten, the ebony ocean receding at dawn's approach. There, in the growing light at the far side of the meadow, Jim saw something. An exhausted smile touched his face. Sil and Moonlight stood at the edge of the timber, gazing at the smoldering campfire. Even a hundred yards away, Jim could see that the pack saddle on Moonlight sat at a strange angle. Her lead rope was torn, just short of her halter. Sil looked unharmed, but he would need to draw closer to see if her saddle and tack were intact. Jim detached Comanche's lead rope from the blood-soaked halter.

With a purposeful stride, he crossed the park, though the grass and uneven ground slowed him a bit. He was determined to catch the horses, to do this one thing right. He knew the accident was his fault. He hadn't tightened Moonlight's cinch when he knew he should have.

"Damn you Jim," he hissed at himself. "You are such an idiot!"

With each step, his self-loathing grew. It was all his fault, both the mound of rocks covering Comanche's body and Tom lying there broken and grieving, miles from help. This anger grew as he neared the horses. As he approached, he reached out like he always did back in the corral at Tom's place. His eyes locked on Sil. Just another inch and he would have her. The horses thought otherwise, jumping back and trotting off, loose reins, rope, and the remains of panniers dragging behind. Jim ran after the fleeing horses, which only caused them to increase their speed.

For fifteen minutes this tortuous game played out until, exhausted, Jim stopped. He struggled to catch his breath after running all over that alpine meadow. He bent over with his hands on his knees. At nearly seven thousand feet above sea level, the lack of oxygen taxed his lungs. He looked up in time to see the horses stop just thirty yards away. Jim wanted to scream at the two frightened mares who seemed to taunt him by staying just out of reach. It was then that he remembered Tom's lesson on catching horses, about how they were used to being hunted.

If they feel threatened they will run. That's why if you're catching one, you can't act like a predator. You gotta be calm, which means keeping your emotions in check if you're having a bad day.

Standing up straight, Jim allowed his breathing to return to normal. This time, not looking directly at the horses, he walked slowly towards them, calling their names in a soft voice. Moonlight started to walk away, but Sil didn't. Beautiful, wonderful Sil. She stood still as her rider approached. Drawing close enough to touch her, Jim let his hand run along her mane, petting her, calming both the horse and himself. A few more cautious steps and his fingers curled around the lead rope.

"Thank you, Sil," he whispered as he wrapped his arms around the horse's neck, embracing her in gratitude. After seeing her companion calmly following Jim, Moonlight was amenable to his approach. The black mare even took a few steps toward Jim as he came closer. He took hold of the tatters of her lead rope and attached Comanche's lead to her halter.

Keeping both horses close, he adjusted Moonlight's halter and her pack saddle. The blanket was gone, fallen in the woods somewhere. Jim led the two horses back to where Tom lay. Pepsi wagged her tail against the slicker, waking her master.

"They okay?" Tom asked, his voice still weak but stronger than it had been last night.

"I think so, they have some scrapes, but they're walking fine. Moonlight lost her blanket, but we can use that one." Jim didn't dare mention Comanche's name as he pointed to the blanket under Tom's head. "We're a couple miles from the first trail camp.

If we head west, staying south of the ridge, we should run into the trail. Do you think you can ride?"

Tom looked at him, eyes lucid and voice firm. "Son, the day I can't ride is the day they're putting dirt on me. Now help me up so we can figure out how to get the hell out of here."

CHAPTER 21

When Jim caught Sil and Moonlight early that morning, Tom had hope. Though perhaps only a fool's hope. The pannier that had held their bedrolls had been ripped open and its contents strewn only God knew where. At least the other pannier, the one that held their food and cook gear, was intact. If, by some miracle, they actually got out of the mountains today, the loss of the bedrolls would be of little concern. Tom knew that they couldn't stay another night. They had to get out. He knew just enough about injuries to know that they needed to make it back to the truck and get to a hospital. The broken leg was the least of his worries—it was the constant skull-splitting pain in his head and the coughing of blood that troubled him.

After Jim had caught the horses, Tom tried to sit up. It was as though the entire world, the sky, the trees, and the mountains, were picked up and spun around him violently. Laying back down, Tom rested his hand on Pepsi for comfort, the dog faithfully by his side as usual. From that position, Tom directed Jim on what to do for the next several hours. He had the boy start by unsaddling both horses and checking for sores and injuries, then fixing the tack and resaddling them. Finally, they needed to eat something.

Tom passed on the simple meal of Spam and hard rolls. The stomach-churning dizziness killed his appetite. He told Jim to give his share to Pepsi. Both Jim and Pepsi would need their strength to help him out of here. He had no other hope but that of the boy. Tom could see that Jim realized it too. The teen followed every direction perfectly, asking whenever he needed clarification. Once the saddles were readied, Jim sat at the edge of the near-dead fire and ate his Spam sandwich, tossing every other bite to Pepsi.

"I'm thinking that if we follow the ridge west we can catch a drainage that'll take us down to the new trail," Jim said between bites. "If we're lucky, we might come across a few game trails to make the going easier. What do you think?"

"It's what I'd do. It'll be slow going, and you'll have to pick the trail well. You might have to walk a bit to do that."

"I was planning on walking the whole way, that way I can move logs and break branches if I need to. Figured I could set Comanche's saddle on top of the pack saddle."

It was the first time that either one of them had uttered the horse's name since last night. Tom gave a single nod, his head pounding with the motion. His lips quivered for a moment. No time for grief. Sure as hell, not now.

"Sounds good to me," he said. "Get that fire out as best you can. Piss on it if you need to, and throw dirt on it as well. I don't want a damned forest fire happening on our account."

Jim did as he was told. Once the fire was completely out, he sat near Tom and tried to patch together the damaged pannier using the reins from Comanche's bridle. He strapped the panniers to the D-rings on the Decker and distributed their few remaining supplies between the two so that the load was even. Then he lay Comanche's saddle over the top and used its latigo and cinch to tie it to the Decker.

After watching all this work, the torture began for Tom. He grimaced as Jim put his arms around his chest, forcing him into a standing position. Though he did his best to hide it, he knew that Jim could see his distress.

"Where's my hat?" Tom barked.

"Don't worry about that, I'll get it for you in a bit."

Using Jim as a crutch, Tom hopped over to the rock ledge that he wanted to use to mount Sil.

"Can you stand for a second while I lead Sil over?" Jim asked.

Tom nodded, but the moment Jim let go his head spun and he began to fall. Jim quickly caught him.

"Here, sit back on this rock." Jim eased him down, and Pepsi drew close as he slumped on the rock. She had kept her distance while Tom was being moved, but the moment he was seated, she was back at his side.

Tom nodded, though he was far from okay. It took all he had to not cry out in pain at the slightest movement, or to fall over because of the incessant spinning of the world. Even sitting on the rock with his arm supporting him was nearly too much to tolerate. The splint on his leg dug into his skin, but it was doing its job. Not bad work, really. Jim led Sil over to the rock ledge. How the hell was this going to work? To get into the saddle was one thing, but to ride for several miles through rough terrain seemed impossible. At least he could be thankful that the break was in his lower leg and not his femur; he'd really be up a creek if that had been the case.

Jim let Sil's lead rope hang loose, lacking someplace to tie her. She wasn't going anywhere though. That beautiful horse clearly knew she was needed. Jim climbed onto the rock shelf to help Tom to his feet once more. Slowly, with Tom hanging his weight almost entirely on Jim, the two made their way to the edge of the rock, where Tom could grab hold of the saddle horn. The feel of the leather helped stabilize his swirling head.

"Nice and easy," Tom said. "Go slow with me." Delicately, carefully, Jim helped him lift his broken right leg up over the saddle.

Halfway over, the end of one of the sticks in the splint caught on the saddle bag, nearly sending Tom into unconsciousness from the pain. He swallowed the scream, not wanting to spook the horse. Jim freed the leg, then muscled under Tom, lifting him up the rest of the way. Finally, Tom's weight was square in the saddle. Sil had not moved during the effort—entirely foregoing her usual annoying habit of walking the moment she felt weight in the saddle. Yeah, she knew.

Tom's muscles quivered, but the longer he sat on the big roan mare, the more the pain in his leg eased. "Take some of that rope from the saddle bag and lash me on here," he said, his words raspy and terse.

Jim looking at him as if he was nuts, did nothing.

"Listen, boy, I'm near faint as it is. If I fade out, I don't want to fall off. Tie. Me. On."

Jim grabbed the rope and helped Tom tie a rigging across his waist and shoulders, connecting that to the saddle at four points, two on each side. "That'll do, now hand me my hat and Moonlight's lead rope so we can get the hell out of here."

Jim handed Tom's hat up to him. Though when he tried to put it on, he found that it barely fit because of all the matted blood. The raw, abrasive pain from pulling the hat over his head was a trifle compared to the throbbing everywhere else. With Tom squared away, Jim untied Moonlight and walked her over to Sil. He was about to hand Tom the lead rope when he hesitated.

"What you waiting for? Give me the rope," Tom demanded.

"You don't look so well," the boy stammered. "How about we just tie her up with a breakaway string off the back. That way if she spooks she won't pull on you."

The kid had a point. Tom nodded. "Yeah, I suppose you're right."

Jim removed the quarter inch braided rope from the back of Moonlight's Decker. He tied it to the thin leather straps that held the rain slicker on the back of Sil's saddle and then tied the lead rope to that. The twine or leather would break loose if the horse reared, but it was secure enough to motivate the trailing horse to follow.

"You ready?" Jim asked as he picked up Sil's lead rope.

"Yeah," Tom said and steeled himself for what he knew was coming. The pain that hit him with Sil's first step was of such an intensity that he nearly fell off. The rope rigging, thankfully, held him fast. At least he knew the rigging worked. With each subsequent step, Tom's suffering expanded. His splinted leg rubbed against the stirrup and against Sil's belly. The gentle sway of her walk made his world spiral in fresh sadistic ways. The throbbing in his head spread down into his shoulders and joined forces with the agony in his ribs. Back at Monte La Difensa in Italy, he'd been carried down on a litter by two medics. That had been a slight bit less painful than this current circumstance. At least then he had been given a couple hits of morphine. No such relief now. It wasn't that Sil had a hard gait or stumbled often. It was just that motion, any motion, sent Tom reeling with pain and nausea. His occasional need to cough only made things worse. Searing blades shot from his ribs on his right side, and his head nearly burst with each cough. More than anything, it was the blood that concerned him. He tasted it every time he coughed, and he spit it out when Jim wasn't looking. The kid had enough on his plate. He didn't need to know how bad things really were, not with miles still to cover. Jim looked back and Tom gave the boy a thumbs-up. That's right kid, no one's dying today. Tom kept that thought in mind with each agonizing step.

Normally, Tom would be incensed by delays on a ride, but each time Jim paused to pick a new path, Tom experienced a sweet, though brief, reduction in the pain and vertigo. He watched from behind as Jim played the role of trailblazer. Each path he chose was a good one, and not once did they need to backtrack as they carved their way slowly through the dense timber. Occasionally, Jim stopped to heft away a log or break branches to ensure that the horses and Tom could pass through unhindered. The kid was tired, Tom knew that. He probably hadn't slept for two full days, and now he was breaking trail for two horses and a cripple. Tom felt useless and humbled as he watched Jim, the boy who didn't care about anything but himself just a few months ago. Jim pressed on, kept going, refusing to stop to rest even when Tom suggested it. For the first time, Tom saw it—the kid didn't have any quit in him.

During one of the longer pauses, as Jim went on ahead to scout a path, Tom found himself torn between admiration and spite. He wondered what had really happened with Comanche. He knew that Jim had shot his horse, he'd been told that much. But the blood on the kid's jeans and the withdrawn look in Jim's eyes told Tom that it had not been a clean shot. He didn't want to know the details. He didn't need to. His horse, his friend was gone, and nothing could change that now.

After over two hours of picking their way from game trail to game trail and working further down the mountain, Jim turned around with a hopeful smile.

"We made it," he said, panting. "There's the trail."

Tom raised his head and saw the earthen scar of the path just a hundred yards away, on the hillside. They were not far from the first camp, and from there it was less than an hour down to the truck.

"Good job kid," he said. "Good job."

With newfound enthusiasm, Jim pressed on, Sil and Moonlight seeming to catch the teen's excitement, their steps a little faster—much to Tom's discomfort. Once on the trail, though, the going was easier. Even ground and a gentle grade made the descent smoother, but the bright sunlight of the open slope forced Tom to clench his eyes shut. The radiant illumination set his brain on fire. He gripped the saddle horn with all his remaining strength hoping he could remain conscious till they made it to the truck.

Even in the timber leading through the cliff gates of Refrigerator Canyon, Tom's eyes were tightly closed. He had little sense of time or place, but he stayed alert, awake to the pain. The sound of horses walking through the creek told him that the truck was just a few hundred feet away. Glancing at his wristwatch, he saw that it was ten minutes to three. He raised his head, looked forward and saw the faded, baby blue paint of the low cab forward truck, the chipped and rusted stock rails in the back. It was a beautiful sight.

Stopping at the side of the truck, Jim untied Moonlight's lead rope from Sil and tied the black mare to the side of the truck then led Sil to the loading ramp. The ramp was the perfect height for Tom to reach out with his good leg and lean his weight onto it. From there, with Jim's help, he disembarked from Sil. This time he could lift his broken leg high enough to clear the saddle, but the pain was still intense. Gravity worked against the splint for the brief moment that his leg was horizontal. Once Tom was off the horse, Jim again acted as his crutch, leading him down the ramp and over to the passenger side of the truck, one painful hop at a time.

"Okay Tom, let's get you into the truck and to the hospital."

"You're gonna load the horses, aren't you?" Strange panic washed over him. "Ain't no way we're leaving without the horses!"

Jim looked at him funny. "I wasn't planning on leaving them," he said, calm and steady like he was talking to an irate child. "Just figured you might be more comfortable in the cab is all."

"Oh," Tom said. His head hurt. "Yeah, I suppose so." That knock he'd taken to his head must have jarred some of his sense loose. Jim opened the door while Tom balanced on his good leg, his arms grasping the corner of the stock panels. Pepsi leapt into the cab the moment the door opened, ensuring she would not be left behind.

Tom shimmied to the door and grasped the door and seat-back. With no fear of spooking a horse at this point, he yelped in pain as hefted himself up and into the cab of the truck. His butt on the seat and his legs still hanging out the door, he paused, breathing deeply. When he was ready, he had Jim steady his broken right leg as he pulled both legs into the passenger side footwell.

The heavy door slammed and Tom leaned his head back, his breathing fast in rhythm with the pulsing throughout his body. The footwell of the cab allowed no room to take pressure off the leg. No matter how he shifted his weight, the burden on the bone through the splint tortured him. It was a visible pain, flashes of light appearing at the corners of his eyes.

The truck shuddered and rocked as Jim loaded the horses. Shit, if that vibration alone aggravated his head, what would the drive be like? With the stock gate secured, Jim climbed into the truck and rummaged around for the key hidden underneath the instrument panel. There, he found it, just left of the ashtray. He started the engine and turned to Tom.

"Which hospital should we head to?"

The boy's question brought Tom back to almost full consciousness. "Saint Pete's is closest. 11th and Logan, up by the cathedral. You know where that is?"

"Yes, got a cast on my arm there when I was ten."

"Good, good," Tom said. Then his world went black.

CHAPTER 22

As the stock truck crossed the city limits, the "Entering Helena" sign filled Jim with both dread and hope. It had been fifty minutes since they left Refrigerator Canyon. Tom had passed out before Jim could even get the truck moving. With two horses, snaky roads, and a low-geared truck, the trip into town had not been fast enough for Jim's liking. The slow pace of the horse ride out had eaten precious time that he hoped he could make up for in the truck. At the end of the gravel road, Jim thought about stopping at the York Bar to call for help, but decided the time would be wasted waiting for anyone to arrive. No, he would get Tom to town himself. Once on paved roadways, Jim gunned the truck, the big block engine roaring in response. Tom's face had taken on a ghostly pallor as he slumped against the passenger door. Was he alive?

"Don't die on me, Tom," Jim whispered. A cough, followed by a low moan, offered proof that Tom was indeed alive, at least for the moment. The truck was no race car, built for hauling heavy loads, not for taking fast corners and exceeding posted speed limits. But the urgency of the situation forced Jim to take risks, pushing the truck hard. Should he stop? He second-guessed himself as he spotted a house just off the road. But again, he didn't want to slow the momentum of his travel; he had to keep moving forward. Was that a sheriff's car? Jim glanced in his mirror as a car rushed by. No, but it sure would have been easier if it had been. It would have been a welcome relief to be pulled over and to turn Tom's care over to someone who knew what they were doing.

It was just after four as Jim coaxed the big truck up Montana Avenue. Traffic was light for late afternoon on a Wednesday, but it was thick enough to tighten Jim's grip on the wheel whenever he wasn't shifting gears.

"We're almost there, Tom," Jim said, more a reassurance for himself. It certainly elicited no response from his passenger. After turning onto 11th Avenue, Jim glanced up at the trees lining the street, hoping the overhanging branches were not hitting Sil and Moonlight as the truck passed underneath. Jim ignored the surprised glances of the people walking down the sidewalk as the large truck rolled to a stop in front of the hospital entrance. Shutting off the engine, Jim had just enough presence of mind to make sure the truck was in gear and the parking brake set before getting out and running across the street and into the hospital.

The ornate entrance opened immediately into a long hallway. Where was he supposed to go? Jim looked each way and finally saw a nurse come out of a room about fifty feet to his right. Calling out for help, Jim ran towards her. At the sound of his shouting and pounding boots, she raised a finger to her lips and cast a scolding look his way. What was her problem? Wasn't this a hospital?

"My boss is hurt; he was thrown from a horse! I need some help!" Jim blurted out. The woman's disdain immediately transformed into urgency. Jim told her that Tom was unconscious in the truck outside, and she called for a couple of orderlies to join her. When they approached the truck and opened the door, Pepsi's frantic barks competed with the nurse's commands to the orderlies as they extricated Tom from the passenger seat. The soda pop dog nipped at one of the men as they handled Tom's limp body. Jim watched from the sidewalk, useless and numb. All he could do was rush to the truck door when Pepsi tried to jump out to be with Tom. Jim slammed the door shut before the dog could escape. More nurses arrived with a stretcher, and Tom was ferried across the street. Pepsi leapt over to the driver's side door. Her barking fit exploded in intensity. She growled and flashed her fangs—something Jim had never witnessed in the normally timid dog.

"It's okay, Pepsi." Jim tried in vain to reassure her through the window. He left the enraged and fearful dog inside the truck. At least she was safe in there.

Tom was carried into the hospital and down the hall to a side room. Jim followed and was immediately bombarded with questions as nurses removed Tom's clothes and cut the stick and rope splint free from his leg. As best he could, Jim described the accident and how he had found Tom unconscious on the rocks.

"I had to shoot the horse," Jim confessed at the end. The doctor acted as though he hadn't heard, or didn't care.

"Are you injured?" the doctor asked as he glanced at the matted hair under Jim's hat.

Jim shook his head no.

"Very well, you'll have to wait outside. Does he have any family we should contact?"

Jim thought about Pepsi and the horses outside, as well as the rest of the herd back home. "No, no one I know of."

The doctor ushered Jim out the door where a nurse touched his arm to get his attention. In a stupor, Jim followed her to a desk. She handed him several forms and a pen. Patient's Name. He wrote Tom McKee on the appropriate line. Patient's Address. He knew that too and jotted it down quickly. On down the list, Jim filled out what he knew about Tom, which proved to be very little. He twirled the pen between his fingers nervously as he tried to think of answers. The line asking about relatives bothered him. Tom had mentioned that he would die alone. Did he really have no family, no one to come to his side? The pen continued its dance.

"If you don't know an answer just leave the line blank," the nurse said and gave him an empathetic smile.

Without a word, he handed the forms back to her.

"You may have a seat over there. Someone will be out in a bit to talk with you." The nurse motioned to a long wooden bench along the wall of the hallway. Jim slumped onto it, exhausted. He took off his hat and held it in his hand as he wondered what to do. Thoughts of his mom and dad entered his mind. He considered calling them, but what would they do? Dad would pace and check with the nurse every five minutes, till he would go outside and smoke his pipe in frustration at feeling useless. Mom would pray. Her faith was as much a part of her daily routine as was feeding her family. Jim had never prayed until yesterday.

"God, please help Tom," he whispered once more. Defeated, Jim leaned over with his elbows on his knees, his hat hanging from his fingers as he looked at the intricate pattern in the tile floor. Hard-heeled footsteps passed up and down the hall. He didn't even look up. Minutes passed. Maybe ten. Maybe twenty. The entrance door opened. A heavier set of footsteps approached. Boots. The footfalls passed, paused, and then turned around.

"Redmond, Jim Redmond isn't it?" a voice inquired.

Jim looked up to see the face of the police officer who had arrested him almost three months before. Jim's stomach twisted up like a packer's knot with a couple of half-hitches thrown in for good measure. Dumbstruck, he nodded yes.

The officer took a step forward, "I thought you were doing community service up in the mountains. You're not supposed to be back in town until school starts."

"Yes sir, that's true."

"So, what are you doing here?"

"There was a horse accident up in the mountains. My friend was hurt bad." Friend, yes, Jim had used the word friend, not in hope of gaining leniency from the officer but because he truly thought of Tom as a friend now—a friend who might be dying because of his mistake. Jim told the story of going into the mountains with Tom to mark trails, even admitted how he was the one who hadn't tightened the cinch. The accident was his fault. Staring at the opposite wall, Jim disclosed how he'd had to shoot Comanche and get Tom out of the mountains. His eyes welled. He looked down and away to blot the tears on his sleeve.

"That's why I'm here," Jim finished. He looked up at the officer.

The officer offered a nod of his head, turned, and continued his path to the nurse's station. The officer spoke to the nurse, both occasionally eyeing Jim, voices hushed, preventing him from hearing their conversation. The officer finished whatever business had brought him to the hospital, and he walked back down the hall toward Jim.

"Good job getting your friend down the mountain. I hope he recovers fast." The officer touched the brim of his hat with a soft salute and said, "See you around, Jim." With that he walked down the hall and out the door.

Half of Jim was purely relieved the officer decided to overlook his obvious breach of parole. The other half choked on the commendation. *Good job?* Was that what he'd done? In all honesty, he'd only cleaned up a mess of his own making. He rested his head against the wall behind him, stared at the ceiling. Waited. Suddenly he remembered the animals in the stock truck. As much as Jim wanted to wait for someone to come and tell him how Tom was doing, his job wasn't finished just yet. He walked to the nurse's station.

"Can I help you?" The nurse wore her practiced smile. Did she even remember his situation?

"I've still gotta take care of the horses," he said. He scribbled Tom's number on a piece of paper and handed it to her. "Can someone call me at this number when you know how my friend is doing?"

She said she'd make sure of it. That was all he could do. He couldn't leave the animals any longer.

Outside at the truck, the horses stomped when they saw him. They knew something was wrong. Pepsi whined. At least she'd given up the vengeful dog routine. The sun was still high above the Continental Divide to the west, but in only a few hours it would start to cast the shadow of Mount Helena over the city. Jim needed to get home and care for the stock before dark.

He climbed into the cab, turned the key, and brought the truck to life. He looked back at the hospital and at Pepsi seated near the passenger door, then dropped the truck into first gear, starting the journey home. To Tom's place, that is. Home enough. Pepsi remained on the passenger side of the bench seat during the entire ride. He could tell that she was confused and he couldn't blame her. He was confused too. At least he had something to focus on; he had animals to tend to.

Back at Tom's place, Jim got Sil and Moonlight unloaded, unsaddled, brushed out, and released into the corral. The piles of fresh hay in the feeders told him that Tom's neighbor had come to care for the herd that day. Jim watched them all, how the returning horses were brought back into the fold with curious sniffs and nudges. Did they know? Did Sil and Moonlight somehow convey to the rest of the herd that Comanche was dead? No one bucked or nipped or whinnied loudly like they usually did upon reuniting. The way they acted almost convinced him that they did know. Jim closed the metal gate latch and tied it down with a length of baling twine, double-checking that it was secure. He took his time looking over the saddles and putting them away exactly as Tom would want. At least this gave him something else to focus on. He then walked around the entire barnyard, checking fences and water tanks, all while keeping an eye on Sil and Moonlight to ensure they were not showing a limp now that they were home. Thankfully, both appeared to be walking fine as they mingled with their herd.

The sun was setting. Jim had wasted enough time and needed to head into the house. He didn't want to, but he needed to eat. After one last look at the horses and mules, he turned to the house and saw Pepsi sitting near the stock truck. He'd left the passenger side door open for her, but she had refused to leave the truck. At least she was outside the vehicle now. That was progress.

"Pepsi, come here girl," Jim called.

The dark dog didn't move. She was nearly invisible in the shadow of the big vehicle.

"You hungry?" That got her attention. "Come on then." He headed to the house and held the door open. The dog caught up to him and trotted inside. Jim filled Pepsi's food and water dishes before looking for a meal for himself. With no energy to cook, Jim pulled out the Tom McKee staples: Swiss cheese and summer sausage. Cutting off several thick pieces, he ate quietly, listening to Pepsi alternate between crunching on her food and lapping at her water.

Jim stared at the phone on the wall, willing it to ring with news of Tom's condition. Not able to sit and wait, he left his meal, pulled the phonebook down from the top of the refrigerator, and looked up the hospital's number. Five rings later his call was answered. He gave his name, asked about Tom, and waited again, his finger tapping nervously against the wall next to the phone.

Finally, the nurse returned. "Your friend is in surgery but I don't have any other details," she said.

Silence.

"Sir?"

"Yeah, I'm here."

"You should call back in the morning."

More silence. How could she know nothing more than that?

"Are you there, sir? I'm afraid I have to get going."

"Yeah. That's really all?"

She assured him she had absolutely no details about Tom, then bid him goodnight, not waiting for him to reply. Beyond frustrated, Jim forcefully hung up the phone, but the look on Pepsi's face tempered him from any more expressive, physical venting. He returned to the table to finish eating and continued wondering what else he could do.

The clock on the wall told him it was too late to call his parents. He didn't want to wake them, though he knew he needed to pass the news on. Tom was their friend as well. Still, ten o'clock was way too late, and he had no actual news from the hospital. He would succeed only in worrying them. It could wait until morning.

His simple meal complete, Jim shed his blood-covered jeans in the laundry room and switched off the kitchen light. He showered. As if any part of the past two days could be washed away. Exhausted, Jim retreated to his room. A flick of the light switch left him in darkness as he groped across the room to his cot. Dim light from the half-moon revealed the storage boxes in his path. Finding his bed, he collapsed. His mind immediately danced at the edge of sleep and, for a few minutes, he became convinced that the last two days had been a terrible dream.

Sleep quickly consumed him, but only until a bright flash and the noise of a gunshot jolted him back to consciousness, his body jumping at the sensory memory. Jim's heart pounded like the hooves of a hundred horses. With deep breaths, he tried to calm himself. His eyes drifted shut, only to be greeted by Comanche's panic-filled brown eye. Again, the gunshot jarred him. He could smell the spent gunpowder. The tang of blood-soaked dirt. The horses in his chest returned.

So, this was how Comanche would haunt him.

Jim lay there, staring at the ceiling, terrified to close his eyes again. His rapid gasps and pounding heart were the only sounds in the house. Then he heard something else: the unmistakable click-clack of Pepsi's claws as she made her way down the hall. In the dim light, Jim saw Pepsi's shadowy form push through the partially closed door. She hesitated at the side of the cot for a moment then jumped up and curled into a ball near his feet. He felt her breath and warmth through the blanket. In one last attempt, Jim closed his eyes and found sleep, if only for a few hours.

⊶⊷

The next morning, Jim completed his chores as always, though more slowly than normal. Three more times during the night, the terrors had returned. Every time, he had to slowly breathe his way back to a normal heart rate. At least he was able to fall back to sleep. At least Pepsi was there with him the whole night.

Jim was outside cleaning the float valve of the stock tank when he heard the phone ring. Sprinting across the yard, he nearly tore the screen door off its hinges as he rushed inside. Answering the phone with heavy breaths, he struggled to hear the doctor identify himself on the other end of the line.

"Yes-this-is-Jim," he blurted out. "How's Tom?"

"Mr. McKee is one lucky man. The broken leg was the least of his worries. He has three broken ribs, a bruised lung, and a hairline fracture of his skull," the doctor said. "But he's alive and stable."

"He's gonna be okay, right?"

"Yes, he'll live, but he won't be going anywhere for several weeks. Are you his son?"

"No, just a friend helping with his horses."

"Is there any family we need to contact?"

Jim told the doctor no, but he said he would call his own parents to let them know of Tom's condition. "They're his closest friends," he explained. "They'll probably stop by the hospital today."

The doctor agreed that visitors would be fine as long as they didn't stay too long. Jim hung up the phone and leaned against the wall. So, Tom would live. What a tough old bird. Jim quickly dialed his parents' number.

His mom answered, and he tumbled headlong into recounting the incident and having to shoot Comanche, though he withheld the details of him being the cause of it all. "Mom, I'm not supposed to go into town till school starts, could you and Dad check in on Tom, and let me know how he's doing?"

"Of course, but do you need your father to come out and get you? I'm sure we can talk to the judge about making an exception, given what's happened."

"No, I want to stay out here and take care of Tom's place till he gets back. The judge doesn't need to know, does he?"

"Jim... I'll need to talk to your father. No promises. I'll go to the shop now, and then we'll go to check on Tom. We'll call you later today."

"Okay. Thanks."

"I love you."

"I love you too." Jim spoke the words without thinking, then realized he meant them.

Hanging up the phone, he wondered if he should call anyone else. He didn't know who to call at the Forest Service. He remembered that he and Tom were scheduled to make a supply run up to the trail camp tomorrow. He looked at the numbers and names scribbled on a pad of paper hanging from a nail on the wall near the phone. None looked familiar. Someone would have to take the supplies in. He had to call someone to cancel the run, didn't he?

Or did he? Jim knew how to saddle the horses and mules, drive the truck, load the panniers, and lead a string in the mountains. Why couldn't he do it? He rummaged through the drawer of an old desk in the TV room where Tom did his bookkeeping—often accompanied by a beer and lots of cursing. There, in an old cigar box, was the cash. Jim pulled out a couple fives, just enough to get gas—which meant he could do the run himself.

Jim spent the rest of the day getting ready. He checked the oil, brake fluid, and coolant levels in the stock truck and added a quart of oil, which was needed after every trip. Then he looked over all the Decker saddles for the pack mules, as well as his own saddle for Sil, making sure all the buckles and straps were sound. That task required the most time, pulling each saddle out and setting it on the hitching rail near the tack shed, and then meticulously examining each part. Dry leather was given a dose of saddle oil, and straps that looked questionable were replaced. While looking over Tom's saddle, he found the pistol in the saddlebag. The dried blood was black on the faded steel frame. Jim wiped as much of it off as he could, then took the pistol to the house. He left it on the dresser in Tom's bedroom. At almost two in the afternoon, he finished with all the tack and allowed himself a lunch break.

Afterwards, he went to the corral and caught Sil and the three mules he would use on the ride. One at a time, he led them out of the corral to the hitching rail where he brushed them. He closely examined their legs for cuts or injuries, even pulling up their hooves, as Tom had taught him, to ensure that all their shoes were still on and secure. Sil was the only animal of real concern. Her recent run through the timber had left her with several minor scrapes on her sides and one small cut on her front left leg. The cut looked good though, not oozing or puffy, and the scab was forming well. Jim decided that she would be okay, especially after a good day of rest. Besides, he needed a horse he could trust. He needed the big silver roan.

His work done, Jim sat on the porch with Pepsi by his side on the bench swing. The steel chains creaked as he pushed back and forth. As always, the wide valley stretched out to touch the distant mountains, golden fields contrasting with the dark evergreen forest climbing the steep slopes. He could see why Tom liked to sit there.

Almost two hours before sunset, Jim went inside and glanced at the chessboard. They'd paused a game the night before their trip. Jim had begged off, claiming he couldn't keep his eyes open. It was still Tom's turn to move. Yeah, Jim had been tired, but he'd had the old man on the run in this game, and he knew that Tom had been frustrated by that fact. Jim had only beaten him twice so far. He examined the board. He could have him in the next seven moves if Tom didn't protect his queen. That was assuming he would want to finish the game when he came home from the hospital.

A little after seven, the phone rang. It was Dad. His voice was calm, but Jim could tell he was measuring his words, holding some emotion back.

"Your mom and I visited Tom and talked with the doctor a bit. The good news is he'll be okay, but it was lucky you got him out of there when you did. They had to go in and stop some bleeding in his lung. That must have been one hell of a fall he took." Dad paused for a moment. "Your mother told me a little about what happened. About Comanche. Are you okay?"

"Yeah Dad, I'm okay. I need to run a string of supplies up to the trail crew tomorrow, but I'm sure I can do that. Do you think the judge will let me stay out here until Tom comes back?"

Dad was quiet in response. "I didn't talk with the judge. I wanted to talk to you first, to see if you could manage things out there. Hearing you're thinking of going into the mountains by yourself, I'm not so sure."

"I can do this, Dad."

"If you want, I'll have Zack watch the shop and I can ride up with you."

"I can do this. Really. I'll be alright." For several seconds Jim could only hear his own breath as he waited for his dad's reply.

"Alright, be smart and be safe," he said. "You call us immediately when you get back, you hear me?"

"Yes sir. I will."

The next morning, when Jim pulled up to the loading dock at Refrigerator Canyon, the Forest Service worker waiting in the pick-up truck with the supplies looked on in disbelief. Jim backed the truck up to the ramp and got out with Pepsi to start unloading Sil and the mules.

"Where's Tom?" the man asked.

"Had a horse roll. Tom broke his leg and a few ribs," Jim said as matter-of-fact as Tom would have. "He's in the hospital in Helena." Jim's focus was on getting the animals unloaded and tied up, not on chatting.

"You taking this string up yourself?"

"Yep," Jim said. He glanced at the man, making eye contact.

"Okay, I'll help you load up."

Together the two men stuffed the panniers with a variety of cans, boxes, and bags meant to feed the trail crew for the next week. Jim lifted each pannier to ensure that the weight was evenly distributed. He shuffled items from one pack to the other to level out the weight, then closed the panniers and, with the help of the Forest Service worker, hefted them up to the pack saddles. Jim walked the string and pushed each pannier to ensure they were stable and their straps were tight. He tightened and retightened every damn cinch. Following a final check, Jim mounted Sil and the string was off on their long ride up to the camp. Just before slipping into the narrow rock canyon, Jim turned around and gave a quick wave toward the Forest Service truck.

Once clear of the canyon, Jim felt himself settle into the motion of Sil's steps. His left hand stayed on the lead rope, which was looped over the saddle horn. He could feel every bit of tension in it as the string headed up the trail. Every few minutes Jim looked back and checked on Cecil, Maggie, and Bart to ensure that the packs were centered. When he wasn't looking at the trail ahead or at the string behind, he was noting Pepsi's position. He realized his head was always moving. Tom did the same, always watchful, always mindful of the string. He understood that now.

The mules kept in line and in pace with Sil, the years of packing for Tom showing in their stable, easy-going gate. Jim felt an odd peace even with the weighty duties of the ride. The task, the horses and mules, and the mountains all helped to dampen the memory of the accident.

After three hours, they reached the camp. The trail crews were out working, as always, leaving just the cook, cook's helper, and Roy. The trail boss' greeting was less than friendly as he stormed out of his tent.

"What the hell are you doing here alone?" he demanded. "Where's Tom?"

"He was hurt marking trail Tuesday," Jim said as he dismounted and tied Sil to a tree. He didn't bother to look at Roy, who towered just a few feet away.

"How? Where?"

"A couple miles east of the first basecamp. Horses spooked and got into some rocks. Tom's horse rolled; Tom got banged up real bad. He's at Saint Pete's in Helena." Jim hooked the left stirrup of his saddle up on the horn so he could loosen the latigo of Sil's cinch.

"Horses hurt?" Roy had simmered down. He seemed genuinely concerned.

Jim stopped working for a moment and looked at the man. "Comanche broke his leg."

255

Roy muttered something under his breath as he glanced down to the ground. He kicked softly at the dirt. "Damn, Tom loved that horse, as mean and ornery as that pale beast was."

"Yeah, he did." Jim turned back to the work of tending to the pack mules.

"That still doesn't answer my question. What are *you* doing here?" Roy's head was cocked to one side. The glint of his cold blue eyes was barely visible between the slits of his eyelids and the shadow of his hat.

Jim looked at him—not in fear, not even in anger, but simply with a steady gaze, one man to another.

"My job," he said, "I'm doing my job."

CHAPTER 23

"Damn it, woman, I don't care what the doctor ordered, there ain't no way I'm letting you stick that thing up my ass!" Tom yelled from his hospital bed. Even with his leg in a cast and his head spinning and throbbing, he was more cantankerous than usual. The portly old nurse, wearing a white dress and apron and a humorless scowl, stood next to him with her hands on her hips.

"Mr. McKee, you've thrown up twice already today, we need to give you this suppository so you can hold down some food!"

"I'll puke a lung before I let you defile me, you evil woman!"

"If I have to, I will call the orderlies."

"You just call them and we'll see how things turn out." Tom glared up from the bed, hoping like hell she didn't call his bluff. He was in no condition to fight anyone. Even those pansy orderlies.

"It will be a great relief when you are transferred to the VA!" the nurse said and stormed out of the room.

"I'll be happy to go," he shouted after her, "that way I won't have to see your hideous face, you old battle axe!"

Tom grimaced. The rant had triggered that throbbing pain in his head again. Even after a week, his head still hurt if he moved too quickly. His bruised lungs seemed fit enough to holler. But they still hadn't let him have a cigarette, which didn't help his mood any. Tom's tirade didn't benefit the aching or the dizziness, but he had no regrets. His tolerance for being bedridden had reached its limits.

Memory of his arrival at the hospital was spotty at best. He remembered the horse ride down, and he could recall Jim helping him into the truck. The last recollection he had was that of the door slamming and feeling Pepsi nuzzle his left hand. After that he had only vague images of being carried into the hospital, nurses removing his clothing, and waking up two days later in a hospital gown, lying in a bed with an overly-starched white curtain surrounding him.

The pounding between his ears was worse than any hangover or shell shock he'd ever experienced. For the next three days, he hadn't had the energy to resist the changing of IVs or to argue about having to piss and crap in a bedpan. He just wanted his head to stop hurting.

The morphine helped, but not as much as the doctors thought it did. Having been wounded twice in the war, Tom had taken more than his fair share of the opiate, and his body had grown tolerant with each dose. He didn't want to ask for more than what they were already giving him though, because the misery of the pain was better than how he felt on the morphine, at least during the times he was awake.

The drug set his mind adrift in strange realms, and his body felt as though it was melting. He was repeatedly visited by the witch from The Wizard of Oz. The green-faced hag would fly into the room and hover over his bed, cackling at him. Tom had experienced such hallucinations before. It was for this very reason he didn't want more of the drug. That and he knew of too many other vets who had fallen prey to the drug's all-consuming ways. He welcomed it only when he truly needed it, so he could sleep. Tom quickly learned to allow himself to retreat into sleep right after the nurse injected the drug into his IV. The sting of the painkiller in his veins was worth the benefit. With each pump of his heart, the drug spread. Soon the anguish ceased, allowing him to close his eyes without seeing Comanche and without feeling as though a grenade was detonating inside his cranium. Sleep helped, lying entirely still in bed helped, and the occasional visits from Frank and Abby and his neighbor, Walt, helped. Dealing with the head nurse did not. Recalling the events that precipitated his current state was not helpful either.

For two days now, Tom had tried to piece things together. Why had the horses panicked as they did? In his foggy memories, Tom saw Jim and Sil jump the log. No problem there. Then he saw Moonlight. That's when it started: Moonlight had bucked, but her Decker was out of sorts, high on her shoulders. Why? The cinches, it had to be that. The cinches had come loose. Or had they never been tightened? That lazy, good-for-nothing bastard! How many times had he told the boy to check the cinches? That was the only explanation as to why Moonlight bucked, causing the chain of events that led all the way to Comanche breaking his leg. Had his leg even been broken? Tom began to wonder if Jim would have known a broken leg from a sprain. He feared that Comanche had been shot for no good reason. His anger festered the more time he spent thinking about the accident. Alone in that bed, the rage grew, to the point that he took it out on the first person he could justify. Today it had been the nurse with that nasty ass pill.

A woman's voice—not the nurse—pulled him out of his stewing. "You know Tom, I could hear your foul language clear out on the street."

Well shit, if it wasn't Abby Redmond. There she stood, with Frank, in the doorway to the room. A look of mock disapproval crossed her face. It faded quickly into a smile. Tom didn't know what to think of them anymore. The Redmonds. Loyal friends. Good people. Parents of the bastard who killed his horse. The rage wrenched in his gut. He remembered that allowing Jim onto the trail crew and taking him into his home had been his own idea. Holding a firm poker face, Tom talked himself down internally. Frank and Abby hadn't been there when Comanche died. They weren't responsible for that.

"I'm sorry," he said. "I'm just a bit irritable is all. They're stickin' and pokin' me every which way. Can't get a wink of sleep without someone coming in and violating me. Wonder if they ain't trying to kill me off at times."

"I think you've done a good enough job of trying to get yourself killed already. These folks are just trying to slow down the process," Frank said and shook his hand. "If your temper is any indicator, you seem to be feeling better."

Tom glanced away, not wanting to reveal the rage still simmering. "I'm fair. Head hurts still, and I can't stand up without the world startin' to buck on me. Leg's got another couple weeks in this itch blanket they call a cast. How's my spread? Pepsi and the stock?" Tom asked the same every time the pair visited.

"They're fine. We stopped by your place yesterday to bring Jim some food and to let Vi see the horses," Abby said. She gave Tom a hug and quick kiss on his cheek then opened the blinds to let in a bit more light. She said she wasn't staying. She had to leave to pick Vi up from piano lessons. She'd come back to pick up Frank a little later. Abby gave her husband a kiss on the cheek then headed out the door. "Try and rest Tom," she said, "for the sake of the nurses at least."

"You in pain?" Frank pulled up a chair next to the bed. "You seem out of sorts today."

Tom didn't answer, his mind still mulling over the specifics of the accident, the anger about the truth.

Frank leaned back in the chair. "I talked with the judge last week and told him all that had happened. Everything is okay. Jim's sentence is complete this coming weekend with school starting Monday. Judge said Jim could stay out at your place until you get back. He can drive himself to school. I finally got his truck up and running."

"That won't be necessary," Tom said, keeping his emotions in check. He didn't want that brat near his animals for even a day longer. "I'll call Walt, from down the road, and he can come take care of the place till I get back."

"You sure? Jim said it won't be no trouble."

"I'm sure. But, I'd prefer that Jim not be around when I come back."

Frank was silent, obviously shocked. Then he leaned forward in his chair with a hard look. "What the hell is that supposed to mean?"

"I think he's done enough damage," Tom said. It was time to call a spade a spade. "So, it's best if he not be there when I get home."

"Damage? Jim saved your life, getting you down the mountain. He's kept up with supply runs this past week. He's not getting paid for that contract, you are. I'd say you owe him your thanks."

"He killed Comanche."

"It was an accident. Your horse's leg was broken. What the hell else was he supposed to do?" Frank shook his head then walked to the window.

"Was it an accident?" Tom said to Frank's back. "I know my horses, and they don't just get to bucking. Jim did something. And was Comanche's leg even broke? I doubt that kid would know a broken leg if he had one himself."

Frank turned from the window, his eyes wide in disbelief. "You stubborn fool." He took a step toward the bed. "Jim told me all about the accident. Comanche had bone sticking out. That boy did exactly what you would have done in the same situation. He did it, and then he got your cantankerous, ungrateful ass out of the mountains."

Tom matched Frank's determined glare, neither willing to look away. "I don't want him on my ranch when I get there. That's final."

Frank's lips tightened. His right fist clenched. After several seconds he gave a sharp nod. "Fine, he'll be out of there this week-end when the court order expires."

Tom dropped his chin slightly—that was as much movement as he cared to waste on showing his approval. Then he looked out the window to the parking lot. He had nothing more to say.

"I've been friends with you a long time. This is the first time I've wanted to punch you. My son saved your life. He's owed more than you're giving him." Frank grabbed his chair and slid it back to the wall none too gently. He shook his head in disgust then put on his hat and left.

Frank and Abby didn't visit again following that confrontation—not in the next two days that Tom remained at St. Pete's and not after he was transferred to the VA hospital either. Once at the VA, he could rest more comfortably and more importantly, he had access to the outdoors, meaning he could enjoy a cigarette from the makings that his neighbor, Walt, delivered. Tom didn't blame the Redmonds. He wasn't even angry at Frank and Abby. But he couldn't just go and ignore the facts. Jim was the reason he was beat up, and he was the reason Comanche was dead.

Two weeks of recovery at the VA were all that Tom could toler-ate. At least it was all the time that the doctors were willing to put up with him. With the cast removed and a rubber stamp check-up saying he was well enough to be discharged, Tom was granted release.

Walt was kind enough to give Tom a ride home from the VA. Upon arrival, Pepsi danced and barked in excitement as Tom opened the passenger door of Walt's truck. The soda pop dog leapt onto Tom's lap, not bothering to wait for him to exit the vehicle. After several minutes of licking and whining, he convinced her to hop down so he could get out of the truck and make his was to the house. The five-yard walk to the porch was slow going. The cane kept him upright but did nothing for his speed. Though the cane was clearly needed for now, he hoped to ditch it much sooner than the doctors had prescribed. Once Tom made it to the front porch, Walt made sure he had everything he needed and that the horses were cared for, then he left Tom to the merciful solitude of his ranch.

Carefully lowering himself onto the porch swing, Tom patted the cushion next to him. Pepsi jumped up and curled up at his side, her head resting on his leg, Tom looked across the drive to the corral. He counted each animal, mouthing their names as he visually made his way down the line. All were accounted for, all but Comanche.

CHAPTER 24

APRIL 14, 1966

"Jim, don't forget to dust Trigger," the manager of DeVore's Saddlery called out from behind the counter.

"I won't sir," Jim said as he finished sweeping the floor near the shelves of cowboy boots. Putting away the push broom, Jim grabbed the large feather duster and headed to the front of the store, where a full-size plastic palomino horse modeled the latest in western saddle design.

The equine mannequin, affectionately named Trigger by the store staff, was now the closest Jim got to anything that resembled a horse. Cleaning away the thin layer of dust and the occasional cobweb, he couldn't help but miss the times he'd brushed down Tom's horses after a long ride. With his typical Saturday morning duties nearly complete, Jim looked forward to finishing at the store and then heading out back to the saddle shop, where he'd help the master saddle maker with his craft.

Having been banished by Tom eight months ago, there were few options that allowed Jim to be around the smell and feel of horse tack and to chat with people who lived the horseman's lifestyle. At first he'd been shocked, angry when his dad told him of Tom's demand.

"You're gonna have to give Tom some time to sort this out. You can't take it personally, son. It's just who he is." Dad had come out to the ranch the weekend before Jim was to start his senior year. Jim's anger was intense; he'd looked to punch a hole in the nearest wall. But he didn't give into the rage. Leaving Dad standing on the front porch, Jim walked over to the corral. Once the horses and mules came to the fence, the anger waned. It had to.

The horses both calmed him and reminded him of the horrible reality: Comanche was gone. After several minutes, that cold fact gave him a bit of an understanding of Tom's decision. He didn't want to leave the ranch, the horses, Pepsi, the constant sense of purpose. But it wasn't his land. It wasn't his choice. Jim conceded. He'd returned to Helena the Sunday before school started.

Jim discovered he could use the anger. He headed into the school year determined, ready to prove that he wasn't the same person he had been a year ago. Every one of Jim's greetings or responses to a person of authority now included a 'sir' or 'ma'am', homework was no longer avoided but finished early, chores were done quickly, and invitations to parties with friends were declined. Everyone had thought he was destined to be worthless. A drunk. A criminal. He quit fulfilling their expectations with a vengeance. He settled in well to this disciplined existence. Still, he longed to be around the horses, to take Sil out for a ride, and to work on the saddles.

It was his Mom's idea that he apply for a job at DeVore's next to the Ford garage. It was only a few blocks from his father's stone shop. Every day after school and each Saturday, Jim could be found at DeVore's, sweeping, serving customers, and working in the saddle shop. Though it occupied his free time and provided spending money, DeVore's was only a temporary patch over the hole left in his life, a hole that could only be filled by riding.

With essentially no spare time, Jim's senior year rushed by. In April, everyone in his graduating class was scheduled to visit with guidance counselors. Jim attended the usual presentation and heard about the options: college, trade schools, or the military. He didn't mention anything to his guidance counselor, though he had decided the direction for his life six months prior. There was only one person he wanted to talk with first, the one person who had cut him off.

That weekend, in mid-April, with both fear and determination, Jim drove out to Tom's place. The spring rains rolling over the divide toward the west had left the drive a rutted mud pit. He parked as close to the house as he could. Tom was out, sitting on his porch swing, having a smoke and petting Pepsi. The downpour obviously prevented any work from being done. Making a quick dash to the cover of the porch, Jim removed his hat and shook it a few times. Through a haze of tobacco smoke, Tom's cold eyes pierced Jim.

"Afternoon, Tom." Jim greeted his old mentor. Wind-driven rain bombarded the ground and porch roof.

"What brings you out this way?"

"No reason, just figured it had been a while." Jim glanced through the rain and toward the corral then looked back at Tom. "I thought, well, I was wondering if I could ask you something." There was so much Jim wanted to ask: why he had been told to leave and why any effort to come out again had been rebuffed. For now, he set those questions aside to stick to the main reason for his trip. "Mind if I sit down?"

"Go ahead," Tom grunted and motioned to a chair in the corner. Jim grabbed the chair and pulled it close to the bench swing. As he sat, Pepsi jumped off the bench and trotted over to him. She propped her front paws on his lap, licking his face in greeting. As he petted Pepsi, Jim noticed Tom's glare.

"Pepsi. Come here," Tom patted the cushion on the bench next to him. His stern voice made Pepsi jump. But she immediately returned to Tom. "What's your question kid?"

"Why did you join the Army?" Jim probed.

Tom raised his eyebrows, causing his old Stetson to lift slightly. There was the faintest sigh. "Seemed like the thing to do at the time."

"When you joined the Devil's Brigade, was it the same? Just seemed like the thing to do?"

"Mostly. It was special duty. I fit what they were looking for, and it paid well."

"Was that all?"

Tom took several drags from his cigarette, the tip glowing red with each pull.

"I hated the boredom of being a soldier. It was all too mundane. Everyone looked the same, acted the same, and did the same job. The Force was something special. I knew that if I made it, I wouldn't be just a soldier, I would be elite. I liked that idea."

Jim liked that idea as well. "You told me that you saw the Green Berets once, and that they were elite."

"Yep, they're a different breed, for sure."

"Do you think I could be one?"

Tom looked at Jim, removing the cigarette from his lips. His mouth tightened as he stared out to the corral. "It takes a man of honor to do a job like that, one that others can trust."

The rain slowed and finally stopped. Mountain storms always passed quick. A patch of blue sky appeared through the clouds. Tom's words smoldered between them.

"The accident was my fault," Jim said. There, it was out.

Tom was silent. A slow drag on his cigarette caused the end to glow bright.

"I didn't tighten Moonlight's cinch like I was supposed to. I knew it was loose, but I figured it wouldn't matter since she had a light load. I'm the reason you were hurt and the reason that Comanche is dead. I'm sorry. It was my fault."

Jim waited for Tom to stand up and slam him into the wall like he had that first day. Even though he knew he was stronger than Tom and could fight him off, he'd already decided that he wouldn't. He would let Tom exact his revenge in exchange for the life of his horse. But Tom didn't move. His eyes fixed on the corral as his left hand petted Pepsi. Come on Tom, do something. The old man remained still.

"You feel mighty brave getting that off your chest, don't ya?" he said. "Been burning at you all this time, I suppose. Probably think you deserve a big handshake and pat on the back, don't ya?"

"No, I just…"

"You think I didn't know it was your fault? I figured it out last summer. After all this time you just now get the balls to come out and tell me?" Tom flicked the remnant of his cigarette into a rusty coffee can near the door. "You're a coward and a liar. You ain't got what it takes to be a soldier, let alone a Green Beret."

Jim had braced himself for a physical attack. He hadn't anticipated that Tom could hurt him in a far more painful way. Standing up, Jim walked to the edge of the porch. Shaking, he reached into his pocket. He returned to the chair and set the patch and Italian coin he had taken last summer on the now-empty seat.

Tom looked at them, laughing and shaking his head. "And you're a goddamned thief too. Get out of my sight. I never want to see your face again."

Jim gave a final glance to Pepsi and one last look toward Sil and the other horses and mules in the corral. They were the only goodbyes he could offer. His welcome had been more than worn out. Walking to his truck, Jim kept his eyes on the horses and mules. They were huddled together, the sun causing steam to rise from their rain-soaked hides. He didn't look back at the house, at Tom. Instead, as he drove down the drive, he looked at the herd, wishing them a silent farewell.

CHAPTER 25
SEPTEMBER 26, 1969

C ancer. At least that's what the doctor had told Tom that morning. Lung cancer, specifically, and it had spread so much that he, at best, had twelve months to live. The chronic cough had started over a year ago. It wasn't till he became winded doing chores that he bothered to schedule a visit to the VA. It had been just over four years since Comanche died.

That evening the reality of the news gripped him as he lay upon his bed in the darkness. He moved his foot, hoping to feel the familiar, comforting warmth of Pepsi, but she wasn't there. Tom knew he wouldn't find her, but his foot still tried every night. The dog's ashes sat upon his dresser along with Tom's pictures. First Comanche. Then Pepsi just six months ago. A neighbor friend had brought over a half-broke gelding for Tom to work with. The beloved soda pop dog had caught a hoof kick from the unruly beast. Losing her was as painful as it had been to lose Comanche, worse even, because Tom hadn't watched Comanche die. But he'd had to rush his broken Pepsi to the vet, only to watch her die on the truck seat next to him.

He couldn't bring himself to bury her, wanting to keep her close, if only as ashes. Who had ever heard of cremating a dog?

Not knowing how else to accomplish this, Tom had bribed the funeral home operator. So there the dog sat now, on the dresser, still keeping watch over him.

In recent weeks, he'd actually been thinking of getting another pup, but today's news put a stop to those plans. Given how quickly he had gone downhill physically, he wasn't sure how much longer he could take care of himself, let alone a new dog. Then there was the matter of the horses and mules. What to do with them? In macabre examination, Tom considered all the tasks that needed to be completed before he lost the ability to do them. As long as he wasn't sleeping tonight, he might as well make use of the time. Yes, he thought about ending it all, taking out the pistol and making it quick, but that wasn't his style. No, he would finish this ride as best he could, even though he knew that this bronco couldn't be broke.

Of his list of things to do, making sure the horses and mules would be cared for was at the top. He could start making calls in the morning to see about selling them. There were plenty of packers who would love to have such reliable animals. Just the house and the land would remain, along with his personal belongings. Tom laughed: never had he thought he would be required to account for such things. Yet here he was, in the darkness of his room, pondering just that. The fearful truth of it all wrapped around him as if he was already in the grave. He could feel the dirt pouring in around him. Given all he had gone through in life, he hadn't feared death much. He had figured it would come so quickly it wouldn't matter. But that wasn't the case now. Death was on its way more like the cold of winter—there was no stopping it, but it sure wasn't sudden. Tom couldn't help but wonder about the specifics, what would happen at the end.

The sleepless night left Tom drained when the sun finally rose. Everything took so long to do nowadays: getting dressed, shaving, making coffee. His despair smothered what little appetite for food he had. The slow walk to the corral, with the required rest on the hay bales, at least allowed him to sit quietly in the company of his beloved horses and mules. After catching his breath, he would feed them, until another break was needed. Part of Tom wanted to defy death, to hold onto his life, his home, and his animals as tightly as he could. Would he be permitted to die at home? If he couldn't do that then he wanted to retreat to the mountains and die in a beautiful place of his choosing. In his mind, he heard a cowboy drawl, "*Well, there are some things a man just can't run away from.*" Tom had always liked that John Wayne quote but not now. As much as he wanted to run for the hills, he knew that he was only thinking of himself and not the herd. The doctor had been very blunt about what Tom's final time on this earth would be like. The grim process would leave the herd uncared for. He couldn't do that; he wouldn't.

The hour he now spent, tossing hay over the fence, would have taken him five minutes just a couple years ago. The need to rest and, occasionally, shed a few tears while petting the herd demanded extra time. With feeding done, Tom made the slow return to the house. The screen door had barely closed when his legs gave out. He seized the chain that held the porch swing and gasped as he pulled himself to the bench so he could sit down. Catching his breath, he looked out at the horses and mules eating and milling around the corral.

Doctor's orders be damned, Tom rolled a cigarette and lit it. He relished the sharp familiar taste until it triggered the cough. It always did that lately. He reached his hand over to where Pepsi would rest, but felt only the wool blanket stapled to the wood slats. The cough hurt greatly. For the remainder of his cigarette, Tom just let the smoke linger in his mouth and then escape into the cool fall air.

When he felt strong enough, he got up and made his way to the kitchen, moving a chair over to the phone. Sitting down, he thumbed through his pad of numbers until he found the one he hadn't dialed in years. He paused, wondering if he should make the call and whether they would even talk to him. His didn't want any damned sympathy; it only seemed they deserved to learn the news from him rather than reading about it in the paper or hearing it through the rumor mill. With pride swallowed, Tom dialed Frank Redmond.

"Morning, Frank. This is Tom McKee. Sorry to bother you on a Sunday."

"Well, Tom. Been a while. To what do I owe this pleasure?"

"Yeah, I apologize that it's been so long. I was wondering if you and Abby might come out for a visit? I need to talk with you about something, if you don't mind."

"Of course, is everything alright?"

"Yes, I'd just prefer to talk in person."

Frank excused himself to talk to Abby. Tom could hear the muffled conversation but couldn't make out the words. When Frank's voice returned, he said they'd be happy to come out that very afternoon. That was fine in Tom's book. Best to get this conversation done soon.

After hanging up, Tom began calling all the packers he knew to see if anyone might be interested in buying his mules and all the saddle horses and their tack, minus Sil and Moonlight. He would hold out on selling those two until he had a chance to tell Frank and Abby the news and offer the horses to them. During the calls, Tom never told the potential buyer why he was selling and never implied he was selling all of them. "Oh, I'm just thinning the herd a bit," he said over and over. He kept the calls short, not wanting to be chatty with anyone. He didn't want to break down, and he didn't want anyone to know the truth just yet. Tom simply wanted to ensure that every animal would have a place to live with good riders and packers, and no one buying them out of guilt or sympathy.

It was nearly four in the afternoon when Frank's car pulled off the highway and onto Tom's dirt road. As soon as the car stopped, Vi leapt out through the back passenger door and ran to the corral. Good God, she was a young woman now. But, she climbed the fence and jumped down to say hi to the horses just as she always had. Tom stayed seated on his porch swing, not out of disrespect, but only because he was too tired to rise to his feet. Frank and Abby laughed at Vi then headed straight to the house. Frank held the screen door for Abby, who greeted Tom. Friendly, but cautious. Couldn't blame her. Tom didn't get up.

The Redmond couple seemed older. It had been four years. Surely it was a strain to raise a teenage daughter, run a business, and have a son fighting overseas. All those things must have exacted their costs in terms of gray hairs. Tom hadn't been in contact with Frank or Abby, but he'd heard news from other horsemen who frequented DeVore's. He knew that Jim had joined the Army and even managed to make it into the Green Berets.

Frank shook Tom's hand, a stilted and brief gesture, more like meeting a stranger. Abby, who used to greet Tom with a hug and a kiss on the cheek, stood back near the screen door.

"She sure has grown up," Tom nodded towards Vi who mingled with the horses as if she hadn't missed a day.

"Yes, we were lucky she was around today," Abby said. "She's usually off with her friends." Abby brightened talking about Vi, but her arms were crossed tightly across her chest. She narrowed her eyes in scrutiny when she looked at him. Curiosity? Spite? Maybe both. He deserved it. Perhaps he could set things straight now.

"Pull up a chair," Tom said, then coughed, "please."

"Is everything alright?" Abby asked.

"Have a seat and I'll tell you." Tom wanted Frank and Abby to hear the news first. Despite the last four years of division, his connection to their family was strong, going back over twenty-five years. He'd certainly strained their friendship, maybe even destroyed it. He hoped that wasn't the case and that he could mend things once and for all. He looked at them. Well, time to dive in.

"I'm dying," he said, "cancer. Doc says I've got a year if I'm lucky." He let the words sink in. He looked away from them, to the mountains, but out of the corner of his eye, he saw Abby shake her head in disbelief, heard her sharp inhale. Frank leaned forward, as if he hadn't heard correctly.

"Isn't there anything they can do? Surgery or something?" Frank asked.

"Nope. They could try and cut it out, but they'd have to gut me like a fish," Tom said. He looked back at Frank then. "That's why you're here. I need to sell my stock. I can't care for them anymore, and I wanted to give you first dibs on Sil and Moonlight. I'll take whatever you think's fair, so long as they have a good home."

Frank looked at Abby, her mouth still open slightly in shock.

"I know I've been an ass. I can't change that at this point. I'm trying to set things right and trying to make sure my stock are cared for. The others are spoken for but—" Tom swallowed hard and composed himself, "but I know that Vi loved those two horses. And Jim did too."

"Tom, that's a thoughtful offer," Frank said. "I'm just not sure—"

"We'll take them," Abby interrupted. "We'll find a place to keep them, so don't worry about that."

"Abby, how will we?"

"We'll make it work. You've been talking about getting some property outside of town, maybe even a part of the old ranch. Well, here's as good a reason as any to move on that. Besides, you know how much those horses mean to Vivian and Jim. And to Tom."

Frank gave a helpless smile and nodded in agreement. "We'll do it then. Can I have a few weeks to sort things out?"

Tom's single nod settled the deal. There. That was done. There was one more matter to discuss. "How's Jim?" he asked. "I hear he went and made himself a Green Beret." Tom inquired. The kid had made it into an elite unit. Believe it or not, Tom didn't mind being proven wrong now and again.

Frank shared a little about Jim's time in Vietnam. "In all honesty, he doesn't tell us much. He can't," Frank said.

Tom expected no less given the unit he was a part of.

Abby jumped in. "Jim did want us to pass along a message to you, from a letter we got a couple weeks ago."

"Did he now? What would that be?"

"He said to tell you that you were right about the stains, and that you would know what that meant."

Tom's mind rushed back to the night by the campfire. That awful night. The boy hunched over the dried blood on his jeans. Tom nodded to Abby and said nothing. Frank and Abby looked at each other, but didn't ask for clarification, not that he would have offered any. They wouldn't understand. Few could.

A hush smothered the conversation. Eventually, Vi's giggles and trotting hoofbeats broke the silence. The three turned their attention to the corral. Vi had climbed aboard Moonlight and was riding her bareback around the enclosure.

"If there is anything we can do, let us know," Frank said, still watching his daughter. "We want to help."

"I know. I'll ask when it's needed. If you don't mind, I'd prefer not to have to tell Vi myself."

"We'll tell her," Abby promised. "I'll write Jim, too, unless you want to do that yourself?"

"No, go ahead. I've never been good at correspondence. You two know that."

Tom and Frank and Abby were silent once more, watching Vi ride around the corral. It might have been ten minutes. Or an hour. Who was counting? At some point, Abby stood and walked over to Tom. She squeezed his shoulder and kissed him on his cheek. She looked down and discretely dabbed at her eyes with a hanky.

"I'll pray for you," she whispered.

Tom didn't see how that would help any, but he smiled at her. "Thank you," he said, "it means a lot."

Frank came over and shook his hand, a little more heartfelt this time. The Redmonds left the porch and called Vi in from the corral. Soon the dust of their departure hung lazily in the breeze-less air.

CHAPTER 26
DECEMBER 3, 1969

"The war is over for you, Sergeant," the doctor smiled and patted Jim on the shoulder. Jim fought through the fog of post-operation stupor to comprehend the words. Before he could respond, the doctor had moved on to another patient in the long, narrow recovery room of the 12th Evacuation Hospital near Cu Chi, Vietnam. His vision still foggy, Jim looked down at his body, his right leg, his chest, and both arms all heavily bandaged. He wrestled with his memory, attempting to recall the events that had landed him here.

It had been a quiet night at the A-Camp when one of the perimeter trip flares went off. It was triggered by sappers who were attempting to reach the barbed wire that made up one of many layers of camp defenses. Almost immediately, flashes of rifles were visible in the heavy vegetation just outside the edge of the base, about one hundred fifty yards away. Jim remembered running to a foxhole to help defend the base, when mortar rounds exploded around him, tearing through the dark. After that, Jim had only flickers of memory.

One of his teammates had yelled for a medic. He recalled brief flashes of the helicopter ride to the evac hospital. The olive drab fatigues of the soldiers who carried his litter into the surgery Quonset hut. The light blue gowns and caps of the surgical staff. The beautiful blue eyes of a nurse who tried to calm him as she held an anesthesia mask on him. Her surgical garb had hidden her face and hair, but her eyes and sweet voice convinced him to stop struggling till blackness overtook him.

Coming out of anesthesia, he felt panicked and confused. The recovery room nurse, with her short blond hair and green eyes, helped Jim to focus, to breathe, to cease struggling against the bandages and restraints that held his body still. Only after Jim showed signs that he was well out of the anesthesia and no longer fighting, did she leave to attend to the other patients.

Still groggy, Jim looked around at the interior of the stretched building with its curved roof, beds lining both walls, and a narrow walkway down the middle. The center footpath was large enough to allow a nurse to pass by with her stainless-steel cart. All the beds were occupied by men in similar postoperative states. Some were missing limbs. Some bodies were so bandaged they looked like mummies. Jim heard someone moaning in pain. The metal cart wheels hurried across the room and the moaning ceased. A shot of morphine. Or some other drug. For thirty minutes Jim's mind cleared and he became more aware of his surroundings. It was then that the doctor came and delivered the strange news before hurrying off on his rounds.

"Nurse," Jim called out. His voice was so hoarse. "Nurse?"

The green-eyed lovely came into his field of view.

"The doc says the war is over," he slurred.

She chuckled. "For you dear," she said, "your injuries are the golden ticket. You're going home."

"No, I need to get back to my unit. Just have them patch me up, I need to get back."

"We did patch you up, soldier, but you're still going home." The nurse explained, in fair detail, all that had been done to try to make Jim whole again. The prognosis wasn't great, but it was better than it could have been. The damage to his arms was minor, comparatively, several shrapnel fragments having been taken from each arm and one small artery repaired. The three penetrations within his torso had perforated his bowel and nicked his liver, but all of that was survivable. Jim's leg hadn't fared so well. It was broken in two places with severed tendons. Even after being repaired, he would always walk with a limp. It was also probable that he would never regain the ability to run. Other injuries included burns to his arms and neck. "Those will leave scars," the nurse said, "but over time they shouldn't be too noticeable."

To hell with the scars. Those didn't matter. But not being able to run? If he couldn't run, he couldn't fight, and if he couldn't fight, then he couldn't return to his unit. He was, indeed, done, only two years into his Green Beret career.

"What now?" he asked.

"Stateside."

"Where?"

"Your rehab will take a couple of months. You'll probably be at the Naval station in Chicago or one of the others back east."

"Any chance the doc can get me sent to Fort Harrison in Montana?"

"He'd have to find out if they provide the rehab you need. Is that close to home?"

"Yeah, I'm from Helena. If someone could make that happen, I'd really appreciate it."

"No promises, but I'll talk to the doc." She jotted a note in his chart, patted his hand, and then turned toward another patient. Another one moaning.

"Hey nurse? One more thing. Who's handling my footlocker?"

"Your C.O. will handle that. All your belongings will be on the flight back to the States. Is there something you need?"

"Yeah, there's a Bible my mom sent with me. If I don't come home with it she'll make me come back for it."

She smiled. "One of us will call your C.O. and make sure they get that for you. None of us want you coming back here again."

For the next ten days, Jim lay in the hospital at Cu Chi while his wounds were left open to prevent infection. Jim flirted as best he could with the nurses, but most politely told him to save his strength. The green-eyed nurse who had greeted him after surgery at least spoke with him when time permitted. She offered him her first name after two days of pestering: Samantha, from Minnesota. She worked the twelve-hour night shift. One night, while most of the patients slept, Jim was wide awake. He heard the cart wheels squeaking as Samantha walked by.

"Hey Samantha?" Jim called out, ignoring Army protocols about addressing her as Lieutenant given she was an officer.

"Are you in pain?" she whispered, not wanting to wake the other patients.

"No, just bored. I hate being bored." He kept his voice quiet like hers. Really, most of the other guys were asleep with the help of heavy doses of painkillers. A little conversation wasn't going to wake them.

"Try to sleep."

"Can't. I keep thinking of home."

"Montana, isn't it?" She sat on the edge of the bed. "Is it nice there?"

"Yeah, not flat like it is here. Not humid or hot either. There are mountains all around. Big blue sky with lots of places to ride horses and get lost in."

"That sounds wonderful. I've never ridden a horse before."

"Really? Well let me get up and running, and you can come out to visit. I'll give you a riding lesson."

"You have horses of your own?"

"I do now," he said, feeling suddenly ashamed at the brag. A letter from Mom a couple months ago had informed him about Tom. Jim explained the situation to Samantha. It came out so sad. He didn't want her to feel sorry for him. He wanted her to ask for his address, to really look him up after she got back to the States. He tried to lighten the tone. "My folks bought two of the horses, Sil and Moonlight. They're big, tame mares, gentle as can be and perfect for a first time rider like yourself."

"They sound nice. I'm sorry to hear about your friend."

"Yeah, me too," Jim said, though he wondered if the word friend still applied. He knew Tom was a stubborn man, but Jim had never expected the anger Tom held to spill over to his parents. For four years he had shut them out. Jim hoped he never became that stubborn.

"Well, you'll be home soon enough," Samantha said. "In a few more days they'll close the wounds, and then you can be transported. What will you do when you get back?"

"I'm going to run," he said, daring her to counter him. "And I'm going to ride horses again."

"Jim... I don't want you to get your hopes up," she said, her sweet face full of concern. "I've read your chart. You might be better off accepting things as they are."

"I've never been too good at that. Besides, if you don't like something, you change it. It's just like riding a horse that swallows its head and gets to buckin." Jim remembered the life lesson Tom had interjected while he had been learning to ride.

"What do you mean?"

"When a horse goes bronc, you've got a few choices: you can grab the horn like a city dude, step off like a coward, or rein, spur, and get rattled, and see how the ride ends," Jim said and winked at her. "I'm gonna ride this one out and see how it ends."

Samantha patted Jim's shoulder, told him to get some sleep. He might have no chances with that gal, but Jim was sure he'd run someday. Thoughts of being on horseback again made sleeping easy, even with the pain. Anticipating his homecoming proved a more effective opiate than anything a syringe could deliver.

The journey from Vietnam was a long one, starting in Saigon and continuing to Japan. From there, Jim headed to Hawaii, then on to Chicago, where he stayed for three weeks of rehab while the government figured out where to send him next. Yet another Christmas that he had to spend away from home. It was with Jim's consistent encouragement—or antagonizing, as the doctors called it—that he was finally transferred to Fort Harrison in Helena on the eighth day of the new year. He would finish his recovery there, near family and friends, and near the mountains he missed so dearly.

Once back in Helena, Jim was allowed to stay home with his parents and sister. He was glad to be there, though navigating the narrow stairs to his room on crutches proved to be a struggle, especially with Timber, the family dog, insisting on following him everywhere he went.

His first day of physical therapy at Fort Harrison was as he expected: painful. All Jim had endured through his training under Army drill instructors was gentle compared to the torture he suffered at the hands of the adorable redheaded physical therapist. That first session started gently enough, with stretching to loosen tendons that were bound tight due to scar tissue. After stretching, the real pain began. The physical therapist, Sheila was her name, demonstrated how he was to stand between the parallel bars, lower himself down to a squat, then stand using only his injured leg. A pleasant demonstration. He was not half so graceful. Could he manage ten reps? He tried and maxed out at six. For the next hour, Sheila guided him through countless other exercises. They paused only occasionally to stretch. Huffing and puffing and wincing as much as he did, there was certainly no opportunity to flirt. That would have to wait.

When freed from the day's torture, Jim headed to the pay-phone to call home for a ride. He hesitated as he neared the elevator beside the phone. Mom had told him that Tom was just two floors up from him, in this very hospital. Part of Jim wanted to walk into the bastard's room and shove his Special Forces patch in the old man's face. Jim shook his head and smiled. That anger was old and decayed; it no longer held the fire that had pushed him through boot camp, advanced infantry training, jump school, and finally the Special Forces program. Anger had served him well then, but it no longer held the weight it once did. Staring at the elevator door, Jim remembered Tom's last words to him. He never wanted to see Jim's face again. That so? Was it still the case? What the hell. Jim crutched his way over to the elevator and pushed the up arrow.

CHAPTER 27

B reathe. Today was one of those days that demanded all of Tom's effort for that simple, life-sustaining task. The oxygen mask that helped keep him alive amplified the noise of his already raspy, shallow breaths. At least he was still breathing. Tom had been in the same bed for twenty-two days now, moved there from another ward of the veteran's hospital at Fort Harrison. He had stayed at his ranch as long as he could after his diagnosis, long enough to see all the stock safely sold off to good homes and to set his affairs in order. But his physical decline had accelerated. It was winter and, in his condition, the dream of heading to the mountains to die was forfeited. He was forced to surrender his view of the mountains for that of the sterile hospital walls.

Each day he wondered how much longer it'd be before the struggle to breathe would not be enough. It was amazing actually, how persistently his body summoned the strength needed to fill his lungs just one more time. As hard as it was to breathe, it was even harder to stop. When would he finally draw that final breath? Apparently not today. With every inhale, Tom thought: *No one dies today.* He silently laughed at himself. How many times had he uttered those words when faced with dire circumstances? Yet now, today, the old chant seemed to mock him.

Tom looked out the third floor window of his room and could just make out the tops of the snow-covered mountains in the distance, knowing this was as close as he'd ever come to them again. What he wouldn't give to have just one more chance to ride into deep and unspoiled wilderness, to gaze down to lush valleys from the rocky peaks.

A touch on Tom's right shoulder brought him out of his daydream.

"Tom, are you feeling well enough for a visitor?" The nurse asked politely.

He nodded his head, hoping it was Frank. It had been a few days since his friend had last visited, and Tom hoped to hear news of Jim. Apparently, the young man had been injured and was somewhere in the Midwest recovering. At least he was alive though.

Outside of Frank, only a few others had taken the time to stop by after Tom's condition had exiled him to this bed. Roy had stopped by once. Jim's neighbor, Walt, stopped by three times as well. The looks on their faces were all the same: concerned and uneasy at seeing him in his deteriorated state. He must look awful. Their visits were made out of respect, which Tom appreciated, but their eyes betrayed their discomfort, maybe even fear. He couldn't blame them. Who would want to spend time with a dying man? Frank had been consistent though, visibly the most unaffected by Tom's dramatic decline.

The nurse waved in a man who had been standing just outside the door. The fellow hobbled into the room at her signal. Hell, it sounded like the drum of a Scottish dirge, the slow and steady tempo of crutches and a single working leg. The nurse left the room, and Tom focused on the crippled man. His face was familiar, though older and darker. The eyes were what struck him, that steely glint Tom had seen in his own mirror for decades—the scars of terrible things both seen and done. Now the eyes were not his own but those of Jim Redmond, himself. The man stopped next to Tom's bed and waited. Tom managed to smile beneath the mask and gave a nod of approval.

"I wasn't sure you'd want to see me. We didn't exactly part on good terms."

Tom lifted his frail, ashen hand from the covers. Jim grasped and shook it, asking if he could sit down. Tom nodded his assent, and Jim brought a chair near to the bed.

One by one, Tom rationed out his words: "I hope the fellow you tangled with fared worse than you."

"Mr. Charles and I did a dance or two. I'd say we ended in a draw."

"Home for good?"

"Yes, the war is over for me."

Tom nodded. He was glad to have the young warrior by his side. The man shared briefly about his injury and how he would be completing his physical therapy at the hospital every weekday to get his leg working again. He kept the conversation brief, which Tom was thankful for, since the effort to communicate this much had already taken its toll.

Oh. Breathe. The morphine was wearing off, and the pain in his back and chest had returned. Jim could tell. He rang for the nurse and stood up. Time to call it a day.

"You suppose I can stop by each day when I'm done down-stairs?" he asked.

Tom ignored the pain and nodded. Then, with some effort, he made his right hand into a fist with his thumb pointing up, raising it a few inches off the bed.

"Fair enough. I'll see you tomorrow then."

True to his word, Jim stopped by the next day and chatted for about twenty minutes. It was just the amount of time it took, Jim explained, for Vi or his mom to arrive at the hospital after he'd called for a ride. Tom was fine with the brevity of their talks. The morphine kept the pain at bay, but it also made it a struggle to stay awake. Each day after that Jim would visit, even on the weekend when he didn't have physical therapy. On those days, Frank came too, father and son bantering about horses and various world events. Tom rarely had energy to join the conversation but he enjoyed listening. The stories distracted him from both the pain and the growing struggle to breath.

The following week, Jim didn't try to get Tom to engage, but instead shared about his physical therapy session—specifically about the cute redhead who was in charge of his rehabilitation. Tom nodded occasionally to assure Jim he was still listening, but it was becoming harder with each visit.

"So, don't tell anyone but I'm working hard to get my physical therapist to go out with me," Jim confessed with a sly grin. "I figure anyone as cute as she is, that can hurt me too, is a keeper."

Tom cracked a smile behind the oxygen mask. He wasn't surprised at Jim's intentions. Each time the young man visited, Sheila was the first conversation topic. By Thursday, Tom found himself drifting off during the latest installment about the potential romance.

"Well, she said yes," Jim beamed. "She kept shooting me down when I asked her to a movie or dinner, but promising a drive out to see the horses did the trick."

Tom snapped back to full consciousness at the mention of horses. "She loves horses, I guess, but she doesn't own any herself, so I invited her to see Sil and Moonlight up at the old homestead. It's too cold to ride, not that my leg would let me anyhow. But this weekend is it."

Jim's words had become harder to hear. Tom's mind wandered. He saw Sil and Moonlight running across an open meadow.

"You still with me, Tom?"

Tom barely heard him and couldn't give his usual thumbs up. The young man kept speaking these odd soundless words.

Strangely, the pain let up. There was Jim, the kid, the young man, the soldier. His head bowed. Oh, one more breath. It was time. Mountain valleys lush and green. Galloping hooves on the wind. A dark speckled dog and a proud, pale horse.

CHAPTER 28

JUNE 23, 1970

The letter arrived five months and a day after Jim watched Tom take his final breath. He had picked up his mail after finishing his weekly physical therapy appointment at Fort Harrison and hadn't thought much about the package as he hobbled into his apartment. He was still limping, though the limp was markedly reduced compared to how he'd gimped along back in January. It had improved so much; the crutches were no longer a necessity. While awaiting the determination of the Medical Evaluation Board regarding his future with the Army—desk job or medical discharge—Jim rented a small apartment on North Park Avenue. Although he was uncertain about where his life was going, he was pleased that it was at least returning to some semblance of normalcy. Then this package arrived with its legal letter inside. In it was the old man's name.

Dear Mr. Redmond,
    The Worley Jacobs Law Firm represents the estate of the late Thomas Logan McKee, who passed away on January 22, 1970.

He couldn't help but remember Tom's final day and the funeral that followed. The Redmond family had been there, along with half a dozen of Tom's fellow horsemen and almost twenty former members of the First Special Service Force, who served the duty of honor guard for the internment. In the cold and snow, Jim had stood in full uniform too, crutches and all, saluting as three volleys of rifle fire pierced the cold, dry air. As the casket was lowered, Jim knew that Pepsi's ashes were inside it, at Tom's feet, fulfilling the man's final request to Frank. As a final tribute to his friend, Frank had also carved Tom's headstone. It was one of his greatest works, simple and beautiful. Beneath Tom's name and the dates marking the beginning and end of his life, ran a herd of horses, galloping along the bottom of the smooth granite stone. Jim pulled his thoughts away from that solemn day and continued reading.

> *In accordance with his last will and testament, the enclosed package was to be sent to you, James Clayton Redmond, upon his passing and the settling of his estate. The contents of the package are unknown, as Mr. McKee's wishes were clearly detailed prior to his decline in health. Please accept our condolences on your loss.*

Jim reread the letter, then set the box on his kitchen table. He pulled the package toward himself and unwrapped the brown paper. Inside was a shoe box. Opening it, Jim pulled out a string-tied manila envelope. From inside the envelope, he removed the red First Special Service Force patch and the Italian coin he had once stolen. Jim felt the rough stitching on the patch and smiled. He held the patch against his left arm, imagining how it would look on a uniform. Setting it back on the table, he again looked into the package and found a small wooden box with a faded checkerboard-patterned metal veneer. Opening it, Jim discovered tiny, well-worn chess pieces with magnets on the bottom of each piece. The interior of the lid had places and dates carved onto it.

Ft. Harrison Helena, MT, September 12, 1942
Camp Bradford, Virginia, April 16, 1943
Ft. Ethan Allen, Vermont, June 23, 1943
Aleutians, August 15, 1943
Italy, October 30, 1943
Anzio, February 10, 1944
France, August 14, 1944

Jim removed the white knight piece and held it up in the light, admiring the horse head. So regal and proud. He wondered how many moves had been made with it, what strategies it had been a part of, and how many days it had spent on a transport ship or in a foxhole, helping to pass the time.

Closing the chess set, Jim looked into the shoe box once more and removed the crumpled newspaper comics that had been stuffed inside as packaging. At the bottom, straight and true, was the dagger. A small slip of paper was tucked between the handle and the leather sheath. In Tom's hard cursive were the words:

From one warrior to another. Manu Forti.

AFTERWORD

Thank you for taking the time to journey through *Lost Horse Park*. This is the second book that follows the Redmond family, generation by generation. At the time of this publication, I've started research on the third novel in this series and concept work on the fourth.

I write to share stories that touch the heart and soul of my readers. Your feedback and your recommending my work to others is the greatest reward I can hope for. Being a self-published author, my ability to write and publish is entirely dependent on people hearing about my books from readers like you. If you have enjoyed this or my first novel, *Stranger's Dance,* then then please encourage others to buy a copy. Thank you and God Bless.

ABOUT THE AUTHOR

Troy B. Kechely spent his youth on a ranch west of Helena, Montana. His years of working with animals and on horseback are evident in his novels, *Stranger's Dance* and *Lost Horse Park*.

Kechely has written articles for *Dog and Kennel* magazine, as well as numerous canine rescue group newsletters and websites. Kechely's blog, *The Beautiful Bond*, has over ten thousand views. Additionally, Kechely is a nationally recognized dog behavior expert and is the author of *The Management of Aggressive Canines for Law Enforcement*, which helps law enforcement avoid using deadly force against dogs worldwide.

Kechely lives in Bozeman, Montana, with his rescue Rottweiler, Carly.